PRAISE FOR *THE VERY BEST OF KATE ELLIOTT*

"Elliott's delightful first collection contains pieces set in the worlds of her major fantasy series . . . serves beautifully both as an introduction to Elliott and as a treat for fans who want more of her marvels."
—*Publishers Weekly*, starred review

"*The Very Best of Kate Elliott* does an excellent job of displaying Elliott's multifaceted creativity, her huge talent for inventing a variety of worlds without ever sacrificing the sparkling little details in each one that make her writing so compelling."
—Katharine Kerr, author of the Deverry Cycle

"If you're a fan of Kate Elliott's fantasy novels, then you know she knows how to tell an epic. But remarkably, Elliott is one of those rare writers who is also able to distill that sense of an epic fantasy novel into the short form. For fans of epic storytelling, this is a collection not to be missed."
—John Joseph Adams, series editor of *Best American Science Fiction & Fantasy* and editor of *Lightspeed Magazine*

"Kate Elliot fits more rich and complex writing into her short pieces than many authors manage at novel length, tackling the social fabric of SF&F with clarity and grace."
—Tanya Huff, author of the Keeper's Chronicles

"Intricate and enthralling. This really is the *best* of Kate Elliott."
—Seanan McGuire, author of *Rosemary and Rue*

PRAISE FOR KATE ELLIOTT

"A gripping and enthralling fantasy epic."
—*London Times* on Crown of Stars

"Elliott pulls out all the stops in a wildly imaginative narrative that will ring happy bells for fans of Philip Pullman's His Dark Materials trilogy."
—*Publishers Weekly*

"The Crossroads trilogy is a breathtaking achievement that places fantasy back in the center of political fiction."
—*Strange Horizons*

"The most fabulous part of Elliott's series is how perfectly crafted the characters are, each with their own flaws and blind spots, as well as their honor or lack thereof. . . . Rebellion and unrest provide plenty of opportunity for plot surprises, and the conclusion is delicious."
—*RT Book Reviews*

"Elliott's writing keeps getting better. She handles a cast roughly the size of *The Iliad*'s and still makes each personality distinct, and she excels at depicting quiet character moments."
—*Starlog*

"An exuberant narrative with great energy and inventive world building . . . I utterly loved it."
—*Fantasy Book Critic*

"Elliott has concocted something very special and original here, with elements to tweak sci-fi and fantasy fans of nearly any stripe, from alt-history and steampunk aficionados, to lovers of intrigue, romance, and swashbuckling adventure."
—*New York Journal of Books*

"A fantastic exploration of an alternate world, complete with a spirit world, Mages, an alternate geography, an alternate history, and lots and lots of cool ideas."
—*SF Signal*

"The Spiritwalker trilogy contains many of the qualities that I love to see in a fantasy novel—a richly detailed, vivid world; well-developed characters with unique personalities and histories; and a first-person narrator whose sparkling words bring the story to life. Books like these are why I read speculative fiction, and the three books in the Spiritwalker trilogy are keepers."
—*Fantasy Cafe*

"Fans of steampunk and alternate history will enjoy this heady mix of magic and technology."
—*Library Journal*

"If you need your fix of secret enclaves of sorcerers attempting to turn the world into its puppet, Mesoamerican elves and their time-traveling ghosts, Woman of Color protagonist with bookish habits and complex motives, political intrigue of the best and worst sort, White-farm-boy-who-might-have-a-destiny protagonist, Non-human yet oddly relatable protagonist, Noble Knight Man of Color protagonist with simple desires and complicated loyalties, enormous cast of interesting and terrible people, the beauty of war, the horrors of love, heresy and power-mad Clergyfolk, Matriarchs who abuse their power and those that lead revolutions from prisons, Hack-N-Bash Knights in Full Plate and Kings who go forth in the land, Prophecies, Curses, Magic Cities that Aren't There, and spoiled child empresses who like to get dirt on their gowns, welcome to staying up WAY past your bedtime for the foreseeable future."
—*Medievalpoc* on Crown of Stars

The Very Best of Kate Elliott
Copyright © 2015 by Katrina Elliott

Introduction: The Landscapes That Surround Us copyright © 2015 by Katrina Elliott
Introduction: Four Essays copyright © 2015 by Katrina Elliott

Cover art by Julie Dillon
Cover and interior design by Elizabeth Story

Tachyon Publications
1459 18th Street #139
San Francisco, CA 94107
(415) 285-5615
www.tachyonpublications.com
tachyon@tachyonpublications.com

Series Editor: Jacob Weisman
Project Editor: Jill Roberts

ISBN 13: 978-1-61696-179-4

Printed in the United States of America by Worzalla
First Edition: 2015
9 8 7 6 5 4 3 2 1

THE VERY BEST OF
KATE ELLIOTT

Other Books by Kate Elliott

Court of Fives (2015)
Black Wolves (2015)

The Spiritwalker Trilogy
Cold Magic (2010)
Cold Fire (2011)
Cold Steel (2013)

The Crossroads Trilogy
Spirit Gate (2007)
Shadow Gate (2008)
Traitors' Gate (2009)

Crown of Stars
King's Dragon (1997)
Prince of Dogs (1998)
The Burning Stone (1999)
Child of Flame (2000)
The Gathering Storm (2003)
In the Ruins (2005)
Crown of Stars (2006)

The Novels of the Jaran
Jaran (1992)
An Earthly Crown (1993)
His Conquering Sword (1993)
The Law of Becoming (1994)

Standalone
The Golden Key (1996, with Melanie Rawn
and Jennifer Roberson)

Originally published as Alis A. Rasmussen

The Labyrinth Gate (1988)

The Highroad Trilogy
A Passage of Stars (1990)
Revolution's Shore (1990)
The Price of Ransom (1990)

THE VERY BEST OF
KATE ELLIOTT

WITHDRAWN

TACHYON | SAN FRANCISCO

Contents

Four Essays

TO THE MEMORY OF
MY BELOVED FATHER,
GERALD RASMUSSEN (1926–2013)

Introduction:
The Landscapes That Surround Us

As a teen growing up in quiet rural Oregon, I fell in love with the vivid and worlds-shaking landscapes of epic fantasy and science fiction. Yet seen through the filters of the world as I was taught to know it then, I understood without needing to be told that the grand stories were almost exclusively about men. More than that, they were necessarily about men. Men were the actors on the great stage of history. Men were the adventurers. Men were the warriors.

The story I fell in love with did not include me, not really. It was a landscape meant for someone else. The story I wanted to be part of was a landscape of "you don't belong here" and "this can't be your tale" and "you are at best a minor player, a spectator, a helpmeet, or a reward."

Think for a moment about how we see and understand the landscapes that surround us.

The physical landscape of my childhood happened to be a river valley with rich soil, plenty of rain, and foothills in the distance with a glimpse of mountain peaks on very clear days. Before the Willamette River was engineered with revetments, dams, and reservoirs into its current banks, the river had many channels that shifted with the spring floodwaters. It sprawled along multiple branches and spilled down backwaters that had once been the main current.

I grew up on farmland bisected by a long narrow lake that is a remnant of one of the river's ancient beds. The field directly behind the house boasts a solitary old oak right out in the middle, seeming out of place until you realize it reveals the existence of an old river bank. On this slight ridge my spouse found an arrowhead and evidence of an encampment of Native people.

In 1856, as more settlers of European ancestry arrived in the valley, the remaining Kalapuya were forcibly removed to a reservation. The land was divided up and parceled out according to an alien view of ownership. In the mid–twentieth century the plot I grew up on was bought by my grandparents. Who the people were who set up a camp on what was then a river bank is unknown to me. I can only see the barest traces of a life that the life I grew up living had overrun.

All through the many fields you can see the ebb and flow of a topography marking higher ground and lower ground, the banks and shallows and depths of what came before. If you don't look for it, if you don't know it's there, all you will see are crops: wheat, mint, grass-seed, strawberries, cherry and filbert orchards.

Narrative gets engineered until we start to believe it has always run that way.

Grim stories are bowdlerized and their watered-down versions accepted as if they were the originals. Academic histories elide the existence of noblewomen who signed charters next to their brothers and women who ran businesses and negotiated contracts. Received wisdom leads people to make such absurd claims as that there were no women composers or artists in pre-twentieth-century Europe (I was told this in college as if it were a well-known fact). Some claim that epic fantasy based in a "medieval Europe-style setting" can't realistically include people of color because there weren't any in medieval and early modern Europe, which simply isn't true.

Eventually people believe the river is bounded by these artificially created banks.

My first serious attempt at a fantasy story, written when I was fourteen, followed the adventures of two men, partners in rollicking escapades that unfolded across a narrative landscape of men. The fantasy I read at that time followed only a few sorts of (almost exclusively male) characters: the thief, the rogue, the prince (corrupt or good), the wizard, the scheming merchant, and so forth. Men were the only people who could "realistically" be major characters, with the exception of a few women who usually existed in the story solely in relationship to the men. This is why Éowyn, for all the problems people may justly see with her depiction today, was such a revelatory character for a teenage girl back in the day.

Even as I was writing my first "ambitious" fantasy tale I felt something missing.

I was missing.

Not me personally, as if I had to be the hero of every story I wrote, although it was certainly at this time that I decided to start writing adventure stories in which girls and/or women were the main characters. What was really missing was the topography of how I experienced and saw the world.

A local farming family rented out the arable acreage of our land and planted various crops over the years. On the other side of the lake (the former river channel) was a pasture where we kept a few head of cattle. This place contained plenty of trees and space for an outdoorsy child to invent adventurous games and stories in her head. My society wasn't kind to strong-willed girls in the '60s and '70s (it is often still unkind to them and indeed to anyone who doesn't adhere to a binary gender essentialism). In those days I was labeled a tomboy, a word used to describe a girl who liked to do things which at that time were explicitly and demandingly associated with boys. Climbing trees, playing outside, running, being active and liking to explore, playing sports as I did because athletics for girls was just then opening up due to Title IX: All these were claimed as peculiarly masculine traits for some definition of what "masculine" needed to mean to fulfill cultural expectations of a "male role."

At this time I couldn't get the best-paying summer jobs working in the fields moving irrigation pipe or driving tractor because I was a girl, a strong, active, physical girl perfectly capable of the work but a girl nonetheless. In that day girls didn't do that work, just like they didn't have those adventures. You see how this trickles down.

I felt like an impostor trying to walk in shoes not meant for me, wearing my desires for adventure and physical activity like stolen garments that I could only provisionally possess. At the same time I carefully refused to learn the skills and engage in most "typical girl" activities. I thought that by rejecting what my culture labeled "girl things" I could prove I was "not-girl" and therefore be allowed to provisionally identify with the preferred and superior "boy" status. Only later did I come to understand that my rejection of "girl things" was a form of negating myself. It was just another way of partaking in the diminishment of women.

One of the peculiarities of the actual space in which I lived was that the forty-five acres, although mostly farmland, had four domiciles: The home—formerly a barn—in which I, my parents, and three siblings lived, always with a dog and usually one or more barn cats. A small apartment attached our house that had once been the milk shed, which was lived in by different people over the years. My father's parents' home (always called "the other house") next door. For a stretch of many years a temporary trailer sat between our house and the other house in which lived a nurse about the same age as my grandparents. When I knew her she was a widow with a grown-up child. This older single woman who had a job, practical wisdom, and a wicked sense of humor was a fixture in my landscape, yet such women weren't mentioned in the histories or fantasies I read. But there she was. She existed. She was real.

She happened to be friends with my doctor's nurse, a woman I never knew well but whom I always liked in that distant way a child may like a grown-up whose life seems so removed from her own. Only as an adult did I learn that the nurse I saw for my regular checkups had been a nurse in the European theater during World War II. I never knew this woman had participated in the war in a profound way even though I was always acquainted with the stories of the many male veterans of my parents' generation. The participation and experience of women in war, in whatever capacity, was not just ignored but set away, papered over; it was another channel lost to view.

My childhood landscapes stretched into the past and also across the ocean. My father grew up in an enclave of Danish Americans. As a child he went to "Dane School," where he learned the language of his immigrant grandparents. It happened that he was raised as much by his grandmother as by his own parents; his connection to the nineteenth-century struggles they came out of was part of his childhood, and so it connected to me. I assumed everyone was surrounded by a net of older relatives whose memories reached into a past they could briefly illuminate. My great-uncle remembered the first time he saw a car. I heard firsthand stories of how people made their way who had very little money and no expectation of more. Their memories made the world they had been part of not so distant from my own because it was part of the story of how mine had come to be. The Depression and World War II were my touchstones as a child not because I was alive then but because these events were central to the lives of my elders.

One consequence of my father's ethnic upbringing was that, after the war, he went to Denmark to study for a year and returned home with a Danish bride. She was a young woman bold enough to leave her family behind and embark for a new country where she did not (yet) speak the language. In our household, a second language was spoken. We ate different foods and had customs that mainstream American culture viewed as peculiar or charming. This upbringing contributed to creating a view of myself as fractured. I belonged to the mainstream culture because I was white and had an enthusiastically approved European ancestry (Scandinavian Americans being among that small group of foreign immigrants to the USA who never had to "become white" but were always accepted as white), but I sensed that other topographies influenced my personal landscape as well.

After I wrote that initial story with its two generic male protagonists having adventures in a world filled with men, I made a conscious decision to write stories with girls or women as the lead characters. I knew I would be told that I was merely writing "wish-fulfillment," and at that time I believed it *was* wish-fulfillment to populate my stories with whatever characters I wanted, especially ones who represented people like me.

That the standard stories I read provided their own form of wish-fulfillment to the men reading and praising them hadn't yet occurred to me.

At the same time, elements I took for granted from my own limited yet unique understanding of the world crept into my stories. I wasn't yet conscious that writing about a woman who had to journey from her homeland to a foreign land was a story I knew by heart because I grew up with it. I wasn't yet conscious that women not specifically tied to their relationships to men appeared in my stories because in my tiny world they were visible to me. Elders played a role in the narrative, as did continuity and connection between past and present and between old places and new ones. My slow groping toward an architecture of what I thought made for gripping and "realistic" world building filled in around channels I wasn't at that time aware had scored so deeply into my creative heartland.

Attending a women's college in Oakland, California, was a profoundly eye-opening experience for a white girl from rural Oregon, a window into the ways race and class and gender shape America. I trained in martial arts. I married a man from a different religion and converted to that religion not as a favor to him but because I found my spiritual home there. Having children layered on yet more perspectives. Opening the door to the idea that the world was far larger than what I had been told in school and by the culture at large altered my sense of the world. Realizing that the "truths" laid on the table were almost without exception incomplete and at times outright falsehoods forced me to dig deeper into the unexamined assumptions I lived with. Today I keep adjusting my way of looking at the world as I continue to listen, look, and learn.

I never fell out of love with SFF and its landscapes of heroism, adventure, discovery, the numinous, the intangible, the idea of being part of something larger than yourself. It's an odd thing, falling in love with a story, especially when that story itself sometimes defines and creates problematic elements. Especially when that story denies you an existence.

Most often the cultural landscapes we are familiar with dictate the approach we take to writing and the worlds we write about. Often the true contours of these landscapes remain unseen because they hide beneath the fields we expect to encounter. Often we are not aware that we have unexamined expectations about what we will find in the narrative. These unexamined expectations in fictional terms can be called a "default" of preselected options.

For example, what if a reader genuinely believes that there were only a handful of "exceptional women" in the past and that the rest were passive, ignorant, oppressed bystanders? If this is the story the reader has absorbed through historical stereotypes, revisionist history, and bad television and film, they will approach each narrative with an idea of what a "realistic" landscape looks like (regardless of how many dragons and FTL spaceships it has in it). That reader may call "unbelievable" a fantasy story that includes a guild with women as members; a royal daughter who rides out with her imperial father on a military campaign; a literate woman who administers an archive, composes poetry praised by a court, or writes the first known novel; harem women who control extensive commercial interests; a single woman supporting herself in a trade; Amazons or any woman who fights; and women as leaders of religious establishments and revolutions.

Like air, this default remains invisible if it is not examined by other instruments, just as we do not see the river's history in its fullness if we only measure the engineered banks.

One place to start is to tear apart the idea that there is a single authentic story that can have legitimacy for all people, one with a universal message that speaks to everyone and thus to everything. A classic example of a narrative often seen as being a "universal story" in epic fantasy is that of a white man (working within European or USA cultural antecedents) with daddy issues who has to overthrow or surpass his father. Usually he gets laid along the way *and* receives a woman as reward, although she is not as important as his final triumph in the hierarchy of menfolk.

By what standard can this story (and others like it) be claimed as universal? Of itself it is particularist, limited, and superficial when applied to the wide-ranging experience of human beings across time and place.

The trappings and tropes we are told are "realistic" are in fact selective realism.

Many hold to the idea of science fiction and fantasy as a progressive genre, one that can continually open up new spaces, new paths, new visions that have to do with humanity. But if new spaces and new paths are only inhabited by the same people as were valorized in the stories before, then they aren't new and they aren't progressive, if progress means anything.

Now and again people bewail how fantasy is an inherently conservative genre but in fact most fantasy has little to do with the actual past. The myths layered on top of the past get more rigid the more they are needed to reinforce the status quo. Modern fantasy has less to do with nostalgia for monarchy and more to do with protecting the status quo of today, the desire to protect the privilege of those who have held on to it for so long. The male main character who through genius or magical skill succeeds at his quest or takes or regains a throne is less about catering to notions of aristocracy and more about essentialism and perhaps even social Darwinism. Both notions are part and parcel of the same way of organizing the universe: rationalizing that some people deserve better than others regardless of how it came about that they got it. Modern science fiction rarely fares much better than fantasy even if its trappings may seem more democratic or industrial (I won't say technological because periods of technological innovation exist throughout human history, a fact much ignored by people who love to excoriate "fantasy" for its "pastoral traditionalism").

In the end I chose to write the epic fantasy and science fiction I wanted to see, not the epic SFF I had been sold as the only authentic brand. I chose to write women at the center of my narratives. I chose to create space for myself, by which I meant all of the people I did not see in these stories. Instead of landscapes of received wisdom, of ossified expectation, and of unchallenged assumptions, I chose to build landscapes of possibility and expansion. What had been labeled trivial and unworthy could be exposed as important and necessary. Those who had been invisible through omission and prejudice would become visible and inevitable at the heart of the narrative.

This is my landscape, the heart of everything I have written.

I do belong here. This can be my narrative, and yours too. The landscapes of the fantasy and science fiction genre are not owned by a few, nor can they any longer be defined by a few. The river has many channels, some running strong, some hidden and hard to see, some yet to be carved. We can explore them all.

Thanks to Katharine Beutner, Liz Bourke, Daniel José Older, and N. K. Jemisin for reading and comments.

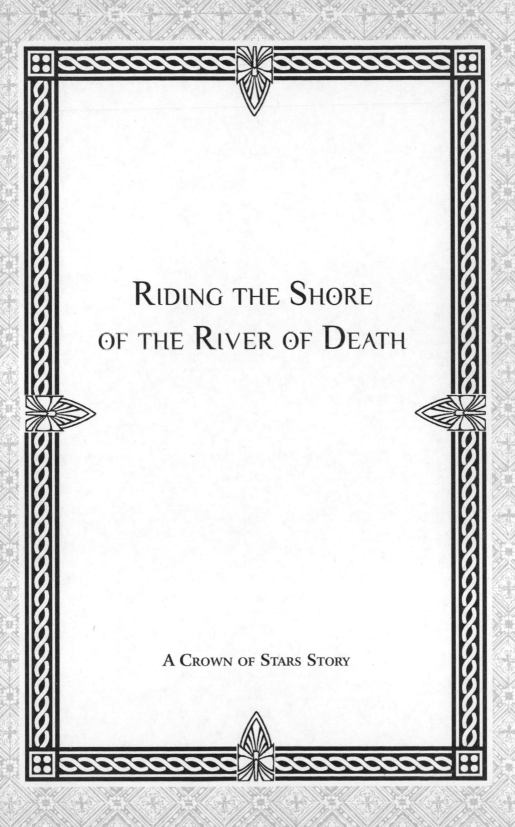

RIDING THE SHORE
OF THE RIVER OF DEATH

A CROWN OF STARS STORY

This wooded western country far from their tribal lands in the east smelled raw and unpalatable to Kereka, but the hawk that circled overhead had the same look as hawks in the grasslands. Some things were the same no matter where you went, even if you had to ride into the lands where foreigners made their homes to get what you wanted. Even if you had to journey far from your father's authority and your mother's tent to seize the glory of your first kill.

The reverberant thunk of an axe striking wood surprised her; she'd thought it was too early to hunt because they had yet to see any sign of habitation. Ahead, barely visible within the stretch of pine and beech through which they rode, her brother Belek unslipped his spear from its brace against his boot and urged his mare into a run. Kereka rose in her stirrups to watch him vanish into a clearing occluded by summer's leaves. Birds broke from cover, wings flashing. The clatter of weapons, a sharp shriek, and then a man's howl of pain chased off through the bright woodland.

Edek, riding in front of her, whipped his horse forward. His voice raised in a furious burst of words as he and Kereka broke out of the woods and into a clearing of grass, meadow flowers, bold green saplings, and a pair of sturdy young oak trees.

Belek's mare had lost her rider. She shied sideways and stood with head lifted and ears flat. Beside the oaks, two had fought. Belek's spear had thrust true, skewering the foreign man through the torso, but the farmer's axe had cut into the flesh below Belek's ribs before Belek had finally killed the man with a sword-thrust up under the ribs. Edek stood with mouth working soundlessly, watching as Belek sawed off the head of the dead man with his bloodied knife. Blood leaked from

Belek's gut, trailing from under his long felt tunic and over the knees of his leather trousers, but he was determined to get that head.

If he could present the head to the *begh* before he died, then he would die as a man rather than a boy.

His teeth were gritted and his eyes narrowed, but he uttered no word that might betray how much he hurt. Even when he got the head detached so it rolled away from the body, blood spilling brightly onto the grass, he said nothing, only uttered a "gah" of pain as he toppled over to one side. His left hand clutched the hair of the dead man. With his gaze he tracked the sky, skipping from cloud to cloud, and fetched up on Kereka's face. He seemed about to speak but instead passed out.

Kereka stared. One of the young oaks had a gash in its side, but the farmer hadn't chopped deep enough to fell it. Bugs crawled among the chips of wood cut from the trunk. A cluster of white flowers had been crushed by the farmer's boots. His red blood mingled with Belek's, soaking into the grass. This could not be happening, could it?

Every year boys rode out of the clans to seek their first kill, and every year some did not return. Riding the shore of the river of death was the risk you took to become a man. Yet no lad rode out in the dawn's thunder thinking death would capture *him*.

Edek dismounted and knelt beside Belek to untie the heavy tunic, opening it as one might unfold the wings of a downed bird. Seeing the deep axe cut and the white flash of exposed rib, he swore softly. Kereka could not find words as she absorbed the death of her hopes.

"He'll never get home with this wound," said Edek. "We'll have to leave him." He started, hearing a crack, but it was only Belek's mare stepping on a fallen branch as it turned to move back toward the familiarity of its herd.

"We can't leave him." Kereka knew she had to speak quickly before she succumbed to the lure of Edek's selfish suggestion. "He is my brother. The *begh's* son. It will bring shame on us if we abandon him."

Edek shrugged. "If we take him back, then you and I have no chance of taking a head. You must see that. He can't ride. He's dead anyway. Let's leave him and ride on. Others have done it."

She set her jaw against his tempting words. "Other boys who were left to die hadn't already taken a head. He's taken his head, so we must give him a chance to die as a man. We'll lose all honor if we leave him. Even if both of us took a head in our turn."

"I don't want to wait another season. I'm tired of being treated as a boy when I'm old enough to be a man."

"Go on alone if you wish, Edek the whiner." Kereka forced out the mocking words, and Edek's sullen frown deepened with anger. "You'll sour the milk with your curdling tongue. You can suckle on your grievances for another season. You'll get another chance to raid."

As she would not.

Last moon the *begh*'s son from the Pechanek clan had delivered six mares to her father, with the promise of twenty sheep, ten fleeces, two bronze cauldrons, a gilded saddle, three gold-embroidered saddle blankets, five felt rugs, and a chest of gold necklaces and bronze belt clasps as her bride price. Her father's wives and the mothers of the tribe had been impressed by the offer. They had been charmed by Prince Vayek's respectful manners and pleasing speeches. Perhaps most of all they had been dazzled by his handsome face and well-proportioned body displayed to good effect in several bouts of wrestling, all of which he had won against the best wrestlers of the Kirshat clan. Her father and uncles had praised his reputation as a mighty warrior, scourge of the Uzay and Torkay clans, and all the while their gazes had returned again and again to the deadly iron gleam of the griffin feathers he wore as his warrior's wings. Other warriors, even other *beghs* and their princely sons, wore ordinary wings, feathers fastened with wire to wooden frames that were riveted to an armored coat. Only a man who had slain a griffin could fly griffin wings. Such a man must be called a hero among men, celebrated, praised, and admired.

Her father had decreed she would wed Prince Vayek at the next full moon. Wed, and be marked as a woman forever, even unto death.

This was her last chance to prove her manhood.

When she spoke, her voice was as harsh as a crow's. "We'll weave a litter of sticks and drag him behind his horse."

Dismounting, she turned her back so Edek could not see her wipe away the hot tears. Honor did not allow her to cry. She wanted to be a man and live a man's life, not a woman's. But she could not abandon her dying brother.

Grass flattened under the weight of a litter as Belek's mare labored up a long slope. Kereka rode at a walk just in front of Belek's horse, its lead tied to her saddle. Her own mare, summer coat shiny in the hot sun, flicked an ear at a fly.

She glanced back at the land falling away to the west. She had lagged behind to shoot grouse in the brush that cloaked a stream, its banks marked at this distance by the crowd of trees and bushes flourishing alongside running water. She squinted into the westering sun, scanning the land for pursuers, but saw no movement. Yesterday they had left the broken woodland country behind. Out here under the unfenced sky, they'd flown beyond the range of the farmers and their stinking fields.

From ahead, Edek called her name. She whistled piercingly to let him know she was coming. The two birds she'd killed dangled from a line hooked to the saddle of Belek's horse. Belek himself lay strapped to the litter they had woven of sapling branches. He had drifted in and out of consciousness for four days. It was amazing he was still alive, but he had swallowed drips and drops of mare's blood, enough to keep breath in his body. Now, however, his own blood frothed at his lips. The end would come soon.

Maybe if he died now, before they reached the tents of the Kirshat clan, she and Edek could turn immediately around, ride back west, and take up their hunt in fresh territory. Yet even to think this brought shame; Belek deserved to die as a man, whatever it meant to her.

She topped the rise to see hills rolling all the way to the eastern horizon. Dropping smoothly away from her horse's hooves lay a long grassy hollow half in shadow with the late afternoon light. The ground bellied up again beyond the hollow like a pregnant woman's distended abdomen. Edek had dismounted partway up the farther slope. He'd stripped out of his tunic in the heat and crouched with the sun on his back as he examined the ground. Above him, thick blocks of stone stood like sentries at the height of the hill: a stone circle, dark and forbidding.

The sight of the heavy stones made her ears tingle, as though someone was trying to whisper a warning but couldn't speak loudly enough for her to hear. A hiss of fear escaped her, and at once she spat to avert spirits who might have heard that hiss and seek to capture her fear and use it against her. She whistled again, but Edek did not look up. With its reins dropped over its head, his mount grazed in a slow munch up the slope toward the looming stones. He had his dagger out and was digging at the dirt. His quiver shifted on his bare back as he hunkered forward. What was he doing, leaving himself vulnerable like that?

She nudged her mare forward. When the reins tightened and pulled, Belek's mare braced stubbornly, then gave in and followed. The litter bumped over a rough patch of ground. Belek grunted, whimpered. Eyes fluttering, he muttered spirit words forced out of him where he lay spinning between the living world and the world of the spirits. A bubble of blood swelled and popped on his lips. The head of the farmer he had slain bumped at his thigh. Its lank hair tangled in his fingers. The skin had gone gray, and it stank.

Edek did not look up when she halted behind him. She touched the hilt of the sword slung across her back. Once they reached the tribe, she would have to give it back to her uncle. Only men carried swords.

"What if I had been your enemy?" she asked. She drew the sword in a swift, practiced slide and lowered its tip to brush Edek between the shoulder blades.

He did not look up or even respond. He was trying to pry something out of the densely packed soil. The sun warmed his back as he strained. As the quiver shifted with each of his movements, the old Festival scars on his back pulled and retracted, displaying the breadth of his back to great advantage. She didn't like Edek much; he was good-looking enough to expect girls to admire him, but his family wasn't wealthy enough that he could marry where he pleased, and that had made him bitter, so in a way she understood his sulks and frowns. And she could still ogle his back, sweating and slick under the sun's weight.

Suddenly he hooked his dagger under an object and with a grunt freed it from an entangling root and the weight of moist soil. When he flipped it into plain view, she sucked in breath between teeth in astonishment.

The sun flashed in their eyes and she threw up a hand to shield herself from the flare. Edek cried out. From Belek came a horrible shriek more like the rasp of a knife on stone than a human cry. Only the horses seemed unmoved.

She lowered her hand cautiously. At first glance, the object seemed nothing more than an earth-encrusted feather, but as Edek cautiously wiped the vanes with the sleeve of his tunic, the cloth separated as though sliced. Where dirt flaked away, the feather glinted with a metallic sheen unlike that of any bird's feather.

"It's a griffin's feather!" said Edek.

Kereka was too amazed and humbled to speak, awed by its solidity, its beauty, its strength. Its sacred, powerful magic. Only shamans and heroes possessed griffin feathers.

He shifted in his crouch to measure her, eyes narrowed. "Even a humble clansman can aspire to wed a *begh*'s daughter if he brings a griffin's feather as her bride price."

Kereka snorted. "Even one you dug up from the dirt?"

"The gods give gifts to those they favor!"

"You'll set yourself against the mighty Vayek and the entire Pechanek clan? Who will listen to your bleating, even with a griffin feather in your hand to dazzle their eyes?"

"Who will listen? Maybe the one who matters most." How he stared! He'd never been so bold before! She shook a hand in annoyance, like swatting away a fly, and he flushed, mouth twisting downward.

The feather's glamour faded as the shadow of afternoon crept over their position. And yet, at the height of the hill to the east, a glimmer still brightened the air.

How could they see the setting sun's flash when they were facing east, not west?

"Look!" she cried.

A woman stood framed and gleaming within the western portal of stone and lintel. Sparks flowered above the stones in a pattern like the unfurling of wings sewn out of gold, the fading banner of a phoenix. So brief its passage; the last embers floating in the air snapped, winked bright, and vanished.

Edek stared, mouth agape.

The woman, not so very far away, watched them. She had black hair, bound into braids but uncovered, and a brown face and dark hands. She wore sandals bound by straps that wound up her calves over tight leggings suitable for riding. A close-fitting bodice of supple leather was laced over a white shirt. But she wore no decent skirts or heavy knee-length tunic or long robe; her legs were gloved in cloth, but she might as well have been bare, for you could imagine her shape quite easily. She wore no other clothing at all unless one could count as clothing her wealth of necklaces. Made of gold and beads, they draped thickly around her shoulders like a collar of bright armor.

A woman of the Quman people who displayed herself so brazenly would have been staked down and had the cattle herd driven across her to obliterate her shame. But this woman seemed unaware of her own nakedness. Edek could not stop staring at that shapely bodice and those form-fitting trousers even as the woman hefted her spear and regarded them with no sign of fear.

"Chsst!" hissed Edek, warding himself with a gesture. "A witch!"

"A witch, maybe, but armed with stone like a savage," muttered Kereka in disgust. Anyway, even a woman who carried a spear was of no use to her.

A shape moved behind the foreigner: broad shoulders, long hair, sharp nose. Of course no woman would be traveling alone! Edek did not see the man because he was blinded by lust. Let him hesitate, and she would take the prize. This was her chance to take a head and never have to marry the Pechanek *begh*'s son.

Kereka sliced the halter rope that bound Belek's horse to her saddle, and drove her mare up the hill. A Quman warrior rode in silence, for he had wings to sing the song of battle for him. She had no wings yet—only men were allowed to wear armor and thereby fly the honored pennant of warrior's wings—but she clamped her lips tight down over a woman's trilling ululation, the goad to victory. She would ride in silence, like a man.

The horse was surefooted and the hill none too steep. Edek had only a moment in which to cry out an unheeded question before he scrambled for his mount. Ahead, the woman retreated behind one of the huge stones. The man had vanished. Kereka grinned, yanked her mare to the right, and swung round to enter the stone circle at a different angle so she could flank them.

"*Sister! Beware!*"

The words rasped at the edge of her hearing.

It was too late.

She hit the trap with all the force of her mare's weight and her own fierce desire for a different life than the one that awaited her. A sheet of pebbles spun under its hooves. A taut line of rope took her at the neck, and she went tumbling. She hit the ground so hard, head cracking against stone, that she could not move. The present world faded until she could see, beyond it, into the shimmering lights of the spirit world where untethered souls wept and whispered and danced. Belek reached out to her, his hand as insubstantial as the fog that swallows the valleys yet never truly possesses them. It was his spirit voice she heard, because he was strong enough in magic for his spirit to bridge the gap.

"*Sister! Take my hand!*"

"I will not go with you to the other side!" she cried, although no sound left her mouth. In the spirit world, only shamans and animals could speak out loud. "But I will drag you back here if it takes all my strength!"

She grasped his hand and *tugged*. A fire as fierce as the gods' anger rose up to greet her. She had to shield her eyes from its heat and searing power. She blinked back tears as the present world came into focus again.

It was night. Twilight had passed in what seemed to her only an instant while she had swum out of the spirit world.

Pebbles ground uncomfortably into her buttocks. A stalk of grass tickled the underside of one wrist. Tiny feet tracked on her forehead, then vanished as the creature flew. She sat propped against the rough wall of standing stones, wrists and ankles bound. How had this happened? She could not remember.

The scene before her lay in sullen colorless tones, lit by a grazing moon and by the blazing stars. Each point of light marked a burning arrow shot into the heavens by the warrior Tarkan, he who had bred with a female griffin and fathered the Quman people.

The flaring light of a campfire stung her eyes. The man crouched before it, raking red coals to one side. He had a thick beard, like the northern farmers, and skin pale enough that it was easy to follow his gestures as he efficiently scalded and plucked *her grouse* and roasted them over coals. Grease dripped and sizzled, the smell so sweet it was an insult thrown in her face.

Where were the others?

Edek lay well out of her reach, slumped against one of the giant stones. The horses stood hobbled just beyond the nimbus of light; she saw them only as shapes. Belek's litter lay at the edge of the harsh and restless flare of the fire. Still strapped to the litter, he moaned and shuddered. The woman appeared out of the darkness as abruptly as a shaman's evil dream. She crouched beside him with both hands extended. Lips moving but without sound, she sprinkled grains of dirt or flakes of herbs over his body.

Fear came on Kereka in the same way a spirit sickness does, penetrating the eyes first and sinking down to lodge in the throat and, at last, to grasp hold of her belly like an ailment. There are ways to animate dead flesh with sorcery. She had to stop the working, or Belek would be trapped by this creature's magic and never able to find his way past the spirit-lands to the ancient home of First Grandfather along the path lit by Tarkan's flaming arrows. But she could not move, not even to push her foot along the ground to kick the corpse and dislodge Belek's spirit.

Mist and darkness writhed between dying youth and foreign woman. With a powerful inhalation, the woman sucked in the cloud. Belek thrashed as foam speckled his lips. The witch rocked forward to balance so lightly on her toes that Kereka was sure she would fall forward onto Belek's unprotected chest. Instead, the woman exhaled, her breath loud in the silence; the air glittered with sparks expelled from her mouth. They dissolved into the youth's flesh as the witch settled smoothly back on her heels. She lifted her gaze to look directly at Kereka.

No matter how vulnerable she appeared, indecently clothed and armed only with a stone-pointed spear in the midst of the grasslands, she had power. As the *begh* Bulkezu, ancestor of Kereka's ancestors, had wrapped himself in an impenetrable coat of armor in his triumphant war against the westerners, this woman was armed with something more dangerous than a physical weapon. She was not the bearded man's wife or slave, but his master.

She nodded to mark Kereka's gaze, and spoke curtly in a language unlike any of those muttered by the tribe's slaves.

Kereka shook her head, understanding nothing. It would be better to kill the witch, but in the event, she had no choice except to negotiate from a position of weakness. "What do you want from us? My father will pay a ransom—"

As if her voice awakened him, Belek murmured as in a daze. "Kereka? Are you there?" Rope creaked as he fought with unexpected strength against his bonds. He looked up at the woman crouched above him. "Who are you? Where is my sister—?"

The witch rose easily to her feet and moved away into the gloom. The bearded man stood up and followed her. Kereka heard them speaking, voices trading back and forth in the manner of equals, not master and slave. Two warriors might converse in such tones, debating the best direction for a good hunt, or two female cousins or friendly co-wives unravel an obstacle tangling the weave of family life within their tents.

Belek tried again, voice spiking as he tried to control his fear. "Kereka? Edek?"

"Chsst!" Kereka spoke in a calming voice. She adored her brother, son of her father's third wife, but he was the kind of person who felt each least pebble beneath him when he slept, and although he never complained—what Quman child would and not get beaten for being weak?—he would shift and scoot and brush at the ground all night to get comfortable and thus disturb any who slept next to him. "We're here, Belek. We had to tie you down to keep you on the litter. You'd taken a wound. Now, we have been captured by foreigners."

"I feel a sting in my gut. Ah. Aah!" He grunted, bit back a curse, thapped his head against the litter, and yelped. These healthy noises, evidence of his return from the threshold of the spirit world, sang in her belly with joy. "I remember when I charged that dirty farmer, but nothing after it. Did I get his head?"

"Yes. We tied it to your belt."

His hand groped; he found the greasy hair. "Tarkan's blessings! But what happened to me?"

He deserved to know the worst. "The woman is a witch. She trapped us with sorcery. I think she must have healed you."

"Aie! Better dead than in her debt! If it's true, I am bound to her and she can take from me whatever she wants in payment."

His fretful tone irritated her. "No sense panicking! Best we get free of her, then."

"It's not so simple! The binding which heals has its roots in the spirit world and can't be so easily escaped. Her magic can follow me wherever I go—"

"Then it's best we get back to the tribe quickly and ask for the shamans to intercede. There's a knife at your belt. You should be able to cut yourself loose."

Obedient as always to her suggestions, he writhed under the confining ropes. "Eh! Fah! Knife's gone."

Night lay everywhere over them. The fattening moon grazed on its dark pastures. Kereka clenched her teeth in frustration. There must be some way to free themselves!

Only then did she see a stockpile of weapons—*their* good Kirshat steel swords, iron-pointed arrows, and iron-tipped spears—heaped beyond the campfire, barely visible in the darkness. A stubborn gleam betrayed the griffin's feather, resting atop the loot in the seat of honor.

The foreigners ceased speaking and walked back into the fire's aura. The witch still carried her primitive spear and she was now brandishing a knife that gleamed in black splendor, an ugly gash of obsidian chipped away to make one sharp edge. She had not even bothered to arm herself with the better weapons she had captured, although the bearded man wore a decent iron sword at his side, foreign in its heft and length.

The woman crouched again beside Belek.

Anything was better than pleading—that was a woman's duty, not a man's—but the knife's evil gleam woke such fear in Kereka's heart that she knew such distinctions no longer mattered.

"I beg you, listen to my words. Belek is the honored son of the Kirshat *begh*'s third wife. He has powerful magic. The shamans have said so. He has already entered the first tent of apprenticeship. To kill him would be to release his anger and his untrained power into the spirit world. You don't want that!"

Where there is no understanding there can be no response. And yet, the woman weighed her sorcerer's knife and, with a flicker of a smile, sheathed it. Instead, she slid a finger's-length needle of bone from a pouch slung from her belt.

Leather cord bit into Kereka's skin, tightening as she wiggled her hands and only easing its bite when she stilled. She could do nothing to spare Belek whatever torture this creature meant to inflict on him. Witchcraft had bound her to the rock.

The woman caught hold of her own tongue. With exaggerated care she slid the fine needle point through thick pink flesh. Then, with a delicacy made more horrifying for the sight of her bland expression in the face of self-mutilation, she slid the needle back out of her tongue, leaned over Belek, and let those drops of blood mingle with the drying froth on Belek's lips.

He struggled, but he too was bound tight. He gasped, swallowed, grimaced; then he sighed as if his breath had been pulled out of him, and abruptly his head lolled back. He had fainted. Or been murdered.

"Tarkan's curse on you!" Kereka shouted. "I'll have my revenge in my brother's name and in the name of the Kirshat tribe! Our father will drive his warband against you even to the ends of the earth—"

The woman laughed, and Kereka sputtered to a halt, her mouth suddenly too dry to moisten words. The skin on her neck crawled as with warning of a storm about to blow down over the grass.

The witch gestured, and the bearded man came forward, knelt beside

Belek, and dribbled water from a pouch into his mouth. Belek sputtered, choked, spat, eyes blinking furiously. The bearded man stoppered the pouch and dragged the litter over to rest in the lee of the great stone to Kereka's right. He offered water to Kereka, wordlessly, and she tipped back her head to let the cool liquid flow down her parched throat. She knew better than to refuse it. She needed time to think about that knowing laugh.

He returned to the fire. Tearing apart the grouse, he ate one, wrapped the rest of the meat in a woven grass mat, then curled up on the ground beneath a cloak. The woman settled down cross-legged to stare into the fire. Occasionally she fed it with dried pats of dung.

Night passed, sluggish and sleepy. Kereka dozed, woke, tried to worm her way out of her bonds but could not. No matter how hard she tried to roll away from the monolith, she could not separate herself from the stone. She hissed to get Belek's attention, saw his eyes roll and his mouth work, but no sound emerged except for a faint wordless groan.

The witch woman did not stir from her silent contemplation of the campfire. Now and again a bead of blood leaked from between her lips, and each time as it pearled on her lips she licked it away as if loathe to let even that droplet escape her. She did not speak to them, did not test the bonds that held them, only waited, tasting nothing except her own blood.

Very late a sword moon, thin and curved, rose out of the east. Soon after, the light changed, darkness lightening to gray and at last ceding victory to the pinkish tint of dawn.

The woman roused. Picking up the pouch, she trickled water into Belek's mouth; he gulped, obviously awake, but still he said nothing. She approached Kereka.

As she leaned in to offer water, Kereka caught the scent of her, like hot sand and bitter root. She tried to grab at her with her teeth, any way of fighting back, but the woman jumped nimbly back and grinned mockingly. The man chuckled and spoke words in their harsh foreign tongue as he flung off the cloak and stretched to warm his muscles.

The brilliant disc of the sun nosed above the horizon to paint the world in daylight colors.

From the bundle of gear heaped by a stone, the bearded man unearthed a shovel and set to work digging a shallow ditch just outside the limit of the stones. It was hard work, even though he was only scraping away enough of the carpet of grass and its dense tangle of roots to reveal the black earth. The woman joined him, taking a turn. The grasslands were tough, like its people, unwilling to yield up even this much. Both soon stripped down to shirt and trousers, their shirts sticking to their backs, wet through with sweat. It was slave's work, yet they tossed words back and forth in the manner of free men. And although the woman's form was strikingly revealed, breasts outlined by the shirt's fabric, nipples erect from the effort and heat, the bearded man never stared at her as men stared at women whose bodies they wanted to conquer. He just talked, and she replied, and they passed the shovel back and forth, sharing the work as the ditch steadily grew from a scar, to a curve, to a half-circle around the stones.

Kereka waited until they had moved out of sight behind her. "Hsst! Belek? Edek?"

Yet when there came no answer, she was afraid to speak louder lest she be overheard.

The sun crept up off the eastern horizon as the foreigners toiled. Shadows shortened and shifted; the sloping land came clear as light swallowed the last hollows of darkness. It was a cloudless day, a scalding blue that hurt the eye. Kereka measured the sun's slow rise between squinted eyes: two hands; four hands. A pair of vultures circled overhead but did not land. The steady scrape of the shovel and the spatter of clumps of dirt sprayed on the ground serenaded her, moving on from behind her and around to her right, closing the circle.

The sound caught her ear first as a faint discordance beneath the noise of digging. She had heard this precious and familiar music all her life, marked it as eagerly as the ring of bells on the sheep she was set to watch as a little girl or the scuff of bare feet spinning in the dances of Festival time.

The wind sings with the breath of battle, the flight of the winged riders, the warriors of the Quman people. It whistles like the approach of griffins whose feathers, grown out of the metals of the earth, thrum their high calls in the air.

Kereka scrambled to get her feet under her, shoved up along the rough surface of the stone. She had to see, even if she couldn't escape the stone's grip. Their enemies heard Quman warriors before they saw them, and some stood in wonder, not knowing what that whirring presaged, while others froze in fear, knowing they could not run fast enough to outpace galloping horses.

Belek struggled against the ropes that bound him but gained nothing. Edek neither moved nor spoke.

The woman and bearded man had worked almost all the way around the stones. The woman spoke. The man stopped digging. They stood in profile, listening. She shook her head, and together, shoulders tense, they trotted back into the stones straight to Edek's limp body. The bearded man grabbed the lad by his ankles and dragged him down to the scar. The body lay tumbled there; impossible to say if he was breathing. The woman gestured peremptorily, and the bearded man leaped away from the bare earth and ran up to the nearest stone, leaning on the haft of the shovel, panting from the exertion as he watched her through narrowed eyes.

The obsidian blade flashed in the sun. She bent, grabbed Edek's hair, and tugged his head back to expose his throat. With a single cut she sliced deep.

Kereka yelped. Did the witch mean to take Edek's head as a trophy, as Quman lads must take a head to prove themselves as men?

Belek coughed, chin lifting, feet and hands twitching as he fought against his bonds. He could see everything but do nothing.

Blood pumped sluggishly from Edek's throat. The witch grabbed him by the ankles and, with his face in the dirt and his life's blood spilling onto the black earth, dragged him along the scar away around the circle. All the while her lips moved although Kereka heard no words.

The bearded man wiped his mustache and nose with the back of a grimy hand, shrugged his shoulders to loosen the strain of digging, and dropped the shovel beside their gear. With the casual grace of a man accustomed to fighting, he pulled on a quilted coat and over it a leather coat reinforced with overlapping metal plates. He set out two black crossbows, levering each back to hook the trigger and ready a bolt. After, he drew on gloves and strapped on a helm before gathering up a bow as tall as he was, a quiver of arrows, an axe, and his sword and trotting away out of Kereka's line of sight, again carrying the shovel.

The woman appeared at the other limit of the scar, still towing Edek's body. Where they had ceased digging, a gap opened, about five paces wide. He gestured with the shovel. She shook her head, with a lift of her chin seeming to indicate the now-obvious singing of wings. The two argued, a quick and brutal exchange silenced by two emphatic words she spat out. She arranged the body to block as much of the gap as possible. With a resigned shrug, the bearded man took up a defensive position behind one of the stones to line up on the gap.

Brushing her hands off on her trousers, the witch jogged over to the gear, hooked a quiver of bolts onto her belt, and picked up both crossbows. Women did not wear armor, of course; Kereka knew better than to expect that even this remarkable creature would ever have been fitted with a man's accoutrements. Yet when she sauntered to take a measure of cover behind the standing stone nearest the gap, her easy pace, her lack of any outward sign of nervousness, made her seem far more powerful than her companion, who was forced to rely on leather and metal to protect himself. She propped one crossbow against the stone and, holding the other, straightened. The sun illuminated her haughty face. As she surveyed the eastern landscape and the golden hills, she smiled, a half twist of scornful amusement that woke a traitorous admiration in Kereka's heart. Someday she, the *begh*'s daughter who wished to live a man's life, would look upon her enemies with that same lazy contempt.

A band of warriors topped a far rise, the sound of their wings fading as they pulled up behind their leader to survey the stones beyond. The captain wore the distinctive metal glitter of griffin feathers on his wings, their shine so bright it hurt the eyes. They carried a banner of deep night blue on which rose a sword moon, dawn's herald.

"Belek," Kereka whispered, sure he could not see them, "it's the Pechanek! Curse them!"

Belek coughed and moaned; turned his head; kicked his feet in frustration.

She, too, struggled. Bad as things were, they had just gotten worse. Belek was healed; if they could escape or talk their way free, they had a hope of riding out again to continue Kereka's hunt, or maybe tricking their captors into a moment's inattention that would allow Kereka to kill the bearded man. Tarkan's bones! How had the Pechanek come to this forsaken place? Only a man who had killed a griffin had earned the right to wear griffin's wings. The *begh* of the Pechanek clan was not such a man. But his son Vayek was.

No *begh*'s son of a rival tribe would be out looking for three youths who must, after all, make their own way home or be judged unworthy of manhood's privileges and a man's respect. Had all her attempts to train herself in secret with her brother's aid in weapons and hunting and bragging and running and wrestling and the crafts and knowledge reserved for men now come to nothing?

A bitter anger burned in Kereka's throat. Her eyes stung, and for an instant she thought she might actually burst out of her bonds from sheer fury, but the magic binding her was too powerful.

The leader raised his spear to signal the advance. They raced out, wings singing, and split to encircle the stones. Waiting at a distance, they watched as their leader trotted forward alone. He was that sure of himself. His gaze scanned the stones, the two foreigners, the corpse, and the prisoners. Spotting Kereka, he stiffened, shoulders taut. He bent slightly forward, as if after all he had not expected to find her in such a predicament.

He absorbed the shock quickly enough. He was a man who knew how to adapt when the tide of battle turned against him; his cunning retreat in the face of superior numbers that he had twisted into a flanking ambush as the enemy galloped in reckless pursuit had defeated the Torkay, a tale everyone knew. He swung his gaze away from Kereka and addressed the bearded man, punctiliously polite.

"Honored sir, I address you. I, who am Prince Vayek, son of the

Pechanek *begh*, scourge of the Uzay and Torkay clans, defender of Tarkan's honor, Festival champion, slayer of griffins. If you please, surrender. Therefore, if you do so, we will be able to allow you to live as a slave among us, treated fairly as long as you work hard. If we are forced to fight you, then unfortunately we must kill you."

"You are not the man who arranged to meet me here," said the woman, her voice so resonant and clear that it seemed the wind spoke at her command. Had she always known their language? For unlike the foreigners enslaved by the clans, she spoke without accent, without mistake, as smoothly as if she had taken someone else's voice as her own.

Belek coughed again, and Kereka glanced his way as he opened and closed his mouth impotently. Was this the payment—or maybe only the first of many payments—the witch had ripped out of him? Had she stolen his voice?

"Women are consulted in private, not in public among men," Vayek continued, still looking toward the bearded man. "I do not wish to insult any woman by so boldly addressing her where any man could hear her precious words."

"Alas, my companion cannot speak your language, while I can. Where are my griffin feathers? For I perceive you have them with you, there, in that bundle." She gestured with the crossbow.

Kereka had all this time been staring at Vayek, not because the conical helm seemed shaped to magnify and enhance the shapely regularity of his features but rather as a dying person stares at the arrow of death flying to meet her. But now she looked in the direction of the gesture to see one horse whose rider was slung belly-down over the saddle, a bulky bundle of rolled-up hides strapped to his back.

Fool of a stupid girl! How was she to free herself if she could not pay attention, observe, and react? She was still on the hunt. She wasn't married yet.

Vayek's warband rode with a dead man. And it was this man, apparently, whom the witch had been waiting for. Kereka and the others had merely had the bad fortune to stumble upon their meeting place.

"I am willing to pay you the same reward I offered to the man I first dealt with. I presume that the bundle on his back is what he was obliged to deliver to me."

Vayek struggled; he truly did. He was famous among the clans for his exceptional courtesy and honor, and he made now no attempt to hide his feelings of embarrassment and shame, because true warriors expressed rage and joy and grief in public so that others might live their own struggles through such manly display. He looked again toward the bearded man, but the bearded man made no effort to intercede.

"Very well." As unseemly as it was to engage in such a conversation, he accepted the battleground, as a warrior must. "I will speak. I pray the gods will pardon me for my rudeness. I discovered a Berandai man skulking westward through the land with this bundle of griffin feathers. It is forbidden to trade the holy feathers outside the clans. He has paid the penalty." He gestured toward the body draped over the horse. "How can it be that such a meeting transpired, between foreign people and a plainsman, even one of the lowly Berandai, who like to call themselves our cousins? How can any foreigner have convinced even one of them to dishonor himself, his clan, and the grass and sky that sustain us?"

"Have your ancestors' tales not reminded you of that time, long in the past, when the Quman clans as well as the Berandai and the Kerayit made an agreement with the western queen? When they sent a levy to guard her, so the sorcerers of their kind could weave paths between the stones?"

"We clansmen do not send our warriors to serve foreigners as slaves."

But Kereka had seen the flash of light in the stones. Could it be true that the witch and her companion had used sorcery to weave a path into these stones from some other faraway place? That they could cross a vast distance with a single step? The old tales spoke of such sorcery, but she had never believed it because the Quman shamans said it could not be accomplished. Yet what if they had only meant that *they* could not weave such magic?

"Maybe *you* do not remember," the witch went on, "but some among you have not forgotten the old compact. This man had not. He was one among a levy sent into the west by his chiefs ten years ago. I saved his life, but that is another story. His debt I agreed could be repaid by him delivering to me what I need most."

"But I have already declared that it is forbidden! Perhaps an explanation is necessary. Griffin feathers are proof and purchase against sorcery. They are too powerful to be handled by any man except a shaman or a hero. They cannot be allowed to leave the grasslands. Long ago, griffin feathers were stolen from our ancestors, but the fabled *begh* Bulkezu invaded the western lands and returned the stolen feathers to their rightful place."

"Bulkezu the Humbled?" Her laughter cut sharply. "I see your clans do not learn from the past, as ours do in our careful keeping of records."

"Bulkezu was the greatest of *beghs*, the most honored and respected! He conquered the western lands and trampled their riders beneath his feet, and all the people living in those days knelt before him with their faces in the dirt."

She snorted. "He died a hunted man, killed by the bastard prince, Sanglant of Wendar. How small your world is! What tales you tell yourself! You don't even know the truth!"

Belek squirmed and grimaced, looking at Kereka with that excitable gaze of his, full of the hidden knowledge he had gleaned from the shamans who favored him and had shared with the sister he loved so well that he had secretly taught her how to fight.

She was accustomed to silence in the camp, but the witch's confident tongue emboldened her: *how small your world is*. Her own voice was harsh, like a crow's, but she cawed nevertheless, just to show that not all Quman were ignorant and blind. "I heard a different tale! I heard the great *begh* Bulkezu was killed by a phoenix, with wings of flame!"

Vayek's bright gaze flashed to her, and maybe he was shocked or maybe he simply refused to contradict her publicly before his waiting men because such correcting words would shame them both. Maybe he just knew better than to reveal to his enemy that he knew their prisoners. No doubt he was waiting to attack only for fear of risking Kereka's life. He himself need not fear the witch's sorcery; with his griffin wings, he was protected against it.

"Lads," he said instead, pretending not to recognize Kereka in her male clothing, "where did the witch come from?"

"Prince Belek was already wounded." Kereka choose her words slowly. Through desperate and thereby incautious speech, she and her brother had already betrayed their chiefly lineage, so all that was left them was to conceal Vayek's interest in her specifically. Yet she could not bear for Vayek to think she had given up, that she was returning meekly to the clans having failed in her hunt. "He was wounded taking a head. We had to help him reach his father the *begh* so he could die as a man, not a boy. Any other path would have been dishonorable. When we were riding back, we saw a flash of light like the sun rising. After that, we saw the witch standing up among the stones. We didn't see where she came from."

"Prince Vayek!" the witch cried, laughing as would a man after victory in a wrestling bout. "And this lad, the one whose spirit is woven with magic, he too is a prince!" Her gaze skipped from Belek to Kereka, and as the woman stared, Kereka did not flinch; she met her gaze; she would not be the first one to look away! But the woman's lips curved upward, cold and deadly: she was no fool, she could weave together the strands lying before her. She looked back toward the *begh*'s son. "Why are you come, Prince Vayek, son of the *begh* of the Pechanek clan, scourge, defender, champion? How have you stumbled across my poor comrade who so dutifully gathered griffin feathers for me? Were you out here in the western steppe looking for *something else?*"

He could not answer in words: he was too intelligent to give Kereka away, too proud to show weakness in public, too honorable to reply to a charge cast into the air by a woman who by all proper custom and understanding must be deemed insane and her life therefore forfeit.

He was a hero of the clans, seeking his bride. He had a different answer for his enemies.

He signaled with his spear. His riders shifted from stillness to motion between one heartbeat and the next. His own horse broke forward into a charge.

But the witch had guessed what was coming. She flung a handful of dust outward. When the first grains pattered onto the scarred earth sown with Edek's blood, threads of twisting red fire spewed out of the ground. Their furious heat scorched the grass outside the stones, although within them the air remained cool and the breeze gentle. Within two breaths, her sorcery wove a palisade impossible to breach.

Except for a man wearing griffin wings.

He tossed his spear to the ground and, drawing his sword, rode for the gap, where Edek's body, encased in white fire, did not quite seal the sorcerous palisade.

The bearded man released an arrow, the shot flying through the narrow gap.

Vayek rose in his stirrups and twisted, feathers flashing, and the arrow shredded to bits in the metal wings. He settled back into the saddle, lashing the horse, and with a leap they cleared the opening between the fiery palisade and Edek's burning feet. Again, and again, the bearded man released arrows, and again Vayek's quick reflexes shielded him as the arrows shattered in the feathers. He pressed hard, slamming a sword stroke at the bearded man, who hastily flung up his wooden shield to protect himself, taking such a solid blow that his legs twisted away under him and he stumbled back. Yet he was a strong and canny fighter, not easily subdued; he threw himself behind one of the great standing stones for cover as Vayek pulled the weight of his horse around in the confined corral made by the stones and the ring of sorcerous fire. Carrying a crossbow, the witch ran down to Edek's body and with her stone knife scraped the drying dregs of his blood out from Edek's head toward the far end of the scar. She meant to close the circle.

Kereka tugged at her ropes, hating this helplessness. All her life she had hated the things that bound her, just as poor Belek had hated his warriors' training so much that their father had once joked angrily that it would have been better had they swapped spirits into the other's body. Now, too—of course!—Belek had given up trying to break free; he had even shut his eyes!

"Belek!" Kereka whispered, hard enough to jolt him. "Is there no magic the shamans taught you? Anything that might help us—?"

Hoofbeats echoed eerily off the stones. She heard the snorting of a horse and then the horse loomed beside her, Vayek himself leaning from the saddle with a griffin feather plucked from his own wings held in his gauntlet. His gaze captured hers; he smiled, the expression all the more striking and sweet for its brevity.

"Boldest among women!" he said admiringly. "You have a man's courage and a man's wit! You alone will stand first among my wives, now and always! This I promise!"

What promises he made, he would keep. How could it be otherwise? He was a hero.

And so he would rescue her, and the tale's fame and elaboration would grow in the telling to become one of the great romantic legends told among the clans: his story, and she, like his noble horse, attendant in it.

A bolt like a slap of awakening clattered on the stone's face above Kereka's head and tumbled down over her body: another arrow. He sliced with the feather toward her. Ropes and magic slithered away. As she collapsed forward, released from the stone, he reined his steed hard aside and clattered off at a new angle to continue the fight. Kereka's hands and shoulders hurt, prickling with agony, but she shoved up against the pain. She had to watch. Movement flashed as a spear thrust from behind a huge stone monolith standing off to her right; steel flashed in reply as Vayek parried with his sword.

Over by the fiery palisade, the witch cursed, rising with blood on her knife, the gap between Edek's head and the scar now sealed. She raised the crossbow and released a bolt, but the missile slammed into stone to the right of the two warriors as they kept moving. She cursed again and winched in another bolt, then spun around as a bold rider tried to push through the remaining gap but was driven back by the intensity of the sorcerous flames.

Vayek fought the bearded man through the stones, using the stones and his wings to protect himself while the bearded man, with the agility of a seasoned fighter, used the stones to protect himself, trying to get close enough to hook his axe into Vayek's armor and pull him off the horse.

But in the end, the foreign man was just that: a man. He was not a hero. He was already bleeding from several wounds. It was only a matter of time before Vayek triumphed, yet again, as victor. What glory he would gather then!

All for him, because that was how the gods had fashioned the world: hawks hunted; horses grazed; marmots burrowed; flies annoyed. A man hunted glory while a woman tended the fires.

So the elders and shamans said. Their word was truth among the clans.

What tales they told themselves! How small was their world?

Legs burning as with a hundred pricking needles, Kereka staggered to the pile of gear and grabbed the haft of the griffin's feather Edek had found. Where her skin brushed the lower edge of a vane, blood welled at once. She grabbed the first leather riding glove that came to hand and shoved her bleeding hand into it, and even then the griffin feather bit through it; tugged on a gauntlet—Edek's—and at last she could grasp it without more blood spilling. She sliced Belek free and hauled him up, the farmer's head bumping against his thigh, still tied to his belt. She shoved him toward the flames consuming Edek's corpse.

"Run! Quickly!" She pushed him before her, and after a few clumsy steps he broke away from her and, clutching his belly, limped in a staggering run as he choked down cries of pain. Kereka easily kept pace beside him, and as the witch swung around, braids flying, bringing her crossbow to bear, Kereka leaped in front into the line of fire.

"Do not kill us!" she cried, "and in exchange for my brother's life and his debt to you, I will fetch you the griffin feathers you seek. I swear it on the bones of my father's father! I swear it on the honor of Tarkan's arrows."

A sword rang, striking stone, and sparks tumbled. A male voice shouted; a thump was followed by the straining howls of men grappling.

The witch stepped aside.

With the griffin feather held before her to cut away the searing heat of the palisade, Kereka dragged Belek through the breach. The cool breeze within the stones vanished and they ran through a haze of hot smoke and blackened grass to burst coughing and heaving into clearer air beyond. The sky throbbed with such a hollow blue like the taut inside of a drum that she wondered all at once what the sky within the stone circle had looked like. Had it even been the same sky? She looked back, but smoke and the weave of fire obscured the area.

The Pechanek men closed around them, spears bristling, faces grim.

"Don't harm us!" Belek cried. "I'm the son of the Kirshat *begh*!"

She gave Belek a shove that sent him sprawling in the grass. Waving the griffin's feather, she shouted in her crow's voice.

"The foreign witch is almost vanquished, but her magic must be smothered once and for all! I come at Prince Vayek's command to take to him the bundle of griffin feathers he captured. At once!"

Women did not command warriors. They sat beside their fathers, or brothers, or husbands, and a man knew he must listen to the advice they dispensed lest he suffer for having foolishly ignored female wisdom. Yet a *begh*'s daughter cannot be trifled with, however unseemly her behavior. Nor would a common warrior wish to offend the future wife of his future *begh*.

The horse with its corpse and cargo was brought swiftly, the thick bundle wrapped in leather cut free. She grabbed the cords and hoisted the bundle onto her back, its weight oddly light given the power of what lay concealed within. Brandishing the griffin feather to cut a path for herself through the witch's sorcery, she ran back into the smoke before they could think to question her, although which one would have the courage to speak directly to her, who was neither kin or wife, she could not imagine. Grass crackled beneath her feet; soot and ash flaked and floated everywhere; the tapestry of flames rose as if to touch the pastures of the heavens, but she did not hesitate. She plunged into the maelstrom of scalding magic. Stinging hot ash rained on her cheeks and forehead.

"Sister! Don't leave me!"

But her and Belek's lives had been severed on the day Prince Vayek had ridden into the Kirshat clan with her bride price. It was the only reason cautious Belek had agreed to let her hunt with him: he was more afraid of losing her than of being beaten for taking her along where no one intended her to go.

Blessed breathable air hit her chest so unexpectedly that she was gulping and hacking as tears flowed freely. She blinked hard until she could see.

At the far edge of the circle, Vayek had caught the bearded man and pinned his axe against stone with his spear. The witch, her back to Kereka, loosed a bolt toward his magnificent profile, but he could not be taken by surprise. He twisted to bring his wings around to shield himself, and with the motion cut his sword down on his hapless prey.

The bearded man crumpled.

The witch shrieked.

Kereka shoved the bundle against the woman's torso and, when the witch flinched back, grabbed the crossbow out of her hands.

"You're not warrior enough to defeat him!" she cried. "Even I am not that! And there's no glory for me in being dead! Here are your griffin feathers. If you want to escape, pretend to fall at my feet."

She tossed the crossbow to one side as she screamed in as loud a voice as she had ever used. "Husband! Husband! The witch weaves an evil sorcery even now. She means to wither my womb! Hurry! We must escape this wicked, evil trap or I will be barren forever, no sons born from your siring to join the Pechanek clan! Hurry!"

He reined his horse hard away from the stone, casting a glance as swift as an arrow toward her. The bearded man lay slumped along the base of the black megalith. It was too late for him. But not for Kereka.

The witch had not moved, caught in a choice between clutching the precious bundle of griffin feathers or lunging past Kereka for the crossbow.

Kereka tripped her neatly, using a wrestling move she'd learned from Belek, speaking fast as she released her. "If it's true there are paths between the stones, then open a way now with your sorcery. But wait for me! Remember that I have fulfilled a debt and I want payment in return. Remember to trust me."

She leaped back as if fleeing something she feared more deeply than death itself. Vayek thundered up behind her, sword raised for the running kill, but Kereka held her ground with the griffin's feather shielding the witch's body.

"I've killed her!" she shouted. "Your courage has emboldened me! Now it won't be said that you laid hands on a mere woman! Quickly, let us go before her sorcery sickens me!"

She bolted toward the fire like an arrow released from Tarkan's heavenly bow, praying that Vayek would dismiss the woman as not worthy of his warrior's prowess. She ran, and he followed.

The fire's hissing crackle, the horse's weight and speed and heavy hoof-falls as it plunged toward the wall of fire; the high thrumming atonal singing of the wings in the presence of powerful magic; all this perhaps distracted Vayek as she raced ahead and dashed through that flaming gap in front of him. Fire roared. The smoke poured up to greet her, and because she was only one small human on two small feet, she darted to one side even as the clothes on her back grew hot and began to curl and blacken. He galloped past like the fury of the heavens, not even seeing her step aside because he was blinded by the tale he had long since learned to believe was the only tale in all the world.

But it wasn't the only tale.

She could follow Vayek back onto the sea of grass into a life whose contours were utterly familiar and entirely honorable. Handsome, brave, strong, even-tempered, honorable, famous among the clans for his prowess, with two secondary wives already although he was not ten years a man, he would be the worst kind of husband. A woman could live her life tending the fire of such a man's life. Its heat was seductive, but in the end its glory belonged only to him.

She spun, feet light beneath her, and raced back through the gap.

To find the witch already in action. She had bound the bundle of griffin feathers to her own back. Now she had her arms under the bearded man's shoulders, trying to hoist him up and over a saddled horse. Kereka ran to help her, got her arms around his hips and her own body beneath him. Blood slicked her hands and dripped on her face, but his rattling breaths revealed that he still lived.

The woman spared her one surprised glance. Then, like a *begh*, she gestured toward the other horses before running to a patch of sandy soil churned by the battle and spotted with blood. She unsheathed her obsidian knife and began, as one might at the Festival dance with Tarkan's flaming arrows, to cut a pattern into the expectant air.

A distant howl of rage rang from beyond the sorcerous fire.

Kereka ran to fetch the three remaining foreign horses that had come with the witch and the bearded man as well as her own mount. The other horses were already saddled and laded, obedient to the lead. She strung them on a line and mounted the lead mare as an arch of golden fire flowered into existence just beyond the obsidian blade. The witch grabbed the reins of the bearded man's horse and walked under the fulgent threads.

Into what she walked, Kereka could not see. But riding the shore of the river of death was the risk you took to find out what lay on the other side.

Wings sang. The shape of a winged man astride a horse loomed beyond the fire. Vayek burst back past the writhing white fire of Edek's corpse and into the circle. The complex weave that gave the arch form began to fray at the edges, flashing and shivering.

Griffin feathers are proof against sorcery.

She flung Edek's griffin feather away; it glittered, spinning as on a wind blowing out of the unseen land beyond the arch, while Edek's gauntlet fell with a thud to the dirt. Then she whipped her mount forward, and they charged into a mist that stank of burned and rotting corpses, of ash and grass, of blood and noble deeds.

Her eyes streamed stinging tears; heat burned in her lungs.

The foul miasma cleared, and she was trotting free down the slope of a hill with blackened grass flying away beneath the horses' hooves and the sun setting ahead of her, drawing long shadows over the grass. The witch had already reached a familiar-looking stream, and she was kneeling beside the body of her comrade as she cast handfuls of glittering dust over his limp form. Saplings and brush fluttered in a brisk wind out of the west.

Kereka twisted to see behind her the same stones, the very same stone circle, rising black and ominous exactly where they had stood moments before. Vayek and his warband had vanished.

Did the witch possess such powerful sorcery that she could pluck men from the present world and cast them into the spirit world?

No.

The carpet of burned grass had cooled; its ashy stubble had been disheveled by strong winds; green shoots had found the courage to poke their heads above the scorched ground. She dismounted, tossed the reins over her mount's head. Her mare nipped one of the pack horses, who kicked; she separated the steppe horse and hobbled her, then trudged on aching feet back up into the stones. The soles of her boots were almost burned away. Her clothes shed flakes of soot. Her hands oozed blood from a score of hairline cuts. Her chest stung with each breath she inhaled.

There lay what remained of Edek, flesh eaten away by the unearthly fire and skeleton torn and scattered by beasts. Cut ropes lay in heaps at the base of three stones; the litter had been mauled by animals but was mostly intact. Their gear was gone, picked up to the last knife and bridle and leather bottle. The ashes of the campfire were ground into the earth. The wind gentled as dusk sighed down over them.

The moon shouldered up out of the east, round and bright, the full moon on which she was to have been wed. The moon could not lie. Half a month had passed since the night of the sword moon. The witch had woven a path between that time and this time, and they had ridden down it.

A whistle shrilled. Standing at the edge of the stones, Kereka saw the witch, standing now and waving to catch her attention. Trusting fool! It might well be easy to kill her and take the bearded man's head while he was injured and weak, before the witch fully healed him, if he could be healed. She could then ride back to her mother's tent and her father's tribe and declare herself a man. She knew what to expect from a man's life, just as she knew what a woman's life entailed.

So what kind of life did these foreigners live, with their sorcery and their crossbows and the way they handed a shovel from one to the other, sharing the same work, maybe even sharing the same glory? It was a question for which she had no answer. Not yet.

She went back to the litter and grabbed the leather towlines. Pulled them taut over her own shoulders and tugged. Like uncertainty, the burden was unwieldy, but she was stubborn and it was not too heavy for her to manage.

Could she trust a witch? Would a witch and a foreigner ever trust her?

Pulling the litter behind her, she walked across the charred earth and down through the tall grass to find out.

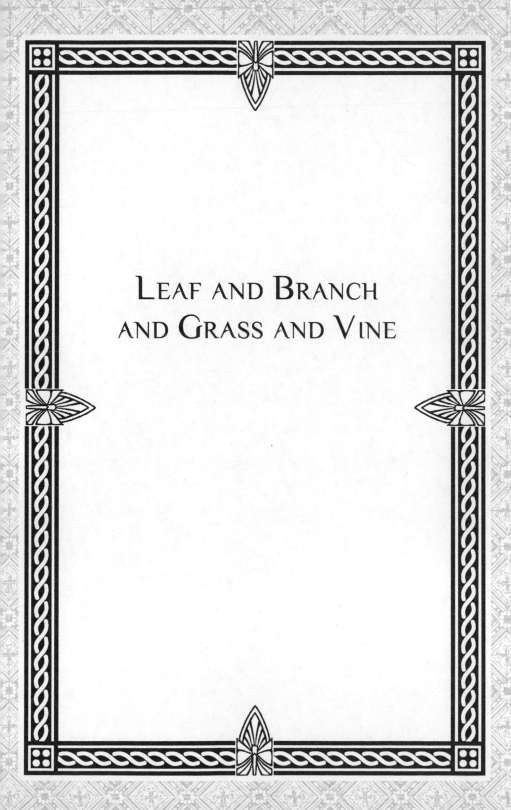

LEAF AND BRANCH
AND GRASS AND VINE

A hand pounding on her cottage door woke Anna, just as it had that terrible night almost three months ago. Jolting upright, she wiped a hand across her mouth as if to wipe away the taste of fear and grief but it did not go away. Beside her on the wide mattress, her two youngest children slept like the dead, and she was glad for it. No sense in cringing and stalling; the bad news would come whether now or at dawn, and she did not want the children to wake.

From the other room, where she had long slept with her husband, rose a murmur of voices: her daughter and her new husband waking to the summons.

She wrapped her well-worn bride's shawl over her shift and padded to the barred door. Pointless to bar the door, really, since she had left the glass window unshuttered. The light of a full moon bathed the plank floor in a ghostly light, enough that she need not grope for a precious candle. By the measure of the shortened shadows, she knew it was barely past midnight.

She set a hand on the latch. "Who is there?"

"Anna, it is Joen. No trouble here, but I need you at once."

Her brother's familiar voice calmed the pounding clamor of her heart. She let him in just as the door into the other room opened and Hansi stuck his head out, holding a lit candle in one hand and his butchering knife in the other.

She said, "Holding a light in the darkness means the other man can see you but you can't see him."

Hansi chuckled. He was a good-natured young man, slow to take offense to his pride. "My apologies, Mother Anna. Is that Uncle Joen I hear?"

"It is," said Joen, "and I would ask you to get everyone dressed."

Anna grabbed Joen's thick forearm. "I thought you said no trouble."

"There's been a skirmish fought in and around West Hall. Rumor says the Forlangers are involved. The family should hide in the caves until we are sure they've moved on."

Anna's daughter Mari appeared beside Hansi, resplendent in her bride's shawl and so heavily pregnant that she lumbered. Her face was solemn as she took the candle from her young husband and examined first her mother and then her uncle by its smoky light.

"We'll get the children up and go at once," Mari said.

Hansi brushed his fingers down Mari's forearm, and the gesture of affection made Anna glad all over again that her daughter had found a good man.

Joen nodded, shifting his crutch. His empty trouser leg swayed. "Take provisions, everything you can carry and cart, but be quick about it. But I need you, Anna, if you will. There are dead and wounded at West Hall."

She turned on him, her mood gone bitter at once. "I will sew up none of those cursed Forlangers. They can die in their own rot."

"Truly," he said, patting her shoulder, "but it was General Olivar's men they fought."

"That changes matters then. For the sake of the general, I will do everything I can to help. I'll get my things."

Now that she was awake, the sour morning taste was rising in her stomach, a reminder that her husband's death had not left her entirely alone. But she did not speak of it. Mari suspected, but it was ill fortune to count on the harvest of fruit that might not ripen. If the gods willed it, then they would bless her with his last child.

Hansi rousted the children as Anna dressed and afterward collected her bag. She kissed them all and left, Joen shifting impatiently as he waited. The full moon bathed the world in a glamour. She had many soft memories of this time of night, for summer's tide had washed her youth in many sweet meetings. But now he was dead.

The houses of the village sprouted in clusters along a cart track that led to the tavern and the temple and, most magnificently, the new market hall built under the supervision of General Olivar ten years ago. She had to measure her pace to allow Joen to keep up without it seeming she could easily out-stride him and, because he was her older brother, she dared not joke with him about it; he would take it amiss, for he had been a soldier for ten years under the general's command before he had lost his foot.

Her husband would not have cared. His sense of humor had never failed, even as he was dying of a rotting wound her herbs and wise nursing could not heal.

The treacherous Forlangers had the king's ear and bragged that they were his most loyal subjects. But out here beyond the King's City people knew them for the greedy, cruel mercenaries that they were, always ready to steal from villages wherever they guessed the king would not notice. Only the general and his men stood between the villages and the raiders.

Someone had lit the crowing cock lamp atop the market hall's steep roof. This beacon called to the folk hurrying forward now, carrying their children, cages with chickens, and bags stuffed with grain and such produce as they could carry. It was not late enough in the season that beasts had been slaughtered for the winter's meat, so the older boys and girls were being dispatched to drive the animals out to the far pastures where they might hope to bide unseen until the danger was past.

The headman's daughter, standing among a cluster of whispering women, saw Anna and broke away from the others to meet her.

"Mistress Anna, if you will, can you go with my husband to West Hall? He is taking ten men."

"If the Forlangers walk the road, ten men will attract their attention. Give me your brother as escort, and we'll go through the forest. He knows the woods as well as I do. No Forlanger will see us."

"But alone, Mistress? My brother is no help in a skirmish. He will just run away and hide, but hiding did not save him then and will not now."

"He is braver than you think. Anyway, we cannot fight the Forlangers with swords and spears. If we have our wits, then that is our weapon against them."

The cool autumn night air did not bite, but summer was irrevocably gone. Because it had rained the day before, the leaves slipped instead of crackled underfoot, making it a quiet passage. With a clear sky and the moon's merciful light a bounty laid over the world, they did not bother with a lantern. Both she and young Uwe knew the nearby animal trails well enough that the full moon gave them all the light they needed to follow familiar ground. She kept her eye open for night-blooming woundheal, at its strongest here at the end of the year and especially under a full moon, but saw none of its pale blossoms.

Uwe slipped in and out of shadow ahead of her. The young man was light on his feet and very shy. He glanced back now and again to make sure she was on the right track, for there were places in the wood where a person might fall into harm's way and never know until it was too late to climb out.

That was the way of the world: usually the worst was already on you before you knew your throat had been opened and you were bleeding out. So her husband's death had come, its end determined before she had even known he was injured.

Ahead, Uwe halted, a hand raised in warning. Anna stopped, careful with her feet as she felt a branch bend beneath her shoe, shifting carefully so as to make no noise.

Men's voices shattered the silence with shouts and a ringing clash of weapons. Sound carried oddly at night, seeming both near at hand and yet impossibly distant. Uwe merely shrugged and began walking again. This trail swung away from the main road and around the back of Witch's Hill to the back pastures of West Hall's cultivated lands. No one liked to go this way. As they neared the haunted clearing that sheltered Dead Man's Oak, Anna listened for the hooves of the Hanging Woman. All she heard were the last dying shrieks of a skirmish away north, then nothing at all except for the wind rattling branches and the chirp of a night sparrow in a nearby tree.

Maybe the Hanging Woman walked elsewhere this night.

As they entered the big clearing with the oak, Uwe slowed his steps until he was walking beside her, keeping her between him and the ancient tree. An old reddened scar like a ring around his neck marked him as one of the few who had survived an encounter with the Hanging Woman. The meeting had changed him, for no one could meet the Hanging Woman and not be changed.

Uwe grabbed Anna's arm, fingers a vise.

A body lay propped against the oak's gnarled trunk.

Uwe shrank back into the brush, but Anna knew better. You never retreated from what could not be changed. What was the point? If the Hanging Woman came, you could not hide from her.

Anyway, a sword rested on the ground at the body's feet, and the Hanging Woman always took weapons for she was a scavenger of lives. As Anna moved into the clearing, she crumbled a bit of dried lavender in her outstretched hand, letting its dust sweeten her steps, taking no more than three steps at a time, pausing between to whisper the prayer that the old woman of the wood had taught her. "Moonlight make a shade of me, daylight make me whole."

So she came to the oak untouched. Its trunk was as wide as her cottage, and its bark wrinkled and knobby. The huge branches of the oak draped like arms waiting to crush her if she did one wrong thing.

The body was that of a soldier. He was alive, unconscious and bleeding, and at first glance, seeing an officer's sash bunched up across his chest, she thought he was a wounded Forlanger. She hefted her walking stick to bash in his head before he woke.

But then the light changed, shifting through the branches to illuminate his face clearly: an older man, dark hair sifted with white. A face she knew and would never forget, although she had only seen him once in her life, on the day ten years ago when the market hall had been dedicated and given over to the village.

She would never forget the crookedly healed nose, the scar on his cheek, the metal brace he wore on his left leg. She knelt cautiously and eased the bloody glove off his left hand: yes, his left little finger was missing, as it said in the song—*He was last to get on the boat and yet all the Forlanger wolf got of him was his smallest finger.*

The wounded soldier was General Olivar.

Struck down and somehow abandoned or lost by his own men.

She was so stunned that she sat with a grunt and pressed both hands to her belly, panting softly as she tried to gather her scattering thoughts. Ten years had aged him, as it had aged her: ten years ago her eldest child Mari had been a mischievous girl always singing some silly song, her eldest son had still been alive, for that was before the shivering sickness had taken the boy, and her two youngest not yet even born.

A hoof-fall sounded, gentle as mist, and then another.

So the Hanging Woman announced her coming.

She looked up. At the edge of the clearing Uwe hid under an evergreen bitterberry shrub, crouching with arms wrapped around knees. All she could see of him was his face like a frightened baby moon. Moonlight collected in the open space as magic into a bowl.

The hoof-falls touched as lightly as the light itself.

Shadows tangled, stretching and winding, coming into life.

The Hanging Woman's noose took shape as a rope of darkness coiling across the grass.

The old oak had a cleft, and in its hollow many years ago an old cunning woman well versed in herbcraft and mystery had lived for several winters. That was the old woman of the wood, the witch for whom the hill was named, although there had been another cunning woman before her according to the stories told to Anna by her grandmother when she was a child.

Anna glanced once more toward Uwe and, as she hoped, he had not moved, trusting to the bitterberry's prickly scent to shield him. Rising, she grasped General Olivar by the armpits and dragged his limp weight halfway around the tree, whispering the chant of protection she had learned from the old woman: "Leaf and branch and grass and vine. Let me be like them, what the eye sees but does not notice."

Just in time she hauled him in through the cleft, into the dusty dry shelter of the tree's heart. The smell of smoke still lingered. He gasped softly, and his eyes opened.

"My sword," he said in a hoarse whisper, as if he already knew what she was about.

She had to risk it. The sword would betray their presence. The narrow cleft had been barely wide enough to admit the general's shoulders. She squeezed back through it now and to her horror heard the creaks of men shifting on saddles and the thump of many ordinary horses rather than the eight-legged steed ridden by the Hanging Woman. Pulling her bridal shawl up over her head gave her cover, of a sort, as she glided around the base of the tree. Four riders emerged into the clearing from the path that led, through thickets, to West Hall. They were too far away yet to see the ground clearly but if she moved again they would see her, so she did not run but instead placed herself to stand squarely over the fallen sword, letting her skirt cover it.

Their pale tunics and dark sashes marked them as Forlangers, a fine lord and three of his retainers to look at them all agleam in their pride. But the moonlight showed their faces: a wolf and his gaunt and ugly brethren, hard of heart and bitter of blood.

Night and the ill-omened tree made them nervous. Battle had strung them taut. She had no trouble hearing their too loud voices.

"... said they saw someone running in this direction, my lord."

"I want him dead," said the lord in a high coarse voice. "This is all for naught if he is not dead."

"My lord, we came the wrong way," said a second retainer, his tone brittle with nerves. "This is the witch's tree, the hanging tree. It has an angry and hateful spirit."

The Hanging Woman was already here. Her shadows swelled with the rope of fear. The horses shifted nervously, ears flaring. In the sky above, clouds crept toward the moon.

Why not? What weapon had she, except her wits?

She raised her arms to make the shawl flutter like dark wings.

"Here are you come, so which is it who will offer himself to my rope?" she said in a voice that carried across the clearing lit with a gauzy glamour. "I take one for my noose."

The moon slid beneath the cloud. A gust of wind shook through the vast branches. An owl hooted from the verge, and there came out of the forest the sound of a clop of horse's hooves, slow and steady as the approach of death.

The Hanging Woman was coming.

Night, and the oak's mighty shadow, did the rest.

The Forlangers turned tail and rode back the way they had come, toward the fields and buildings of West Hall. Brush rattled around them, marking their passage, and one man shouted as he lost control of his horse.

The cloud passed, and the moon reemerged. The shadows untangled, and Uwe rose with wide eyes from the bitterberry where he had been hiding and dashed across the clearing to fetch up beside her.

She hoisted the heavy sword. "Was that you, with the owl call? I reckon I have heard you test that other times."

He grinned, then popped his tongue in his mouth to make the clop-clap hoofbeat sound.

She laughed, then frowned, for it was dangerous to insult the Hanging Woman. "They will come back," she said. "If not at night, then at dawn. You must help me carry him to the rose bower."

Uwe did not want to enter the cleft. Into that cleft one night several years ago the Hanging Woman had dragged the person Uwe had been before, and he had emerged changed, become what he was now.

Anna grasped his elbow and shook him. "The wounded soldier is General Olivar himself. The Forlangers mean to kill him. If they do, there will be nothing but theft and indignity for us and all our kin. You see that, do you not?"

He nodded. They all knew it was true.

The general had fallen unconscious again, although he was still breathing. They dragged him as gently as possible out of the cleft. In the moonlight, Anna unclasped his coat of plate armor and cut away padding and under-tunic to lay bare the wound. It was just above his hip, in the meat and muscle of the torso. She bent to sniff at it, and while the scent of blood was strong, it seemed the blade had missed his gut for there was no fetid sewage breath from the cut.

That meant he might live.

If they worked quickly and covered their tracks.

They got his coat of plates off him, which woke him up, but he was a soldier who did not complain or panic. He just watched, eyes fluttering with pain, as she bound the wound with strips cut from his tunic.

Because he was awake, it was easiest to drape him over Uwe and let the slight man walk with the general's weight on him. Anna followed with the sword and the coat of plates. They halted beyond the clearing so she could go back with a branch and confuse the ground to make sure no one guessed they had been there.

"Leaf and branch and grass and vine. Let them see but see nothing."

The old cunning woman had lived for six years in the wood, wintering in the oak and living the other seasons in a hidden refuge. During the time she had bided at Witch's Hill, the Hanging Woman had never once ridden out.

There is more than one kind of power in the world.

They made their way into the trees, following trails in the dim light all the way to a rocky spine of land where boulders made a great jumble of the forest floor. A stream burbled through the undergrowth, running low at this time of year.

In the other three seasons, the old woman had lived deep in the forest in this rocky dell within an astounding growth of sprawling evergreen rose trees that were more shrub than tree. Sticks woven into the arched branches made a house of remarkable grandeur, one so artfully concealed that you could not see it unless you knew it was there.

Anna had herself lived here off and on for five years as a girl, because the old woman had demanded an apprentice from the village, someone to fetch and carry for her, and Anna had been the only girl bold enough to volunteer. She had been paid with learning. The old woman had instructed her in herbcraft and many other cunning skills, although Anna had not passed some subtle test and so had never been taught any deeper secrets. Most of all, she had been given the gift of freedom, able to speak her mind, to ask any question she wanted regardless of whether the old woman answered it, and to run where she willed on summer nights. She had met her husband in the forest, for he was a woodsman's son and became a woodsman himself in time. So they had set up house together after she got pregnant. By then the old woman had vanished, never to be seen again.

"Uwe," she said. "Go back and make sure no trace remains of our trail."

He left his heavy pack behind with its store of grain, for they had known they would have to depend on feeding themselves if the stores in West Hall were burned or looted.

Anna visited the rose bower several times a year to sort out its store of firewood, rake the ground, lay in grass, clear out any animal nests. The old woman had taught her that a fire must always be laid, ready to light. She was glad of that teaching now, for even in darkness she could start a fire on the old hearth. By its golden light she shifted the general onto a layer of grass.

His eyes were open but he did not speak. By the reckoning of his cold glare, she suspected he was in so much pain he dared not speak. Perhaps he was barely conscious, half sunk into the blinding haze that separates life from death.

She opened her bag and got to work. After peeling back the temporary bandage and his bloody clothing and giving him a leather strap to bite on, she cleansed the gash with a tonic of dog rose and whitethorn. Afterward she sewed it up with catgut as neatly as a torn sleeve. A poultice of mashed feverbane leaves she bound over the wound with linen strips. That he did not pass out again during all this surprised her, but it took men like that sometimes: the heart would race and keep them wakeful despite the pain. She therefore lifted up his head and helped him drink an infusion of willowbark and courage-flower. She then fortified herself with the cider and bread she had brought for herself, since the old woman had also taught her that no one could keep their wits about them if they were starving or thirsty, especially not those who were needed to care for the ill and injured. He watched her from the pallet of grass. Being evidently a polite man, he did not speak until she finished eating.

"Where am I and how did you come to find me?" he asked in a voice made harsh with weakness and pain.

"You are in the forest between West Hall and Woodpasture, my lord general."

"You know me?"

"I live in Woodpasture, my lord. We have a market in our fine market hall every week."

"Woodpasture?" He murmured the word, seeking through his memory. "Ah. Bayisal."

"That is the name they call it in the king's court, I think," she said kindly. "But it is not our name. How came you to fall under the Forlanger sword, my lord?"

He breathed in silence for a time, measuring the pain in his hip or perhaps simply fishing back through the last few days. "Treachery. They and I are ever at odds in court. Lord Hargrim is ready to steal my command and my lands. I must get back to court. Have you men in your village who can convey me?"

"We have men, my lord. My husband died in your service, and my brother lost his leg."

He slanted a look at her, shifting a moment later to notice that she had placed the sword near his side, where he could reach it.

"I blame the Forlangers. Not you, my lord. In case you are wondering."

His smile had a force that cracked the distance between them. "Generously spoken, Mistress. May I know your name?"

"Anna, my lord."

"And the other one. There was another woman, was there not? The one who was supporting me as we walked?"

"No other woman. A man."

"I was sure, for my arm was wrapped around . . . I meant no offense by it. . . ." He rubbed a callused hand over his eyes. "I suppose I was delirious. Perhaps I am roaming not on earth but in the shadows cast by the gods."

"No, my lord. You lie on earth. If men from the village convey you to the King's City, my lord, what is to stop the Forlangers from killing you all?"

"They could hide me in a wagon. . . ." He shook his head at the same time she did. "They'll be watching the roads. They will not rest until Hargrim can throw my corpse before the king and claim me as a traitor."

"How will he claim you as a traitor when all know you serve the king loyally?"

"Men lie, Mistress Anna. They tell stories that are false."

"So they do, my lord. All but my husband. He was a good man and never lied to me, except for the time he had to come tell me that my son was dead."

"I hope your son did not die in my service too. I would hate to think I had repaid you for this by having measured so much grief into your life."

"No, my lord. He was a boy and died of a sickness, as children do."

"Sad tidings for a mother. What of you, Mistress Anna, do you lie?" He paused, a hand probing the linen bandage. "Can you heal me?"

"I have some knowledge of herbcraft and have done what I know how to do. I have a tea that should help with the pain and any fever. It is a bad wound, and you may yet die of it, but you may live. It is not for me to say. That is the choice of the Hanging Woman."

"Who is the Hanging Woman? Some country name for death?"

"Death is death, my lord, not a person. Do they not know that at court? The Hanging Woman has a rope and will hang you in it if she chooses to capture you. Those who are hanged are changed. Maybe that change will be life into death or maybe it will be something else, something you never expected."

He gave a rough cough, then winced. "This is not the work of your Hanging Woman, then, for I have been expecting an attack for months now. Ever since the poison has reached the king's ear, a rumor that I plan to raise my army against him and place myself on the throne."

"Do you, my lord?"

All at once the pain and exhaustion and blood loss overwhelmed him, or perhaps the infusion finally took hold. He looked so tired, as if the fight had dragged on too long and he wondered if he had the will to keep struggling. "No. Never. But it may be too late. The rot of that story may already have tainted the king's heart."

"Can you rest, my lord?"

He twisted and turned as well as he could, restless and aggrieved. Lines of pain wrinkled his forehead. His lips were pale, and his eyes shadowed by the effort of speaking. "If only . . . if I could get to the king and not be murdered on the way. I was on my way to court now, and you see what has happened. Lord Hargrim's people control the roads. I will never get through."

"Have you no allies in court?"

"The king's sister has the king's ear. He trusts her. And I trust her." He paused and looked at her. A yellow-beak's whistle chirred twice from out among the leaves. "We were not lovers. It is nothing to do with that."

"I did not think it was," she said, surprised at how quickly he had hastened to deny an unasked question. "It is no business of mine."

"She was married to Lord Hargrim's brother back once. She knows what they are."

"Wolves," said Anna, for they had returned to a subject she cared about. "Winter wolves, on the hunt."

A smile tightened his mouth. "That's right. They are wolves. They want to kill me so they can eat the herd at their leisure once I am no longer there to protect those the king has given me to guard."

He looked up, seeing Uwe duck into view, but since Anna had heard the bird call she did not turn.

"This is Uwe. He is my friend, the one who carried you," she said.

The general stared for a long, uncomfortable while at Uwe's beardless face and the loose layers of clothing that hid his slender body.

Anna rolled up a blanket against the general's side. "Rest a little," she said. "You can go nowhere tonight or tomorrow or any day soon."

"Do me this one favor," he said, touching his throat.

There was a humble iron chain there, well made but nothing fancy. When he fumbled at the chain, she realized he had not the strength or dexterity to pull it out, so she hooked fingers around the links and eased it from under his tunic.

A hammered tin medallion in the shape of a swan hung from the end of the chain, odd to see around the neck of the general because it was a cheap trinket, the kind of thing peddlers sold when they came through the village with their carts in the summer and autumn. She turned it over. On the back were scratched markings.

"Do you see what it says?" he asked.

Uwe stretched forward to look and, like Anna, shook his head.

"I cannot read, my lord," Anna said. "I thought a lord like you would wear gold, not tin."

A smile brushed his lips. His gaze seemed to track back into memory, or else he was about to pass out.

"It says 'one foot in the river.'" His voice was hoarser now, fading as the infusion dulled the pain. "Elland Fort is where I saved the kingdom, even though people say my great victory was at Toyant Bridge. But the ones who I trust know the truth of it. They know I wear this to remind me."

"Who are those, my lord?"

"My young wife. My brother. My three captains, of whom one is now dead. My two aunts. The king's sister."

"And where are these people, my lord? Can they not rescue you?"

"The king's sister is at the palace, close to the king. The others are far from here, for we heard a rumor that the Forlangers were going to strike. My wife is pregnant, so I sent her to my aunts' stronghold in the south. I was riding to the palace with proof of the Forlangers' treachery. That is why they cut me down even so close to the court. Once the king knows, they will be ruined."

Anna pressed another swallow of the tincture down him. His breathing was getting a ragged edge as his body fought him down into the rest he needed if he wished to heal.

"They will lie about me, about what I did here, how I died here. They will lie about my disloyalty to the king. But whatever else, this is my token. Do not let it fall into the hands of the Forlangers. Better you should have it, if it cannot be returned to my wife."

She tucked the tin swan into his hand. His fingers closed over the medallion.

His eyes fluttered closed, as if the swan comforted him.

For a moment she thought he would finally sleep, but he struggled awake again as a man struggles to climb a slippery hillside. He glanced around the space but because of the darkness beyond the glow of the hearthfire he could see nothing except a glimmer of smoke pooling against the leaves as it sought a way heavenward.

"No one will find this place," she said. "And we will keep a watch over you. You can trust Uwe as you can trust me. The Forlangers killed my husband. I will not turn you over to them. I give you my oath by the water of the gods. Let that content you, my lord. You must rest if you are to have a hope of healing."

It did content him, or else blood loss and the herbs pulled him down.

Slowly, the sun came up, although it remained dim beneath the leaves. The heavy cover of branches would disperse the smoke by so many diverse channels that it would be hard to see it, but a good nose might smell it and it was not yet cold. So she let the fire burn down and smothered its scent with crumbled leaves of lavender and fennel while Uwe fetched water from the nearby stream to fill the two covered jars she always left here.

She tidied herself and considered the situation.

"So here we are, Uwe," she said. "He will die here, or he will live. If he dies, then he is dead. If he lives, though, what then?"

Uwe rarely spoke for he preferred the forest and solitude, where he could live within the patience of the trapper and hunter and not have to trouble himself with the difficult passages that a changed man must negotiate among people. His voice had a lightness that made it hard to hear, but Anna knew how to listen. "My sister's husband can take him to the King's City in a wagon under guard of a company of men."

Anna shook her head. "No. They will be stopped and the general killed."

"They can carry him through the forest. I can show the way."

"The forest does not grow all the way to the gates of the King's City. They will still catch you."

"Then we can carry him to the other place he spoke of. In the south." Uwe bit a finger, sorting through thoughts. Anna had rarely seen him so animated. "The lord can write. We could fetch a bit of paper from the priest and have him write a message."

"One written word is like another," said Anna. "How can anyone trust that the message truly came from him and is no trick of the Forlangers? Ten men may write the same word and it will look the same, but each man speaks in a different voice."

The general's hand had relaxed in sleep and the tin swan slipped from his fingers, dangling just above the dirt where the chain caught and tangled through his lax fingers. His hands were callused and scarred as by the lash of a whip. From far away, chased to their ears by the mystery of how the forest weaves sound, they heard a horn call, soldiers about their pursuit.

She fished the tin swan out of General Olivar's hand. "I will go."

Uwe blinked at her, then pressed a hand to his throat as if he wished to cry out that she could not, dared not, must not, but knew the words would be spoken in vain.

"Yes, I will go," she said more firmly, for she saw it was the only choice. "It is three days' walk. I have food enough if I take all the bread and cheese. You know enough of herbcraft to stay with him."

Uwe nodded, silent, acquiescing because he had been her pupil once, learning the herbcraft handed down from woman to woman. That was before the Hanging Woman changed him into the man he had secretly known himself to be. So Anna felt assured Uwe could care for the patient while she was gone. She thoroughly described the regimen necessary to keep the wound from rotting, and advised him to brew up a stout broth from whatever grouse he could catch and to boil up barley to thicken the general's blood.

"But only cook at night. Douse the fire in the day. Stay away from the village until you are out of food. If I am not back in seven days, then go to my brother Joen."

She did not like to think about Mari and her other children. She hoped they were well, hidden in the warren of caves where the villagers of Woodpasture had for generations taken refuge in times of strife. She hoped they would not worry on her behalf, but if the general died, then the steady depredations of the Forlangers would make life worse for everyone. West Hall would just be the beginning. Better they suffer a few days' anxiety now than a lifetime of misery after.

She took her humble bag and set off, skirting along the edge of West Hall's fields. No smoke rose, a better sign than she could have hoped for because it meant no houses were being burned. No doubt the Forlangers hoped to be given this grant of land once the general was disgraced and dead; only a fool burned the grain that would feed him. How many West Hall villagers had died or been injured she could not know, but she hoped her relatives had been spared. The Forlangers knew that if they caused too much damage the king would notice that strife troubled the isolated corners of his peaceful realm, so they prowled lightly and struck only for the necessary kill.

She made good time on woodsmen's paths that wound through the trees and heavy undergrowth. Twice, on hearing men's shouts and horses, she found concealment and waited until all sound of soldiers' presence died away. Once she heard the ring of an axe, and she paused in a copse of trembling aspen. All the woodsmen in this region were some form of relation to her dead husband, sworn to aid each other. But the sound and presence of an axe might bring down the notice of the soldiers, so she walked on.

West Hall and Woodpasture lay on quiet tracks well off the King's Road, which led from the large town of Cloth Market direct to the King's City. Just after midday she came down out of the woods as if she had briefly retired there to relieve herself and was now simply resuming her journey. The traffic on the road was intermittent but steady for all that, no long stretches between a wagon drawn by oxen or a group of travelers striding along. She fell in behind a group of mixed journeyers, kinfolk by the look of them.

One of the women at the back of the group smiled tentatively at her, for Anna looked neat and tidy, no sores or sickness apparent on her skin.

"Good day to you, Mistress," said the other woman in a merry voice.

"It is a fine day," Anna agreed. "What a busy group there are of you, out in all your cheer."

"We are off to a wedding, my cousin's son." The other woman spoke with the clipped 'd' of the villages closer to Cloth Market, so the word sounded like "wetting." She glanced past Anna and saw no one walking behind her. "What of you, Mistress? Walk you alone?"

Anna gauged her interest and that of the other women, young and old, who turned to listen, for she was something new and interesting to pass the time. The men in the party saw her worn bridal shawl and drawn face and went back to their own conversations at the front of the group.

"I am recently widowed," she said in a low voice, and their murmured commiserations gave her the time she needed to settle on which story might be most convincing for such a company. "I am going to the King's City to get work as a spinner. My cousin said there are workshops there that will take a respectable woman like me."

They had opinions about that! They came from a village that lay athwart the King's Road near to Cloth Market and had heard many a sad story about girls and women from the villages being promised decent work and then finding themselves in far worse conditions, forced to work day and night for a harsh master who took all the profits for herself or, so one heard, sometimes even trapped into indecent work and abused by men. Yet other women did well for themselves! You had to be cautious, prudent, and hard-headed.

"But come walk along with us as far as Ash Hill," they said.

So she did, and heard about all the family gossip, and spent the night in comfort with some of the girls in the hay mow of the cousin's farm just outside the village of Ash Hill. Late that night a party of Forlangers clattered up to the farmstead, but after they spoke to the farmer and to all the men in the party, they rode away again.

Soon after dawn she took her leave and set out, pleased that the weather was fine. No friendly party of relatives appeared. She was careful to always walk close to or alongside other groups of people. For the entire afternoon she shadowed a suspicious group of carters pushing along baskets of apples who allowed her to walk close behind them after she explained that she was going in to the city to live with her sister who was a laundress. That night she slept rough, but it did not rain and it was not cold and she knew how to make a pleasant haven with a cushioned bed of old needles and grass under the evergreen branches of a thick spruce, although she badly missed her husband who would once have shared such a quiet bower with her.

In the morning she tidied herself as neatly as she could, braided her hair freshly back, and perfumed herself with a bit of lavender to hide the smell of forest. The road was quieter today, and she found herself a place to walk about a stone's throw behind a trio of wagons bearing threshed grain bound for the king's granaries. When the wagoners halted to take their midday break on a long spur of grass alongside the bank at the confluence of the Wheel River and the chalky colored

White, she sat down away from them, far enough away that they would not walk over to question her but close enough that she was not alone on the wide road.

The last rind of cheese made a tough meal, and she was out of bread, but she hoped to make the King's Gate by nightfall. The sky remained clear and the air cool but not chilly, so hearing a roll as of distant thunder made her frown. Worse yet came the sudden appearance of outriders wearing the dark sash of the Forlangers. The wagoners quickly leaped up and raced to get their oxen unhobbled and their wagons moving, but it was too late. A company of Forlangers marched swiftly into view.

The outriders caught up with the wagoners before they could get out of sight down the road. A dozen soldiers searched the wagon beds, but most of the infantrymen swarmed the bank to take a drink of water and sit down to rest their feet and eat a bite from their stores. They were mostly young men, respectful in their way and quite uninterested in a careworn woman old enough to be their mother, but because there was only so much nice grassy space, a half-dozen seated themselves near to her and opened their kit to get out dried fish and round flatbread suitable for the march.

"A good morning to you, Mother," they said in the way of lads, politely offering her a quarter of bread. "Where are you off to?"

"The King's City to make my fortune as a herbwoman making love potions for the heartsick," she answered. "And where are you off to?"

They liked her cheeky reply.

One said, "Have you advice for me, Mother? For there's a girl who has said no to me three times. Is there any hope?"

She considered the youth's merry smile and dashing eyes. "Is she the only girl, or just the only one wise enough to refuse you when she sees you are quick to find solace from her hard heart elsewhere?"

His comrades laughed uproariously at that, and soon they were all telling her their troubles and asking her advice in the way of chance-met travelers who will confide to strangers what they would never tell their own kin, for it was sure she would never have opportunity to repeat the tales to anyone they knew. Despite their northern accents, she could understand them well enough. In truth, she wondered at them, for they were decent lads for all that they were Forlangers. Maybe it was their lord who made them wicked, not any of their doing.

A new party rode up at a canter, from the direction of West Hall.

Her heart froze, and her mouth turned as dry as the stubble of a mowed field in summer's heat. The lord she had seen in the clearing of Dead Man's Oak arrived with all his anger riding as a mantle draping him. He was accompanied by ten mounted soldiers. The infantry leaped to their feet, hastening to pack away their flasks and bread.

"Why do you loiter here?" he demanded. "We have reports of a remnant of General Olivar's company that escaped us and is even now making its way cross country to reach the court. Get up! Get up!"

He reined up by the flustered lads dusting off their backsides and shouldering their packs. His eye lit on her, sitting at peace among them.

"Who is this?" he asked them in a tone that snapped.

"My lord," said the merry one hastily. "Just a herbwife who chanced to be resting her feet here when we halted."

"Get on the march," commanded the lord.

As they hastened away, that stare came to rest on her. He had the eyes of a fish, moist and deadened, and thin lips that might, she hoped, never waken desire in a lover so that he would never know what it is to share true affection.

"What are you about on the road, herbwife?" he demanded.

Kindness would make no shift with a man like him. He could only see what he expected.

"I am but a poor widow," she said, pitching her voice to whine like her youngest would do in a tone both grating and harsh, "for my husband is dead of drink and my daughter married. The wicked girl promised I could live with her, though she didn't mean a word of it even though she took my marriage bed, so what am I to do when her ungrateful brute of a husband said he wanted nothing to do with me, and him a drinker, too, I'll have you know. But mayhap you have a coin to spare for a sad widow."

"Which I daresay you will spend on ale the moment you reach an alehouse, you old shrew," he replied with a sneer. But he tossed her a copper penny and rode away. That quickly they were all gone, riding at speed away toward the city while she sat shaking.

Finally, when she could breathe calmly again, she picked up the copper for all that it had the taste of his evil hand on it. Old shrew! Not that old, surely, but then she looked at her work-chapped hands and she supposed her sun-weathered face appeared little different. There was certainly gray in her hair, for her comb told her that, although still plenty of the auburn that Olef had said was the fire washed through her that made his heart warm. Not just his heart.

She pressed a hand to her breast, feeling the tin swan tucked within her bodice.

A league more brought her to a small river whose name she did not know. She had only traveled to the King's City twice in the whole of her life, and while there were landmarks she recognized from her other trips, she did not know what they were called.

The road wound through coppiced trees. Ahead of her, she heard the harried voices and the grind of wheels just in time to step off the road. A shout chased along the wind. A half-dozen men trotted into view, pushing carts laden with sheepskins. They cast frightened looks back over their shoulders.

"Here, Mistress," called the eldest, seeing her. "Trouble at the bridge. Best you hurry back the way you came."

"What manner of trouble?" she asked, but then she heard thumping and screaming, and she knew.

"A fight on the bridge," said the oldest man, slowing to a walk as the rest kept moving. "Don't go down there."

"But I must get to the King's City."

He gestured in the direction of the carters as the last vanished around a curve in the road.

"Did you see the big ash tree with the blaze on its north-facing trunk? There's a trail there that carries on upstream to Three Willows village. They keep a small bridge, though they charge a penny for a crossing, so we don't like to go that way. But better a penny than dead."

He hurried on after the others, but Anna crept forward, careful to stay concealed in the undergrowth. She had to see.

The bridge in quieter times had a watchman and a gate flanked by two posts, each with a carved hawk on top whose talons held lanterns at night.

The watchman was dead, and dead and wounded men sprawled on the bridge's span, caught while crossing. A body bobbed in the sluggish water, dark hair trailing along the current. Several saddled but riderless horses had broken away and now sidestepped skittishly through uncut grass, not sure whether to bolt or to await their lost riders.

The skirmish had swirled onto the other bank, a few last desperate men trying to break away from the Forlangers, but they were outnumbered. Anna stared in horror at the melee.

The outnumbered soldiers were the general's men by their colors: pine green and white. There were only six left, and two of those were badly wounded. A horse stumbled and went down with a spear in its belly. Lord Hargrim himself directed his men as they moved to encircle the last survivors.

At once, five of the general's soldiers charged with shrieks and shouts while the sixth drove his horse into the water and flung himself into the current to swim. It took a while for the Forlanger archers to loose arrows because the last of the general's soldiers had spread out, killing themselves by disrupting the Forlanger line for just long enough that the swimming man could get out of range.

Shouting curses down on their enemy, they too fell to lie bleeding at the feet of the Forlangers. The riderless horse made it across the river and stumbled up the bank, then headed straight for the other horses as for home.

"Follow him!" shouted the lord. "He must not get away."

A half-dozen Forlanger men were left behind to pick through the survivors, kill any who still breathed, and drag away their own wounded.

She turned her back on the slaughter and walked as quickly as she could, shaking, afraid at every sound, sure they would come galloping up behind her and lop off her head. But the ash tree with its half-hidden blaze was still standing, and she cut into the forest and was well into the trees when she heard horses pass on the road. Her heart pounded so hard that she walked without tiring until at length she caught up with the carters.

The older man nodded to acknowledge her.

She said, "Your pardon, but might I walk with you the rest of the way? Seeing that blood-soaked bridge has taken ten years off my life."

"I pay no mind to the fights the king's men have among themselves," he said, "and nor should you. Not as long as they do not bother us. Why your haste to reach the King's City? You should just go home."

"I'm off to visit my daughter in the city, for she is to have her lie-in soon. Her first child. And while I do not like to speak ill of any woman, I must say that her husband's mother does not treat her in a generous way. Rather she lets my daughter do all the work while she sits in a chair and gives orders."

He was a chatty man, happy to talk about his own wife's mother and how she had been a scold unlike his own dear mother, both now long passed. He was just friendly enough that she did not mention she was a widow, and his younger kinsmen were polite but preoccupied at having seen slaughter done right before their eyes.

The path led upriver for about a league to a small bridge she would never have known existed but for the carters. A watchman at the bridge demanded the penny toll, and she handed over the coin the lord had thrown at her.

There was a party of Forlangers guarding the bridge on the far bank, but after they searched the carts for smuggled men, they let the wagoners pass and her with them, for no one paid her any mind in her worn shawl and with her worn face.

So she came to the city gates just as dusk was coming down, later than she had hoped. She knew well how to make a dry nest in the forest whatever the weather, but how to find a place to sleep in the city seemed a fearful mystery. The place was so crowded and so loud, and it stank.

She made her way to the river bank's stony shore. There, the last laundresses were heaping their baskets with damp cloth to haul back to their households.

"My pardon, good dames, but I'm wondering if you know where I can find my cousin's sister. She is laundress to the king's sister, so they tell me. I walked here from the village to let her know that her brother is gravely ill."

They laughed at her country accent and her ignorance.

"The king's sister's laundry is done indoors in great vats with boiling water, not out on these cold rocks," said the youngest of them, who was almost as pregnant as Mari. "Those women don't talk to us. You have to go round to the Dowager House beside the King's Palace. The king's mother has been dead these five years, so the sister has set up housekeeping there. And a good thing, too."

"Shhh," said the other women, and many of them hurried away.

"Why do you say so?" asked Anna, watching the others vanish into the twilight. Smoke made the air hazy. Everything tasted of ash and rubbish and shit.

"My pardon, I didn't mean to say it," said the girl. "It's dangerous to speak of the troubles in the court. You know how it is."

"I am up from the country. We hear no gossip there."

"Better if I say nothing," said the girl as she shifted the basket awkwardly around her huge belly.

"Let me help you," said Anna, taking the girl's basket. "It is a shame for you to carry such a heavy load so near your time."

The girl smiled gratefully and started walking. "The work must be done. Where are you from, Mistress?"

"Just a small village, no place you'll have ever heard of. By the forest."

"Isn't the forest full of wolves?"

"Yes, it is."

"Aren't you scared all the time that they'll come and eat you?"

"Wolves are no different than men. They hunt the weak. But maybe in one way they are kinder. They only kill what they eat."

The girl had a wan face, and hearing these words she looked more tired than ever.

"Here now," said Anna, regarding her sadly, for it seemed a terrible burden to be so young and look so weary. "If you'll tell me how to find the Dowager's House, then I will teach you some bird calls. Like this."

She trilled like a lark, and the girl laughed, so entirely delighted that she looked like a child on Festival morning waiting for a treat of honey.

"If you'll carry the basket I'll walk you there. It's not so far from where I work and live."

"Do you wash all this laundry for a family?"

"That I do, Mistress. I'm lucky to have the work with a respectable tailor and his household. The lady of the house has said she will let me keep my baby in the kitchen during the day as long as I keep up my work." She named a name that she clearly thought would impress Anna, but Anna had to admit she had no knowledge of this well-known tailor and how he had once made a coat for the king's sister's chatelaine's brother. Anna's ignorance made the girl laugh even more. Anna was glad to see her cheerful.

So they walked along cobblestone streets as Anna taught her the capped owl's hoot and the periwinkle's chitter and the nightlark's sad mournful whistling "sweet! sweet!" until some man shouted from a closed house, "Shut that noise!" They giggled, and in good charity with each other reached a wide square on which rose the Dowager House, with stone columns making a monumental porch along the front and a walled garden with trees in the back.

The girl checked Anna with an elbow, keeping her to the shadows. "There are soldiers on guard," she said, bitterness staining her tone to make it dark and angry. "Those are not the king's men. They belong to the Forlanger lord. He has people watching the Dowager House. He licks the king's boots, so I wonder what he fears from the king's sister."

Anna knew what he feared, but she said nothing.

The girl took her hand, anger loosening her tongue. "My man soldiers with General Olivar's company, a foot soldier. That is why I do not like the Forlangers. I thought they were to be back by now. He and I are to be wed next month."

The words took Anna like a blow to the heart, reminding her of Olef's last day, of his last words, of his last breath. Of how the Forlangers had been responsible, of how they took their war against General Olivar to the back roads and the isolated places where their actions would remain hidden from the king.

She thought of the market hall, and how folk from all around came there on market day. Now that he could no longer push a plough, her brother Joen had been able to set up a stall selling garden produce that his wife and children tended, together with rope he braided from hemp. What went on in the king's court she did not know, but if the general trusted the king's sister, then the king's sister it must be.

But she could say nothing of this to the young laundress. She could only pray to the gods that the man who had escaped down the river might be her man.

A single guard wearing the mark of a white swan stood guard at the service door, around by the alley. When she touched the tin swan in her bodice, she knew she had to brave this last leg of the journey.

"Go on, child, go home, then, and my thanks to you." She handed over the heavy basket. "May the Hanging Woman loosen your womb and let your child come easily."

"My thanks, Mistress."

Anna watched the girl's waddling progress into the dusky streets and hoped she would get home without mishap, but the King's City was a peaceful place on the whole. Folk were still about, so she was able to cross the square by tagging along behind a pair of young apprentices hauling a butchered pig between them. The Forlanger soldiers glanced at the pig and made crude comments about what the lads were like to do with the sow, but their gaze skipped right over her. They took no notice of her at all, right up to the moment she cut sideways and strode up to the side gate and its single swan-marked guardsman.

"I pray you," she said in a low voice, not hiding her distress as a pair of Forlanger soldiers broke off to trot toward the gate, "if your lady wishes to save the life of General Olivar, then let me inside before they catch me. And tell them this tale, that I am. . . ."

Fear made her words fail and her thoughts sluggish. The guard was staring at her as the footfalls of the Forlangers closed in. The poor young man looked as stupefied as she felt. A breath of wind brushed her neck, like the stroke of a sword.

So she got mad, for she had not trudged all this way just to have her corpse tossed into a rubbish heap and the general left for dead in the forest.

"Stupid boy, let me in! Tell the soldiers I am your poor mother come to beg a loaf of bread in the kitchen and that I will scold you if you don't let me in. I will see that the lady knows you helped me. But General Olivar will die if you do not act now."

He was so surprised by her harsh tone that he opened the gate and, as soon as she slipped through, slammed it behind her.

The Forlangers ran up as she hurried across a courtyard to the servants' door. "You! Who was that?" they demanded.

The youth's voice was shaking, but it could as well have been from annoyance as fear.

"My mum, as if it's anything to you. Cursed woman keeps coming to beg bread off the kitchen. I'm that ashamed of it, but if I don't let her in she stands outside and scolds me. And she's drunk as usual. Best day of my life when I walked out of her cursed filthy hovel."

Their argument faded as she reached the door. She whispered thanks to the gods when the big latch pushed down easily, not locked. The door opened onto an entryway bigger than her cottage. She closed the door and stood there gaping at a high ceiling and wood paneling illuminated by oil lamps, the richest ornamentation she had ever seen, such fine carving as put the headman's house in the village to shame. The heat and smell of the oil in the lamps drenched her; the fierce light after the dark streets made her blink. A riot was happening somewhere down the hall, a clattering like a battle and many voices talking over each other.

Something about a roast.

A girl in a neat skirt and blouse covered by a linen apron dashed down a length of stairs with a tray in her hands. Seeing Anna, she stopped.

"Where is that careless girl?" bellowed a voice from the room where a mob was evidently destroying every piece of furnishing.

The girl ran into that other room. Anna tried desperately to get her bearings, but the long corridor, the many doors, the stairs, and the echoing sound confused her more than forest, road, or city streets had.

The girl appeared again, stared at her again, and ran down the corridor to vanish into another room. She reappeared with a radiantly handsome woman behind her who might have been Anna's age and was wearing the most fashionable clothing Anna had ever seen, a gold gown that shone like sunlight and a finely embroidered bridal shawl draped over her shoulders. Anna stood stunned, not knowing how to show honor to a great lady, the king's own sister!

The woman approached her with a stern gaze. "Who are you, Mistress? How have you gotten through the gates this night? I am surprised that Roderd allowed you in, for he knows better. On the new moon, the lady gives out alms. You must come back then."

"You are not the king's sister?" Anna asked.

Those lustrous eyes opened wide, and the woman smiled. "I am her downstairs chatelaine, the keeper of the kitchen and lower hall. Where are you from? For you have a country accent and a country look about you."

Anna looked toward the girl, a little thing no taller than her second daughter but lively and as smartly dressed as the headman's three proud daughters who liked to traipse around the village showing off their expensive garb.

"Go along," said the chatelaine with a gesture. The girl scurried off into what Anna at long last realized must be a kitchen so large that the headman's house would fit inside it. That explained the echoing clamor of many cooks and servants at their work, making ready for some manner of feast.

"Do not make me call a guard to throw you out, Mistress," said the chatelaine more kindly, as if suspecting Anna was slow of wit and perhaps drunk besides.

"I beg pardon for my manner," said Anna, recovering her tongue at last, "but I have never seen such a fine house as this one."

The chatelaine sighed.

She went on hastily, seeing the woman's patience wane. "I pray you do not throw me out. I am come many days' walk from a distant village with news I can only trust the king's sister to hear."

"You must imagine such a tale will fall coldly on my ears."

Anna did not know what to do. What if the Forlanger soldiers pushed past the lone guard and rushed into the house? She had to trust that the mark of the king's sister being a swan and the general's mention of her meant that the lady's servants were also loyal to the man. Her voice dropped to a whisper. "News of General Olivar."

The chatelaine's eyes opened wide. From the courtyard, shouting broke out.

Anna reached into her bodice and pulled out the tin swan.

The chatelaine gasped. "Hide it!" she said, then grasped Anna's wrist and tugged her along up the stairs in such haste that Anna stumbled twice before they reached the top. There, a pair of bored young men wearing swan-embroidered tabards straightened up as if caught doing what they were not allowed.

"Get down to the door and by no means allow any outsiders farther than the entry until I return," the chatelaine snapped. "Send Captain Bellwin to me at once in the library."

The young men grinned, like hounds eager to the scent, and pounded down the stairs just as some manner of altercation erupted at another door. But Anna had scarcely time to think, for the dazzling corridor down which they hurried was like a palace of the gods, all studded with gold and silver and color. There were people walking and standing and hunting and dancing along the walls too, so like to people that she wanted to reach out and touch them, only she knew they were paintings like the one in the market hall that depicted the king being anointed and crowned.

The chatelaine pulled her into a room so filled with books that it smelled different than any room Anna had ever been in. She did not know there were so many books. Even the priest at the temple, who bragged of his treasure-house of six books, would lose his ability to speak could he have seen the shelves and shelves of them. Who made so many books? What was their purpose?

What was going to happen now?

The chatelaine released her wrist and glowered at her until a neatly clad servant girl peeped in. "Get me water to wash," she ordered.

They waited a bit longer. The girl returned with a bowl and pitcher and towel, and poured and rinsed the chatelaine's hand where she had touched Anna, then took everything away. As the servant went out, a soldier dressed in a swan tabard strode in.

"There is trouble at the gate. I did not know Roderd's mother is a drunk beggar." His gaze fell on Anna. A glint of humor in the slant of his lips gave her hope. "Is this the dame?"

"I am not the lad's mother," she said. "It was a lie so that the Forlangers did not take me."

"She says she has news of General Olivar." The chatelaine turned on Anna, and her fierce stare was the most frightening thing Anna had seen on her entire journey, for she could not tell if it promised or threatened.

It was only now that she realized it might all be for naught. She might have walked into a trap, and her life forfeit. Yet then she would join Olef on the other side. Mari and Hansi had the wit and strength to take care of the little ones. So be it.

She fished the tin swan out of her bodice and displayed it.

The chatelaine and the captain exchanged a foreboding glance.

"How come you by this token?" asked the captain. "What is your name, and where are you from?"

"I am called Anna, my lord. I have taken this token from the general. If you wish to save his life, then you must rescue him from the place where he is hidden."

"Word came last night that he is dead," said the captain in a flat voice.

"He is not dead. He lives, but is wounded and hidden. I brought this to show the king's sister, for he said that she would be able and willing to aid him. The Forlangers mean to kill him."

"They have already struck," said the captain to the chatelaine. "I thought it must be Lord Hargrim's doing, but we cannot establish he is the one behind the attack."

"General Olivar is proof," Anna insisted. "But the Forlangers control the roads."

The two servants conferred in low voices, and then the chatelaine left. Anna knew perfectly well the captain remained as a guard to make sure she did not escape. What surprised her was that he did not attempt to take the tin swan out of her hand. Nor did he speak. He went over to the desk and, still standing, opened a book and looked at the scratchings just as a priest could. Anna watched him but he did not move his lips as the priest did when he read; only his eyes moved, tracing left to right and then skipping back to the left and so on, a pattern as steady as that of a woman knitting.

The door opened to admit the chatelaine escorting two women. One was a magnificent noble beauty dressed in a gown of such splendor that she might as well have been dressed in threads spun of gold and silver. Her small, ordinary companion wore simpler garb sewn out of a midnight blue cloth so tightly woven it shone. They studied Anna, who did her best to stand respectfully, for she was not sure how to properly greet a king's sister.

The small, ordinary woman spoke to her, her speech so colored by odd pronunciations and words Anna did not recognize that she could make no sense of it. The king's grandparents had come from a distant place to establish their court here; that no doubt accounted for their strange way of speaking.

The chatelaine translated. "Her Serenity addresses you, Mistress. She wishes to see the token you hold."

Anna held out the swan. The tin badge was such a cheap thing, a trinket any girl could buy at a summer fair as a remembrance of her journeying there. Yet both ladies gasped, and the ordinary one stepped forward, took the swan out of Anna's hand, and turned it over. Her cheeks flushed when she saw the scratchings. Her gaze fixed on Anna in a fearsome way that made Anna see that she had mistaken the beautiful woman for the king's sister when in fact it was this unremarkable one who had the power and majesty.

Her snapped question had no word in it Anna understood, but she comprehended what the lady wished to know.

"The Forlangers attacked the village of West Hall, my lady. I went at night to give what aid to any wounded that I might, for I have some herbcraft. We found the general lying beneath the Dead Man's Oak. I recognized him, for he came once to our village to dedicate a market hall. Woodpasture, that is, but he called it Bayisal. Our people have always lent our support to the general. Our men fight when they are called. We have lost men in his service, killed by the Forlangers. My own husband...."

She faltered, choked by grief as she rested a hand on her belly.

The king's sister passed the tin swan to the beautiful woman, who perused it and handed it back, nodding.

The king's sister spoke and the chatelaine repeated it.

"How are we to know you did not find this token on a corpse and are come at the behest of the Forlangers to trick us into some rash action?"

"*One foot in the river* are the words he told me with his own lips. At Elland Fort he saved the kingdom, not Toyant Bridge. So he told me. He was wounded, and he may yet not live, but I did what I could to ease his wound, and if the rot does not take him, then I think it likely he will live. I know where he is, and I can take you to him."

Even the silent captain looked around at that, first startled and then, as his wrinkled brow cleared, brightened by hope. The king's sister caught in a sob, grasped the beauty's hand, and shut her eyes. When she opened her eyes, the four of them fell into an intense discussion filled with many exclamations and objections and finally a forceful declaration by the king's sister that ended the argument.

She and the beauty left. The captain and chatelaine remained, looking as impatient as if Anna was the last chore that had to be done before a girl could run off to the Festival night and the promises of a lover. Brisk footfalls sounded in the hall and a soldier appeared.

"The cursed Forlangers are still hammering on the front gate, Captain," said the man. Like the laundress he was a little difficult to understand with his quick rhythm and city accent, but he spoke the language she knew. "They demand to be admitted to speak to Her Serenity."

The captain nodded. "I will come in a moment and send them off with my boot in their ass." The soldier left. "She must be guarded without making it obvious we are guarding her. Make all ready. You heard what Her Serenity commanded. We leave at dawn. Lord Hargrim and his faction must be given no reason for suspicion."

The chatelaine said, "I will hide her among the servants."

So she did, giving Anna the finest clothes she had ever worn and feeding her the finest meal she had ever eaten, so rich with thick gravy that it made her stomach queasy. The meal ended with a sweet flour cake that was indescribably delicious, like nothing she had ever before eaten. She was given a pallet to sleep on among the other kitchen women, a decent bed, but this at least was not as comfortable as the marriage bed she had shared with Olef.

She slept soundly but woke at once when the chatelaine rousted her. An impressive cavalcade of outriders, carriages, and wagons assembled outside. Anna was tucked in among the gaggle of women servants in one of the wagons, all wearing the same swan-marked midnight blue livery with their hair tucked away beneath cloth caps. With a great blaring of horns, the company rolled down the widest avenue in the city and out the main gate. The wagon with its padded seats was at first jarringly uncomfortable; Anna would rather have walked. But after a time she got the rhythm of it. The women around her gossiped and laughed for all the world as if this were a delightful excursion, and it did seem from their talk—those of them she could understand—they all believed their lady had suddenly taken a longing to visit the cloth markets of Ticantal, which name Anna eventually understood to be the same town she called Cloth Market.

But abruptly the whole long procession lurched to a halt. When she craned her neck to see, she realized they had reached the bridge where the last of the general's company had died. Soldiers blocked the bridge, and to her horror, Lord Hargrim himself could be seen in his sash and his brilliance speaking to the king's sister. The lady was riding a horse; he was standing, at a disadvantage because of the horse's bulk. The king's sister waved a hand, indicating her procession. Anna's hands tightened to fists as the lord walked down the length of the cavalcade, ordering his soldiers to peer into the closed carriage, to poke among the wagons carrying luggage. He ordered the wagon full of women servants to disembark, and Anna climbed down not ten strides from the man who had contemptuously tossed her a copper penny and called her an old shrew, but he looked right at her and did not recognize her. His soldiers looked under the benches and checked under the wagon, and yet when their rude inspection was over, even a lord as powerful as Lord Hargrim had to allow the king's own sister to pass, for she was powerful in her own right.

Thus they came after two more days' travel to the turning for West Hall and Woodpasture. Anna herself led the king's sister and Captain Bellwin and a few stout soldiers past the outer pastures of West Hall and down the overgrown trail to Witch's Hill and the Dead Man's Oak. The clearing lay quiet in the midday sun.

Now, after all this, the secret nest which she had cherished all these years would be betrayed, but it was in a good cause, surely. She hoped the old woman would forgive her the trespass.

Off her horse the king's sister strode along as well as any of the men as they pushed on into the forest. When they approached the rocky tumble and its dense watershed of thick rose tree, Anna whistled the bird song she and Uwe had set for a signal.

There Uwe came, one moment hidden and the next appearing as out of nowhere, startling the captain so badly that the man drew his sword.

"He is a friend, the general's guardian," Anna said, anxious as Uwe shrank away, for the fear in his face might be fear of reprisal. Yet if the general were dead, why would Uwe still be here?

"Lives he still?" she asked.

"He lives," said Uwe.

She showed them the way in and allowed them their reunion in private, for it was what she would have wished, were it her own self.

They gave her coin, as such folk did, and although she and her family had never had much coin before, she was glad of it, for her brother Joen could use it to expand his rope-making and Mari had long wished for a new loom, her being clever with her hands and mind in that way, and now they could pay the carpenter to make one.

The general himself thanked her.

"I have thought much about our conversation," he said to her. "I cannot return your husband to you. Not even the gods can do that. But I have a thought that there is something else I can give you that may repay the debt I owe you."

Then they were gone.

After this the people of Woodpasture came out of the caves where they had hidden and life went on with the late-season slaughtering and all the many chores that needed doing to get ready for winter. Mari had her baby, a healthy little girl, and they made a feast for the mother and child.

Over the next few weeks peddlers came through the village on their last pass through the area, selling needles, delicate thread much finer than what the village women spun for themselves, lamps, knives, and wool and linen cloth from Cloth Market, everything necessary for the kind of work women could do across the long closed-in days of winter. The traveling men had stories, too; stories made peddlers more friends than the goods they had to sell.

General Olivar, the hero of the country, had been treacherously attacked by the northern traitor, Lord Hargrim. Although wounded, the general had escaped by swimming down the river and had been rescued by his loyal captain Bellwin. The king had exiled Lord Hargrim for disturbing the king's peace and sent the Forlangers back home to the north.

It was a good story. Everyone told it over and over again.

One night a scratching on the door woke Anna out of a sound sleep. She checked to make sure the children still slumbered, then swung her feet to the floor and lit the fine oil lamp she had purchased. The shutter was closed against the cold but the lamp's warm light lit her steps to the door.

"Who is there?" she whispered.

"It is me, your friend Uwe," said Uwe.

She set down the bar and opened the door. A full moon spilled its light over the porch. Uwe had on his familiar and well-worn wool cloak and a new sheepskin hat pulled down over his ears. The frosty chill made his cheeks gleam.

"Can you come?" he asked, his forehead knit in a frown and his lips paled by cold.

It was such an odd request that she merely nodded and dressed in silence, waking no one. They walked the forest track, their path lit by the splendid lamp of the moon. An early snow had come and gone, leaving the northern lee of trees spotted with patches of white. Branches glittered, as beautiful as any painting on a wall. Dry leaves crackled under their feet, and in the distance an owl hooted.

She soon knew where they were going. When they came to the clearing, she saw that a man was hanging from the tree, naked, cold, and dead. It was Lord Hargrim. No sign of battle marred his skin, no wounds, no bruising, no broken bones. He was just dead, except for the crude mark of a swan carved on his back.

Uwe stamped his feet against the chill. Shadows tangled across the grass. Anna rested her hand on her round belly.

"Well, then, there comes an end to him," she said. "They'll make a good story of it. Now we have hope of peace."

She turned and, less cold than she had been before, set back for home.

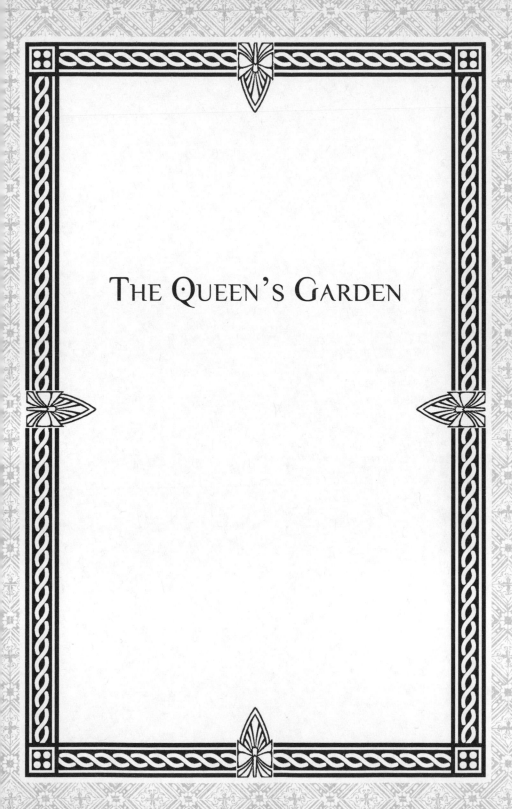

THE QUEEN'S GARDEN

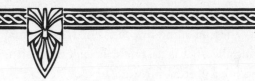

Please sit down, the youngest girls in front and the older on the pillows behind. Close the doors so no one is distracted by the blooms and by the sunbirds and peacocks in the garden. The only blooms I want to admire are your attentive faces. Now that I have lit the incense and we have said the prayers to our divine ancestress, I can begin.

Listen carefully to what I am about to tell you.

On the day their father the king Karanadayara gravely insulted the envoys of a powerful emperor, his daughters Princess An and Princess Yara awoke from their complacency. In the years since their mother's death they had allowed his affection to lull them into thinking all would go forward as it always had down the generations since the first queen, the Lady Rhinoceros, had established her sacred presence in the queen's garden.

An and Yara sat on pillows on the balcony that had been built for their mother, Queen Karan, in the king's palace. The sisters were twins who shared everything equally except that they were entirely different in stature and disposition. An had a cleft in her chin and the ability to listen to what was not being said. Yara was small of frame and she kept her hair cut short so it would not ever fall in her eyes when she most needed to see.

Through an elaborately carved teak panel they watched the proceedings in the king's audience hall. Elevated upon a dais, the king their father sat on a gold brocade couch embroidered with male peacocks parading in brilliant sprays of blue-green feathers while drab peahens lingered half hidden along the backs.

"Goodness!" Yara exclaimed as she studied the startling scene unfolding below. "I knew our father could be volatile but even I did not expect him to act so provocatively."

An squinted, for her eyesight was as poor as her hearing was keen. "When an emperor sends envoys to demand tribute from a king who is not already his vassal, he is expecting either to receive submission or to create a pretext for war."

The three envoys knelt, arms held behind their backs by the king's soldiers. Blood spattered their silk robes. Their cries wove through the golden pillars that lined the hall. The fleshy knobs of two severed noses had come to rest on the marble floor; the third man's nose hung by a strip of skin. The captain of the guard calmly placed the three severed ears into a linen pouch. Threads of blood seeped through the cloth as he handed them to the king's sorcerers.

The king's herald spoke on the king's behalf. "Let it be known to the Emperor of Saro that His Excellency Karanadayara is master of the kingdom of Karan. Your master's impolite demand that our holy majesty bend his knee to a foreign king and pay him a vassal's tribute can only be met with refusal. Being merciful, the king has left you each your tongues with which to carry these words back to your master, and each one ear to hear what answer your master may give you for the trouble you took to come here."

The groaning envoys were dragged out, the one man's severed nose still flopping against his cheek. Two royal custodians hurried forward to clean up the blood with its offending tang. Incense was lit. The royal pig-keeper took away the noses for they were of little use to the sorcerers, not like the ears which could be tuned so the king could listen in on all conversations the envoys heard.

The teak panels with their carvings of vines screened the sisters' sacred power away from the sight of foreign men. It also allowed the sisters to observe the king's clenched expression and fisted hands without him knowing they were watching.

"He has become too full of himself." Fine lines wrinkled An's delicate brow as she frowned. "Ever since Mother's death he has forgotten to rule wisely as our regent and instead rules pridefully. We should have seen it before it came to this."

"But he is right to refuse to pay tribute!" objected Yara.

"Not so loud. That may be, but we cannot defeat the Empire of Saro in open war. There are quieter ways to deflect the empire's interest. When the envoys return home, the emperor is required to avenge the insult or he will look weak to his own court. This will be the excuse he desires."

Yara fidgeting and An pensive, the sisters watched their father gesture for the next supplicant to come forward. The king's color was heightened and his back straight with energy and tension, or so Yara described him to An. The mutilation had put him in a good mood, and with a generous smile he welcomed each new group of visitors come to pay their respects.

A consortium of merchants sought royal permission to open up an exchange with the port of Emerald Island and they had brought the fifth son of the Emerald Prince to assist them in negotiations together with a substantial offering for the temple. A prince from the upland province of Golden Hill had sent his third son to be admitted to the royal guards. Envoys from the Ruby Baron, the king's distant cousin and former rival for their mother's preference in marriage, brought bolts of lambent silk and waterfalls of jewelry wrought of gold and gems to remind their father that the king had daughters of an age to be married and the baron had sons of an age to marry them.

Pearls hung from the bottom of the curtain that separated the balcony from the corridor. They clacked softly as Lady Norenna, supervisor of the court kitchens, swept the outer curtain aside and entered the balcony, a privilege she had earned through years of tireless service. She sat on her heels on the far side of the inner curtain whose translucent silk did not hide the towering beaded headdress she wore as a mark of her importance in the royal household.

"Your graces," she said. "What of the matter of the banquet we have prepared for the envoys of the Emperor of Saro?"

"Let the food be distributed at the hospital," said An. "Princess Yara and I will dine in private with the king our father."

"But with less variety than the pigs savor today," said Yara.

Lady Norenna coughed once, hand covering her smile, but when she lowered her hand her expression turned somber. "There will be trouble in the provinces when the princes and barons and lords hear the king has insulted an emperor. Saro will now send a fleet to castigate the man responsible for such disrespect. The sword will fall on everyone in the kingdom not just on one man's pride."

"This has occurred to us as well." An touched a finger to her own lips. "Have you some recommendation?"

"Go to the palace of the ancestors and pray to the Lady Rhinoceros for guidance, and to your mother and grandmother who still have wisdom to impart. But if I may, let me be given permission to recover the noses from the pig-keepers."

Yara raised an eyebrow to show interest but Lady Norenna offered no further morsel.

An slipped an oblong gold bead stamped with the royal horn of the ancestress from one of her braids and handed it over to the lady. "Do what you believe to be prudent. We will call you when we need you."

Lady Norenna withdrew. With her went the scent of musk and flowers she wore dusted into her ornately knotted clothing.

Yara sneezed, sniffed, and wiped her eyes. "We could invite the invaders to a banquet and poison them," she said with a hopeful lift of her eyebrows.

"Poison leaves a tainted trail. We must find a path that avoids war before it is too late to turn the conflict aside."

Below, the king departed with his guards and custodians and sorcerers. Afterward the courtiers, supplicants, and visitors lined up in a complicated pattern according to ancestral rank to take their leave through the far doors. Yara had leisure to study their faces and describe them in detail to An, since no man could turn his back on the king's couch even if the king was not seated in it.

There were tall men and short men, stocky men and slender men, men wearing the long wrapped skirts and embroidered jackets of the Fire Islands and men garbed in the flamboyant robes or sober tunics of far-off lands. The prince's son from the Emerald Island had a pleasing face and a ready smile, Yara said, which An pronounced suspicious. The prince's son from Golden Hill wore the somber expression and neat garments appropriate to a warrior, which An thought proper but perhaps meant the man was hiding something. Among the envoys from the Ruby Baron stood a young man remarkable for the scar on his neck, the embroidered sunbird on his tunic, and the turquoise stone embedded in the socket of his right eye. This meant, An said, that he was worth watching for a hint of his true purpose at court.

Many men lived in the land of Karan, whose territories had been strung together like so many beads into a headdress through the efforts of King Karanadayara. Their father had built upon the wealth and authority that Queen Karan had bestowed on him when she had married him in their youth. Merchants beholden to his fleet for protection from pirates enriched his treasury with the taxes they paid for the privilege of trading. Many were his cousin princes and rival chiefs, and none loved him, for he had bound many once-independent principalities and baronies into the folds of his royal garment. But they obeyed him and paid tribute, just as the distant Emperor of Saro was now demanding obeisance from him.

After twenty-five years as preeminent king in the Fire Islands, he was not about to bow down before another man. He was still vigorous enough to prosecute any war he pleased and would do so without regard to what it cost the people he ruled.

An scooted closer to the balcony railing and gripped it to push herself up onto her withered legs. "War will bring nothing but ruin on the land. We must prevent it."

Yara tucked a crutch under her sister's arm and gave her an arm to lean on. "I think you already have an idea."

"Perhaps I do. But we cannot proceed without asking for the blessing of the queens who came before us."

A note written on a scarf of floral silk awaited them in their private rooms. The letters were brushed by a masterful hand in the form a man uses when he gifts poetry and fine cloth to a woman he is courting.

"In the king's garden, two kiss-of-elegance flowers bloom but there is no sunbird to harvest their nectar."

Yara laughed so hard that she cried and afterward dabbed tears from her cheeks with one corner of the scarf. "I would be ashamed to write something so baldly obvious. He even wore the mark of the sunbird on his clothing, as if he feared we might miss his meaning. As a marriage proposal, it lacks subtlety and refinement."

An pulled the silk from her sister's fingers and examined the brushstrokes. "The man who wrote this is too ambitious, or his opinion of us is too low."

"Furthermore I would never marry a man who makes such a crude and insulting error," added Yara. "It is not the king's garden. It is the queen's garden."

"We do not need to marry him to make use of him. We must discover where his ambitions lead him."

A fleet of devoted women serve the queen's garden, then as now, some of them kinswomen and some loyal attendants. An called for their chief chatelaine. She was their deceased mother's much older sister, born without the queen's mark and thus free to live outside the palace in her youth. In widowhood she had returned to live in the palace. Because of her wisdom and age, it was she who knew if a blade of grass was blown under any door in the palace or if a glance was shared between hopeful lovers or budding rivals.

It took some time for the woman to appear, striding in from outside with her sleeves fluttering. Her decades of travel and diplomacy had given her a brisk, confident manner, although her skin was quite weathered from sun and wind and sea.

"Who brought this, Lady Aunt?" An asked.

Lady Aunt examined the scarf, spoke to several of her own attendants, then nodded. "A courier from the guest wing, Your Excellencies. I had him followed. His master is called Prince Ejenli."

"One of the sons of our father's cousin, the Ruby Baron?"

"The eldest son. He has won renown in several sea battles against the sea pirates who plague the North Strait. He lost an eye in battle and replaced it with an ensorceled piece of turquoise. It is said he can see the movements of enemy ships in the stone and thus can never be ambushed or surprised."

"Prince Ejenli is an ambitious man," Yara remarked.

Lady Aunt nodded. "A trifle too ambitious, we may surmise. Yet it is known his family's holdings are poverty stricken and shabby. It is rumored he seeks to restore the family fortunes."

An smoothed the scarf along the table. The unmarked side of the cloth promised a fallow field for words should she wish to sow them there. Before she wrote, she addressed her aunt again. "Lady Aunt, what do you know of the son of the prince of Golden Hill?"

Lady Aunt gestured for the young attendants to go out to fetch tea and rice balls baked with coconut milk, bean curd in a sweet ginger sauce, and dumplings. She walked a circuit of the spacious chamber where the princesses, their attendants, aunts, cousins, and friends often spent evenings playing chess and reciting poems. One side of the room was open to the queen's garden, where kiss-of-elegance bobbed in a breeze and streamers of purple sky-blaze hung in curtain-like sheets from trellises. When Lady Aunt was sure no one could possibly overhear, she returned to the princesses.

"I was just now hurrying to speak privately with you on this very matter, for I have heard the most unexpected news. The third son of the prince of Golden Hill is called Lord Kini. I have it on good authority that when a boy Lord Kini was betrothed to Lady Nasua. She is the second daughter of the neighboring Seven Falls principality, which is the mountain land ruled by the descendants of Lady Snake. The auspicious days for the wedding had been set years ago, but I have just heard the marriage is to be set aside because your father the king has decided to take the young woman to wife instead."

These tidings reduced both sisters to speechlessness. For a while there was silence but for a hummingbird flitting among the sky-blaze, wings a blur.

"Father means to marry again!" exclaimed Yara at last, grasping An's hands in hers. "We heard no whisper of his intention here in the queen's garden. All these years he has properly contented himself with concubines. What can it mean?"

Lady Aunt had a smile that stung more the brighter it got. "Your father saw a portrait of the girl and desired her. He claims it is as simple as that."

"Nothing with our father is simple," said An slowly. "Now it seems his desire is enflamed in more than matters of war and trade. Perhaps his cook is spicing his food too heatedly."

"Do not forget that in my younger years I traveled all over the Fire Islands as ambassador for your mother the queen," said Lady Aunt, not that anyone could forget it for she still wore her hair in the simple style of fisherwomen and trade widows, never adorned with beads and towering headdresses. "It was I who interviewed and negotiated for a husband for her. Remember that your father comes from an island where the king is succeeded by his favored son."

"Are two daughters born with the queen's mark not riches enough for him?" Yara cried. "Can he believe any son could replace us?"

Lady Aunt tapped two fingers to her own lips to remind Yara to keep her voice low. "No daughter can replace you who does not come from the lineage of the Lady Rhinoceros. Yet an ambitious man may forget the proper order of life and the honor of the ancestors in favor of greed and pride. He was a good husband to your mother. But he has changed since she passed into the palace of the ancestors."

Yara shifted restlessly on her pillow, not knowing what to say.

An's gaze was fixed on a hazy distance only she could see. "I would like to know what manner of match it was for Lord Kini and Lady Nasua. What have you heard, Lady Aunt? Are they glad to be free of the marriage? Indifferent? Resigned?"

"The match was arranged in the usual manner when both were children. It is in all ways an unexceptional alliance between neighboring principalities: a third son and a daughter who lacks her divine ancestress's royal mark. Rumor has a sharper tongue, however. She tells me that over the years the two were allowed to spend a great deal of time together and have come to genuinely love each other. My informants whisper that when your father the king's decision was made known to them, both objected passionately to any suggestion they must dissolve the match. That your father has kept his intentions a secret cannot bode well. Likewise, he is the one who demanded Lord Kini be brought to the palace and sealed into life service in his army. A handy way to be rid of the young man, if you ask me."

Yara leaped to her feet, taking a turn around the pillows on which she and An sat. "Is it not cruel to ask Lord Kini to serve in the palace guard and watch the woman he loves be paraded as queen in front of him?"

The royal bell rang, announcing their father's approach.

Yara flung herself back on the pillows, hastily tidying the strings of beads in her headdress that had gotten tangled during her outburst.

Lady Aunt calmly rang her hand bell to summon the servants, but she continued speaking in a low voice. "Lord Kini will be sent on campaign, not kept in the palace. Before this new trouble with the Saroese, your father has been talking of nothing except his desire to expand his influence yet farther."

"He wants to bring more ports under his sway," said An.

Lady Aunt nodded. "You can be sure the independent islands are aware of this, and have sent their own informants to court to sniff out his plans. You saw the envoy from the Emerald Island. His name is Lord Varay, the fifth son of the Emerald Prince. He came in the company of the merchants but I think he is not here to assist them in bargaining for trade rights."

"The carelessly smiling man?" said Yara with a laugh, for she was not one to dwell on bad news for more than a few breaths. "Hard not to notice him! I described him at great length to An, and I am sure she asked me to repeat myself several times!"

An's frown made Yara giggle again. "A man who smiles too much may be slow-witted, careless, bored, or too enamored of himself," An said in a tart voice quite unlike her usual fathomlessly cool demeanor.

"Write Lord Varay a note," advised Lady Aunt as she craned her neck to see if the king's attendants had yet appeared on the garden walkway to announce the king. "I believe your father intends to conquer Emerald Island to get control of its red-leaf plantations. Perhaps the Emerald Prince suspects and has sent his son to determine what risk his people face. Or perhaps the young man is here for some other reason, one his father the prince knows nothing about. Now, tuck your secrets away into the folds of your garments and speak of safer topics."

Footsteps approached along the garden walkway. Lady Aunt rang the hand bell again, and their ladies hurried back into the airy chamber to sort seating pillows and clear tables strewn with books and chess pieces. The doors to the inner walkway were opened. Their father the king strode in, having shed his audience robes and now wearing a lustrous silk robe of wave-churned blue, embroidered with fiery phoenixes burning up out of the white ocean foam. He sat on the pillow reserved for him, which had been placed on a mat by the balcony so he could enjoy a lovely view over the orchids. An quickly settled beside him because he did not like to see her struggle to walk. While everyone else retired to a respectful distance, Yara took charge of the tray of delicacies and poured the tea.

He lifted the cup to inhale the heady scent of ginger and peach. He had great dignity of presence but the disturbing intensity of his manner betrayed a man made restless by a constant storm surging within. At first he had a great deal to say about the Emperor of Saro's attempt to insult him and why it had required him to react as he did lest he be diminished in the eyes of the men at court and indeed the world at large. He spoke at length and neither of his daughters interrupted him. After a while he paused to eat a dumpling and drink more tea.

"Your Excellency," said An. "Perhaps you have considered what trouble may be brought down upon a peaceful land."

He set down his cup quite emphatically. "You are still a child, Daughter. This is the king's duty. It must be left to the king to act."

An's eyes fluttered in a way Yara recognized as the heat of her anger fanning imprudent words that Yara knew must be left unspoken. She slid the platter of aromatic bean curd with its ginger slices directly in front of the king, distracting him while with her other hand she pinched An into silence.

"Is there some news you bring, Your Excellency?" Yara asked in a voice so bright it lightened the chamber. "How eager you look!"

His gaze held a smile that saw not them but a brilliantly feathered dream invisible to all others. When he told them the news they already knew, they clapped their hands and pretended surprise.

Yara plied him with more dumplings, smiling fixedly. "What wonderful news, Your Excellency! I have long harbored the most heartfelt desire to welcome a new woman into the palace, for I miss my mother quite sorely."

"How soon may this longed-for arrangement come to pass?" added An in a tone only half as sour as she felt, but her father did not notice the way she blinked too much and meanwhile crushed a rice ball flat with the bottom of her spoon.

The priests, he informed them, were even now calculating the matter, seeking the most beneficent days to hold the wedding festivities. Because Lady Nasua was born into a different divine lineage than that of Lady Rhinoceros, the temple must show exceptional attention to the phase of the moon and the rising time of certain stars.

Yara poured more tea.

He was not a man inclined to dwell on any matter for long, once it was decided. An had at last recovered enough to be able to delicately direct their conversation down more amicable channels. He wanted to know how the tapestries commemorating his victory three years ago over the Golden Hill principality were coming along in the weaving hall. Had they received the silk thread he had sent them from his recent expedition to the west? Were the colors and patterns acceptable? How did the royal hospital fare?

An detailed her work administering the royal hospital she had founded. He listened attentively, as he always did. Afterward she and her father played a game of Walls, which was sadly interrupted before its conclusion by a message calling the king to meet with his council over the matter of the Saroese ambassadors whose ship had departed with the turning tide.

The messenger was one of the women of his household, an elderly woman who had served in the palace since she was a child. "Your Excellency, the royal sorcerers have sent me to tell you that the ears have begun whispering."

An and Yara leaned forward, eager to hear more, but the king merely glanced at his daughters and then departed with his attendants exactly as he would have done when they were small.

When he had gone and the room cleared of all trace of his presence, Yara said, "He would have discussed the matter with our mother. The sorcerers would have been brought to the queen's audience hall so she could hear their words. With his own words he treats us as if we are still children. Can it be our father does not honor us as he ought?"

An considered the red and gold sprays of flowers which to her appeared more as smears of color than petals and leaves. "At any time within the past three years we have been of proper age to be anointed as queen. Yet he has never once encouraged the temple to inquire as to an auspicious festival for our ascension. Why have we been content to remain as princesses rather than ascend to our rightful place?"

"He is a responsible administrator and a bold commander. Under his regency, the land has prospered."

"If the Saroese invade, it will go ill for the people and the land. As for you and me, Yara, who can say what will become of us if that happens?"

"It is a dreadful thing to consider! If I were the Emperor of Saro, I would delegate a prince to marry us and thus hold the land in our name."

"If the Saroese care for the ancestors at all, which we cannot be sure they do," retorted An grimly. "For I have had a worse thought."

Yara bent closer to hear. "What could be worse than a Saroese invasion?"

"The noblewomen of the hill country hold their power through their holy foremothers just as we do. What if our father means to bury the sacred relics of the Lady Rhinoceros and erect a temple to a new ancestress? To replace our lineage with that of his new queen?"

Yara's hiss startled a cat just then curling up to nap on the king's pillow. The animal bolted outside to vanish among the blooms.

"This will not do," Yara said in a hard tone.

"No, indeed, it will not. It makes a person wonder if he has more than one kind of desire on his mind when he seeks a new bride. Perhaps he seeks to overthrow the power of the Lady Rhinoceros. Or of the divine ancestresses altogether, for if a new queen is beholden to him for her power then he may believe the land is his, and not in her keeping."

"What do we do, An?"

"We have allowed our affection for our father the king to lull us into a false peace. It has been so comfortable to go on in this way."

"It is true we have shirked our duty," Yara said with a lightning frown. "However much we may suffer, the land will suffer more. We must act, An."

Sorrow had drained the light from An's face but now she straightened her shoulders and gestured for an attendant to set out her writing desk. "We discover what allies and weapons we have. The robe of our plan must be seamless. Fetch out the new inkstone."

With a needle she pricked her finger and Yara's and with two drops of blood mixed a blue-black ink on the untouched stone. Because An had an especially graceful hand despite her poor vision, she wrote the notes.

In answer to Prince Ejenli she wrote, *A bath of salt water kills flowers but a bejeweled fish may carve the seas at will.*

"Are you sure that is not too obvious?" Yara puffed light breaths onto the wet ink to hasten its drying as it set into the weave.

"He must be answered in the same manner he wrote. A man of his temperament will expect such unsubtle treatment. I am willing to offer him what he truly wants, which I do not believe is marriage to us."

To Lord Kini she wrote, *The kite will fly higher with a longer string.*

"Very good," agreed Yara. "If Lord Kini wishes to be free of his betrothal or honestly desires Lady Nasua to gain a nobler station in life than marriage to him, then we cannot rely on his aid."

To Lord Varay, she wrote, *The banquet table.*

"Goodness, that is elusive even for you, An," said Yara as she slipped the messages into silver tubes inscribed to look like bamboo. "Even I am not sure what you mean by it."

"What the man makes of it will tell us what we need to know about him."

They gave the messages into the hands of trusted ladies and sent them off.

Because An and Yara wore the mark of the queen, they were too sacred and holy to walk about in the world like ordinary people. A queen's faithful sisters and cousins and aunts and nieces and ladies act as her hands and ears and eyes to the world outside the palace complex while the man she marries acts as her spear and public voice. A queen's responsibilities are legion, for it is her duty to see that the land and the people flourish.

Thus, after their afternoon devotions at the temple, Yara spent the last of the day's light weaving at her loom among the other women in the royal weaving hall, because every notable event was commemorated with garlanded tapestries. Meanwhile An stripped out of her finery and, wearing humbler garb, was carried to the hospital she had founded. The hospital lay at the edge of the vast palace grounds, reached by crossing three bridges, traversing two orchards, and passing alongside the reed-skirted Western Lake with its waterfowl and fish.

The hospital building was of An's design, a long building built of wood with raised floors to keep damp and bugs and snakes and scorpions away. All the male patients were housed at one end, women at the other, and children in their own dormitory amid the fragrant medicinal herb garden. An's eyes were weak but she had discovered that if she touched a person and listened with her ears and her heart and the caring that dwelt in the pit of her belly, she could hear something about their illness. From palace doctors and city surgeons and village healers she encouraged to come speak to her, she continued to learn. More importantly, in the hospital she could bring the people to her, and thus the garden of their fears and hopes was opened to her.

Now, sitting in the children's dormitory beside a slack-faced child shivering with fever, she heard the bubbling strain of lungs filling with liquid. She was listening so intently to the child's labored breathing she did not at first notice a rumble of footsteps at the entrance, not until they ceased and a pleasing male voice murmured, as to a guide, "Who is that lovely young woman?"

She looked up to see a smear of bright colors at the other end of the long dormitory room, sky blues and palm greens with splashes of sun yellow and searing orange. A company of foreign men had come to tour the hospital; visitors to the kingdom often did, for the palace hospital was already famous for being open to any person who needed care.

Her sight was too weak to make out distinct faces but she felt their gazes on her. Most moved away politely but one man took several steps closer to her. His gaze she felt as a pressure on her face. If smiles were fragrance then his bloomed as with flowers.

Would a man be so rude as to smile at a noblewoman he could not know and ought not converse with? Or did she, in her brown hospital robe worn to conceal stains, appear as something else entirely, an ordinary woman whom a charming man might gently flirt with?

She blushed.

Just as he took in a breath to speak, the guide hurried back to fetch him. "My lord, if you please, the party has moved on to the next building. It is not permitted to remain behind."

"Is it not? For I have questions that only an intelligent person who knows this place intimately might answer."

Because he was still looking at her as he spoke in exactly the sort of laughing voice An found most suspicious, she blushed more deeply. Yet she refused to avert her face as she ought as he cast a last glance toward her and finally followed the rest out.

Trembling a little, she gave instructions to ply the sick child with cold baths and a tisane of firebane. In the curtained carriage on their way back to the queen's garden, she asked her attendants what party of visitors had trampled so discourteously through the hospital.

"The delegation from the Emerald Island, Your Excellency. Everyone on the staff was talking about it. There was a prince with them, a pleasing manner of man so everyone said. He asked a great many questions about how the hospital was established and if its presence in the city had reduced the incidence of disease."

An's annoyance boiled, and she had to fan herself to cool down her cheeks. For the worst of it was that she had been pleased by the man complimenting her intelligence. She had to wonder if he had guessed who she really was.

The carriage rolled to a stop beneath the sprawling canopy of the sacred fig tree that stood outside the double gates leading into the queen's garden. Lady Aunt clambered into the carriage and signaled for the attendants to disembark to give them privacy. As the oxen started up again, she spoke so as not to be heard above the rumble of wheels on stone.

"I have yet more news which the king has attempted to keep from me. The Saroese know nothing of our sorcery so they speak freely among themselves. The commander of the ship that carries the envoys back to the fleet has praised the envoys' courage in provoking the king to this degree of insult. To create a pretext for invasion was their intention all along. Once they return to the emperor's court, it is expected that the emperor will order a fleet to sail here, overthrow King Karanadayara on the grounds of scorning and insulting the empire's envoys who arrived under the banner of peaceful diplomacy, and take the kingdom for himself."

An held the beaded curtain away from the window and let the fragrance of the garden kiss her face. The blur of trees was overladen with the depthless blue of a shadowless sky. Perhaps until that moment she had hoped for a different outcome, but if her father was concealing even this news from them then she knew they had to proceed.

"Let us go to the weaving hall," she said at last.

Lady Aunt nodded, making no further comment.

In the royal weaving hall An left her aunt in the carriage. Yara sat apart from the main weaving hall on a span of floor where the afternoon light spilled gold over the loom with its warp and weft but left Yara seated in shadow beneath the high beams of the roof. The weight of the sun faded the cloth even as she wove it but display was never her purpose. Nor was her weaving ever finished.

She rose from her stool and hurried over so that An should not have to limp across the expanse of polished plank floor on which her crutch might slip.

An took her hands. The memory of the blurred colors in the hospital, the gaudy clothes, the brilliant presence, still made her tremble. Not even the garden's expansive grounds and the song of wind in the branches had wiped away that memory.

"How does your work go?" she asked, hearing a quaver in her own voice.

"It will serve our purpose. If we are truly determined on this end."

"We must be," said An, and told her what Lady Aunt had discovered. "To do anything else would dishonor the queens who came before us."

With a sigh of resignation followed by a deep inhalation for resolve, Yara agreed.

That evening they called Lady Norenna and Lady Aunt to their garden room. Once the women were settled for a game of four-handed dice, the princesses set their ladies to singing a long excerpt from the Opera of the Phoenix-Haunted Ship. The robust choruses and effortful arias drowned out the players' soft voices.

Lady Norenna placed first stakes of a single ivory comb on the table.

"Did you acquire the noses?" Yara asked in a whisper.

Norenna rolled the bone dice. The four sides came up as two cups, the sign of boundless abundance, a mortar and pestle, and a ship. She touched each one with the tip of a finger. "This is a throw appropriate for the supervisor of the kitchens, do you not think? Properly dried, a nose can be ground to powder with a specially treated mortar and pestle. Food flavored with this condiment will cause the one who eats it to have his desire heightened for that which smells best to him."

"Ah," said Yara.

An reached for the dice. "Perhaps I may send you red-leaf powder to flavor this meal as well. It is very expensive, which is why we use it at the hospital only for the most sickly cases, to thicken weak blood. But it is also known to thicken a man's desire."

"That will inflame his desire, truly," remarked Norenna. "But the dish must also be spiced with a kingly savor, to encourage his other lusts."

An slid a gold bracelet off her royal arm and pushed it under the low table. "Flakes of gold touched by royal skin."

Norenna tucked the bracelet into one of the ornate knots of her wrapped dress.

After placing a stake of two silver brooches on the table, An shook out the dice for her own play. They fell as a calligraphy brush, a mortar and pestle, a stalk of rice, and a knife.

"You are a predictable person," observed Yara with a flicker of the eyelids that made her seem ready to laugh. "Each of these represents an aspect of your work at the hospital. Also, two cups defeats your one knife, so Lady Norenna defeats you."

Lady Aunt placed three silver sticks shaped as bamboo on the table as her stake. As the old woman carefully weighed each of the eight-sided dice to measure how much power burned in them, An slipped a curled strip of rice paper from each of the ornate silver tubes Lady Aunt had just set down.

On the first paper Lord Ejenli had written: *The sea wind knows no walls. The waves are its bride.*

"As I hoped," said An, nodding. "He will take our offer. He is more interested in his own quest than in our garden."

Lord Kini had written: *Past the weir lies the empty pond gilded in sunlight.*

"He means the fish will be trapped in a golden cage that offers no sustenance or companionship," murmured An. "The mountain bride does not desire to become queen."

Yara looked pensive, studying Lord Kini's formal hand, which was correct in all its curves and angles but too precise to be beautiful. "The man's passion is not for brushwork, but his metaphor is good."

"More importantly I believe his heart will be willing to do what needs to be done. Yet all turns on this last." Her hands had begun trembling as they did when her thoughts became agitated and so she had to nudge the last paper to her sister.

Yara unrolled the last message, read it quickly, then silently passed the note to An.

Lord Varay had written in a hand as elegant as An's lovely script. The letters wore the crowns and curlicues customary to the more elaborate writing style of Emerald Island, almost too decorative, yet on the page he made it joyful, like a laughing smile.

He had written: *A man savors the first two fish brought to his table and eats his fill of them. The rest he throws to the pigs.*

An frowned and Yara read the note again. "Is he calling us fish?" Yara whispered.

Lady Aunt picked up the dice. "I interpret the message otherwise. He is speaking of sons, not daughters. A fifth son holds little interest for a prince already surfeited with healthy boys. Such a prince may even have tried to kill or exile the extra boys to protect the ones he favors so there is no struggle for succession. It is no wonder a fifth son travels with humble merchants, for like best quality silk he may be worth a good price to the right buyer. Or he may simply have escaped an untenable situation."

She rolled the dice with so much force they slammed into the silver sticks, flipping to rest with a wheel, a ship, and two knives on display.

"Two knives defeat two cups," said Lady Aunt with a triumphant smile. She flashed a teasing glance at Yara as she reached out as if to collect her winnings.

Yara affectionately tapped Lady Aunt's arm with a closed fan. "Not so fast, for I have not yet played."

She set out her own stake of four silver bracelets. She scooped up the dice, shook them in her cupped hand as she murmured a charm under her breath, smiled at the other three women, and tossed. The bone pieces clattered over the table and came to rest.

Four knives.

"That looks ominous, does it not? Every blade will meet its target." With a lazy smile, Yara swept in her earnings.

Over on the cushions where their ladies played flutes and lutes, a woman was singing the lament of the dying phoenix as it melted into sea foam and dissolved into the ocean.

"I am sorry for it, but he has driven us down this road by his own choices," said An, wiping away a tear. "Let me write answers to each man using the same inkstone. Then we must shatter the stone into pieces and seed the fragments into the garden gravel. After that we will pull apart the brush and feed each separate hair to a separate fire. We must be careful to be sure the king's sorcerers cannot possibly steal from stone or brush the truth of what we wrote and planned."

To Prince Ejenli she sent nothing except a small seal, its stamp depicting the royal horn of their ancient ancestress who was both a woman and a rhinoceros.

To Lord Kini she wrote: *The bird will fly home if its tether comes unleashed.*

To Lord Varay she wrote: *A subtle dish graces the banquet table.*

So it was done.

That night Lord Kini escaped the palace barracks with his face concealed beneath a veil. A string of remounts gave him speed toward the mountains.

The next morning, unaware that his hostage had absconded, the king ate his dawn soup of rice, fowl, cilantro, and pepper, cooked to its usual perfection in the royal kitchen tended by Lady Norenna's gracious expertise. Afterward, nose twitching, he expressed an urgent desire to ride at once to Seven Falls to collect his bride. Because much of his army had already been mustered to march to the coast where they would set up defenses against the expected invasion from the Empire of Saro, he took only the palace guard as escort.

Three days later, at the turn of the tide, Prince Ejenli departed in his sunbird-haunted ship, bearing the seal of the noble lineage of the Lady Rhinoceros.

The sisters waited, watching. In the warp and weft of the loom a vision unfolded, for Yara had woven the eyes of peacocks' feathers into her threads. With this magic they could see across the whole of the land that prospered under the protection of their sacred ancestress.

The king's company leaves behind the dense green farmlands and golden temples of the lowland and rides up into the mist-shrouded mountains. As the road steepens the company straggles out into a long line, the winged lancers in the vanguard with their rainbow banners flooding the air with streaming color and the night guard bringing up the rear in their rich indigo uniforms sewn with an ornamentation of silver vines. The king himself is carried in an elaborately carved litter whose roof and curtains are sewn of many layers of gold and purple silk so that like wings they seem to fold and unfold with each step.

Soon the company slows to a crawl as it picks its way up toward a cloud-capped pass along a narrow valley surrounded by steep hills.

Suddenly rocks tumble and crash down onto the road. Earthquakes are common here in the Fire Islands, not that anyone felt a tremor this day. When the rumble subsides and the dust settles, the survivors scramble to claw twisted bodies out of the rubble. The rocks have split the party into two groups, one before and one behind the new barrier. In the ensuing confusion men and women wearing the stripes of forest cats and the dappled skin of mountain wolves rush as if out of the rock itself, although in truth it is just that armed people had secreted themselves in caves and brush-hidden overhangs to carry out their ambush.

The men carrying the king's litter fall as their group is overrun.

A woman armed with a bow and painted all green in the manner of a whip snake steps onto the road. It is her arrow that pierces the king's eye as he stumbles out of silken draperies, and it is Lord Kini's knife that finishes their father off.

The soldiers who surrender are allowed to live and are sent back to the lowlands with the king's body wrapped in the silk he died in. With the rockfall still blocking the road behind them, the mountain people stride up into the mist and rain of their ancestral home.

The woman wearing the snake's aspect pauses before she departs. She looks up into the sky as if she can see the brilliant feathered eyes that see all. Around her neck she wears the token of her ancestress, a gold neck ring bearing the face and tail of the whip snake. With a green hand she makes the sign of "peace," and then Lady Nasua follows the others out of sight into the rugged wild slopes.

An wept when Yara released her hand. Dust motes sank through strands of light. The rustle and chatter of women in the adjoining weaving hall drifted in to ease the silence.

"I love him because our mother loved him and because he treasured us," An said. "But this is our land, not his."

Yara shed no tears. Unraveling the pattern took her the rest of the day while An made her usual rounds at the hospital, her tears watering every sufferer she attended.

In the sorcerers' garden, the ears whispered the words spoken aboard the Saroese ship as it flew over the waves on its way to the emperor's harbor far to the south. "King Karanadayara will pay personally for his insult to the emperor. Afterward the riches of the Kingdom of Karan will belong to the empire."

Three days later the remnants of the palace guard returned bearing the king's body. The day after King Karanadayara's funeral, Lord Varay tossed the first torch onto the roof of the palace founded and built by the deceased king in the first years of his reign. The entire court watched from afar as the palace burned to the ground, all the while placing bets on which chambers and structures would collapse in first.

Before the ashes had cooled the sisters married Lord Varay in a quiet ceremony. In this way the least of the sons of the Emerald Prince became King Anyaravaray by means of his marriage. An ceased speaking ill of his smiles when she discovered he indeed had a particular interest in the hospital because his mother was a mountain woman who had taught him her healing lore. That he truly thought her lovely was no small inducement even if she pretended otherwise. Yara encouraged their attachment; she had her own paramours among her ladies and loved the king well enough in her own way.

After the burning, the new king commanded the royal architects to measure out the grounds of a new king's palace upstream past the third bridge and thereby close to the royal hospital. Breaking with tradition, he asked for Queen An's input because she had some ideas about better plumbing and running water that she wished to put into practice.

Gifts were delivered from Lord Kini and his mountain bride: a bow and arrows for Yara and for An a set of bat-haunted calligraphy brushes made with hog, badger, civet, mongoose, and weasel hair. The new king received an ally's knife with an ivory hilt and a blade engraved with promises.

Some weeks later the king's sorcerers brought the whispering ears before the king and queens in a temporary hall hung with tapestries and roofed with palm fronds. The envoys had reached the imperial court of Saro. They all listened as the emperor swore that with a mighty fleet he would avenge the insult and punish the impertinence of King Karanadayara by invading the kingdom of Karan.

So they prepared.

Thus it happened that half a year later when the winds shifted front to back in their usual pattern, the Saroese fleet sailed with its golden sails and gull-haunted ships across the Fire Sea and up the river to the new palace.

King Anyaravaray sat clothed in gold and purple on the peacock couch in the king's audience hall. He received the invaders with an easy smile. Queen An and Queen Yara watched from the queens' balcony as three men strode forward in the manner of conquerors: a Saroese general clad in silver-gray, a Saroese admiral marked by the badge of the sea-swift gull, and a Saroese ambassador with his hair plaited into three tiers.

"We are come to chastise King Karanadayara and the kingdom of Karan which he rules," announced the ambassador. "King Karanadayara is required to make personal restitution for the insult he gave to the Emperor of Saro."

The king acknowledged the ambassador's heavy words with a gracious wave of his purple and gold silk scarves. "Then you have journeyed a long distance to the wrong place, for this is the kingdom of Anyara, not Karan. King Karanadayara is dead, most grievously murdered by his enemies. Indeed, his palace was burned at the order of a prince of the Emerald Island. What an outrage that you have come so far to find that others have taken your righteous act of justice away from you! How can I aid you?"

Trapped by their own words, the envoys felt obliged to join in an uneasy friendship with a man who presented himself as their new ally. They drank with the king at a banquet prepared by Lady Norenna. Inspired by the feast they swore vengeance on those who had stolen their revenge. Vengeance first, whatever they might secretly plan about invading this rich land afterward.

The Saroese fleet set sail.

Out on the Fire Sea, Prince Ejenli saw them coming with the magic he held in his turquoise eye. After the Saroese fleet had sacked the Emerald Island, Prince Ejenli used the gusting winds and his knowledge of the shoals to drive their ships onto the rocks near the coast. Then, having been given permission by the queens' seal to take what he wanted from those ships he defeated, he pillaged the Saroese fleet and became wealthy enough to restore his family's holdings.

So it was that the kingdom of Anyara prospered, at peace. In time a daughter named Raya was born with the queen's mark on her breast. It is Queen Raya who now dwells in the queen's garden, the sacred heart of the land, while I, her sister, have traveled all these years as her ambassador and am now returned to guide you, all you girls of the palace, as you come into your womanhood.

This story is the first and most important lesson I teach you. The Lady Rhinoceros understood the dangers her daughters and their descendants would face. The queen's garden is open to any we invite in, and it is a garden well worth sharing, but it belongs to us. Never forget it.

It belongs to you.

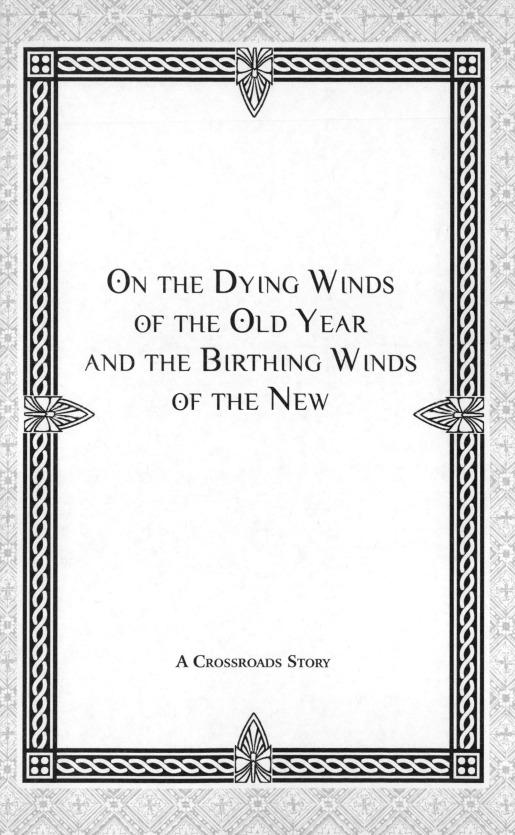

On the Dying Winds of the Old Year and the Birthing Winds of the New

A Crossroads Story

Out on the water, paddling a canoe, the four women could speak without fear of being overheard. It was a windy day, sloppy water instead of steady swells, and their canoe battled an east wind blustering in over the bay. Mai set paddle to water, pulled, and lifted it out and forward to cut back in again, following the rhythm of the woman in the first seat.

"There's a spy in Bronze Hall," said the woman in the seat behind Mai.

"What makes you think so, Tesya?" Mai called the question back over her shoulder.

"Yesterday Marshal Orhon's courier bag went missing. The bag contained his orders for which reeves were to shift stations, which to come home to roost, and which to stay where they were and what routes they were to patrol. Good information if you were wanting to trap reeves stationed out in isolated eyries."

"Orders can be changed," said the woman in the first seat, Zubaidit.

"Neh, it's worse than that," said Tesya. "There are eyries which are well hidden. Observation posts known only to Bronze Hall reeves. Not even fawkners like me know them. Those places have been kept secret for generations. Furthermore, the marshal's cote is locked and guarded at night. There's no shoreline to bring up a boat, and no lights anyway. No one could have stolen it except someone who lives on the island."

Mai blinked eastward into the wind. The barrier islands lay too far away to be seen except for scraps of cloud caught on their low peaks. "So you believe a reeve, a fawkner, or one of the hall-sworn stewards stole it. If that's so, then who is the spy working for?"

"I think we all know the answer to that, don't we, Mai?" said Tesya too sharply.

Before Mai could answer, a set of choppy waves rocked the canoe. The long float lashed by wooden arms to the left of the canoe skipped twice on the water's surface.

In the last seat, steering, old Fohiono spoke brusquely. "Get your minds back in the boat, sisters. Weather's coming up. Best we turn back to shore."

The steerswoman angled her paddle against the curve of the hull. The canoe swept a wide half circle. Mai called a change, and they each swung their paddle over to the other side, Mai paddling opposite Zubaidit and Tesya. As the canoe straightened, Zubaidit set them a steady pace for the town of Salya, barely visible as a scar of brown walls and white stone against the vibrant green of the mainland.

They paddled for a while in silence. Sweat and sun and spray glistened on Zubaidit's brown back. Out on the bay Zubaidit usually stripped down to just her linen kilt. It was easy to see her muscles working as she cut the paddle in and out of the water.

Eventually Mai felt obliged to speak.

"It's exactly the kind of information King Anjihosh will want. He does not like what he cannot control. He will do whatever he feels is necessary to bring Bronze Hall under his command. He believes it is best for the Hundred to be ruled by a strong man with a clear vision and a firm hand."

"It's true he saved us from a terrible civil war," said Zubaidit.

"I was there when Copper Hall was burned down and my comrades slaughtered," added Tesya. "That was a dark day. I admit I was glad when King Anjihosh and his army of outlanders stood up to fight the Star of Life and its cruel army. I cheered their victory."

"He did not act alone," remarked Fohiono.

"He did not," agreed Mai. "Many acted. They just acted under his leadership."

"You had some part in it, I have heard," the steerswoman continued.

"Maybe I did. And Anji might thereafter have chosen to retire to a quiet life, as I have. But that is not the kind of man he is."

"By all accounts, you could have been his consort and ruled beside him here in the Hundred," said Tesya.

Zubaidit flashed a glance back over her shoulder.

"Watch your rhythm!" said Fohiono with more tartness than usual.

Once the memories might have brought tears to her eyes and a lump in her throat. But the wide waters and hard winds of coastal Mar had scoured the remnants of regret right out of her.

"I could have remained his possession, however well I was treated and no matter how beautifully I was dressed. Honestly, my friends, even though I was offered a palace of my own and all the fine silks and sweets and soaps and tender kisses I could desire, I would rather be out here in this wind paddling with you and with my back screaming and my hips like to freeze up. Just a dawn paddle to catch a few fish and discuss matters of life and death! I didn't think you would take us out so far, Fo."

That got them laughing.

"You're the youngest among us," barked Fohiono, chuckling. "When the year turns, you'll be able to count twenty-six years, won't you? You ought to be ashamed to complain."

"I am! You can be sure I am bitterly ashamed! But I still hurt!"

Waves slapped the hull. The float skimmed the tops of wavelets. The sun glowered in a sky beginning to turn the sulky blue-green that marked a storm blowing in from the ocean.

"You know the man best," remarked Fohiono. "If the theft is his doing, what does he want?"

Mai considered the character and ambitions of the man she had once called husband. "He has had eight years to settle his new government in the north. According to report, he's gained control of the major trade roads so all is peaceful and secure and to his liking. Now he'll turn his gaze to those regions of the Hundred that have not fully bent their heads to his rule. He already has agents here in Salya."

"Watching *you!*" cried Tesya. "We would have a quieter time here in Salya and at Bronze Hall if *you* hadn't settled here."

"Yes, he has agents in town watching me." Mai had accepted the consequences of leaving him but she knew some resented the complications her presence brought despite the success of her mercantile dealings. "But it isn't as if I am the sole reason he keeps spies here. Bronze Hall is the only one of the six reeve halls that has not acknowledged him as its commander. That makes Bronze Hall's reeves suspect in his eyes. They might foment disorder. They might urge the councils and guilds hereabouts to rebel." She glanced again over her shoulder. "Tesya, have you anyone in the hall you distrust?"

As a fawkner in the reeve halls, handling the huge eagles, Tesya had earned impressive scars. They glittered like fireling's threads scored across her left cheek and down her neck to her left shoulder. The scars twisted as she grimaced. "A new reeve flew in with his eagle two months ago. I'm sure you've all seen him."

Fohiono whistled appreciatively. "That young, pretty fellow? Sure I've seen him."

Tesya went on, her tone sour. "Folk at Bronze Hall say he's the kind who visits the Merciless One's temple as often as he can. What do you think of him, Zubaidit?"

Zubaidit was the ruling priestess in charge of the local temple of Ushara, goddess of Love, Death, and Desire. Her even stroke did not slacken as she answered, while her tone remained entirely neutral. "You know I can't reveal who enters the temple, nor what is said within the Devourer's garden, but I do know who you mean. What makes you think he might be a traitor and spy, Tesya?"

"He tells a funny story of where he and his eagle come from. The tale doesn't hang together, if you take my meaning. Then after he arrived, little things started disappearing from around the hall. A carry bag. An eating knife. A celadon tea cup."

"That seems clumsy, and pointless," said Zubaidit.

Tesya shook her head stubbornly. "Some of us at Bronze Hall have got to thinking that a spy would start by stealing little things, so we get accustomed to thinking we've got a petty thief on our hands. A spy might hope to cast suspicion onto the boatmen who bring supplies. What a newcomer can't know is the boatmen are never allowed off the dock onto the island."

As Salya's busy piers hove into view, Mai broke into the discussion. "If you know you have a spy in your midst before he knows you know, you can cause the spy's master more trouble than the spy is worth."

"How might one do that?" demanded Tesya.

"I'll think about it," said Mai.

They approached Gull Pier with its pilings encrusted with barnacles to the high-water mark and its banner-posts topped with beautifully carved gulls at rest. Zubaidit released a hand from her oar and scooped up her vest from the sloshing trickles of water running under their feet. She slid an arm through one armhole, flipped the paddle to her other hand, shrugged into the vest, and managed to cut right back into the stroking rhythm the others had kept up. Men at work on nearby piers shouted ribald comments at Zubaidit, to which she replied with insults so bald that the words made Mai's ears burn even as she could not help but laugh. This was not the kind of town she had grown up in! There, a woman would never talk back to a man.

"You're not the catch we went out for," called Fohiono to the men mockingly, for she had no doubt done the same as Zubaidit when she was young.

"At least we caught something," said Mai, still laughing.

The catch amounted to a paltry fourteen muhi-fish, just enough to give the women an excuse for going out on the water on a morning when they might have been expected to be preparing for the Ghost Festival. They slipped past Gull Pier to Gull Beach, being raked clean by a pair of boys. Several young men came running to help them carry the canoe up into the canoe shelter. Fohiono's clan's canoes rested under a thatched roof above the wrack of the high-water line.

Mai gave a kiss to Fohiono and a more formal goodbye to Tesya.

Zubaidit gestured with a quick chop in the hand-talk that meant, *"I'll see you later."*

Mai fetched the cotton taloos she'd left folded atop a crossbeam. She draped the length of cloth around her body and, after shucking the linen kilt she wore when out on the water, wrapped the taloos with the elaborate tucks and folds that turned it into a dress. The short kilt and tightly laced vest were the only practical thing to wear out on the bay. But unlike many of the women here, she could not bring herself to wear kilt and vest while walking around town. She had grown up in a different world, where women young and old covered their legs and never displayed any glimpse of midriff or breast. It was not so easy to leave that world behind even though it had been almost ten years since she had been carried away from her desert oasis home. Certainly she had been accustomed as a girl to selling produce in the market—nothing exceptional in that!—but to show so much skin, in public! That she could not do, not even now.

She grabbed her paddle and her leather bottle, draped a silk shawl to cover her shoulders, and set off. The waterside district was lively this morning as last-day shoppers made ready for the Ghost Festival. Folk greeted her as she passed; a few men greeted her with hopeful grins but she knew how to smile to warn them away. She reached the Grand Pier and headed inland up the wide avenue locally known as Drunk's Lane. The town rose in tiers on the hillside beyond; she could see the sprawl of her porch and the bright yellow walls of her compound against the hillside. Usually walking up an avenue lined with inns and drinking houses posed no problem before midday, but because no ship would be caught out on the water during the Ghost Festival, the establishments were crowded with bored sailors stuck here for three days.

A rather young and good-looking stranger stopped stock still and whistled under his breath, nothing crude, more a comment to himself. Judging by his gear and his clean-shaven chin, he was a sailor from out of town. Beneath his unlaced open vest and snugly tied sailor's kilt he had a stunningly attractive body, all taut planes and wiry muscle. He caught her looking, and recognized immediately the manner of scrutiny she was giving him. A reckless smile flashed on his face. He touched all five fingers together, then opened them with an emphatic flourish, the hand-talk for *"startling beauty!"* as in a flower blooming.

His companion was a woman some years older and similarly fit. She grabbed his elbow and steered him toward one of the inns. "Kellas, that kind of beauty is always dangerous to chase. Anyway, you're not allowed to have sex when you're working. . . ."

They ran up the steps of the Inn of Fortune's Star. The heat in Mai's cheeks faded, although her pulse was still racing. It wasn't as if she could risk inviting a man to her bed, even had she time for one. Anji had taken care of that.

The young man had been wearing a ring, quickly glimpsed when he'd made the gesture. Was its wolf's-head design familiar, or did it only seem so because she was thinking of Anji?

On one inn porch busy with men drinking at low tables, voices raised ominously. A fight broke out with a rolling crash worthy of an unexpected thunderclap. A man slammed against a wooden pillar, the shudder quivering through the whole edifice. This provocation was enough for men already half sauced. Sailors, idle laborers, artisans who had closed their workshops until the dawn of the new year, all swarmed up off the thin cushions they had been sitting on. Drunk already! Think of what a mess they would make, which someone else would have to clean up.

As she tried to hurry past, a pair of tussling men stumbled off the inn's porch. She raised her paddle to fend them off. One's fist connected with another's nose, and blood spattered down his face. The injured man grabbed the other man by the shoulders and began to swing him around; her heart raced as she skipped back, sure they were about to slam into her. A baton swept down from behind her and, with a swift pair of whacks to their shoulders, commanded the attention of the belligerent men.

"Heya!"

The combatants separated and backed up, hands in fists. Up on the inn porch the innkeeper was shouting furiously as his help started to knock heads together.

"My thanks, ver," said Mai to the unseen person behind her but she did not wait for him to reply. She strode onward, wanting suddenly to enjoy the peaceable quiet of her home where she could expect a measure of blessed solitude.

The man with the baton hurried up alongside. "You took no hurt, verea?"

He was a reeve. *That reeve.* Young and pretty enough to look at twice, and with an intangible quality of melancholy that made you look yet again.

She feigned a limp. "No, nothing."

"You are hurt!"

She bit her lower lip as if wincing in pain. "No, it's nothing, truly."

"If it pleases you, verea, I will just walk you up to your home, to make sure you do not falter."

Roping him in was almost too easy. "Yes, with my thanks."

"Can I carry the paddle for you, verea?" he asked as they started walking.

Shouts, laughter, and the blaring whistles blown by the harbor militia floated up after them. "Neh, I can manage. You're newly come to Bronze Hall, are you not? I fear I don't know your name. I'm Mai. People call me Mayit in the local way."

"Mayit," he agreed. "I've heard of you." Then he blushed furiously and stammered something too thickly accented for her to understand.

"You're not from the south," she said encouragingly. "Where did you train?"

"Horn Hall." Now that she knew what to listen for, she heard the way he struggled to form his words so that indescribably thick dialect did not crawl out. "I were born and raised in the far north. It is surely a long way from my home village to all other places in the Hundred. No one has ever been there. I mean, we in the villages live there. But no one ever came there. Then I was jessed, and I was found by—"

He broke off and pinched his lips closed over the name he'd been about to say.

"Were you transferred to Bronze Hall?" she asked with her best coaxing smile.

He frowned, a fleeting expression quickly controlled. "The story of how I came here has many twists and turns."

They climbed stairs to the residential terraces where she made her home. "You never told me your name," she said.

"Badinen. My eagle's Sisit." He glanced skyward, a habitual motion she had become accustomed to in the reeves she counted as friends. She counted three eagles circling, on patrol or possibly just aloft waiting for their reeves to finish business in town.

"For your kindness, ver, surely you'll take tea with us before you go back to your duties?"

"Oh. Eh." He was shier than she expected, especially given that he was a young man about the same age as she was. It was an appealing trait, she decided, watching him sidelong as he matched his stride to hers.

She asked him how he liked Bronze Hall, and piece by piece coaxed out opinions so bland—the food was good but that twice-spicy barsh was an odd thing to eat in the morning; the winds were chancy; the ocean's roar kept him awake at nights—that the answers made her suspect he was hiding something.

As she walked down her own street her neighbors greeted her. Mistress Firuliya was out with her girls decorating the porch with wire baskets filled with sweet rice balls and adorning the delicate potted trees with garish festival hats in bright red for the upcoming year. The woman looked the reeve up and down in a way that made him half trip on a step and again stammer into that incomprehensible northern dialect, while Firuliya's girls giggled.

"Here we are," Mai said, too loudly.

She waved gaily at the red-capped fellow loitering at the corner, one of Anji's silent watchers. The red cap was Anji's pointed reminder to her that things could have been different had she made a different choice. The man lifted a hand to acknowledge her, as this one with the broken nose always did. The others weren't as polite.

She led Badinen up onto the spacious porch with its spectacular view of the bay sparkling in the sun. From this height you could see the weather coming in as a blustery haze. She had some time before the rain came.

She rattled the bell and made a fuss about taking off her shoes by the mats. "Please, Reeve Badinen, sit down."

She gestured toward the quilted cushions that ringed the tea table, little islands of color around a glossy sea. As he hesitated she pulled out her hair-sticks so the wind- and water-mess of her hair tumbled down, its ends reaching to her lower back. She smiled at him, thinking very hard of sex, imagining naked limbs, bellies brushing, sweat and the musk of love-making.

He sat, felled like an ox that has just taken a blow to the head. Cheeks darkening, he looked away.

"I'll bring tea," she said.

The door slid easily, and she left it open behind her so he could see in to the sparsely furnished front room with its low table for doing business and seating pillows stacked neatly to one side on the matted floor. She never entertained visitors there; the porch was her front room, where she spoke to male visitors right out in the public eye. That was the way it had to be.

She felt Badinen's gaze follow her as she crossed the front room and passed through the covered walkway that led to the kitchen. She had given her hirelings the festival off to spend with their families. Her sister-by-adoption, Miravia, was at the market doing the last shopping. Miravia's husband Keshad was at the warehouse doing the final accounting before he sealed the books and the doors for the year. The girls had run around the corner to spend the morning with Mai's former slave, elderly Priya and her husband O'eki, who treated the young ones like grandchildren.

In the kitchen, Edi was sweeping in preparation for the last bout of cooking. On the stove a big-bellied pot simmered, cooking down four chickens whose meat and broth would anchor tonight's feast. He smiled as well as he could with his scarred face. Besides Keshad, Edi was the only male who lived at the house, safe because of his disfigurement and his youth; he was only twelve.

"Go on," she said as she ladled water from the barrel into the kettle and set it over the flames. "I'm just making tea. Where is your mother?"

"Garden." The word was difficult to understand unless you knew how to listen for the consonants. He'd not spoken at all when he and his mother had come to them four years ago; he'd been too ashamed. "Choosing vegetables for slip-fry."

She nodded and walked along the side walkway to the tidy vegetable garden in the back, its obedient rows framed by fruit and nut trees. Derra stood when she saw Mai, her apron sagging under tiny green tomatoes, white radish, pale cabbage, and bold red peppers.

"I was just worrying about Miravia," said Mai. "I should have gone with her to the market, her so close to her time."

"You said you had business down harborside, Mistress," said Derra in her soft voice. "Afterward, I told Miravia I would go with her. But she said neh."

"As if anything I, or you, would have said could have made the slightest difference once she decided to go. Aui! But now I've got to serve tea to a reeve, so I'm wondering if you would go after her. Help her carry things up? She'll not refuse if you're down there. You can say you need—oh, anything—something we're lacking for our feast. I had a sudden craving for durian, maybe."

Derra snickered, knowing perfectly well that Mai had never managed to develop a liking for the fruit because of its appalling smell.

"I'll take this into the kitchen." Mai took the apron from Derra and carried it back to the kitchen, where she set it down on the big table. Then she followed Derra out onto the front porch. The woman gave Badinen a startled look, followed by a polite nod and a skittish smile, and descended the stairs to the street. The red-capped man watched Derra walk away down into town.

Mai settled on a cushion at arm's length from the reeve. "Last minute festival shopping. You know how that is."

"I suppose so." He wiped a hand with charming awkwardness over his short black hair. "Where I grew up, we have no market. We grew and raised everything our own selves. I never saw a market until I came south."

"Is that so?" Mai said, and though she had deliberately set herself to charm him, she did not need to feign astonishment. "You must have grown up in a very out-of-the-way sort of place, truly."

"We had no hirelings, that's for sure," he said as Derra vanished around a corner with a final glance back over her shoulder and an expression that too closely resembled a smirk. "I don't miss home much, I guess. But the weather was a cursed sight better there. Not so hot as it always is here."

Derra's look back had made Mai self-conscious. She grabbed for whatever words came to hand. "You think it's hot here?"

"Here in the south? I should think so! It's all muggy like the breath of a sea monster in your face all the time."

She laughed. "That's a fine way to phrase it. Is that from one of the tales?"

His blush crept up his cheeks as if her laughter was suggestive. "No. Just a way of speaking."

"'Tell me more about where you grew up." A limpid gaze turned on him, the slight cant of her body toward him, brought him alive as water kisses seedlings in a desert garden and brings their passion into bloom.

He told her about where he grew up. She listened as she had learned to do in her childhood home, which lay so far from the Hundred that its dusty confines and rigid customs seemed like a bad dream. But that life had made her what she was; she saw no reason to scorn it. Nor did Badinen complain of his own humble upbringing. He spoke easily and affectionately of those childhood years even though it was clear he had been a superfluous son treated with mild affection and casual disregard. Becoming a reeve had been a more magnificent destiny than any other end he might have hoped for. He had seen terrible things, the massacre of an entire reeve hall, but he had weathered it and kept on.

Really, what else could you do but keep on?

It's what she had done.

A door snapped open inside the house. Dragging footsteps announced Edi's approach with the tea. He came out onto the porch and set the tray on the tea table. At the sight of Edi's grotesquely scarred face, Badinen's eyes widened and his lips tightened.

"Edi, where are the girls?"

He gestured up the street in the direction of Priya's home, unwilling to speak in front of a stranger.

"Can you go fetch them? They need to help prepare dinner." At his look of horror, she laughed. "I know. I know. But they're not really that bad, are they?"

"Are," Edi mumbled.

"Maybe Arasit is," she acknowledged with a sigh. "But your mother is already gone down to the market to help Miravia carry up the shopping. So there's no one else to fetch them. You can wait until they finish whatever Priya has them doing. No hurry."

His glance flickered toward the reeve, who rose.

"I'm called Badinen," said the reeve, straight to his face. "And you?"

"Edi," he said with a sudden lopsided smile that stretched his scars.

He paused, as if wondering what else he could say to an admired reeve who deigned to speak to him, but then grabbed his cane from beside the door and clumped down the steps.

Badinen watched him go.

So did the red-capped man, who knew perfectly well how many people lived in the house and that Mai was now alone in the compound. It was his duty to know such things.

With steady hands, Mai poured tea.

The reeve turned back to her. "What in the hells happened to that poor lad? Blessed Taru! He looks like he fell head first into a fire after having half his face cut up."

"That's about it." She did not look up from the stream of tea as it filled a cup. "His father tried to kill him. Thought another man had sired him."

He whistled sharply. The red-capped man looked around, although the reeve was looking at her, not at the man with the broken nose lounging so still and silent in the shadows that it was easy to forget he was there.

"That's a cursed wrong-headed thing to do. If he had a dispute, surely it was with his wife or with the other man, not with the blameless child."

"It would seem so, would it not? Tea?" She handed him the cup in both hands. His skin brushed hers as he took it with a hopeful smile.

They both sipped in silence. The brew was sharp, fitting for the season. There was more than one way to flush out a spy, to hit Anji back in a way that would spoil his triumph.

She rose as he watched her over the rim of his cup. "Come in and help me prepare a bit of a meal," she said.

Slowly, he set down the cup. She had not even finished hers; a shimmer of heat still spun from its surface. She went to the door. Poised on the threshold, she glanced over her shoulder at him. He rose with a shy smile. Like any man born and bred in the Hundred, he saw nothing odd in entering a house with a woman, even one he was flirting with.

"Eh, truly," he said, the older accent wakening in his voice, "my aunties used to make me chop the vegetables. Said it were best when done by a man."

Then a flush darkened his skin again, as if he had said something he ought not.

As if the words had two meanings, as they often did in the Hundred.

He would go inside with her, all alone into the compound. They would chop vegetables in the kitchen—that was all—and the others would return, and maybe he would take the feast with them and return to the reeve hall after. And at some time in the next few weeks he would die an unfortunate death. Because Anji would order it. He would not be able to help himself, being what he was. He'd have to kill the spy he'd sent to steal Bronze Hall's secrets, for the crime of having been alone with the woman Anji still considered his wife.

That would teach Anji, wouldn't it?

But what if Tesya was wrong about Badinen?

A wave of disgust swamped her, its taste so bitter she wanted to spit. How could she even think of luring this man into a situation he could not understand and was in no way responsible for? Maybe he was Anji's willing and eager agent. Maybe he was just obeying orders forced upon him. Obviously, even if that were true, he had not been warned what would happen to men known to have been alone with her. So even if he were Anji's agent, Anji considered him expendable. No one could look at Badinen and not see that women might find him attractive. Anji might even have sent him to test Mai, without warning the poor reeve.

Eiya! Down these paths branched a maze of possible threats, promises, motives, and outcomes. All she knew for sure was that important documents had been stolen from Bronze Hall.

She stepped back onto the porch, slammed the door shut, and turned to the young reeve. "A thousand pardons, Reeve Badinen. I entirely forgot that I promised to go over to my neighbor's—"

Breaking off, she strode forward, grabbed her cup, and drained the tea. The liquid burned on her tongue, making her eyes water. She set it down so hard on the table that he jumped.

"Why have you come to Bronze Hall?" she said, keeping her voice low.

"I-I beg your pardon, verea?" He took a step away from her, as if just now wondering if she might be demented. "Did I offend you in some way? I had no intention—"

"Surely you know a courier bag has gone missing. As the only newcomer to the hall you are the chief suspect. Did you know people believe you're working as a spy for King Anjihosh?"

His mouth opened, worked wordlessly, and shut again.

"I heard something about a courier bag in the hall at dawn this morning, before I flew here. . . . They think I stole it?" He covered his eyes with a hand, shook his head, and lowered the hand to stare at her helplessly. "No, of course they would blame me. I'm the only new reeve among them. Peddonon warned me this might happen."

"Peddonon? The reeve Peddonon? He warned you what might happen?"

"He and many others transferred from Horn Hall to Bronze Hall after the war. King Anjihosh never trusted them, knowing they had been close companions to the previous reeve commander. But at that time, right after the war, I was a novice reeve. Because I needed training I had an excuse to stay behind. So they left me as their agent within Horn Hall. All these years I've faithfully sent information to them when I could . . . but now that I've finally left there, no one trusts me here."

His words fell like so many leaves scattered by a gusting wind: hard to grasp hold of. "Are you saying you have been Peddonon's spy in Horn Hall all this time?"

He looked as guileless as the unclouded sun. "Yes."

"But then why did you leave there just now . . . ?" She trailed off. His gaze did not leave her face.

After a moment, he said, very softly, "You're the one, aren't you? I didn't realize."

"I'm what one?"

"Discipline is so tight at Horn Hall that there was a joke among the reeves that 'Nothing escapes the King Anjihosh.' Then the rejoinder was, 'Except one.' So if anyone ever made some comment like, 'Everyone knows that,' or 'Everyone must do that,' then someone would always respond, 'Except one.' It's you, isn't it?"

Heat flamed up her cheeks so fast that he looked away.

"My apologies," he muttered. "I should never have spoken it."

"Best you go," she said, more curtly than she intended. "If you see Reeve Peddonon, tell him I wish to see him as soon as he can trouble himself to get here."

Badinen glanced up at the sky. The sun blazed at zenith, clouds parting around it as if afraid to veil its fierce disk. "My apologies, verea," he repeated.

"Neh, neh, do not say so. It was nothing. But I need to speak to Peddonon right away. Do you understand?"

With his hands he sketched the gesture used in the tales to indicate *"good-bye and fare well."* "I'll go at once."

"If you go up this street to its end and through the gate there," she added, "you'll find the hilltop has a perch built out in the open. Your eagle can land and launch from there."

"My thanks," he murmured, still so embarrassed that he could not meet her gaze as he took his leave.

She watched him go and then, at last, met the gaze of the curious red cap. After all, she was not as ruthless as she ought to be. He tipped his cap in mocking salute, a strenuously polished ring glinting on his left hand. A wolf's-head ring. She refrained from grabbing the pole used to raise and lower the lamps, running down onto the street, and smashing him right on his already once-broken nose. How she hated them and their surveillance! But she would not become like the man she had left. She would not. Instead, she went back to the kitchen.

Once a year a spray of plum blossoms was delivered to Mai's door by a cadre of Anji's elite Black Wolves. Once a year she refused to accept the flowers, and the riders left bearing the message implicit in her refusal. That was the only communication between them. She kept hoping Anji would give up but so far he had not. The only thing stopping him from riding into town with his troops and making her a prisoner was his pride.

She had built a fine life as far away from him in the Hundred he ruled as she could manage. In the region of Mar, in the port town of Salya, she had family, a business, friends, and a network of interlacing community in which she was deeply involved and, she believed, was respected. She had a daughter to raise. She had allies, whatever that meant, but it meant something when part of your life involved a rear-guard action fighting to own yourself.

"Mai! You're slaughtering that innocent brinjal root. You must be thinking of Anji."

Miravia lumbered in, belly leading, and gave Mai a kiss on the cheek before she swung the basket she was carrying onto the table. Derra followed with a basket balanced on each hip.

Mai set down the knife, seeing the spray of white tuberous brinjal flesh in splinters across the wooden cutting board. "Oh."

"Yes," agreed Miravia. "Let me do that."

"You should sit down after tramping all over town."

"I can't. I feel very restless."

Mai glanced at Miravia's huge belly. "Do you think the baby is coming?"

"I think so. It's exactly how I felt with the other two."

Mai handed her the knife. "It wouldn't be like this if all ties had been severed. I would simply have moved on. But I am constantly reminded that I can't. For example, I would like to have a man in my arms again someday. I would like to not worry that my friends in Bronze Hall are under constant siege. I fear he may find an excuse to send his soldiers to occupy Salya even though the town council pays taxes faithfully every year."

Miravia smiled ruefully as she lined up scrubbed radish and began chopping, but she made no reply. Her hair was bound back in a scarf, and her cheeks were round and moist with sweat from the excursion. She began to tell Mai the gossip she'd heard in the market, and what news there was of ships and sheep and merchants from exotic lands come to sell exotic wares for a season in Salya in the hopes of earning enough to buy Mar-grown spices and delicacies to take back to their homes.

Mai let the words flow past. What manner of person was she that she had even for an instant entertained the notion of inviting Badinen inside to innocently help her prepare a meal with the full expectation that this unexceptional act would get him killed? She hadn't any proof he was a spy nor any reason to think so except what Tesya had said. Was she so caught up in this silent war with Anji that she would throw the innocent to the wolves just to prove that she could?

The two girls came running in, towing big Edi and little Raida. Arasit's shrieks filled the kitchen area before calm Eiko pulled her away to go set up the dining room for the feast. Raida toddled loyally after the big girls as always. Edi went out to haul in fuel and water and extend the awning so they could leave the dining room doors open on the sunside. Miravia chattered on with an entertaining if far-fetched tale about sea-going ships whose hulls were magically woven with the shadows of birds so that they would fly faster over the ocean.

Keshad returned carrying the accounts books, which he sealed into the chest hidden beneath the floor, to be opened after the Ghost Days, at dawn on the first day of the new year. Then he supervised the girls as they put up the festival decorations on the porch. Within the routine of daily life Mai kept her hands busy, and slowly the churning mire of her thoughts settled.

Late in the afternoon, when she had gone into the garden to harvest fresh shoots for the slip-fry, Zubaidit strolled into the garden, her hair braided and coiled up atop her head and an undyed cotton taloos suitable for the Ghost Days tightly wrapped around her lithe body.

Mai rose and kissed her, holding her dirty hands away from the cloth, then said, "You have something you want to say to me in private about Tesya."

Instead of replying, Zubaidit raised a hand, cautioning silence. Boots thumped on the walkway. Reeve Peddonon trotted down the steps and strode across the walled garden. He was big for a reeve, tall and thickly built without being fleshy. Zubaidit relaxed at once, and gave him a sisterly kiss on either cheek, then stepped aside so Mai could greet him in the same way.

"You got my message," Mai said. "I hope there's no need to look so grim."

"What message? I got no message. I have terrible news."

His mouth had a harsh line she'd not seen since the days of the war. "What's happened?"

"Marshal Orhon is dead."

"Dead?" The word shaped easily, but it made no sense. "But I just saw Orhon last week for our usual tea. . . . There's been no word of sickness. . . . Dead? How can he be dead?"

"He was murdered."

"Murdered? How can you be sure?"

"The knife and the blood."

"Knife? Blood?" She kept repeating words as if Peddonon had lapsed into speaking a language she did not know.

"He was stabbed up under the jaw."

"The hells," murmured Mai, to say something. Her head felt raked clean of all but one word: *Murdered.*

"A knife to the brain is one of the ways the acolytes of Ushara mark their killings," said Zubaidit quietly.

"Have you killed a person in that way?" Peddonon asked, examining her from top to toe.

"No." Zubaidit had the deadly grace of a person whose body is honed like steel, her assured posture very like that of the flirtatious young man Mai had seen on the street. "Neither I nor any of my people in my temple were involved with this death. Orhon was my ally in keeping this region free of King Anjihosh's iron fist. Might a disgruntled reeve or fawkner have killed him?"

Peddonon shook his head. "Unlikely. He was rigid and often unpleasant but he was also fair and consistent. People in the hall grumbled but they respected the way he kept Bronze Hall independent when the other five reeve halls bent under the thumb of the king."

Mai nodded. "Anji met Orhon only once. As I recall it, Orhon flatly rejected his overtures to have Bronze Hall join with the other reeve halls under Anji's command. I'm sure Anji never forgave him for that. It's the kind of thing he can't forgive."

"That does make his involvement likely. But I don't understand how someone could have gotten into the marshal's cote to do it, at night, on an island surrounded by cliffs where no stranger is allowed to stay and where there is only one place to put a boat. The pier is guarded day and night. It makes more sense if it was someone already inside."

"What about that new reeve, Badinen?" Mai said. "This morning Tesya accused him of stealing a courier bag. Could he have murdered Orhon last night and flown here to Salya this morning? Because he was here."

He rocked back on his heels as at a hit. "Tesya accused him! It can't be. Badinen was working for me in Horn Hall."

"Was he?" said Zubaidit, exchanging a glance with Mai. "You never told us!"

Peddonon shrugged ruefully. He was such a good-natured man that Mai could never be angry with him. "It seemed safer that only I and Marshal Orhon knew. What did Tesya say?"

"That there is a spy and a thief in Bronze Hall, and he is the only newcomer so therefore the chief suspect. Do you think he could have turned on you?"

"Anything is possible. But he's old-fashioned, our Badinen, from the upcountry north where the old ways are the only ways anyone knows. This business of an outlander riding into the Hundred and declaring himself commander over all the land is not a thing a country lad like Badinen takes lightly. Nor is he infatuated with the idea of being part of an outlander's army, or the reorganized reeve halls, or the way Anjihosh set himself up as king with spies and soldiers to do his bidding."

"What made Badinen come here now?"

Peddonon's lips curled into a sardonic smile. "There was a woman involved. Threw him over for another man."

"Not that you heard it from me," Zubaidit murmured, "but I might I have heard that story in Ushara's garden. Either it's true, or he's a cursed good liar."

"I believe Badinen," said Peddonon. "We'll miss having an ear in Horn Hall, but I could not force him to stay any longer, him being so miserable. Seven years is a long time to live a lie."

"If I were Anji, I would have been foresighted enough to place a spy or two in the group who left Horn Hall with you seven years ago." Mai brandished her knife, with its one blunt and one sharp edge. "So here's another way to look at it. Tesya might accuse Badinen of being a spy to draw attention off of herself while she stole the bag and afterward killed Orhon."

"Hammerer's Balls!" Peddonon ground a boot into the gravel, rubbing it around like killing the idea. "You've a cruel imagination, Mai."

"I think Mai has a practical turn of mind, myself." Zubaidit reached for a stalk of proudhorn and snapped it off. "But Tesya could not have wielded the knife herself. She spent the night in Ushara's temple with one of the acolytes. If she's the one, then she had an accomplice and we are back where we started."

"I just think it's odd she was so quick to go after Badinen," said Mai. "She could have been setting Badinen up by making little thefts herself."

Peddonon ran a thumb along his short beard. "I've not heard of any little thefts in the hall. But it's not necessarily the kind of thing that would be brought to my attention."

"Send Tesya to Horn Hall for a year," said Mai. "If she's loyal, she'll report back on what she hears, and meanwhile Anji will know we suspect he has had a hand in the disruption at Bronze Hall. If she is the real traitor, then Anji will wonder how much we know and how we knew it."

She thought of the men with red caps who kept watch outside her compound. She thought of the attractive man on the street wearing a wolf's-head ring.

"Or if there is a spy in Bronze Hall, maybe they are only there to pass on information," she went on. "Anji knows about the existence of Ushara's hidden acolytes, the ones who can be hired to kill. We all know he will have considered training his own stable of skilled and lethal people."

Her words produced a simmering silence. A bird flitted like a spy through shrubs of sweet-scented muzz before fluttering off.

Zubaidit began pacing restlessly, odd to see in a woman who usually could absorb any shocking news without a murmur. "The murder has the taste of a deliberate assassination meant to let us know that the man who did it can act whenever he wishes. Even the chief of my order would not act as a lackey to a man who calls himself king when there was never a king before in the Hundred. So I think you are right. He has decided to create his own executioners and spies, who act only on his behalf. Just as a tyrant must."

Peddonon scratched his head. "Why act now?"

Mai caught Zubaidit's wrist and drew her to a halt, so the three of them stood tightly together. "He is giving us notice that he is done letting Bronze Hall maintain its autonomy. He's moving in. This means our uneasy truce is over. We truly are at war with Anji now."

Zubaidit tapped a foot on the ground as she shook her head. "We have always been at war with him, since we all broke with our superiors and came to live here. I'd best return to the temple. I will speak to you both after the Ghost Days."

She kissed Peddonon on the cheek and Mai on the mouth, and left.

Mai resumed picking shoots into the shallow basket set on the earth. Peddonon sat on a bench, tapping one foot on the ground, watching her.

"I should have been able to prevent Orhon's murder," he muttered.

"Can you prevent something you never expected?" She smiled sadly at him. "Do you know, it's my old dreams that plague me most, the story I told myself of how the tale would have a fine, romantic ending. In my heart I guessed that the tales of true love and noble adventure where justice wins and wrongdoing is crushed were a sort of falsehood. I saw the evidence for that every day in the home in which I grew up, for it wasn't a happy place! But I wanted to believe so badly. The bold captain! The shy fruit-seller he plucks out of the market! I thought with Anji that my tale was one of those rare few that would have a happy ending. So after all, it's really myself I betrayed, isn't it, by insisting on something that could not be true?"

"I don't think so, Mai. I think he betrayed all of us, and you most of all when he stole your son. As for the rest of us, he brought us peace, at a cost. But peace nevertheless. He's a fair man in his own way. That he is also a tyrant simply makes the situation more complicated."

"Now that I think about it more clearly, Anji would never agree to send a good-looking man like Badinen to spy on me. His weakness is that he believes he cannot hold onto a thing he desires without a chain to leash it."

Peddonon's was an observant gaze, and he had an even temper even in such circumstances, but his anger was visible in the deep lines at his eyes. "Is peace and order nothing more than a harness that keeps us bound?"

"I can't answer for the other people of the Hundred. I made my choice by leaving Anji."

"You lost your child."

As sharp as a well-honed blade, that pain would never ease. She scooted to a parallel row and began stripping dill for a garnish. "The boy had already been taken from me. I see now I could never have gotten him back." She shook her head to throw off the old sorrow. "I think of my beautiful little Atani every day, but he calls another woman 'mother' and I have to believe that she cherishes him or I would not be able to sleep at night."

"War, then," said Peddonon with a sigh. "I did not much like Orhon but I respected how he ran Bronze Hall. His 'old ways' were what kept Bronze Hall from being absorbed into the new reeve hall structure imposed by King Anjihosh. That, of course, and your presence here in Mar."

"Yes." Her lips twisted as the memory of her months as Anji's wife floated before her. Those days had been sweet because she had been so ignorant and so young. "I still have power over him, of a kind, because he still desires to possess me. But he is not a man who chooses to reveal his weaknesses, so up until now he has held Mar at arm's length because I live here. I suppose that sounds terribly vain, but I fear it is true."

"One thing you are not is vain."

"Certainly not! That is why I own the finest collection of silks in Salya and likely all of Mar. Not liking to risk my complexion being seen contrasted with second-quality silk."

He laughed.

She shook her head as her smile faded. "I'm not minded to acquiesce. Are you?"

"I am not."

"Then we must plan our own campaign."

The bell rang from the kitchen.

"You'll stay for the feast?"

"Of course. Let me go make sure all is settled with my eagle." Broad face creased with a frown, the reeve crunched away over the garden path.

She lingered in the garden and when she was sure he was well gone she entered the house by a hidden entrance that led directly into her private chamber. In a narrow storage room lined with shelves stacked with more gorgeous silk than any one woman could realistically wear—silk was her weakness—she fished a chain off a hook. An iron ring dangled from the chain: the wolf's head that was the sigil of the clan she had been born into in a faraway desert town. She already knew it was the same design as the one the young man in the street was wearing. She studied it for a while, thinking of the man she had married, the son he had taken from her, and the daughter he had left behind.

Then she put the ring back and joined the others.

Old Priya and her husband O'eki walked down from their house for the last meal.

Together the household made the proper offerings, sang the customary songs, and ate their feast in the prescribed order, finishing with the sweet pudding just as the night bells rang down the end of the day, and the end of the year, across the town. Three-day candles were lit in ceramic holders and set one in each room and two on the porch to mark the entry. All the doors were left open so wandering ghosts could exit as easily as they entered. The girls, tucked into bed, made silly jokes about ghosts and giggled a lot. Keshad, Peddonon, and O'eki got into a long and involved discussion about the nature of ghosts as they cleared and washed the dishes with Edi helping. The women sat on the porch, sipping the fermented petal wine that was only drunk during the Ghost Days.

"I hope the baby doesn't come during the Ghost Days," whispered Miravia, stroking her belly. Her gaze shifted inward for a space before she offered them a weary smile gilded by candle-light.

Priya said, "How often is your womb tightening?"

"Just now and then," said Miravia. "I suppose I should never have walked down into the market today."

"The child will come when it will come," said Priya more gently. "Best you rest now. Come inside." She rose with Derra's help and at the door the three women turned. "Mai, are you coming?"

"I'll sit the first watch," said Mai. "I'm not tired yet."

She sat in the gloom beyond the reach of the candlelight and watched the empty street. Strangely no red cap was visible in the accustomed place. Maybe even the red caps feared to walk at night on the Ghost Days. With no red cap to trail her a woman might walk right down off the porch and into the ghostly city and go anywhere, really, walk to the inn where that good-looking young man was staying. But no person moved about at night during the Ghost Days except for the fire watch, who walked in pairs during these ill-omened nights and besides that went attended by picked ordinands of Kotaru specially blessed and trained to cast off ghostly assaults.

On Ghost Nights, after the end of the old year and before the priests of Sapanasu rang in the new year, ghosts walked freely at night. You were only safe if you remained within the boundaries of your own compound sealed by offerings and prayers and with the doors left open so no ghosts got trapped inside. Mai did not worship the Hundred's gods, but she accepted their pre-eminence and followed the customs of her adopted home. So she stayed on the porch and sipped petal wine and listened as the wind sighed over the town.

"Mai?" Peddonon stepped out from inside the house, then yawned, stifling it behind an open hand.

"I'm well enough. You sleep now and take the late watch."

He bent to kiss her in a brotherly way—the only way he would ever kiss a woman—and went back inside to sleep.

She sat as the silence drifted down around her like settling dust. Peace kissed her, as on wings. These quiet Ghost Nights held a special place in her heart now, an interval suspended out of time in which she might allow her worries and aggravations to sleep. She tasted on her tongue the waxy lavender scent of the three-day candles. The bones of the house creaked softly. The world breathed, and if she made herself very very still in the midst of it all she could hear the pulse of the land's bright heart, a thread of blue-white light that tangled with her own being.

"Momma?"

She startled back to awareness. "You're meant to be in your bed, Arasit."

"Couldn't sleep," said the girl with her mouth turned down and one foot scraping on the planks as though sweeping them. She had Anji's features more than Mai's, those brilliantly intense eyes. That absolutely stubborn intransigence was Anji's as well although he had learned to hide it while playing at being the most reasonable of men. "I want to see a ghost. I've never seen ghost, even though I peek every year. I don't think there are ghosts."

Mai beckoned, and the girl snuggled into the curve of her mother's arm. "There are ghosts. Your father could see them."

"I can't see ghosts. And I've never met my father, so how do I know he even exists? He might be a pretend person you made up. I think my father ran away because he didn't want me. Because I'm a brat. I wish I had a father like the other girls do."

Arasit was still young enough that Mai knew how to stroke her scalp so as to relax her. "I tell you what, little one. You close your eyes until I count to ten, but if you open them before I'm done, I have to start over. Then afterward, I'll tell you a story. One. Two. . . . Three. . . ."

By "seven" the girl was asleep, all curled up like a flower in bud, waiting for the dawn to open. Mai despaired of Arasit sometimes. She was a brat, full of wild outbursts usually calmed only by Miravia and Keshad's eldest child, Eiko, who was the same age and as steady as Arasit was difficult. But it was more than that. The girl wore a strangeness about her. If a thunderstorm boomed down over town the girl would rush outdoors and refuse to come in. Once in the midst of a frightening crash of lightning and thunder she had climbed up onto the roof and Keshad, raging and cursing, had had to clamber up and actually wrestle her down, not an easy task for she had kicked and screamed the entire time. She adored Priya, though, and would spend entire days there patiently helping grind herbs and blend medicinal pastes. She and Eiko were old enough to attend the children's school, and Mai would soon have to let her go, although she feared the child would become disruptive or that Anji would send soldiers to kidnap her. . . .

A noise scattered her thoughts into the wind. Her heart lugged, and sweat flushed on her brow, and then she realized she was hearing the unhurried clop of horse's hooves. More than one.

Did spirits truly pass through the streets of villages and towns and drag unwilling victims into their saddles and away into one of the hells? She had heard plenty of tales of ghostly vengeance taken for an old grievance. The tales were full of insubstantial Night Riders who abducted people bold and foolish enough to chance the darkness of a Ghost Night, or who unpredictably left dangerous and precious gifts on porches.

She shivered despite herself. But, in truth, the clip clop sounded like perfectly ordinary hooves. Rising, she stepped in front of Arasit's sleeping form just as the shadowy figures of three riders sifted out of shadow into view on the street. Anger scalded her, succeeded by fear for her child and, if she were honest, for herself. She knew those silhouettes instantly. She recognized the distinctive armor and stocky horses of Qin soldiers as if they were the familiar profiles of kinfolk, and in some way they were. She had grown up thousands of mey from the Hundred in an oasis town ruled by the Qin, nomadic raiders who built an empire by capturing what they desired to possess. She had been married off to a prince of the Qin although at the time she had thought he was a simple captain. She had borne to him two children. Once, she had believed she loved him.

Now, with a long in-drawn breath to steady herself, she walked to the steps and waited for the riders to halt on the street below. The second rider dismounted stiffly, burdened by the thick weight ringing his torso, and approached. He halted at the base of the steps so she could identify his face.

"Chief Tuvi!" Heedless of the strictures of the Ghost Days, she descended the steps in a rush and, without thinking, caught the chief by the shoulders and kissed each weathered cheek. He mewled with a faint noise of discomfort. Startled, she stepped back to see his familiar and much loved smile as he looked her over.

"You look well, Mistress. I am pleased to see you healthy and blooming." His voice sounded perfectly normal, just as she remembered it, not mewling at all.

She glanced past him at the two soldiers, still mounted, but they were not men she knew. "Chief, you and your men must come inside. We have a stable, mattresses for visitors, something to drink. . . ."

Then she recalled that Orhon had just been murdered.

"I cannot stay, Mistress." He watched her with the intent gaze she remembered. He was Anji's most trusted retainer, the man to whom Anji had given the duty of protecting his wife, back when Mai was his wife. "I have been sent by the king."

"Tuvi." She hesitated, not wanting her words to a man she respected to be angry. She could not accuse him of the murder, even though she knew he was capable of killing without regret or hesitation. However, most Qin hated the water, and few of them could swim.

His attention had already dropped to what she had at first imagined was a belly grown large from too much eating and drinking in the palace of the Hundred's new ruler. Instead, he unwrapped a swaddling bundle and held it out before her. The candles gave off just enough light that she could discern the thing he had been carrying against his body as he rode.

It was an infant child, not more than ten days old and boasting a head of coal-black hair.

"Merciful One, cast your blessings upon the innocent," she murmured reflexively.

"Will you take him?" Tuvi asked.

"Take him?" The anger poured out in a rush. "What, does Anji mean to offer a trade? This infant in exchange for Atani, whom he stole from me and allows another woman to claim as her son? Or is this his way of trying to bind me back to him, to make me surrender—?"

"Mistress," he said in that way he had of cutting her off without raising his voice or showing the least sign of irritation. "That is not what this is."

She closed her mouth over the rest of her furious words. With a curt gesture she signaled that she would listen to what he had to say.

"There was another boy-child born before this one, a few years ago. The king's mother got to him first and had him killed."

She sucked in air as if she'd been punched in the stomach.

"She had him killed so no younger son could threaten Atani's place as the heir," he went on, and that only made it worse, knowing that the son she had lost had been the cause of a blameless infant's death. "She feared that if Lady Zayrah raised a son borne out of her own womb she might come to prefer it over one born to another woman. This baby, *this infant boy*, would have met the same fate as the other one, smothered at birth. But the king smuggled the infant out of the palace and told his mother the baby was stillborn."

Rage simmered in her heart. The baby was so small, helpless against the ruthless machinations of the adults surrounding it.

He nodded as if she had spoken her thoughts aloud. "King Anjihosh had to decide quickly whom he could trust to raise the boy kindly and with affection. Whom he could trust to never attempt to bring the child into conflict with his heir. So he thought of you."

"He thinks of me too much, Tuvi," she said, for once allowing her bitterness to leak into her voice.

He inclined his head. "When it comes to you, he will never change."

"What if I agree to take the baby only in exchange for Anji letting go of me?"

"I cannot bargain. You must either accept the burden, or reject it. All else remains as it was."

She was by now trembling. Anji knew her too well. At that instant, the baby stirred. A dark infant gaze fixed on her and the little person smacked delicate rosebud lips, thinking of inchoate hungers. She wanted to take him into her arms but she took a step back instead.

"Maybe you cannot bargain, Tuvi, but I can, and he knows I will. If he sent the child to me only as a way to bribe me back to him, it will not work. I will not raise a child as a hostage. But if he genuinely wishes the child to live and thrive, then he must give me room. Let him keep his red caps watching the house if he is so selfish that he cannot bear for me to ever again have sexual love with a man. However brilliant he is, in this matter his mind is very narrow. I have love in plenty. But let him leave Bronze Hall alone."

"Bronze Hall? The reeve hall?"

"He sent two agents to steal a courier bag and murder the marshal. They're staying at the Inn of Fortune's Star."

He said nothing. Either he was ignorant of the matter, which she doubted, or he knew better than to give away the game too early.

She offered him her market smile, offering much and promising nothing. "I know Anji. If he truly cares for the child he will have given you permission to bargain with me. Bring me the courier bag and your sworn word that he will leave Bronze Hall alone, and I will take the baby as my own. I trust you to fulfill any promise you make to me here."

In the deathly hush, every least sound seemed heightened: a splash of wash water being thrown over stones; an unidentifiable thump, heard once and not repeated, like a body falling heavily onto a floor; many streets over, the clapping sticks of the fire watch on patrol. A night-jar trilled its delicious song like a spark of unexpected joy.

He met her gaze with his steady one. "Whatever else, Mistress, he does truly care about the welfare of his children. Let it be done. On my honor as a man and a soldier, I make this bargain on his behalf."

"Give him to me," she whispered hoarsely, extending her arms. "What is his name?"

He settled the infant in her arms. "He has no name. To give him a name would acknowledge his life, and he is dead to the palace. He must remain dead. The child you hold has no mother but you."

She had already taken in the baby into her heart. In her arms he bided restfully, his earnest infant gaze fixed on her mouth and eyes. She caught Tuvi's gaze and held it. "Please tell me, Tuvi-lo. How is Atani? Is he taken care of? Is he healthy? Is he happy? Does he have companions?"

He sighed as though the words pained him. "He is cherished by all who know him, Mistress. He is a good boy, an obedient boy, perhaps a bit timid."

"Has he any playmates, so he isn't lonely?"

"He is just a year older than the eldest of his sisters. He adores her, and she has courage enough for both. He is gentle and kind with his other younger sisters, and they think he is the sun in their sky. He is intelligent, like his father. He studies hard to master all that he should at the palace school, where there are boys his own age who treat him with the respect he deserves. The Lady Zayrah treats him as her own. She loves him with true affection, if that is what concerns you."

"Does Atani love her as a mother?" she asked, the words bitter on her lips as she closed her eyes against the knife of grief. She'd thought the wound healed, but it would never heal.

"He does, Mistress."

She could not speak. The baby fussed a little, and she opened her eyes as she rocked him enough to distract him. Raggedly, she said, "That is well, then. That is well."

"We must be gone long before the dawn, so none suspect where the child came from. We've been giving him sheep's milk."

"Miravia will give birth in a day or two. She can nurse him with his cousin."

To her surprise, he touched her on one arm, an astonishing display from the tough old soldier. "Be well, Mistress. Do not think I have forgotten you."

"I know where your duty lies."

She wanted to ask if the women of the palace treated him well, if they had found a proper wife for him, to replace the one he had been forced to leave behind in the Qin homeland so many years ago because he had followed his duty, which was his captain. But she thought the question would be cruel, for what if they had not? What if no one but her cared anything for Chief Tuvi except as a weapon serving the commander?

He smiled, as if she had spoken with her expression. "I found a good woman, a widow, an older woman. We deal together very well, she and I. I thought you would want to know."

With tears on her cheeks she embraced him as a niece would embrace a beloved uncle.

"I will deliver what you are owed," he said, handing over a leather pouch with some small items for the baby. "Be well, Mistress."

She let him go, as she must. He mounted, and the riders vanished into the darkness. The fall of hooves on stone faded. The distant shush of the incoming tide swallowing the tidal flats soon became the only sound in the sleeping town except for Arasit's restful breathing. The bag included a leather bottle with a bit of fresh sheep's milk still left. Mai fed the baby as ghosts slipped noiselessly past her on the dying winds of the old year and the birthing winds of the new.

Footsteps scuffed the silence. She looked up to see the young man stroll effortlessly out of the darkness. She was surprised and yet not surprised, at once sorting through possible responses and potential lines of attack. He halted at the base of the steps, unslung a bag from his shoulder, and swung it as if to loft it onto the porch with a flourish.

"Quietly. There's a child sleeping."

Catching it deftly on the backswing, he set it on the ground at his feet and grinned at her. Lamplight caught on the interesting planes of his face. He was a few years younger than she was, still a little raw and unformed except for the absolutely sure way he held himself, a man who could manage any sort of physical feat.

"You wear the wolf's-head ring," she said in a low voice. "It's the badge of the king's elite soldiers, the Black Wolves. They carry out his most dangerous missions, so it is said."

His grin got cockier but didn't lose its essential sweetness.

"Did you murder Marshal Orhon?" she added.

His smile vanished. "I stole the bag. But I would have killed him, had I been given that order instead."

"How did you get on the island?"

"That was simple enough. We paddled out on one of those lovely canoes, and then swam the last part, and climbed the cliffs. Not nearly as difficult as it sounds."

"An interesting statement considering everyone believes it can't be done." She studied him carefully and precisely: taut arms, strong calves, a lean waist, and slim hips. He was still wearing the kilt, although he had laced up the vest, thus concealing his attractive torso. His shoulders were beautiful. "But if anyone looks fit for the part, it would be you."

His eyes widened at this unexpected compliment, and he gave her such a frankly sexual look-over, as if only now contemplating that they might actually find themselves tangling together on a bed, that she felt the heat of his thoughts pour right through her flesh. She had bested Anji once, hadn't she? She had wrested her freedom from his possessive grasp. Anji's weakness was that even though he knew she was as brilliant as he was, he could only see her as a woman who ought to belong to him. He knew only one way to fight.

"Aren't you afraid of ghosts and Night Riders?" she asked, filling the silence.

With a flick of his fingers the man gestured to show he had no worries. "My life is not my own. It belongs to the king. Thus I walk without concern because I am already dead."

"You don't look dead," she retorted, meaning the words in so many different possible ways. It had been years since she had so thoroughly enjoyed ogling a man.

The smile emerged again as he picked up on the energy surging between them. "May I ask your name, verea?"

"If you have to ask, then you're not a very good spy."

A blink acknowledged this hit. His gaze cast around the spacious porch, pausing briefly on Arasit before returning to her. "Are these your children?"

The baby had fallen asleep in her arms, the feel of his little body like balm healing the old pain in her heart. With perfect contentment and an almost blistering sense of triumph, she said, "They are, ver. My daughter and my son."

He caught in a breath, as if realizing he had made a mistake, and took a step back. The night drew its shadows over him so he was half obscured, almost a ghost himself. "My apologies if I have rudely intruded upon you, verea. I will bid you and your family a quiet festival and an auspicious new year."

But she caught him with a look before he could walk away. She hooked him with her market smile. "I have fewer encumbrances than it may seem. Will I not see you again, ver?"

Almost he reeled under this onslaught, but he was well trained and well honed, prepared for the most strenuous challenges. "If that is an invitation, then someday you will, verea. When you least expect me."

She allowed him the last word and thus said nothing as he touched a kiss to his fingers and flew it to her, then padded away into the night. This new armistice between her and Anji was not peace but merely a prelude to a more complicated struggle that she would wage with patience and flexibility in place of swords and spears. She laughed to herself as she went down the steps to the street to fetch the courier bag. Surely a man who could paddle, swim, and climb to reach a reeve hall famous for its inaccessibility could easily penetrate the guard of her red-cap sentries and find a way into her house.

If he did not, her life would not change from what it already was. The expectations, pleasures, and goals she held now were perfectly satisfying.

If he did, then anything might happen. The sex might be tedious, or it might be gratifying. . . .

"Mai?"

Startled, she turned.

Peddonon emerged from the interior, rubbing sleep out of his eyes. "In my dreams I thought I heard the sound of hooves. It woke me, so I came to take my share of the watch . . . Mai! Come up off the street! Don't you know the Night Riders steal beauty when they can catch such people out of doors on Ghost Nights?"

He stepped around the sleeping Arasit as Mai mounted the steps and slung the courier bag at his feet.

"The hells! Where did you get that?" Then he saw the bundle in her arms and gave a confounded second look as he shook himself into full alertness. "What are you holding?"

"A baby," she said. "The Night Riders brought me a perilous and beautiful gift. Just like in the tales."

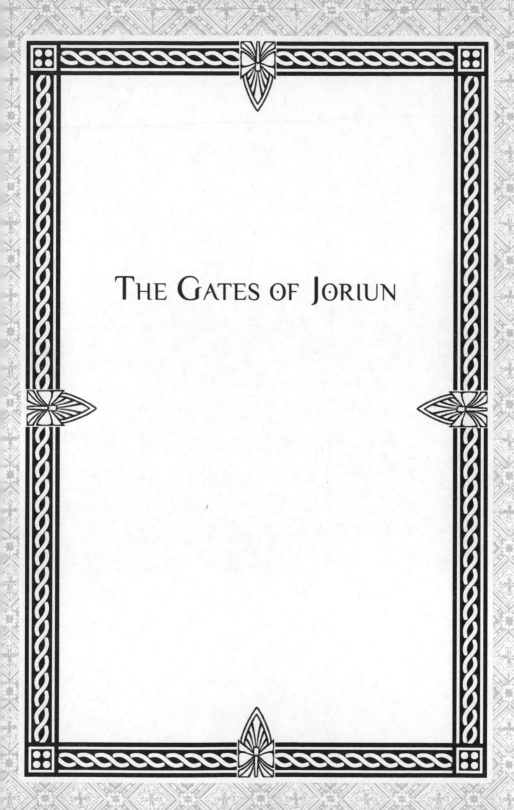

THE GATES OF JORIUN

The magicians say the sun rises every morning, and so far I have found that to be true. I depend on the sun; it is how I mark time, by that and by the food the woman brings me twice daily and by the unending cycle of the moon. I have discovered also that the stars move in the sky each night—when they are not obscured by clouds—and that I can trace pictures in them and see those pictures again and again if only I am patient enough at night and through the seasons. I try to sleep during the day, except for the food. During the day it is worst, for then there are people about and all of them eager to abuse me.

The magicians taught about the stars also, but I did not listen to them about those matters. I was a younger woman—how much younger I no longer know—and newly married. My nights did not involve gazing at stars. Now some of what they said has come back to me and I hoard it. I must hoard what scraps I can because as the days run one into the next, I lose more and more of my past; like the moon my memory waxes and wanes.

But I must remember. If I do not remember, then I become nothing, a mindless animal in a cage hung before the gates of Joriun, and then the king wins and my brother loses.

I remember the magicians.

Duncan was gone, ridden out to raise the Alarn clan behind the standard of war. Anyone would have noticed their entrance, but that day, distracted and feeling sorry for myself because my husband of but one month had been sent away on my brother's errand, I was overwhelmed by it.

They entered like moonlight and sunlight and the twilight between.

The first wore a robe of silver fabric so pale that at first I thought I could see through it. Only later did I realize I could see into it, like staring into the heavens at night. Small of stature, no bigger than a woman, he had neat hands, eyes the bleached color of the noonday sky washed in clouds, and a nose too big for his face. But he had power. It rode on him like a second garment.

The woman towered above the others. As big as a warrior and thicker through the middle, she had skin the color of charcoal, burned black, and robes so voluminous and of such a startlingly piercing gold that she seemed like the billowing sun fallen down to Earth, scorching and bright. I almost could not look at her straight on.

But the third entered in their shadow, like a shadow, and this one's gaze sought and found me in my own shadowed corner where I spun wool to thread and waited for my husband to return. Is that not the lot of women: to wait?

The third waited until I stared, and then beckoned to me while my brother and his advisers were busy with the first two magicians, swarming round them as moths swarm round any bright light—and these lights brighter than most. King in name only, half his countrymen in league with the usurper and the other half too poor to do more than scrabble at the dirt of their farms to save themselves and their kin from starvation, my brother needed help wheresoever he could find it. Even from magicians.

I set down my spindle to rise and cross the long hall. Closer now, I shook off my distraction and studied the visitors: the small moon man, the big sun woman, and the other, the third, the twilight between.

Not tall, not short, this one wore robes that were neither striped yet not of a solid color either, a dusky gray that held night in it and also the coming of morning. Long-fingered hands cupped a deck of cards as another might cup a fistful of gold rings or a child's hand. But it was her face I returned to again and again. Or perhaps I should say his face. Beardless, I might have guessed at once that this was a woman, but upon a second look, despite the lack of beard, I would have said it was a man. His—her—complexion was like to that of a lover seen in half-light as day fades or night lightens.

"You are the sister," he said, her voice so soft I could barely hear it above the ring of voices in the hall, my brother and his captains, lords and fighting men whose loyalty to the rightful heir was greater than their prudence, for certainly our uncle the king had usurped my brother's throne because he had the strength and the riches of the southern lords to back him up. Our uncle the king was not a foolish man, nor did he let ambition rule over common sense. But I was only a girl and my brother an infant in swaddling clothes when first our father died and our mother soon after, poisoned by our uncle so the rumor ran. Made regent, he found it easy enough to take over the duties and privileges of the crown outright and send the poor children—myself and my brother—away to the benighted northcountry; easy enough to put them in the care of a certain ambitious duke who would not be above seeing the two children die of a winter chill or an untimely accident.

But we were stronger than that.

"It is said," remarked the twilight mage, "that you raised your brother. That you led him through dark night and cruel winds to this castle, your safe haven protected through the years by your father's most loyal retainers. Is that true?"

"When he was old enough to walk, we escaped our keepers together," I said, and then added tartly, "though it wasn't in a winter's storm, as some say. Even as a girl I wasn't so foolish as to try such a thing. There was an old woman in the house who pitied us and it was through her offices that we survived as long as we did in the hall of the Duke of Joriun. I waited until a clear warm summer's night, and she gave us bread and cheese and water. She had arranged for a cousin to meet us at a fishing village at the coast, not more than an hour's walk away. The cousin took us north and eventually by one means and another got us to Islamay Castle. I needed only to lead us out of Joriun and out to the village. It was no great journey."

"Nevertheless," said the mage. "Your brother would never have grown to manhood without you."

"Perhaps," I said evasively. I did not like this kind of praise, though I had heard it more than once. My brother was a strong, clean, good man, if rather too fond of pretty young women, and he had to be respected for *his* strength, not for mine. That was the only way he could regain the throne stolen from him.

The mage opened his hands to display the cards. With a deft movement he flipped one over and laid it on the table between two burning candles. The card had a picture on it whose like I had never seen before: a woman, crowned and robed in a simple manner, holding a strong wooden staff in one hand.

"Queen of Staves," the mage said. "She is strong and independent and will gladly fight for that which is rightfully hers."

I snorted, having heard this kind of thing also—before Duncan laid claim to my heart, and my brother, with my approval, granted him my hand in marriage. However desperate my brother's plight, however unlikely his prospects might seem with only a handful of dirt-poor lords as his allies and for his soldiers only common-bred captains and farmers who had but one season in which to march on campaign before they had to return to their farms, there were always a few men who thought to gain my brother's ear through my—well, how shall we say it?—through my favors. I gave them short shrift and had shouted more than one out of Islamay Castle.

"And she is known sometimes to be short-tempered," the mage added with a quicksilver smile that charmed me utterly.

"It's a pretty picture," I said, reaching out to touch the card. But I hesitated before laying my finger on the thin painted card. I felt as strongly as if a voice had shouted in my ear that this was not mine to touch, not without permission.

"You may," the mage said softly. "It is you, after all."

So I did touch her. I felt the film of paint under my finger, touched her stern face and her stout stave that had a single leafing green branch growing from the upraised end.

"We call this card the Significator," the mage continued. "It signifies the person whose fortune we tell with these cards."

I laughed. "Are you going to tell my fortune?"

"Do you have a question you want answered?"

I smiled, thinking of Duncan and of long summer nights. Thinking of our greatest wish, when we whispered together and held each other tight. Was it shameful that, this time, my first thought was not for my brother and our struggle? I don't know. But I was newly wed, and Duncan was, for this summer at least, my world.

"Where will I be next year?" I asked, dreaming of Duncan holding a baby—our baby—while I sat sewing beside him, sewing, perhaps, the child's naming gown or my brother's coronation robes.

The mage's expression turned dour, like a lowering storm. "Very well." I thought the tone disapproving.

I was suddenly apprehensive. "I can ask something else."

"You have already asked," the mage said. And it is true enough, as with my brother, that some enterprises, once begun, must be played out to the bitter end. "If you will, shuffle the deck." He placed the cards in my hands and showed me how to divide them and combine them again, like lords in a dance of evasion and persuasion: Whose side will I come down on this year? When I had finished shuffling them to her satisfaction, he took them from me again and began to lay out the cards into a strange pattern on the table.

I could not help but watch. There was a hall behind us and people milling there, but they might as well have vanished for all the attention I paid them. All *my* attention was on the cards placed so carefully, so precisely, between the two burning candles.

The first card he laid directly on top of the Queen of Staves. "Placed atop the Significator, it represents the current situation. The Four of Staves," he smiled slightly as he spoke the words, "represents marriage. It is crossed by—"

"Crossed by?"

"Crossed by," he repeated placing a card athwart it, "the King of Swords."

"My uncle," I breathed, for although the card did not portray my uncle's actual face it did indeed represent his aspect: a robed and crowned king, stern of face, armed with a sword.

The king's position was unassailable. Many people said so. Those people had no doubt predicted my brother and I would be dead within the year eighteen years ago when our father and mother died. We had proved them wrong.

The mage continued. "At the base of matters, the Ace of Swords, the beginnings of conflict. What is passing away, the Two of Cups, happiness in romance."

I caught in a laugh, not wanting to show him open disrespect—as if what Duncan and I shared could ever pass away.

"What crowns the matter, how the situation appears now, the Nine of Staves . . . a pause in the midst of battle. What is coming into being, the Three of Swords. Heartbreak."

Now, and only now, the mage paused. He hesitated, and I was suddenly afraid. I felt the crawl of the evil eye on my back even as I heard laughter in the hall behind me. The candles burned evenly. The mage turned a gentle eye to me and smiled sadly. "I must go on," she said, "for once begun, a reading must be ended. That is the way of life itself."

"Of course," I said, refusing to surrender to this sudden crawling fear. "Go on." I would not give in to my weakness. Everyone knew that fortunetelling is for the superstitious and gullible, even in such a guise as this, for he asked no coin of me nor nothing in trade, and they say that is the sign of a true magician.

He laid a card to the right of the cross he had made of the others. "This card represents you," she said, "your inner being. Strength." The card depicted a woman, unafraid, holding a lion. "This next card represents what influences you: the Knight of Swords." A fierce and determined knight rode forward into the fray. "Is this your husband?"

"No," I said wonderingly, not knowing how I knew. "That is my brother."

"Ah," said the mage, and turned another card. "Your wishes and fears. The Hanged Man." I shuddered when he spoke those three words, for our uncle had promised us hanging, an outlaw's death, should he ever catch us. He hated us that much for living and surviving and daring to contest what he had gained through treachery. But this hanged man was not a gruesome sight. He hung upside down with the rope around his ankle, and he seemed utterly calm, a light of wisdom shining behind his head. "The Hanged Man represents waiting," said the mage. "Suspension. And the last card lies here, above and to the right of all else. It signifies the outcome."

"The outcome of what?"

"Of your question: 'Where will I be next year?'" He turned it over slowly and I watched, staring, breath held in. His whisper coincided with my hissed breath. "Eight of Swords."

Eight swords stuck point first into the ground and between them, bound by their sharp steel, stood a woman shackled by ropes.

"Mary!" The voice from the other side of the hall startled me out of my shocked contemplation of the horrible card. My brother's voice rang out, strong and true, as he was strong and true, the rightful heir. "You must come and meet our guests."

Mary. That is my name. I remember it now. The folk who come in and out of the gates of Joriun, about their business, on their way to and from the fields or the market, shout it sometimes, but as a curse. *"Mary,"* they shout. *"Hang that whore Mary."* They call me slut and traitor, bastard and demon, apostate, heretic, cunt, and witch. They shouted it more often at first, when the Duke of Joriun's men built and barred this cage and locked me inside it and winched it up to hang, suspended by rope and supported by wooden pillars, beside the central gates that lead into the town and castle of Joriun. They came in packs, in mobs, to jeer at me, and then I was thankful I hung so high above them. Few of them had strong enough arms that the rotting vegetables, the shit, the dirt, and the hail of wood shavings and nails and stones they threw actually hit me. They would have ripped me to pieces had I come within reach of their hands.

War has been hard on the people who live in Joriun. Some of them are refugees from the north. Perhaps a few pity me. I will never know. I never hear those voices.

Now only a few remember my name, or only a few bother to pause and curse me. They are used to me here. But maybe that is worse. I forget my name sometimes for days on end. They don't remind me of it anymore. I cannot turn their hate into strength for myself, living on it as a dog laps water on a hot day, if they do not remember to hate me.

Even the woman who brings me my porridge each day no longer bothers to spit in it before she hands it over to me.

How many years I have been imprisoned here, in this prison hung out like a songbird's cage? The bars are weathering and gray, the bench on which I sleep, swaying in the night wind, cracked and splintered. Gaps in the floorboards show the ground, littered with my refuse and the refuse thrown at me, far below. Too far to jump, even if I could pry open the locked door that abuts the parapet, even if I could break apart the thick bars. Perhaps it would be better to jump and be done with it.

A songbird is treated gently for the song it may sing for its master. I know the song they wish me to sing for all to see.

God help me. Let me not descend into madness.

Let me not weaken. It is so hard.

How many years? One year? Two? Five? I see my hands are weathered, though whether from age or exposure I do not know. I see my nails grow long; filthy and cracked, they curl at the ends. I break them off when they get in the way of eating, of caring for myself such as I can.

I do not know how many years it has been. The woman who brings my food is my only mirror, and she is a new woman every season so I cannot track my days by watching her age. She never ages, because she is always young. I have no knowledge by which to track the time except the round of stars and the procession of spring into summer, summer into winter, and winter into spring. Three winters I think I have been here, but perhaps it is four. I hang in limbo, suspended in this cage, this purgatory.

How fares my brother?

I pray you, God, watch over him and over my husband.

The watchmen tell me sometimes my brother is dead. They taunt me with it, his death, his dead body eaten by crows. I do not believe them. I cannot believe them. They must be lying.

But I don't know. I know nothing but the opening of the gates at dawn and their closing at dusk. I know nothing except that the sun rises every morning without fail and that night comes and passes and comes again.

I must not believe them.

Today I hear a horn. At dawn the gates open. This activity I watch each morning, the opening of the gates below; it is one of my talismans. By this means I remember I am alive.

Today no farmers march out to their fields. No peddlers scurry out with bundles on their back; no carts or wagons roll out onto the morning road.

They come instead, the lords and knights and ladies of Joriun Castle, in their bright procession, their fine clothing so painful that I shade my eyes, for I am dressed now in rags though once this gown was what any decent woman would be proud to wear in her brother's hall, entertaining guests, coaxing reluctant allies to throw in their lot with his desperate cause.

The noble folk of Joriun Castle, no greater in rank than I, flood forth in their brilliant procession. They are off to hunt, I think, for they have hounds aplenty romping beside them or taut under leash and their horses are caparisoned as for a gala festival.

They are not alone.

They are led by their master, the young Duke of Joriun. He is, I see, not yet an old man, so must I be not yet an old woman. The master of Joriun and I were of an age once, and I suppose we remain so now although he walks in freedom and I wait, hanging, in this prison.

My lips are unused to smiling. I feel them crack as the corners turn up as I remember what everyone said: his father, the old Duke, died of apoplexy the night after my brother and I escaped from this castle.

How the son hates me, even after so many years.

He looks up though the others ignore me. I am no longer of interest to them, I am ugly and dirty and mad and lost and sometimes it seems I am a hundred years old, but he never neglects to look up. He always marks me on his comings and goings. He looks, and he *smiles*, in answer to my smile.

I remember his smile.

The magicians stayed for an entire month while we wined them and dined them better than we ate ourselves and then they went away. But they left behind them promises, or so my brother said. I asked him how one can hold a promise and suggested he would have been better off asking for a wagonload of spears and a herd of cattle.

He laughed and agreed. Of course, you see, I could never be angry with him because he always agreed with me. That he then went and did as he wished made no difference to his amiability.

When Duncan rode in empty-handed from the Alarn clan, my brother decided then and there to journey to Alarn himself. It is true he needed the Alarn clan to swell his army, such as it was. He needed their support. He needed the support of every ancient lord and old retainer who had once sworn fealty to our father, especially the ill-tempered and independent lords of the craggy northcountry highlands. If you have not the riches of the south, then you need the rock-hard stubbornness of the north. Gold is not harder than granite.

It was a difficult road into Alarn country. The paths were the known haunts of bandits. So, despite my irritable objections, the ladies were left behind. Even Duncan protested that it might be too difficult for women, though he truly did not want to leave me. His mother and young sister were among the ladies who lived now for part of the year in Islamay Castle and for the rest moved to other estates with my brother or some group of his adherents.

"Of course *you* could make the journey, Mary," said my brother sweetly, "but what of the others? What of Widow Agnes and Lady Dey? They are not strong like you. I must leave someone to watch over them."

So I remained behind. We stayed another month, we ladies—twelve of us and our servants. But as autumn laid in its bitter store of cold and the meager harvest was brought to the hearth to be measured and stored, I knew we would have to split up and move south. I sent Widow Agnes and Lady Dey and most of the other ladies to the western estate of Lord Dey, the lady's husband; it had a milder climate but was more vulnerable to raids from the south. Duncan's mother and young sister I kept by me, for I was fond of them—I knew I could love Duncan soon after I first met him not just for himself but because of the care he took of his widowed mother and his dear sister.

We rode east to the fortress of old Lord Craige, an inhospitable setting but rather safer than the valley manor of Lord Dey.

It was not a trap, precisely. It was only that I did not know that in the skirmishes that raged in the border country, Craige fortress had just fallen to the Duke of Joriun. Few riders dared the high roads alone, and it was easy to miss a fleeing messenger on the road. I did not know, as I rode into the courtyard, where peace reigned and some few men whose faces I did not recognize stared at me in surprise, that but three days earlier Lord Craige had been deposed and sent to the tower.

I did not know until they escorted me with all due respect into the hall and I faced the man who sat in the high chair.

And the young Duke of Joriun smiled *that* smile at me.

"So the woman who killed my father walks like a lamb into my hands," he said when they put the chains on my wrists and neck.

How the son hated me, even after so many years.

But like his father before him, he was ambitious. He wanted reward more than revenge, so he took me south with Duncan's mother and young sister to the court of my uncle the king.

The king had mercy on the old and the young. "Let them be placed in a convent," he said, and I was not even allowed to kiss them nor they me before they were led away.

"But you," he said, turning to look on me, "you I have promised a hanging."

"Hang me if you will," I said, smiling. "It will not alter my brother's cause, nor the outcome, for the just shall triumph and the wicked perish."

"It will give him a martyr," he muttered. He twisted the rings on his hands musingly, for he had many rings, gold encrusted with rubies and diamonds, a black opal set in silver, a ring of green malachite and one of turquoise that had once been my mother's but had failed to change color when danger loomed, as turquoise was said to do. Most impressively, the large seal ring of the king's authority half covered the knuckle of his right middle finger. He wore a houppelande sewn of brilliant blue cloth embroidered with small gold crowns, trimmed with ermine at the neck and lined with a heavy cloth of gold. The hem was beaded with pearls. The crown that rested so easily on his brow I had last seen on my father's head.

At last he stilled himself and came to some conclusion. I was not afraid of him, not then, not yet. I knew my cause was just and I knew I was stronger than he was because I was not afraid of death.

And he knew I was not afraid.

But I should have been afraid. Only a man as cunning as he could have stolen the throne and crown and scepter and husbanded it so well. He smiled oddly and crookedly and beckoned to the Duke of Joriun, calling him before the rest.

These words did the king my uncle the usurper speak.

"Hang her in a cage at the gates of Joriun so that all may see and abuse the sister of the traitor. All may see that I hold captive that which gives him strength."

How many years has it been since I was captured?

It is so cold in the winter.

I am so weary of the cold.

But it is not cold now. It is not even autumn, the season for hunting; I see by the green of the fields and the ripening fruit in the orchard beyond the moat that it is summer, the season for war.

They are not hunting at all. Here they come back, so soon, too soon. They are so cheerful, the young lovers gazing at each other, the men boasting and laughing, the women talking sternly of serious matters or giggling over light ones. I do not exist to them. I am nothing.

I am Mary.

They are no longer alone. They have gone out in such festive attire not to hunt but to greet he who has come to Joriun, ridden north at long last. No army that size has ever marched behind my brother's standard. Great clouds of dust mark their coming, and I see the king my uncle's standard at the head of the army long after I see that an army has come to Joriun.

The duke and his company ride at the head of the procession, flanking the king my uncle. I curse him—all the words I have ever heard cursed and spat at me—but he does not even look up. He does not even seem to know I exist. He does not even glance my way or at the cage, as if I have become invisible. As if I no longer matter.

I must matter. I have to matter. Am I not my brother's strength? Isn't that what everyone has always said?

The nobles enter the town and the gates close behind them. Out, beyond the walls of Joriun, the army encamps. Their tents cover the fields like locusts.

God help me. I am so weary.

The woman brings porridge that night and this night she remembers to spit in it first, as if the king's presence has reminded her that she must hate me. Almost I recoil, too sickened by the gesture to eat, but then I remember that I must eat and that her hatred is a spice to make the bland porridge taste better, to be more nourishing to me in my solitude.

She speaks to me, though this woman has never spoken to me before. "His Majesty has brought the whole army, hasn't he?" she says with a coarse grin. "There's a big battle to be fought, isn't there, and that will make short work of that traitor of yours."

Is that why the king my uncle did not look at me? Does he know I am truly nothing now? That he has pikes and swords and shields enough, soldiers enough, armor and gold enough, to defeat my brother even though I still live? Their campfires burn like stars fallen to earth: I see no end to them as I stare out all through the long long night.

Let me not weaken. Let me not fall into despair.

At dawn the gates open and the mobs come with their curses and their stones and their shit and their rotting meat and fruit. I cower by the bench, arms flung up to cover my face. An ancient mildewing apple splatters against my thigh. A stone grazes my elbow. I have forgotten what their abuse is like. They are themselves the hammer, beating me down. They are themselves the hands strangling the breath out of me. My tattered shawl cannot cover me. I have no armor. I am weaker than I was in the beginning. I begin to cry and, seeing that, their clamor increases. I am peppered with stones, each one a nail driven into my skin.

Please, God, let this cease.

The horns call and at last the mob retreats from the road to let the nobles pass through the gates. They ride in their glory, the men arrayed for campaign and the women with their false brave faces to goad on their menfolk.

He comes, the king my uncle. He draws up his horse below me and yet by every aspect above me. He wears a fine white surcoat over his armor, glittering in the sunlight, magnificent. Gold embroidery traces the symbols of crown and scepter on the surcoat; his sword is my father's sword, the scabbard plated with gold and the hilt fixed with jewels. He is an older man now, silver-haired, and yet by no measure weak.

He raises his gaze to touch me, and it is worse than the stones and all the rotten things that have ever been thrown at me. But I must show a brave false face. He must not sense my weakness and my despair. I dry my tears and strangle my sobs in my throat.

He speaks.

"Mary, Mary, quite contrary," he taunts. "Are you still there, hanging? Or is that another woman, another criminal, who hangs there in fitting punishment for her crime?"

I say nothing. If I speak, I will betray my weakness. He must never know.

"Do you even know your name?" he demands. "Do you remember how to talk or who you are?" He laughs, delighted by this prospect: that I have gone utterly mad. Dear God, how I wish to speak sharply to him while all can hear, for the mob and the nobles and the army all look this way and many can hear his voice.

But I am too weak to answer. My voice will break, if I even have a voice left.

"Do you even know it has been seven years?" he says. "Your brother the traitor is married now and they say he has a girlchild whom he named Mary, but his wife will be a widow soon and the child fatherless. And you brotherless. I am going to hunt him down whether it takes a month or a year or five years. And you shall hang there, my dear niece. You will never know the outcome. That is what I have decreed, that you wait and always wonder. That will be your reward for your treason toward me."

He turns, triumphant, still laughing, and rides away. His army follows him and the clouds of dust that mark their passing are visible long into the day. My voice has vanished. It has fled, along with my reason. Oh, God. Oh, God.

Seven years.

Why fight any more? How can I go on?

How did it get to be night so soon? For it is night, or night coming on. It is twilight, the quarter moon hanging low in the sky, soon to set.

The gates are closing and the last traffic of the day quickens to gain entry before night falls. I sit slumped on the bench, staring. Just staring. Why fight any more? How can I go on? How can my brother defeat such an army? How can he defeat a king who is so rich and so cunning? Why bother to go on? I am so weary. I am mad and lost and a hundred years old. I stare at the stars above, but I see no patterns in their spray of light; I only see the campfires of my uncle's army.

Shadows stir and fragment and coalesce along the roadway. A man— or is it a woman?—emerges briefly from the shadows onto the road and, unable to pass up a last chance on this awful day to insult me, throws a big stone. It bangs against the slats and falls inside to land with a thunk on one of the splintering planks.

But it is no stone. Suddenly I sway forward and grab the thing lying there. My hand touches a small rectangular package of cloth, concealing something hard. I open it, surprised. By the dim light of the quarter moon I see what lies inside: a pack of painted cards.

I look up, but there is no trace on the roadway of that person, half glimpsed, who threw these up here. I see only shadows as twilight fades to full night.

I handle the cards for a long, long time that night, though it is too dark to see them. I feel them, I trace the film of paint on each card and I remember what each one is, for the twilight mage, in his month at my brother's hall, taught me the meaning of each card. I only learned this knowledge then to pass the time while I waited for Duncan to return. I never dreamed I would be glad, someday, to remember it all.

Near dawn, I bind them up again and tuck them into my filthy bodice. Should anyone suspect I had them, they would be taken from me.

I hoard them for seven nights as the moon waxes. I hoard them until there is light enough to see for eyes trained in darkness, as mine are now. The mobs come every day while I wait, but I think only of the cards. I do not hear their voices.

I wait until the watchmen meet and turn on the parapet below and head away from my cage before I shuffle the cards and set them down. I have already picked a Significator: The Knight of Swords.

I lay it down and ask my question: "Where will my brother be next year?" It is the only question I know how to ask.

Placed atop it, the current situation. I turn the next card over. Seven of Swords. It is hard to remember, but here in my cage, memory is all I have. Thievery. Something stolen. I turn another card and lay it athwart the first two. Crossed by—I turn another card—the Wheel. Fate. His situation is going to change.

I pick up another card and set it down below the first three. At the base of matters, Strength. The woman holding the lion. Tears sting me and I brush them back impatiently. Have I not always been strong? Will it still, and always, be demanded of me? Next, what is passing away. The card I turn over now shows a heart pierced by three swords. Three of Swords. Sorrow.

For the first time in many years—years whose count I have lost track of—I feel hope stirring in my heart. Hope is so painful.

The watchmen return on their round, and I must wait in stillness while they pause, stare at the sky, hiss a joke one to the other and laugh boisterously, then at last spin and head back each on their separate slow walk of the parapet.

But I am used to waiting.

What crowns the matter. When I think of crowns, I can only think of my uncle in his crown-embroidered houppelande, condemning me to this cage; I can only think of my father's crown resting on the usurper's head. I can only think of his victory and our defeat, our escape as children into the summer's night that led me at the last to this cage.

But memory is a strange thing, like a fish in the shallows, darting suddenly into view when before it was invisible to the eye. All at once I remember what the magician said, that what crowns the matter is how the situation appears now, what seems to be coming in the near future but which may not be true. I turn the card to see a man standing with his hoe, eyeing a verdant bush now blooming with seven pentangles: reaping the rewards of hard work. Is it for naught? Will my brother's rebellion, now more than seven years old, be fruitless?

Once begun, a reading must be ended.

I turn the next card. What is coming into being. The Hanged Man.

Almost I weep with frustration. But the magician told me that the Hanged Man represents waiting, not defeat. "Bide your time," I whisper to myself, and that voice—*my* voice—gives me the strength to go on.

Now I draw the last four cards.

First, I turn the card which represents my brother, his inner being. A man battles with a staff, six more below him. Seven of Staves: success against the odds.

What influences him. I gasp, for now, appearing in the pale light of the waxing moon on the warped plank floor before me stands the Magician.

His wishes and fears. An angel blows the horn as the dead arise: Judgment. Is judgment not all my brother ever wished for?

But I hesitate before I turn the last card, because it signifies the outcome. I wait so long, trembling, that the watchmen return on their round. One spits over the parapet as the other gossips, and then they turn about and each goes on his way before I gather enough courage to turn that card.

Only the gullible believe in fortunetellers and magicians. But I have nothing left, nothing but this. I close my eyes and turn over the card, fingering the patterns in the paint. At last I look.

The World. Utter success.

My breath comes in bursts and I feel dizzy.

God help me. Let me not fall into madness.

I slide the cards roughly together and shuffle them again, violently. I will read the cards again. I cannot trust myself, my eyes in this moonlight, my terrible hope. I saw the king my uncle ride out with his great army, and I know that as seven years passed without my knowledge, it could take another seven for this struggle to end.

I search through the pack and take out the Knight of Swords, but then I remember what the twilight magician said, that the same question must not be asked a second time on the same day. I am shaking now so hard I drop the card and almost lose it between the warping planks. A cloud covers the moon and I weep in silence—I must never let the watchmen know I weep. It is so hard. Hope is not enough to live on.

But I can ask another question. I can ask a different question.

The moon emerges at last from the clouds. The watchmen meet and move away again. I root through the cards and draw him out, the king my uncle, King of Swords—the little emperor. I place the card firmly in the center place, the Significator.

"Where will my uncle be next year?" I ask.

"Covered by." I flip a card. "The Five of Staves. Conflict." Crossing it, I set down . . . "The Knight of Swords." The whispered words are like a second voice in my ear. Surely this is no coincidence, though I shuffled the cards very very well, too well, too violently in my anger and terror and pain, bending some, chipping off a few flecks of paint on others, before this second reading.

At the base of matters, the Devil. Malevolence. What is passing away, the Emperor.

I glance at the road, visible in the moonlight, but although there are shadows nothing lurks there. No person waits, watching me read. Yet I feel his—her—gaze on me. I feel her—his—presence beside me, even though I know it is impossible. I am alone, as the king my uncle decreed.

What crowns the matter, Eight of Staves. Quick success.

What is coming into being, Seven of Cups. Illusory success.

Yet I saw him march out on that road with a huge army. I heard him, in his confidence, abuse me and promise victory for himself and death for my brother.

There are four cards left to turn. The watchmen come, and gossip, and leave. The moon rides higher in the sky, which is bleached almost gray by its light.

I turn the next card.

His inner being. A man sits with each foot on a pentangle, a pentangle resting on his head, and a fourth gripped in his arms: Four of Pentangles. The hoarder. The usurper.

What influences him. Here, now, floats a hand in the air, cupping a Pentangle, the Ace. Material wealth and success.

His wishes and fears. When I turn over the card, I stare at first, thinking I am only remembering and not actually seeing what lies before me right now. Memory, like a fish, can quickly dart out of view and leave you grasping at shadows. Then I blink. The angel with his trumpet still plays as the dead rise.

Judgment.

So, too, in this reading, does Judgment lead to the outcome.

I turn the last, the final, card to see a dead man pinned to the ground by ten swords.

"Ten of Swords," the mage taught me so long ago, seven years ago and more, I now know. "Complete and utter defeat."

I look at this card for a long time. Then, quietly, carefully, I gather up the cards, bind them in cloth, and hide them away.

Now, for the first time in seven years, I weep as loud and long as I wish. I do not care if the watchmen hear me. I do not care if they curse me, or gloat, or report to my jailers that I have, at long last, broken.

At dawn a messenger rides in at a gallop even before the gates are open. He shouts, jumps off his horse to pound at the gates, and finally they swing open and he hurries inside.

Later, I hear the sounds of celebration.

The woman who brings my porridge makes sure to spit in it first before she hands it to me. "There's come news, hasn't there?" she says, smirking. "There's been a battle and the traitor's folk have retreated up into the hills."

But I only smile, take the bowl from her, and eat the food that is spiced with hatred. The cards nestle, hidden, inside my bodice.

I will be patient. I will wait. I know the usurper is fated to fail and that my brother will triumph in the end. I can endure whatever they throw at me until the day I am freed.

That is my strength, is it not? That I will never give in. That I will never give up.

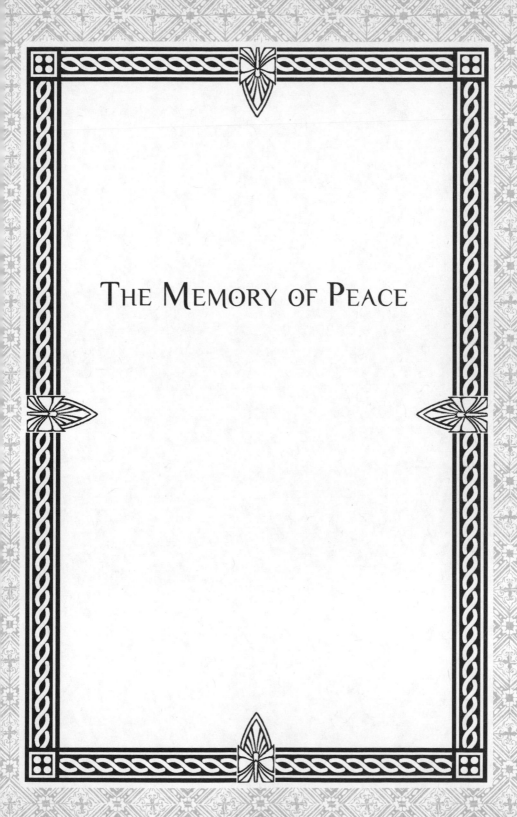

THE MEMORY OF PEACE

Spring came, and with it, clear skies, clear days, and a clear view of the ruins of Trient falling and rising along the hills in a stark curve. Smoke rose near the central market square from a fresh fire sown by the guns of the Marrazzano mercenaries. Jontano crouched next to the sheltering bulk of a fallen column and watched the smoke drift lazily up and up past the wall of greening forest that ringed the city and farther up still into the endless blue of the heavens.

When it was quiet, as it was now, he could almost imagine himself as that smoke, dissipating, dissolving into the air.

"Hsst, Jono, look what I found!"

He jumped, caught himself, and managed to look unsurprised when Stepha ran, hunched over, through the maze of the fallen temple and flung herself down next to him. She undid the strings of her pack.

"You've never seen things like this!"

But Stepha always bragged. Jontano wasn't impressed by the pickings: an empty glass jar, six painted playing cards, a slender book with crisped edges but no writing on its leather cover, a length of fancy silver ribbon, four long red feathers, and ten colored marbles.

"That won't buy much flour," he retorted. "Where'd you find this?"

"You're just jealous I went by myself. It all came from the Apothecary's Shop, the one midway down Murderer's Row."

"You idiot! Not one thing here is worth risking your life for." Murderer's Row had once been known as Prince Walafrid Boulevard, but no one called it that now, since the entire boulevard was well within reach of the cannon and, at the farthest end, the muskets of the Marrazzanos.

"Everyone said Old Aldo was a witch. Maybe these have some power."

"Ha! If he was a witch, then why couldn't he spare his own shop and his own life?" But the cards were pretty. Jontano picked one up even though he didn't want Stepha to think he admired her foolhardy courage.

"No one saw him dead. He could still be alive." Her expression turned sly, and she lowered her voice for dramatic effect. "I heard a noise, like rats, when I was in the shop. Maybe he was hiding from me. Everything was all turned over and broken, except for that old painting of the forest that hangs behind the counter. It was the strangest thing, with the hole in the roof and all, but it still hung there, as if it hadn't been disturbed at all. Not even wet."

"Here, this isn't wet either," he said, showing her the face of the card, "and it has a forest painted on it."

"You *are* jealous! Ha!" But she examined the card with him.

The colors were as fresh as if they had just been painted onto the card: the pale green buds of spring leaves, the thin parchment bark of birches, the scaly gray skin of tulip trees and the denser brown bark of fir; a few dots of color, violet and gold and a deep purpling blue, marked clumps of forest flowers along the ground.

"I don't see how anyone could paint things so tiny," said Stepha.

"They use a brush with a single bristle. Don't you know anything?"

Before she could reply, the sky exploded. They both ducked instinctively. Cannon boomed. A nearby house caved in. A wailing rose up into the air, the alarm, and farther away, smoke rose from newly shattered buildings.

Stepha shoveled her treasures into the bag and scuttled down the hill, dodging this way and that. Jono, still clutching the card, ran after her, not bothering to bend over. Not even the famous Marrazzanos could aim well enough to hit them here, as far away as they were from the lines, but if a ball or shot happened to land close by, then it scarcely mattered whether you were bent in two or running straight up like a man.

He caught up to Stepha just as a great crash sounded from the ruins behind and a column fell, smashing onto the hollow where they had just sheltered. Shards flew. Stepha grunted in pain, and Jontano felt a spray like a hundred bees stinging along his back.

As they darted into the safety of an alley, a double round of shot hit what remained of the roof of the old temple. It caved in with a resounding roar. Dust poured up in the sky in a roiling brown cloud. Then they turned a corner, and another, and ran through the back alleys and barricaded streets, strewn with burnt-out buildings, fallen walls, and an endless parade of little refuges, shelters built from bricks and planks salvaged from once-beautiful houses. In some of those tiny refuges people lived, but most simply served as a hiding place to any man, woman, or child caught outside when a bombardment began.

By the time they got back to their house, in the relative safety of the north central quarter of the city, Jontano could feel tickling fingers of blood running down his back. Stepha was limping.

They burst in through the gate and, panting, walked past the newly planted vegetable garden. Once Mama had grown flowers here, and it had been a lovely place in the spring and summer; she and Papa had entertained guests and laughed and talked and sung to all hours of the night while the children watched from the windows above, faces pressed to the glass. But that had been a long, long time ago. Now most of the windows were covered with boards and the flower garden had been transplanted to vegetables.

Great-Uncle Otto was standing guard over the well. He looked them over with disgust. Stepha yelped when he probed her thigh with his fingers, and Jontano saw a gaping red wound where she had been hit with shrapnel.

"Now your mother will have to sew these clothes up," he said, looking angry as he examined the back of Jontano's shirt. Jontano knew it ought to hurt, but he felt as if Otto's hands probed someone else's body, not his. "There's little enough thread to be had," Otto went on. "Nor do I hold with those who go looting shops. We might as well fall into the hands of the Marrazzanos as become looters ourselves. Look what barbarians this war has made of us and our children!"

Stepha, brave enough up until now, began to snivel. Otto spared her not one sympathetic word and turned his black gaze on Jontano, who squirmed.

"You'll be old enough to go into the militia next year, but I suppose next you'll be saying you'd rather prey on the dead than honor those who have died before you by behaving as a man ought, taking up arms and fighting nobly."

Jontano snorted. "I don't know what's so noble about fighting against cannon and musket with wooden staves and butcher's knives."

Otto slapped him. "I won't say a word against your sainted mother, who has suffered enough, but her mother and her mother's mother were Marrazzanos, and I can see their dirty blood has tainted you."

"What do I care about Trassahar and Marrazzano? I wish I had no blood of either kind! All we do is fight and die. What's the point of that?" Jontano could not help but shout the words. His throat tightened with the familiar lump. "I'd just like to grow up to be a painter like Papa was."

Otto swung his musket around threateningly, but in the next instant he said in a low voice, "Get inside."

Stepha bolted in. Jontano followed her, but just as he crossed the threshold he heard a shot fired, then silence. He turned.

Great-Uncle Otto staggered and dropped the musket, left hand clutching his chest. Jontano ran out to him, shoved him aside to get at the musket, and raised it just in time to stare down the muzzle at a ragged band of men and women, armed with a single musket and several buckets.

"Give us water," said one of the women. She was filthy, skinny, and her hands and arms were a mass of red sores. Beside her, an emaciated man reloaded the musket.

Shaking, Jontano stared them down, but by that time Mama appeared in the door with the pistol and Uncle Martin leaned out of the second-story window, his musket propped on the flowerbox, pushing aside the leafy stems of carrots. He had no legs now, but he had once been a sniper in the militia.

The ragged band retreated. Mama stuck the pistol in her belt and hurried out. With Aunt Martina's help she carried Otto inside, leaving Jontano on guard while Uncle Martin dragged himself down the stairs and together with the two women treated Otto's wound.

It took Otto five days to die, and because of that, everyone was too busy to scold Stepha for looting along Murderer's Row.

"Why shouldn't I?" she whispered to Jontano in the bed they shared with the two surviving youngest cousins, who were asleep. "Why should I care if I get killed, anyway? The Marrazzanos will never leave. And even if they did, I don't have any friends left, and no Trassahar boy will ever want to marry me because I'm just a Marrazzano whore."

They had saved the stub of a candle and they lit it now, while the house was quiet. Great-Uncle Otto's body lay in state in the parlor, until the burial tomorrow. He was the last but one of his branch of the family, having lost wife, sons, and all but one of his grandchildren to the war. He and his surviving daughter-in-law had fled to the city three years ago after their village had been razed, but she had died of a fever last winter, and now only little Judit remained, snoring softly beside Jontano.

Stepha played with the marbles, turning them round so that highlights of bright color caught and winked in the light, yet Jontano could not help but be drawn to the cards once more. They were shaped like playing cards, made of stiff cardboard cut into rectangles as large as his hands, but they were like no deck he had ever seen. A plain hatched pattern of black and white was printed on the backs. The front of each card looked as if it had been painted lovingly by a gifted hand. He spread the deck out to examine them.

A crane stands on one leg in a pool, its form silhouetted in a sunset of red and gold.

A fetid marsh stretches to the horizon, marked by small hummocks and a few twisted old trees.

The restless sea, infinite, surges and swells, without any sign of the safe harbor of land.

A blindfolded woman dressed in a shift runs through a dark forest. Spiders and strange, unsightly creatures peer at her from the branches. As she runs, unseeing, she is stepping on a snake.

Two birch trees bend, their highest branches intertwining so that they form an arch, that leads . . . but here the artist had depicted a haze of golden sunlight in which Jontano could make out only a suggestion, of Trient, perhaps, a golden city where once Trassaharin and Marrazzano lived in peace, together.

And the spring forest, his favorite, the one he never tired of looking at.

As he ran his fingers over the painted surface, he could almost feel the touch of the painter's brush, as if by concentrating hard enough he could become the painter painting the card, as if he could see through the painter's eyes the act of creation, the grinding of the paint, the careful preparation of the brushes and the backing, each brushstroke, each spot of color laid on with exact care.

When he touched the pale green buds of the spring forest, he could feel himself walking there along the path which wound through the wood, darting this way and that through clumps of goldenrod and violets. It sloped down, then crossed a narrow river and ascended a hillside. He walked up. Loam gave under his boots. Wind brushed his face, bringing the scents of the dense forest to him. He heard the rustle of birds above and the little scrabblings of rodents below. A spare outcropping of rock thrust from among the trees. He scrambled up onto it and, turning, saw the land below him, curved like a bowl, filling the graceful little valley with trees and emerald meadows. Suddenly he realized this was Trient—but Trient without the city, without the fighting, at peace, in the quiet of a spring morning.

A crash tore him out of the forest.

He lay in the crowded bed, frozen, feeling Stepha snoring against him—she always had a cold—and listened to the pound of the Marrazzano cannon. They had launched a night attack. Little Judit woke up and began to cry.

Jontano stuffed the cards into his worn but clean pillowcase and gathered the little girl into his arms. After a while she fell asleep, and he did as well, though the cannon boomed intermittently and once an explosion sounded very near them. What did it matter if they were killed in their sleep? At least it would spare them the agony of dying. So he slept, and dreamed of the spring forest.

At dawn as he and Judit walked hand-in-hand to the old central park that was now the main cemetery—all the other graveyards being full—the little girl tugged on him until he leaned down to hear her whisper.

"I dreamed that I was in heaven with Grandpa. It was all the prettiest forest, and a red and yellow bird sat on my fingers. And there were flowers."

Aunt Martina and Cousin Gregor carried the body wrapped in the most threadbare sheet, the only one they could spare for burial. Uncle Martin, ever quick to see the twisted humor in any situation, had waved good-bye to them where he sat on guard in the one unboarded upstairs window and then shouted after: "See, it'll be the last burial in this house—we've got no more sheets to spare!"

They paid the gravediggers three coppers and stood by while a hole was dug next to the others in their family. Jontano led Judit to each wooden cross in turn, Stepha following at his heels: Papa's grave, the oldest one there, Jono's two brothers and one sister, Baby Lucia, cousins, an aunt, and uncles. More men than women, because the men all went to the militia, as Cousin Gregor would go next month when he turned fifteen, as Jontano himself would go next year.

Stepha stared at the graves, dry-eyed. Her parents weren't here. Their graves lay on the other side of the lines, and everyone knew that at least one of her brothers fought in the Marrazzano army, but Mama had taken the girl in because she and Stepha's mother were first cousins, and no woman with even a trace of Trassahar blood in her was safe on the Marrazzano side.

It was another clear day. For once the Marrazzanos weren't shelling Trient. One of the cousins had died while burying his own father. They buried Great-Uncle Otto without much ceremony, and Mama decorated the grave with a few shoots from his beloved potato plants. Here and there on the overgrown grass that was all that was left of the once-manicured park, other families stood, burying a newly lost relative. Dogs nosed at fresh dirt. The gravediggers threw stones at them.

"This park used to be so lovely," said Mama to Aunt Martina as they walked back. The silence lay heavily on them, it was so unusual. "Do you remember?"

"All the trees," said Aunt Martina in her hoarse voice. "I remember all the trees."

Not one was left, of course, not even the stumps, all cut down and dug out for firewood. Jontano remembered the trees vaguely, too, from picnics, from running down by the lake, from Papa's canvases and sketches, flowering tulip trees, elm trees, beech, oaks and birches, ash and aspen, cherry with its spring blossoms and apple and pear.

"It all used to be trees," he said suddenly, and Mama looked at him questioningly. "Trient. The city. Before the city was here it all used to be trees, one great forest. And it was quiet. It was peaceful then."

Aunt Martina snorted. "Except for the wolves howling at night. There are always wolves, Jono. Don't forget them."

"I'd like to be a wolf," said Stepha, "and rip out the throats of my enemies."

Little Judit burst into tears.

"You've scared her, Stepha," snapped Aunt Martina. "I shouldn't have to remind you, but I'll whip you if I've found you went out prowling around Murderer's Row again."

Now Stepha began to cry as well, so they looked properly like mourners as they came home empty-handed.

The house was quiet when they got back. Uncle Martin sat on his chair, elbows and musket propped in the window, and smoked a pipe.

"Where'd you get that tobacco, you good for nothing?" scolded Aunt Martina. "Did you sell the rest of my silver forks?"

Uncle Martin merely grinned at her and flourished the pipe. He had a network of old friends. Once a week they carted him off to a mysterious place in town where only men from the militia were allowed to congregate. When Uncle Martin came home from these jaunts, he always had a new piece of news from the front, and occasionally a trinket for the children or some luxury item for the women—yarn, lamp oil, a piece of fruit, once a pair of good shoes that, with a bit of paper stuffed in the toes, fit Aunt Martina perfectly.

Aunt Martina called him a few rude names, but she was too weary to really lay into him, as she usually did—she and Martin liking good arguments. They argued about everything, the King, the Parliament, the Marrazzano generals, battles fought four hundred years before, treaties signed and broken. Uncle Martin was a good Royalist: He believed in the Trassaharin King, who, Martina reminded him, had escaped years ago to another country where he lived in peace and plenty; he believed in the Parliament, and in the cause. Aunt Martina believed that they were all of them, Trassahar and Marrazzano kings, generals, and ministers alike, scavengers feeding off the body of the farmers and the shopkeepers and the artisans, who had once populated Trient and the surrounding countryside without civil war, marrying each to the other with more attention to economic considerations than to blood ties.

So Mama, half Marrazzano, had married into a good solid Trassahar craftsman's family. No one had thought twice about it, because her own family were craftsmen, tile makers, and she had a good dowry, a fine hand for painting pottery, and liked well enough the man who became her husband. So she had in her turn fostered in her cousin's daughter, Stepha.

So Uncle Martin, Royalist that he was, patted Stepha on the head when she brought him up his dinner of potatoes and onions, and told her that she'd had an offer of marriage.

Stepha dropped the plate. She began weeping, but whether over the shattered plate or the marriage offer Jontano couldn't tell. No one scolded her. Aunt Martina scooped up the precious food and Uncle Martin ate it from a tin cup.

"Who would offer for me?" Stepha asked through her sobs.

"My old friend Zjilo Berio."

"He's only got one arm," objected Aunt Martina.

"Which he lost fighting," said Uncle Martin. "His wife died last winter, and he's got the two little ones now."

"They had the three children," said Mama, having come upstairs to see what the commotion was about.

"They had three, it's true, but he lost the boy to a sniper's bullet one month ago."

"Ah," said Mama. Jontano saw her wipe a speck from her eye. He wasn't sure if it was a tear or not.

"How old is he?" asked Aunt Martina.

"About thirty."

Aunt Martina considered this. "That's not too bad."

"That's *ancient!*" protested Stepha.

Uncle Martin stared her down, and she wiped her nose and clasped her hands obediently in front of her blouse. But she wrung them, twisting her fingers about each other, and Jontano couldn't tell whether she liked or was terrified of the idea of marrying a man as old as thirty. Jontano didn't know what he thought of it. He'd known Stepha so long that he couldn't imagine her being old enough to marry, even though she was almost two years older than he was.

When Uncle Martin spoke again, he measured his words carefully. "Zjilo is a good man. We fought together. He never raised a hand to his wife, though she came from an aristocratic family and spoke down to him once the war came and they couldn't have the luxuries they had before."

"He's rich still!" Aunt Martina leaped on this point. "I thought the family lost their warehouse. I thought they had nothing."

"Or you'd have pursued him yourself?" Martin grinned at her. "The family kept something by, or must have. He's taking the children out of Trient. He can't bear it any more for their sake now that he lost the boy. He's afraid of losing the little girls, too. They've a small estate in Kigori."

"There's no way in or out of Trient," said Mama suddenly. Jontano felt more than saw the pain on her face, in her body. His eldest brother had died that way, trying to get out of the city to fetch the herbs—the apothecary having long since run out of such supplies—that kept Baby Lucia's heart going. So the two had, in a way, died together.

Martin snorted. "How do you think this tobacco got here? There are ways, if you've enough money, or important enough news, and are willing to run the gauntlet and take the risk. It would be a good life for you, Stepha, but if you agree to it, you must understand that you might not live through the crossing. Zjilo's agreed to take Judit, too, now that she's alone, and raise her as his own."

Stepha glanced over at Jontano, but he only shrugged. He tried to imagine what it would be like without her, but could not.

"Why does he want me?" Stepha asked sullenly. "To use me as a servant and a whore?"

Uncle Martin slapped her. This time, though, she didn't begin to cry. Jontano saw something different in the way she stood, as if she had already made a decision but was refusing to give it away easily. "As a favor to me, my girl, and don't you talk back to me again. He needs a wife. A young girl like you will be strong enough to do the work and bear him more children. You're a pretty girl, too, when you're not making faces and acting wild. If we don't get you out of Trient, you'll either get shot or end up in the marketplace with the rest of the goods that are bought and sold."

Stepha flinched.

"Martin!" scolded Aunt Martina, but Martin looked at her gravely. Whatever Martina saw in Martin's gaze caused her to nod her head once, shortly, and gesture at him to go on. Jontano watched in confused silence.

"When Zjilo began talking of leaving, of getting a new wife, I reminded him that you'll be sixteen next month and that you're a good girl and better off out of Trient. He doesn't care that you've got Marrazzano blood. If you agree and are a dutiful wife to him, you'll have a good life, with servants, land, a good kitchen and decent clothes always for yourself and your children."

Abruptly Mama spoke. "Can he get us out, too, Martin? All of us?" Her voice held a passion Jontano hadn't heard in it for years. Ancient memories resurfaced, clawing out of him, growing, consuming, memories of happiness, of Mama and Papa planning the garden, sketching new patterns for plates and vases for the family business, and in her voice as well he thought he heard a whispering note of hope, that somewhere peace might be found, a place where happiness could, grain by grain, brick by brick, be built again.

As if the Marrazzano guns had opened up again, Martin's next words shattered that fragile thread linking Mama, linking Jontano himself, to her dream.

"Do you have a thousand florins?"

She gasped. It was an enormous sum.

"Relatives to go to? We've got nothing but what we have here, Constance. Zjilo stayed this long because of his wife's family, and because of the risk to the children. But they'll die quickly enough in this hell-hole, so why wait? I wish him luck. I wish we hadn't lost everything and everyone, but what's the use? We can't leave."

"We mustn't leave," said Aunt Martina. Her voice, forever scarred by the men who had raped her and then tried and failed to kill her by cutting her throat, sounded hoarser than ever. "That would give Trient to the Marrazzanos. Why else have we suffered? What have our beloved ones died for? I will stand here until the day I die rather than run away and give it to those bastard Marrazzanos."

Stepha stared at Martina. Mama walked to the window and looked out over the city. Her face was pale and the line of her jaw tight with an emotion Jontano could not understand, knowing only that he loved her desperately for her strength—the strength that had allowed her, of all of his family, to survive when the rest had perished. All three of her brothers, her sister, her husband and children, her parents, all gone, leaving her with in-laws and one last child. Uncle Martin got a funny look on his face, and he took Martina's hand in his own and kissed it, as a lord gives respect to a lady.

Martina made a noise in her throat, then pulled her hand free from his. "Huh," she said caustically. "All that fraternizing with former officers is giving you airs above your station, Martin. I hear old Widow Angelit is looking for a new husband."

"Ha! She's buried four already. I'd rather not know my own fate, thank you."

"I'll go," Stepha blurted out.

That simple statement brought its own, new silence to the room. It was so quiet that Jontano heard the distant yell of hawkers in the Wildmo marketplace, where a morning of quiet had brought brave and fatalistic souls alike to set out their wares, to shop, in the ruins of the fine old market stalls.

So it was done.

Zjilo Berio came to the house the next Sunday. He was a quiet man with tired eyes, but he wore a golden pocket-watch and his clothes were neat, pressed, and made of the finest cloth—old clothes, from before the blockade, well cared for and smelling slightly of the cedar chest, where they had perhaps been stored against better days. His daughters were even quieter. They stared at Stepha with great dark eyes. After the brief ceremony, Judit showed them her doll, and with this treasure, while the adults toasted the new bride with precious wine and ate from a table laid with as great a feast as Mama and Aunt Martina could manage, the three girls played together in whispers in the corner of the parlor.

The food was eaten, the wine drunk, and as dusk settled in over Trient, it was time for them to go.

Jontano hugged Stepha, but he could think of nothing to say.

"Take care of my treasures," she said. Then she was gone with her new husband and children.

Jontano gave the marbles to Roman, and the rest of the things from old Aldo's shop he gave to Mama, thinking that she might find some use for them, keeping only the six cards for himself.

At night, the bed seemed enormous with only himself and little Roman, Aunt Martina's youngest child. For the next ten nights he barely slept, wondering, each time he heard cannon blast, each time he heard shots ring out, if Stepha and her new family had won free to Trassahar-held countryside, or if that had been the barrage that had killed them.

"You must accept that we may never hear," said Uncle Martin. "That is the way of things now."

"Why must it be the way?"

Uncle Martin smiled crookedly. "My poor boy. We had a decent life when I was young."

That night Jontano ran his hands over the painted card that showed the forest. Strangely, the trees looked slightly different and it took him a moment to identify what had changed: The leafy buds were no longer tight and pale green. They had begun to unfurl.

If only he could walk the paths that led out of Trient toward the west, and freedom. He recalled once walking with his Papa, years and years ago, when he had been just a little child, up in the woods to the west of the old temple, so that Papa could paint. Jontano traced the painted forest with his fingers, and he felt himself walking there, on quiet paths among the trees. The violets were fading, but now new flowers bloomed in patches of bright sun, flowers his father had names for, names he had known once but now forgotten.

The path wound up into the hills and he followed it, feeling strangely that it was this path that fugitives followed, fleeing the city. He came to an open escarpment and looked out over the valley of Trient. There, across the bowl, lay the rock outcropping where he had stood before, a gray smudge against the distant trees.

Water fell, racing away down the hill. He was alone, except for the animals. There were no bodies, no furtive travelers, no one skulking but a lone fox that darted from cover, then vanished into a thick stand of shrub.

He walked for hours. He saw no one, found no one, heard nothing but animal noises and the flood of wind through the leaves. The silent weight of the sun scattered its light down through budding foliage. It was so peaceful.

"Jono? Jono!"

His mother's voice jolted him out of the forest.

He felt her hands on his arms, shaking him, and he dropped the card and tried to sit up, only she was holding him down and Aunt Martina and Uncle Martin looked on, their faces worn tight with anxiety.

"What is it?" he asked, coming to his senses. "Do you have news of Stepha?"

Mama began to cry. Oh, Lord, they had received terrible news. Pain stabbed in his chest.

"Can you walk?" Aunt Martina demanded.

"Lord, boy, you scared us."

Jontano felt dizzy. What had frightened them? What had happened?"

"Can you stand up?" repeated Aunt Martina.

"Of course." He threw his legs over the side and stood up, and only then did he realize that it was full morning outside. He didn't recall being asleep. Indeed, he felt very tired, as tired as if he had been walking all night.

Mama crushed him against her in a hug. "Jono," she whispered. Then she pushed him away, dried her tears, and straightened her apron and dress. "I don't care what it costs. I am going to send for the doctor."

"Is Stepha back? Was she hurt?"

All three adults examined him so closely that he became nervous. Aunt Martina asked him to raise and lower his arms. Uncle Martin jerked his chair closer to the bed and peered into Jontano's eyes and ears and mouth, and listened to his chest.

"He's never had such a fit before," said Mama in a low voice. "You didn't hear or respond to me, Jono, and you lying there with your eyes wide open, seeing I don't know what. It's as if you weren't there at all."

"I've seen it take soldiers," said Martin, "after they'd had too much. They just go out of themselves."

"If only we had more food," said Aunt Martina. "The boys get little enough as it is. They're all so thin. He needs more meat. And milk. Ah, if only I'd been able to bring the goats. They'd have done well enough on weeds. Then we could have had milk and cheese every week."

Jontano knew he couldn't tell them what he'd really been seeing. He didn't know what they'd do, except he knew they'd take the beautiful cards away from him. "I feel fine. I was just asleep." He sat down on the bed and searched through the rumpled quilt. Finding the card, he tucked it into the drawer of the sidetable—one that had escaped being broken up and burned for fuel last winter.

"What's that?" asked Mama sharply.

"Only some cards Stepha found when she got the other things at old Aldo's shop."

"What kind of cards?" asked Aunt Martina.

Uncle Martin shook his head. "Old Aldo had a way with things. He wasn't the kind of man you cross, or he'd have his revenge, whether in little things or great. I remember the time about eight years ago now, when the girl in his house got into trouble. I don't know whether it was his daughter or granddaughter—no one did, and it wasn't the sort of thing you'd ask a man like that. She'd come from the country when she was a tiny thing, and he'd raised her. He doted on her, which we all remarked on since he was as ill-tempered as a caged wolf. He was the kind of man who would as soon throw a rock at a boy as give him a piece of candy."

He smiled his twisted grin, and Jontano wondered which of the two had happened to Martin. Jontano's own memories of Aldo were hazier, mostly his parents' prohibitions not to bother the old man who stood in the dim doorway of a shop from which wafted the most interesting and bizarre smells.

"But that girl—Lord, I don't even recall her name now—grew into a taking thing. Even we married men liked to stroll down the boulevard just to get a glimpse of her sweeping the sidewalk or grinding herbs into pastes and such. She had two suitors. One was the son of an officer in the Trient militia, a Trassahar boy, back when there was a city militia that any boy from the city could join. . . ."

"One of General Vestino's boys, wasn't it?" asked Mama. "He had six or seven. No one could count them all."

"The youngest of them, yes, I think it was. It scarcely matters now. The other was the son of a Marrazzano merchant, grain and oil, if I remember rightly. That was the proof of how beautiful she was, that sons of good family like that came courting her. But she was a good girl, too, well-spoken, polite. She could read and do figures, and some even said she had the touch of healing in her hands."

"Yes." Mama's voice grew soft with remembrance. "People would bring ailing children to her, and she'd make poultices and drinks for them, and more of them got well than got sicker, as I recall. Girls would go to her for love potions, which I heard she never gave out, but if they would give a tithe to the church or donate some bread for the poor, she'd tell them when they would get married. I remember her."

"What happened to her?" Jono tried to remember a pretty young woman stationed at old Aldo's shop, but he could not, only the old man standing in the doorway, and the musty, inviting scents.

"It came to insults first, between the two suitors, and then to blows. Alas." Martin sighed. "She broke into the fight, trying to stop it, and by one means or another, she got a knife in her side and died. Ah Lord, that was a bitter day. No one knew which boy's knife had taken her. Perhaps they didn't either, but what did it matter by that time? Old Aldo cursed them."

Mama rested a hand on Martin's shoulder, as if to stop him, but he went on.

"He cursed them to be at one another's throats ever after, like dogs worrying at a bone until there was nothing left to be had, and only then would they find peace again."

He lapsed into silence. Mama went to the window and looked out over the city. In the distance, they heard the crack of musket fire.

"Nine months later the war started," said Mama in a soft voice, "as if it was a babe born of the curse. People shunned old Aldo after that, but he stayed in his shop. I suppose he also had nowhere else to go."

"Or nothing to go for," added Uncle Martin. "But the war got him in the end. That's the trouble with curses. They're as likely to rebound on you as to stay fixed on others."

"I haven't heard this story before," said Aunt Martina. "What happened to the two suitors?"

"The Trassahar boy joined the militia and got himself killed in the first month, defending Saint Harmonious Bridge before it was blown to pieces. As for the Marrazzano boy—who knows? He might be up in the hills now, firing down on us. He might be rotting in his grave."

The adults had by now all gone to the window, to look out, Martin bumping his chair over, following the well-worn scratches in the plank floor—this was the window where Martin sat with his musket. The lush greenery of carrots lapped over the windowsill, and Aunt Martina absently thinned a few out as she stared toward the center of the city. Their home stood on just enough of a rise that they could see out over the rooftops below, and the tall boulevard trees that had once obscured the central city from view were now all cut down.

Downstairs, Cousin Gregor sang a counting song to his little brother. From two doors down Jontano heard Widow Angelit singing in her robust voice a tune from an opera popular when he was little—when the opera house in town had still been open. It cheered him, hearing her sing a rousing chorus, even if she was off-key.

Uncle Martin laughed and turned away from the window. "Lord, Martina, you'd want me to marry a woman who can't sing?"

"Better a woman who can't sing than a woman who can't cook, like that woman you courted last year."

"All to no use!"

"Better luck for us!" Martina tilted his chair back and dragged him out of the room. A moment later Jontano heard him bumping his way down the stairs while Martina followed with the chair, hectoring him about his poor choice in sweethearts.

Mama remained. "I don't like you having things from old Aldo's shop."

"Please, Mama. They're so pretty." He opened the drawer and took out the cards, displaying them for her. "Look at the brushwork. Doesn't it remind you of something Papa could do? Please let me keep them."

"Some said the girl wasn't his daughter by the flesh at all, but that he'd created her by sorcery. It's not safe to touch the things of a man who might have worked magic." She sighed, handing the cards back. "But these are just playing cards. I suppose no harm can come from something like that."

"Thank you, Mama." He kissed her on the cheek.

She tousled his hair, then swatted him lightly on the back. "Go do your chores. The rain has made the weeds sprout like flies on a rotten apple."

So the days passed.

But every night, drawn by the lure of green trees and silent paths, he took hold of the card and wandered in the forest. Only now he made sure to keep track of the time; he learned to recognize the path that would take him out of the woods back into his bed, back into the damp spring air of Trient, back to the serenade of intermittent explosions and musket fire, to the wailing of the alarm and the wailing of the newly grief-stricken, to the constant guard they set over their well and garden.

No trees stood within the city now. It was only by walking in the forest hidden in the card that he could watch the trees unfurl their leaves to their full grandeur, only by squinting out over the bare and broken rooftops that he could see the distant line of forest surrounding the city turn a deeper green. There, concealed by the trees, now and again he saw the puffs of smoke that betrayed Marrazzano cannon emplacements as they fired down onto Trient.

"You're tired all the time," said Mama, looking worried, and Aunt Martina braved the marketplace to look for decent cuts of meat. They traded away the sidetable for a slab of pork, so he had to hide the cards in his pillowcase.

Cousin Gregor turned fifteen and left to join the militia. Aunt Martina wept, a little, but she told him to fight bravely, to protect what remained of his father's heritage. Now there were only five in the house, the three adults, the two boys.

Clouds rolled in and settled over the valley. It rained for days.

On the ninth day of torrential rain, when the streets ran with water and the roof leaked, and even the clothes hanging in the wardrobe exuded a damp odor, the Marrazzanos chose to launch a new and brutal bombardment.

"It's taken them that long to build shelters over the guns," said Uncle Martin, "or they'd never fire in such rain. I don't know how they manage it, even so."

Jontano leaned out the window next to Uncle Martin, watching the flash of fire in the hills, hearing muted explosions and watching smoke rise, dense and packed heavy with moisture, and then fall again, unable to catch fire, or to rise up into a sky drenched with rainfall. "I heard from Bobo's son that the Marrazzanos got a new kind of cannon, a better kind."

Uncle Martin only grunted. He peered out at the distant hills. He was renowned for his keen vision, sniper's sight, and now he frowned and shifted the muzzle of his musket through the carrots so that droplets of water sprayed down on his hands. "I don't like it. They're closer than they were a month ago, new guns or no. Our people have lost ground to them, the bastards."

Was he calling the Marrazzanos the bastards, Jono wondered, or the Trassahar militia that had failed to do its duty? He thought about asking, opened his mouth, even. The next instant he was thrown to the ground.

The foundation of the house rocked beneath his body. Whimpering, he grabbed for a leg of Uncle Martin's chair and realized that the chair had tipped over, spilling the legless man onto the ground.

"Curse it!" swore Uncle Martin, scrabbling like a turtle to roll himself from his back onto his chest. "That's taken the widow's house to pieces. Run downstairs, Jono. Get the others into the root cellar."

Even as he said it, a shattering noise deafened Jontano. The wall beside him cracked, splintering.

"Run down, boy!" shouted Martin. "Those bastards have us under their sights and they don't even know it!"

But Jontano grabbed Martin under the arms and dragged him toward the stairs. Just as they got under the safety of the lintel a ball crashed into the window. Dirt and carrots and glass and shards of wood sprayed the room. Jontano yipped in pain. Uncle Martin merely grunted.

Aunt Martina ran up the stairs. "Down, you fools! Can't you come down any faster?" She shoved Jontano aside and heaved Martin up and with him cursing and her shouting, their argument drowned out by the rain of cannon balls on their house and the neighboring houses, by the sudden onslaught of a driving rain, got him down the stairs. They fled to the root cellar and there, huddled together with only musty old potatoes and the few precious remaining bottles of wine and ale, with a finger's-deep pool of water turning the dirt floor into muck, they sheltered while the bombardment went on and on and on. They listened to their house being destroyed, and to the shouts and cries from neighboring houses, and, later, to the silence, except for the endless drone of rain.

At last, when the light began to fade and the bombardment had, seemingly, moved on toward a new neighborhood, they ventured out. Jontano tried to go out first, but Aunt Martina shoved him back.

"I'll go," she said curtly. "I've had a life, a good one, before this war came. You deserve a chance at a decent life, so we won't go taking chances with you yet, my boy." She lifted Roman from her lap, and he wailed and clung to Uncle Martin, sobbing as his mother pushed open the root cellar door and crawled out into the gloomy, wet afternoon.

After a while, when they heard her footsteps overhead but nothing else, she came back. Her face was drawn and white. Her hair lay in wet strings over her dress. She was soaked to the skin, and it still rained.

They crawled out, all except Martin. The house was destroyed. One wall still stood its full height, but the others were shattered. The roof had caved in. The stairs veered crookedly up to a nonexistent floor above.

They stood in silence for a long time, sheltering under a blessedly dry corner, and watched the rain pour down over what remained of their home. Dimly, Jontano heard Uncle Martin calling to them from the root cellar.

Finally, Mama shook herself. "There's no point in waiting here. If we wait until the rain stops, looters may come. Roman, you go down and wait with Uncle Martin. There's nothing he can do until we've salvaged what's left."

"I'll walk down the street," said Aunt Martina. "Perhaps our neighbors need help."

So Jontano and Mama picked through the wreckage. Of their armament—two muskets and a pistol—one musket was dry and still usable and the others were not too badly damaged. The powder and shot had remained dry because they kept it in metal tins, and those in a cupboard which had come through the bombardment mostly intact. Mama set Jontano in the dry corner and put him on watch while she filled bags and blankets with what remained of their possessions: clothing, a few jars of pickled figs that had gotten wedged into the corner of the cupboard, the kettle and three unbroken plates, two pots, silverware, Roman's toy horse and wagon not too dented from its fall from the upper story, a bucket, a shovel, the last of the bread from the morning, a length of silver ribbon, and the butcher knife. She piled the bags and the single intact headboard next to Jontano.

After a while he realized that the street and alley were empty and likely to remain that way. The bombardment had quieted and moved back south again, and the rain had slackened to a steady drizzle. He ventured out of the ruined house to the well. The little roof had fallen in, and a few of the stones had tumbled out, crushing turnips, but as he tugged the boards out, he saw that the well itself remained intact. And though the garden was half covered with debris, as he picked up boards and tossed bricks aside he found that a fair portion of the vegetables were only crushed but not severed. He leaned the musket against the stones of the wall and began to clean up the garden, his heart racing with excitement each time he uncovered an unhurt plant.

Later, as it grew to dusk, Aunt Martina came back. "Widow Angelit is dead. I helped Bobo Milovech pull his daughter from the ruins, but I doubt she'll live. She lost one of her legs below the knee. We bound it up as well as we could, but she's too frail to sustain the loss of blood. Bobita went to see about a doctor, but what's to do when everyone needs a doctor? At least none of us were hurt."

Mama looked at her strangely for a long moment. "Ai," she said at last. "I'm so tired, Martina." She was weeping, but quietly, and Martina hugged her. They stood that way a long time while Jontano watched over them, watched over the well and the garden. Then, leaving Jontano on watch, the two women crouched beside the root cellar stairs to discuss their predicament with Uncle Martin.

Jontano stood in an eerie silence and listened to Roman sneeze and cough, listened to the hopeless sobbing of a woman farther up the street—Bobita Milovech, perhaps—to a single shot followed by a second, then a third, echoing through the empty streets.

"Water," said a child's voice, weak in the twilight. "Do you have water?"

Jontano started around, raising the musket. A small girl stood at the gate, a waif in tattered clothing. She held a battered tin cup in one hand.

He peered down the musket at her, his hands shaking, waiting for the adults who were with her to show themselves.

But there was no movement in the shadows, no threats, whispers, or coughs. The girl had preternaturally pale hair—Marrazzano hair, people called it—and gorgeous brown eyes and a sweet face only partially obscured by dirt. She couldn't be more than seven or eight years old. She was alone.

Jono glanced back toward the shell of the house, but one of the walls hid the entrance to the root cellar from view. Hastily, he dragged away the boards that protected the opening of the well and lowered the bucket, having to winch it hard to get it around, now that a stray hit had bent the axle. The bucket came up half full of clear water, and he dipped her cup in and gave it back to her.

"Now go," he said in a low voice. "I'm not allowed to give any away. Don't come back."

Mutely, she drank the cup dry. He filled it again. This time she padded off, barefoot, down the street, cradling the precious cupful of water against her thin chest. Where were her parents? Lost? Dead? But he heard Mama's voice, calling to him, and as he turned round, he faced the dead house and knew that even if, before today, they might have managed to feed just one more, they had too little left to do so now.

"Martin is going to stay here," said Mama, picking her way around the house. "We'll set him up in the corner, rig a blanket to protect him from wind and rain, and he'll guard the well and the fountain. The rest of us will have to find shelter another place. Roman is getting sicker, the grippe. It's going down into his lungs, I fear. We must find someplace dry and warm for him tomorrow."

"I'll watch tonight," said Jontano. "It's clearing, and I'd rather be up here than down in the cellar."

He caught her answering smile, a ghost in the twilight, and then she went away. So he stood watch, but after the terrible bombardment of the daytime, after the loud, pounding rains, it was now oddly silent. It made him nervous, because unlike the silence in the forest, it was an unnatural quiet.

In the morning, Jontano helped Aunt Martina haul Uncle Martin out of the root cellar. While Martin took the parts of several broken chairs and repaired them into a semblance of one good chair, Mama and Aunt Martina divided up their possessions. Roman huddled in a blanket, coughing so that Jontano's lungs hurt to hear him.

"No sense you staying with me, boy," said Martin when Jontano offered to bide with him. "You'll come over every day and weed the garden and bring me bread, but until this cursed weather lets up, we won't have a chance to rebuild here."

Rebuild! Jontano couldn't reply. How could Martin even think of rebuilding the shattered house? What was the point? If the Marraz-zanos had better guns and better positions, it would just be destroyed again. And yet, Martin had been born here, as had he himself.

"Go to Rado Korsic's shop," Martin added. "That's the first thing to do today, once you get Roman to a safe place. You must give him the musket and the pistol to repair."

Aunt Martina and Mama each gave Martin a kiss on the cheek, then slung bags over their shoulders and set off down the street, Roman trudging between them, his thin shoulders shaking under the blanket. Jontano picked up a blanket wrapped around the cooking gear and the bag containing plate wrapped in a cushion of clothing, said good-bye to his uncle, and with a heavy heart picked his way through the ruined house.

A flash of white, the suggestion of green life, the respiration of trees, the dense scent of unbroken loam . . . he bent down and pulled the six painted cards from underneath a fallen plank.

"What is it, Jono?" asked Uncle Martin sharply. "Are you well?"

"I'm fine," said Jono, straightening up and steadying the bag of plate. He set both bag and blanket down, stuck the cards inside his shirt, and cinched his belt more tightly so that the cards lay snugly against his skin. "Just thought I saw something." He hoisted up his burdens again and left the house behind, following his mother and aunt down the street.

Mama and Aunt Martina were arguing in low voices. Go here? Go there? No, I won't ask Widow Vanyech, not after what she said about Stepha. They'll know in the marketplace. It isn't safe. Nowhere is safe, not after yesterday.

So they walked down into the bowl of the valley, down toward the central marketplace, down toward Murderer's Row. Heavy clouds scudded in, blanketing the sky, and it began to rain again. Roman coughed and snuffled, and began to cry.

"Here, I'll carry you." Jontano lifted the boy up and was aghast to realize how light he was, how slight a burden even with the other things Jontano was carrying. Roman lay his head on Jontano's shoulder and promptly fell asleep.

Even in the rain the marketplace was thronged with other refugees, fleeing their ruined homes. Still holding Roman, Jontano stood guard over the bags and blankets under cover of an empty stall while Mama and Aunt Martina forayed out into the crowd to see if they could find someone they knew who would offer them shelter.

As if they knew and understood—and why not? Why shouldn't they know?—and chose now to launch a new attack because it might demoralize and kill more and even more of their hated enemies, the Marrazzanos opened fire.

The marketplace erupted into cacophony. People screamed, ran, bled, died. Paralyzed, Jontano huddled with Roman in the empty stall. Was it better to stay here, where Mama and Aunt Martina knew he was, and risk being crushed by bricks, if the stall fell in? Was it better to run outside, where rounds filled with shot might explode, scattering like thrown knives into every person within a stone's throw of their landing? He didn't know what to do. He couldn't think. Roman was too terrified and sick to do more than sob quietly against his chest. They were all alone, and outside the panicked crowd surged this way, that, trying to win free of the open market square, but for what safety? There was no safety in Trient, not any longer.

The stall rocked, and a few bricks tumbled down. Roman's sobs cut off, and he lifted his head and stared with a glazed expression at the wall.

"Mama!" he said suddenly.

There! In the crowd, Jontano saw Aunt Martina fighting her way through the mob toward them, but then the press of the crowd shoved her back, to one side, farther and farther away, and she was lost.

"They'll meet us at home," said Jontano with more force than confidence. Another hit nearby sent a second avalanche of bricks tumbling from the stall next door. Jontano eyed the bags, sorting through their contents in his mind: Which to take? Which to leave? He grabbed the firearms and a blanket stuffed with clothes, kettle, the butcher knife, and the last two jars of pickled figs. With Roman clinging to his chest, he heaved the blanket over his back and strode out.

By now the crowd had begun to disperse, fleeing down side streets.

Jontano hesitated. The clouds opened up, and it began to pour down rain. He darted into the nearest boulevard, looking for shelter for Roman. If he could only find a place, he could put the boy there and come back for the other things, come back to find Mama and Aunt Martina. He was halfway down the first block of shattered buildings before he realized he was on Murderer's Row.

Roman, drenched, began to cough heavily. More explosions sounded from the marketplace.

"Mama," whimpered Roman between coughs.

"We'll find a dry place to hide," said Jontano. "Then I'll go back and look for her. Don't worry."

Ahead he saw a doorway. He ducked inside. One wall had fallen in, but the rest of the shop looked reasonably sturdy. It smelled dry, oddly enough, musty, as if perfumed with old herbs. A wooden counter ran along one side of the shop, and he set Roman down in its lee and wrapped him in overlarge clothes and in the two blankets. The boy was shivering with fever, half asleep.

Straightening up, Jontano stared into a forest. If he stepped past the counter, he would step into the woodlands. . . .

Shaking himself, he realized that he was staring at a huge picture, a painting, a painting of a forest. A moment later, he knew he was in old Aldo's shop. Without meaning to, he reached inside his shirt and drew out the painted cards. He held up the card depicting the forest, and in the gray light of the overcast day, he saw that the card and the painting were the same. Except the painting, as tall as he was, was somehow more lifelike. It seemed to pulse with life, as if he could step inside it. It called to him. It would be safe there. If only the trees grew again in Trient, it would be safe. There would be no more fighting.

"Mama," whimpered Roman. Jontano jerked, startled to still be standing in the dim shop. He knelt. The boy was hot, too hot. He needed a doctor. He needed his mother.

Oh, Lord, thought Jontano. What if Mama was killed? I couldn't bear it. I just couldn't bear it.

"Listen, Roman, I must go out and look for Mama and your mother. You must stay here and not move. Do you understand?"

"Yes. Don't leave me."

"Just for a little while. I'll come back."

"Just for a little while," echoed the boy weakly.

Reluctantly, Jontano left Roman and the forest behind. Intermittent shelling still peppered the central city, but the worst of it had moved toward the north. There was more musket fire than anything, as if a skirmish had broken out along the eastern line.

Only a few shapes, more ghosts than people, haunted the marketplace. Jontano hurried, giving them a wide berth, and found the stall where he and Roman had sheltered. It had collapsed, burying their possessions. He scrabbled at the bricks while the musket fire got louder.

"Jono! Oh, Lord, Jono."

He leaped up. It was his Mama.

She crushed him against her. "No time," she said. "No time. They're coming."

"Who is coming?"

"Martina went back to warn Martin. I don't know what they can do. The Marrazzanos have broken past General Vestino's troops. That's what everyone's saying in the streets. I came back, hoping to find you. Ah, Lord, what's to become of us?"

"We must get Roman," said Jontano. "He's down—he's down in old Aldo's shop."

Mama looked at him. A brief spark of something—fear? anticipation? anger?—lit her eyes, and then it fled, leaving her looking tired and resigned. "We'll go get him and try to get back home if we can. We might as well die there as anywhere else."

She said nothing more as they ran down Murderer's Row, hugging half-fallen walls, until she knelt beside Roman, who had by now lapsed into a feverish sleep.

"Poor child," she said. "He deserved a better death than this."

"He doesn't have to die!" cried Jontano. Mama looked up at him, and with a horrid shock, like a claw at his throat, he knew that she had given up, that the years of fighting to survive had all become too much for her to bear.

"I'm so tired," she said. "We'll just rest here a few moments." She lay down beside Roman and between one instant and the next, she was asleep.

She had given up. Jontano shivered. He wanted to cry, for her, for himself, for everything, but he had no tears.

The forest breathed, exhaling its scent around him. His hand clutched the card, the leaves unfurled to their full glory, the spring flowers passing into the blooms of summer—for it was almost summer. Tomorrow would be summer. He remembered that with mild surprise. He smelled, not rain, but the scent of the forest shedding moisture after rain, warmed by the new sun of summer. He heard the rustling of leaves, the scrambling of mice in the undergrowth, not the musket fire, louder now but strangely dull, too, as if from behind the mist, behind an impenetrable hedge.

Once there had been no war in the valley of Trient, though there had always been wolves.

Mama slept, curled around Roman. Perhaps she would sleep forever, never have to wake to the death of all that she had held dear, never have to remember everything she had lost.

Jontano circled the counter and came right up to the painting. It seemed to have grown since he last saw it. It filled the entire wall, as if it was straining, trying to fill the shop. He lifted his arm and pressed the card against it. If only he could find a way through, for himself, for Mama, for Roman and Aunt Martina and Uncle Martin. For the graves, so that the dead could lie in respectful silence, as they deserved.

If only the trees could grow again in Trient, as they once had, filling the parks and the boulevards, filling the once-handsome city with their summer fullness and the stark lines of their winter beauty.

He felt the paper-thin bark of a birch tree under his hand, peeling away where his fingers scraped at it. He felt the flowers blooming under his feet, vines twining up his legs. A glade of sweet grass filled old Aldo's shop, and a lilac bush grew, lush and thick, to shelter Mama and Roman.

Oaks burst up in the marketplace, an ancient grove, watchful and airy. Murderer's Row erupted into an orchard of pears and apples and cherry trees, all mingled together, and the musket fire faded as the Vestino Line, the ruins of Saint Harmonious Bridge, the far hills were swamped by ash and beech. Aspen sunk their roots into the low places of the valley, blanketed with ponds and pools of brackish water left over from the rains. In the northern hills, tulips and elms lifted toward the sky, and in the meadows where blocks of houses had once stood, around springs made by wells, great patches of flowering shrubs spread out into a sea of color. Jasmine, bougainvillaea, and twining wisteria wrapped themselves around the shell of the house where Uncle Martin sat watch and Aunt Martina cooked over an open fire, her eyes red from weeping, and filled the ruined walls with their fragrance.

There were no more than a few startled comments, which Jontano heard on the wind as if from another life, so quickly did the forest take root in lands it had once had all to its own self.

The cannon, the barricades, the buildings whole and shattered, the boulevards, all were subsumed. Trees sprang up where people stood, Marrazzano and Trassahar alike, beech and oak, birch and aspen.

Night fell and passed and with the new sun, summer came to Trient, which was no longer a city but a vast woodland, populated by trees and the many small, quiet inhabitants of the forest.

The valley lay at peace in the calm of a summer morning.

WITH GOD TO GUARD HER

Preface

Now in those days it was not unknown for a man of high birth to put aside one wife, with whom he had become dissatisfied, and marry another. Indeed, when kings indulged in such behavior, then dukes and counts might choose to emulate them. But what seems permissible in the world, God may well judge more harshly, as I shall relate.

One

At this time a man of free birth worked fields adjoining the estate of Duke Amalo, near the River Marne. With him in his house lived his mother, Theudichild, his wife Ingund, his two young sons and a daughter, and a few servants. The daughter was called Merofled.

It so happened that the duty of paying the tax to the church fell one month to Merofled.

She was a girl of good stature, having always been granted good health, and was now old enough to marry. Her family bore a respectable name and they had nothing to be ashamed of in their ancestors. Her mother's father was a canon at Vitry and it was said that his great-grandfather was dedicated in martyrdom in Lyons.

But she had not yet married, nor had her father betrothed her to any man. Some said her father and mother favored her excessively, making her too proud to wish to submit to another man's lordship, others that she was too pious to wish to marry. A few had been heard to whisper that her grandmother, Theudichild, an irascible old tyrant, preferred Merofled's sewing to that of any of her servants or even to that of her daughter-in-law, and would not allow the girl to leave her father's house so that the vain old woman would not have to do without the luxury of finely sewn garments.

On this day, Merofled received the pot of candle wax from one of the servants and, with only a young serving girl as attendant, walked down the road to deliver the wax to the church. In this way, with each household paying its portion of the tax, candles always burned at the altar.

The two young women were forced to move off the road when a great entourage rode by. The serving girl bent her head and knelt at once, but Merofled neither knelt nor looked down.

First walked clerics in their vestments, and after them the kinsmen, friends, and vassals of the Duke, for Merofled realized that this must be the retinue of Duke Amalo. They came in a crowd, kicking up a wide swathe of dust.

She had never seen the Duke except at a distance and so did not recognize him at once when suddenly a rider pulled to a halt and stared straight at her. He was tall, finely dressed, and rode a horse with silver harness and a saddle trimmed with gold. The rest of the column pulled up beside and behind him.

"Who is this girl?" the Duke asked one of his attendants, a certain Count Leudast.

"I do not know," said Leudast, and he turned to another man and ordered him to speak to Merofled.

The servant asked her name and she answered, boldly and not without pride. "I am called Merofled, daughter of Berulf and Ingund."

Having had her words repeated to him, the Duke rode on.

Two

Duke Amalo was a man of sudden passions, the sort who most wishes to have what he does not yet possess, and being unused in any case to having anything denied him.

This is what he had seen: a handsome girl, in the bloom of youth, and wearing dress that was simple yet clean and well-made, which is one of the marks of good family. As well, she had spoken clearly and without flinching.

"Find out about this girl," he ordered his servants.

One of his clerics inquired in the village and returned to him with these facts: That the girl was of free birth and that she came of good family on both sides, including, as I have mentioned before, the grandfather's grandfather who had been granted the glory of martyrdom on this earth. That her father, Berulf, paid his taxes regularly to the church, attended services without fail, and was altogether a man of good character whom God had rewarded with prosperity. That Berulf and his wife gave alms to the poor and had endowed the church in the village with a silver chalice and two finely woven tapestries, one depicting Judith and Holofernes and the other showing St. Martin giving half his cloak to a poor man.

Duke Amalo mentioned nothing of these inquiries to his wife, by whom he had by this time five children, two of which had died in infancy.

THREE

For some days after first seeing Merofled by the roadside Duke Amalo went about his business in the usual fashion, hawking, hunting, seeing to his estate. But more than once he led his retinue along the road that led through the village. Finally, when no more than three Sabbaths had passed, he took his clerics and the rest of his entourage and attended Mass in the village church. There he tended to his prayer assiduously, kneeling in the front rank of benches with his hands covering his face as befits a pious man. However, rather than praying, he used his hands as a screen so that he might stare at the young woman Merofled without betraying his interest to all and sundry.

When Mass ended, he lavished silver and gold vessels on the church and donated a great deal of money to the support of the clergy, so that all spoke well of him when he left and returned to his estates.

Four

By this time, however, Duke Amalo had been seized with a consuming desire for Merofled.

The next day, therefore, he summoned his wife to him. "It is time," he said to her, "that you travel to your estate near Andelot so that you might put your affairs in order there."

By this means he intended to be rid of her.

Now, as her estate in Andelot came to her as part of her inheritance from her father, and as it lay near her relations, she was not averse to going, although the journey was a long one. So, suspecting nothing, she agreed. She took their elder sons with her, leaving the youngest son behind.

Five

From the shelter of an oak grove, Merofled watched the entourage pass, Duke Amalo's wife and all her retinue, her women and servants, her priest and deacons, horses, wagons, and a few dogs. Then she walked quickly home, to her father's hall.

Now Merofled was not a fool, and if she was proud, it was in part because she had a sharp mind and could see what other people sometimes failed to notice.

For this reason she found one excuse and then another to stay near her father's house, never venturing outside the fenced yard that confined the livestock.

Six

Meanwhile, Duke Amalo called his steward to him. He carefully wrote up a deed which would transfer the ownership of one of his estates, near Chalon, to Merofled upon the consummation of their marriage, as was the custom at that time.

He then sent his servants to the house of her father, where they delivered themselves of this message:

"With these words Duke Amalo addresses you: 'I have recently sent away the woman who was my wife, and am now inclined to take a new wife. If this is satisfactory to you, then your daughter Merofled may accompany my servants back to my hall with whatever possessions you choose to settle on her.'"

SEVEN

Berulf was a man of great piety and virtue, but while his good deeds were legion, he was not known for looking over the wall to covet his neighbor's possessions. Thus he was taken aback by this salutation.

He retired at once to his bedchamber and sent for his daughter Merofled. "Is this what you wish?" he asked her, not hiding his surprise.

"Why should I wish to be married to a man who sends his wife away as soon as he sees a woman who appears more comely to him?" she replied. "I would rather be married to a man of my own rank, whom I would not fear. If Duke Amalo should beat me, we would have no recourse, for his relations are more powerful than ours."

Her father saw the wisdom in her words and he returned straightaway to the Duke's envoys and sent them away with his refusal.

EIGHT

Anyone might imagine that this answer did not please Duke Amalo.

He raged for several days, whipped his hounds, and beat several servants who were slow in obeying his commands.

Then he threw himself on his knees in front of the altar at the chapel on his estate and prayed. His father had placed in this chapel some relics of Saint Sergius, and Duke Amalo set a copy of the Psalter atop the reliquary. He spent one whole night in prayer and another two days in fasting and vigil.

After this he opened the Psalter and read from the first verse at the top of the page. It said: "They are utterly consumed because of their iniquities."

These words dismayed him, and he wept.

After this, he did not mention the girl Merofled for ten days.

NINE

As the days passed and nothing happened, Merofled began to believe that she had misjudged Duke Amalo's intent. With a lighter heart, she went about her duties. After some days her father approached her and said these words:

"My child, it is, alas, time that we thought of a worthy alliance for you."

"My lord," she replied, "we must trust to God to provide what is necessary. If a good match presents itself, I will accept it. If it does not, then I am content to devote myself to good deeds and to God's work, and to remain a handmaiden of Christ."

Berulf accepted this answer gladly, since he was in no hurry to lose his daughter.

TEN

One night soon after this it happened that Duke Amalo drank too much at dinner. When he thought of going to bed, he thought at that same moment of the young woman whom he desired. By this time he was completely drunk.

"Go to her house," he said to his servants, "seize her, if she will not come willingly, and bring her to my bed." He went to his bedchamber to await her.

When the servants came, more than ten of them, to Berulf's house, they made their demand.

Merofled stood up proudly and faced them. "I and my father have already given our reply. Now begone from this house, where you are not welcome."

At this, the servants swarmed forward and grabbed hold of her. Her father sent his elder son running to fetch his sword, and even old Theudichild laid about her with her walking stick, but the servants were better armed. Merofled fought against them, overturning tables and chairs, but at last they pinned her arms behind her, tied them, and carried her off like a sack of grain.

No one in the house dared follow, because of Duke Amalo's rank and family.

Eleven

In this way Merofled was brought to Duke Amalo's house. Once in the house they set her down and untied her, thinking that now she would accept the honor of the Duke's attention, but at once she struck about her with her fists and ran for the door.

It took three men at arms to subdue her. They hit her in the face until her nose bled and dragged her upstairs to the bedchamber, where, still fighting, she bled all over the bed, staining the covers red.

Duke Amalo had not waited in tranquil silence while this kidnapping took place. He had taken off his sword and belt and most of his clothing, in anticipation of her arrival. He also had at hand more wine, and when his men dragged Merofled in, he poured a new cup.

"Leave us!" he shouted, and they hurried out, so that Amalo and Merofled were left alone in the chamber.

Stanching the blood from her nose, she climbed off the bed and stared defiantly at him.

"Here is wine," he said, offering her the second cup, "with which we will drink to the consummation of our marriage."

"I refuse it, just as I refuse your offer of marriage, just as I refuse to inhabit your bed."

This was too much for the Duke's uncertain temper. He threw the cup down and it shattered into pieces, the wine staining the carpet a red as deep as the blood that stained the bedcovers. He grabbed hold of Merofled and struck and slapped her. Now he was a man made strong by years of riding and hunting and war, and though Merofled resisted, she was by this time dizzy with the blows she had taken rather than give in to his blandishments, high rank, and threats. Her heart was still strong, but her flesh was weakening from the abuse it had taken, and suddenly she went limp despite her efforts to continue resisting.

As if this was encouragement, he took her in his arms and laid her down on the bed beside him, ready to make her his wife. So overcome was he by her closeness, by the expectation that his desire would now be fulfilled, and by the great amount of wine he had drunk, that he shut his eyes.

Merofled had given herself up to prayer and to her belief in God's judgment. She felt Amalo's grasp slacken just a bit, and taking this as a sign from God she summoned up every last portion of strength that God had granted her. She caught sight of Amalo's sword where he had placed it on the chest at the head of the bed.

Stretching out her hand, she took hold of the hilt and drew the blade from its scabbard. Aroused by her movement, Amalo opened his eyes and began to roll on top of her.

Needing no further encouragement, she struck him as hard as she could with his sword. The blow took him in his naked chest, and he howled in pain.

At once, servants ran into the room. They broke into great clamor while Amalo screamed and moaned. His soldiers grabbed Merofled, disarmed her, and pulled their own knives and swords in order to kill her immediately.

But Amalo, seeing this, took hold of himself. Weeping, he cried out to them.

"Stop! The sin is mine, not hers, for I tried to rape her. She only did this to preserve her honor. Do not hurt her."

As soon as these words left his lips, his eyes rolled up in his head, blood poured from his mouth, and he stopped breathing.

By this time others of his family, relations and servants, had come rushing into the chamber to see what the commotion was about. When he died, a cry of grief and disbelief rose from them all and they were filled with consternation.

Twelve

While servants and family alike stood in the room lamenting, Merofled struggled to her feet and, still dizzy, crept out from the midst of that host. They were all so consumed by grief and astonishment that they did not at first notice her escape.

But with God's help she made her way out of his house and ran home.

Now you may imagine the consternation, of a different kind, that erupted in her father's house when she came in, her clothes torn, her face bloody, her body covered with bruises.

At first her family covered her with kisses, thanking God for her safe return, but when she told her story, they barred the doors and windows and her old grandmother, Theudichild, began to keen with a new grief.

"Ah, child, you have brought ill luck on us. Now Duke Amalo's relatives will ride here and avenge themselves on our house. They will kill my sole remaining son, my grandsons, and no doubt burn down the only house I have ever known. If you had only given in to him, knowing that his power ranks far above ours, you should have had a good marriage gift from him, and we should have had peace."

"It is not I who have sinned!" said Merofled. "I have only protected my virginity and the honor of this house."

"That may be," said her father, "but his kinsmen will avenge themselves on you and your family nevertheless."

"Then I will go to the King himself and plead my case!"

Her family protested at once that she could do no such thing, for she was weak from loss of blood and from the beatings she had sustained, and the roads were not always safe.

"God will guard me," she said. She washed her face and limbs and she put on clean clothes.

Thirteen

At dawn, she took her father's gelding and two servants and without fear set out on the road to Chalon, where it was said that King Guntram was now staying, for in the month of September he liked to celebrate the feast day of Saint Marcellus in the church dedicated to the saint.

A full thirty-five miles she rode, and when she came to the city of Chalon, she went directly to the church. The King and his entire retinue were worshiping in the church, but Merofled walked into the church without hesitation. She begged to be brought before the King. When his guards admitted her to his presence, she threw herself at King Guntram's feet and in plain language told him everything that had happened to her.

Because he was a God-fearing man, King Guntram was filled with compassion for the young woman. He rose. Every person in the church quieted in order to hear him pass judgment.

"God has already passed judgment in this case," he said. "I would not challenge what he has allowed to come to pass. For this reason, I grant you, Merofled, daughter of Berulf and Ingund, your life, for you have lawfully protected yourself against theft."

"What of Duke Amalo's relations, King Guntram?" she asked boldly. "I am of free birth, and my family is a good one, but we cannot protect ourselves against any revenge they might intend, for they are more powerful than we are."

He nodded, for this was indeed a reasonable concern. "Then I place you under my protection, and I prohibit any of the dead man's relations from exacting vengeance on you or your family."

So it was done.

Fourteen

With this royal edict in hand, Merofled rode home, having protected herself from Duke Amalo's brutal attentions and her family from the vengeance of his kinsmen.

Nor have I heard that any other incident disturbed her life, which, with God to guard her, proved both long and prosperous.

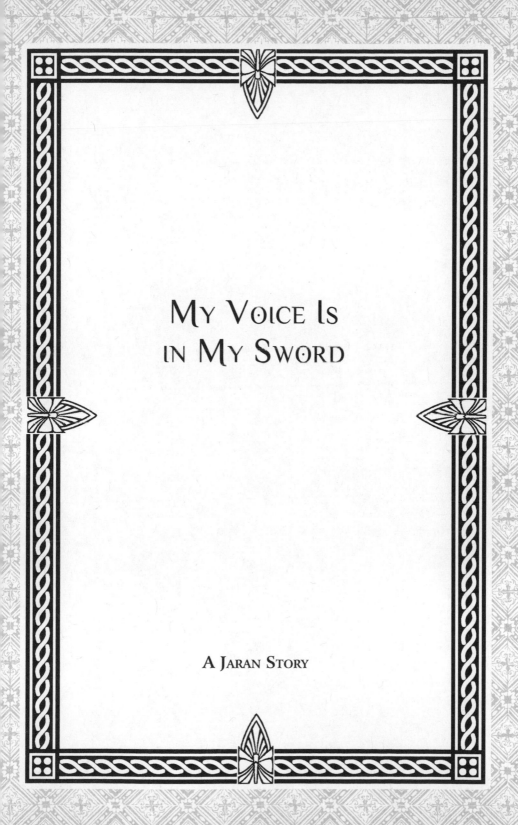

My Voice Is
in My Sword

A Jaran Story

We knew we were in trouble when Macbeth insisted on seeing the witches first.

You know the bit: Banquo and Macbeth enter and Banquo says, "'What are these, so wither'd and so wild in their attire?'" That's his moment, when he points out the three witches to Macbeth and Macbeth sees them for the first time, those three terrible hags who will hail Macbeth as king when of course he isn't king yet and will only become king by murder most foul.

Have you heard about actors who won't let any of the other actors have moments on stage that are theirs alone?

"Hey," said Bax to Yu-Sun, who was playing Banquo in drag, "I'll see the witches first, and then I'll tap you on the shoulder and you see them and say the line."

I propped my feet up on a stool and looked at Octavian and Octavian looked at me, and we both sighed. No doubt you're asking yourself where the director was, who might correct this little bit of scene-stealing. Well, he was right where he ought to be, sitting at a table staring at the taped-out stage where the five actors walked through the scene. He didn't say a word. How could he?

So they went on. The witches say their lines and Macbeth and Banquo say a few more, and just before the witches vanish, Bax got in a feel to Emmi's breast, just grabbed it, and Emmi went all stiff in the face and twisted away from him, and for all you could tell from El Directore's face, he hadn't seen a thing. But Emmi did double time off to the side, looking like steam was about to pour out of her ears. Enter Ross and Angus.

I'm Ross, by the way. The big joke is that I always have to play Ross in the Scottish play because my real name is Ross.

By the time rehearsal was over, Bax had managed to grope another witch and twist King Duncan's arm so hard while offering fealty that it actually brought a tear to old Jon-Jon's good eye. We retired to nurse our wounds, en masse to the hostel where we were sleeping, and Bax made a grand exit with his three lamias—one in each shade—to wherever it was a star of his stature stays on an alien world with a limited number of oxygen-rich chambers in which humankind can breathe.

"Lady Christ in Heaven," said Emmi, massaging her bruised breast while Jon-Jon examined his wrenched wrist with bemused interest. "I don't think I'm going to survive four more weeks of this. Where'd he get you, Cheri?"

Cheri—Second Witch—shrugged. She'd probably endured worse, back when she was a hootch dancer on Tau Ceti Tierce. "Crotch. What a pig."

"But Cheri, my dear," said Octavian quietly, "he's a Star."

Kostas—who should have been playing the lead but was playing Macduff instead—peered down from his bunk. "Why is it that Stars have to prove their legitimacy by doing theater? Can't they stay on their holies and interactives and leave us to do what we've trained for? I still can't believe Bax began directing during the damned read-through. And El Directore didn't say a thing."

"Oh, well," said Emmi. "I'm sure it'll get better. It certainly can't get worse."

Emmi, we all had to agree later, would not be auditioning for the role of Cassandra in *Troilus and Cressida* anytime soon.

We took two days more to block out the rest of the play and Bax behaved himself, except that he ate sandwiches and drank coffee every time he was on stage, walking around with the cup in one hand and his script in the other. When he fought and killed young Siward for the first time, he ate a sandwich during the fight scene and dribbled crumbs onto poor prostrate Ahmed—who was doubling as Donalbain and young Siward—while he said his lines.

At the end of the first week, the diplomat Phalasath Caraglio arrived to give us the official tour of the Squat homeworld. Yes, I know, you're not supposed to call them Squats, but you can't really help it. They seem to spend an endless amount of time sitting around, and whether they're sitting or standing, they only reach hip-high.

Caraglio gave us the standard Squat lecture as we trundled along in a big sealed barge down a canal filled with gold coins. Or, at least, they looked like gold coins. Since humans couldn't breathe the atmosphere, none of us had gotten close enough to check for certain.

"Our hosts are only the second alien group who specifically requested an artistic embassy to their planet, and you will offer them their first glimpse into human art and culture and history. I hope I don't need to remind you that you were chosen for your professionalism and your skill, and your reputation as a first-rank theater company."

We all looked at Bax. He sat lounging in the back, listening to whatever Flopsy and Mopsy and Cottontail were whispering in his ears and certainly not listening to M. Caraglio. Bax had short curly black hair and sported the fashionable tricolor face. His lamias matched the colors. Flopsy was pale white and Mopsy was coal black. Cottontail's skin was a screaming shade of scarlet, which looks okay as a small patch of skin but pretty damned stupid for a whole body. She wore the least clothes—a parti-colored white and black scarf around her hips and a sheer silk blouson—and she must have had enviro work done on her skin implants, too; she never looked cold except, of course, her nipples were always erect. I myself can't believe that happened simply because she found Bax so staggeringly attractive every second of every day.

"May I ask a question?" asked the beautiful Peng-Hsin, who oozed Star out of every pore. She plays Lady Macbeth, and her Star-magnitude is every bit as great as Bax's, with one vital difference: Peng-Hsin Khatun is a professional. M. Caraglio melted in her general direction.

"Assuredly, M. Peng-Hsin. It is by asking questions that we learn, and we hope, of course, to learn as much about our hosts as they learn about us."

"Are we really sailing down a river of gold coins, as it appears?"

"I'm afraid any answer I give will seem inadequate. Chemically, we don't know. But as for appearances—certainly they appear as gold coins to us, but we inevitably impress our own biases onto what we see and experience here, and *their* notion of what these objects are, of what their value is, their notion, even, of how much appearances count at all as opposed to simple reality, we can't know. Ah." He broke off and pointed to his left. "There is the building that we believe is their Parliament, or at least, the seat of their governing body."

Squat Parliament lay on a flat stretch of ground ringed by three circles of flower beds. A simple, regular octagon, it had neither roof nor walls but a plain white foundation marked out by columns and shaded by a perplexing array of what looked like canvas awnings. It was huge, though; four baseball games could have been played simultaneously on that pale surface. The barge ground to a halt and we crowded over to the left to stare out the view windows.

"You may have noticed," added M. Caraglio, pitching his voice higher to carry over our murmuring as we pointed out the clusters of Squats who were, of course, squatting on the green lawns between the flower beds and inside the twin rings of columns that bordered the octagon, "that this, our hosts' capital city, is not large at all by human standards. There's some debate within the xenodiplomacy team stationed here whether that is because they simply have a small population or whether their population base is more agrarian and spread out over the land." He went on, explaining about the relative proportion of land mass to ocean and how that affected their climate and thus their agricultural base and the availability of land for habitation, but something far more interesting was going on outside.

A Squat came trundling along the river bank, spotted our barge, and waded with its splay feet right out over the gold coins to press its nose— if that little turnip of a bulb could be called a nose—up against the window next to Peng-Hsin. They regarded each other. We all regarded it, and it swiveled its squat little head topped with ivory fern ears and took us all in.

"It's curious," said Peng-Hsin, sounding amused.

M. Caraglio coughed, sounding uncomfortable. "This has never happened before," he said. "They've always kept their distance. Very careful about that."

"Aww," said Cheri, who combined the oddest mix of sentimentality and hardheadedness, "maybe it's just a little baby."

From the back, Bax burped loudly. "Fuck, it's ugly," he said. Mopsy and Flopsy tittered. Cottontail said, "Oh, Bax," in her breathless knock-me-up voice.

As if in response to his comment, a whole herd of Squats uprooted themselves from their meditations on the lawn and ambled over toward us. Through the windows, we heard a chorus of hoots rising and falling as the herd of Squats formed a semicircle at the bank of the river. Our Squat pricked up its lacy ears, snuffled one last time toward Peng-Hsin, and then turned and trundled back to the shoreline.

"Oh, dear," murmured M. Caraglio. Bax burped again. The diplomat shot him a look so filled with distaste that it was palpable; then, as quickly, he smoothed over his expression into that bland mask that diplomats and out-of-work actors wear. Caraglio went forward to the lock and made some comment through the translation-screen, and the barge scraped sideways over the coins, following our Squat to the bank. As soon as our alien clambered up onto the sward, it was at once swarmed by other Squats rather like the winning runner is in the last game of the Worlds Series.

"Uh-oh," said Emmi and Cheri at the same time.

"Looks like trouble," Octavian muttered, and we all avoided looking back at Bax. The effect was the same, of course. By not looking at him, we made his presence all the more obvious.

Three Squats inched forward and climbed up the ramp that led into the forward lock. The smoked glass barrier pretty much cut them off from our sight, but I caught a glimpse of a fanned-out fern ear and the trailing end of a bulb nose brushed across the glass from the other side.

Then, like the voice of the gods, the translation-screen boomed out words. "One of our young ones has offended one of your people. We beg your pardon."

I winced. Octavian covered his ears. On the back bench, Cottontail crossed her arms across her breasts, as if the volume might warp their particularly fine shape. Bax pinched her on the thigh, and she shrieked, giggled, and unwound her arms.

Caraglio had a sick look on his face, like he'd just eaten something rancid. "Not at all," he said. "I beg . . . it isn't . . . please don't. . . ." He sputtered to a stop, flexed his hands in and out, and began again. "We are sorry that this incident has interrupted your deliberations, and we were not at all disturbed by the interest of your young one."

Muted hooting leaked out through the glass barrier as the Squats consulted.

"What I want to know," said Kostas in a low voice, "is how from so far away the Squats knew Bax was insulting the poor little thing."

The translation-screen crackled to life, but this time, mercifully, the volume had been lowered. "We consider your words," it squawked in its tinny intonation, not capturing at all the exuberance of Squat hooting, "and will meditate on them. As time continues to flow, you may continue on your journey, but be assured that to our recollection, this incident has not occurred."

Caraglio did not even get a chance to reply before they scooted off the barge and we went on our way. I watched Squat Parliament recede and the Squats amble back up the hill to fall into place in scattered groups like flowers being arranged on separate trays.

"What next?" asked Bax. "They got any dancing girls here?" His lamias shrieked with laughter and he reached over and tweaked Cottontail so hard on her hooters without her even losing a beat in her giggling that I had to wonder if she'd had pain desensitizers built into her skin as well. In her line of work, it might not have been a bad idea.

But Caraglio cut the tour short and we returned to the theater instead. Unsure of what we were supposed to do now, we wandered onto the stage and loitered. Bax and the lamias disappeared into his dressing room. Caraglio headed for El Directore's office. We heard a knock, a voice, and then the door slammed shut.

"Who's going to go eavesdrop?" asked Emmi, and for some damn reason, they all looked at me.

"Oh, hell," I said. Ah, well, once a go-between, always a go-between. I exited through one of the doors in the tiring-house wall and snuck down the hallway to stick an ear up against the door. It was a good thing that wood doesn't transmit emotional heat. I would have been burned.

"The man is a complete asshole," shouted Caraglio in a most undiplomatic fashion. "Why is he allowed to run roughshod over the rest of you?"

"May I be frank with you, M. Caraglio?" said El Directore in a low voice. He sounded tired, and for the first time, I felt some sympathy for him.

"I wish you would be!"

"His studio is bankrolling this expedition as a showcase for him and for Peng-Hsin. You can't have thought that a small theatrical company like ourselves could afford this, even with a government grant?"

There was silence. Caraglio cleared his throat. "Well, then," he said, "he must be confined to quarters and to the theater. We cannot have any more such incidents. Surely you understand that."

"If he is confined, then so must be everyone else."

There was a longer silence.

"So be it," said Caraglio in a resigned tone, and he opened the door so quickly that I had to jerk back to maintain my balance.

"Oh, er, ah," I said as the diplomat shut the door behind himself.

He set his hands on his hips and glared at me. "Star quality," he said, and produced a surprisingly robust raspberry. "Then can you explain to me why M. Baxtrusini acts this way while M. Peng-Hsin, who presumably has the same conditions attaching to her contract and her life, does not?"

I shrugged. "Why are any of us the way we are? Ask Shakespeare, M. Caraglio. He probably had as good an idea of the answer to that question as anyone."

He grunted. "Empathic. Don't you people know how to read? It says so in the packet of orientation materials."

"Empathic?" I echoed weakly. I did not want to admit that the first paragraph of dry prose set beside the first close-grained and utterly confusing diagrammatic map had put me off from the rest. As usual, the government was too cheap to add any decent media values to their official publication.

Caraglio practically snarled. "The Squats—er, the Squanishta—are considered to be empathic by the xenobiological team that identifies psychological and physiological profiles."

"But how can we tell?"

"I don't know how they tell! I'm just a goddamned diplomat, and I can tell you, it's not the aliens I have trouble dealing with! If you'll excuse me." He stamped off down the hall, and I can't say that I blamed him for his bad temper.

El Directore's door cracked open slightly. "Is he gone?" our fearless leader asked tremulously. "Say, Ross, could you let the others know about the new restrictions—er, never mind. I'll ring for Patrick." Lucky Patrick. As the Stage Manager, he always got the dirty jobs.

With the restrictions, we ended up spending a hell of a lot of time in the theater, since our hostel was dreary to the point of sublimity. But it was a nice theater. The Squats had evidently spent some time building a tidy little replica of the Globe with real wood, or what passed for real wood. Since the house wasn't sealed in with the atmospheric shield yet, we could go out and stretch in the yard or sit in the galleries to watch rehearsal or to read or nap or knit, or whatever. It was a good space, as accurate in many ways as the meticulously reconstructed Fourth Globe in London. Certainly the Squats had done their research, and if the theater was any indication, they seemed to care that they gained the fullest appreciation possible of this alien art form.

So meticulous were they that we had to stop for an entire day when Sanjar put his foot through the trap in the banqueting scene. We, the lords, were exiting, and Bax had launched into his monologue a bit early, since he liked to rush his big moments, when Sanjar's foot caught in some loose board and he went through all the way up to his thigh.

He muttered an oath in a language I didn't recognize. Octavian and I grabbed him by the arms and heaved him up. He was white around the mouth, and he winced and then tried to put weight on the foot. Meanwhile, Peng-Hsin, downstage, saw us struggling and she broke away from Bax and came up to see if Sanjar was all right.

Oblivious, Bax continued. "'For mine own good, all causes shall give way. . . .'"

Sanjar tested the foot. Then he shrugged. Nothing broken, or even sprained. The trap gaped in front of him. El Directore had stood up. He hesitated and then sank down again, and we completed our exit. From off stage I looked back to watch Bax finish his monologue: "'Strange things I have in head that will to hand, Which must be acted ere they may be scann'd.'"

And Peng-Hsin, amazingly, came in right on cue with her line. Exeunt. Bax had barely gotten off stage before he spun around and tromped back on.

"What is this?" he demanded, pointing at the trap lying ajar. "How did this happen? I could hurt myself! Tell those damned Squats to fix it!" He marched off, looking deeply offended.

So we took a day off while the Squats fixed it. We played bridge, hearts, and pinochle in our dreary hostel instead of being able to go out and explore a bit more. Not an edifying way to spend the day. In the morning we returned to the theater to find silver leaves inscribed with odd little squiggles in all the dressing rooms. M. Caraglio informed us that these were evidently some kind of mark of apology for the disruption, proffered by the Squat carpenters. Peng-Hsin promptly made hers into a necklace, thus gracing both the gift and herself. Bax insisted the lamias use theirs as g-strings. And when Emmi imitated Peng-Hsin and strung hers as a necklace, too, he managed to rip it in half in one of their scenes. Cheri caught Emmi's arm just before Emmi slugged him, and in thanks got groped again.

"You would think," said Kostas, "that he gets enough groping in on his entourage that he wouldn't need to take it out on them."

I shrugged. Octavian rolled his eyes. "Kost, I don't think it's sex that he's interested in."

"Take a break," called Patrick, thus saving Cheri from Bax's hands and Emmi from doing the deed the rest of us would have liked to do ourselves. "Bax and Kostas in fifteen for their final scene."

But of course, we all returned in fifteen minutes to watch what was now our favorite scene in the play, the one in which Macduff kills Macbeth on the field of battle. We gathered in the yard, sitting and standing in a casual group so as not to seem too interested.

"'Turn, hell-hound, turn!'" Macduff cries when he reenters and sees Macbeth. They fight. Macbeth discovers that Macduff is not "'of woman born,'" and at that moment realizes that he is doomed. We drank it in.

"'Lay on, Macduff, And damn'd be him that first cries, "Hold, enough!"'"

Now it's true that in the text Macbeth is killed off stage and Macduff comes back on carrying Macbeth's head, but it's rarely played that way. Swordplay is a marvelous thing, and we have plenty of ways these days to make the death look real.

They fought, and Macduff drove him back and back—

"Now, wait," said Bax, lowering his sword. "*I'll* drive Macduff back, and when I have him pinned, then I'll drop my sword and allow him to kill me."

"Ah, er," said El Directore.

Kostas stared at a point ten feet behind and two feet above Bax's head, his expression mercifully blank.

Yu-Sun, who was doubling as the fight choreographer, came downstage. "I beg your pardon, but we need to follow the swordfight as it was rehearsed."

They tried it again. Macduff drives Macbeth back and back, and then suddenly and unexpectedly Bax sidestepped and with main force knocked Kostas flat. It took Kost a second, shaking his head, to get his wind back, but then he climbed back to his feet with sword raised. Bax darted away from him, running downstage, and showily impaled himself on the blade. He fell to his knees, paused, got up again, and sheathed the sword. Then he set his hands on his hips, leaving his sword sticking out at an awkward angle. Yu-Sun, coming back downstage, had to dodge the blade as he swung around; it looked like he was trying to trip her with it.

"Or if you don't like that," said Bax, "then instead I could drive him back, like I suggested the first time. You see, I have him at my mercy, but I realize that death is upon me so I let him kill me."

Octavian had his eyes shut, but the rest of us watched in appalled fascination. "Goddess help us," murmured Cheri, "he's so damned swellheaded that he can't let someone else kill him even if it's in the script. He's got to control it himself." She made an obscene little gesture with her left hand.

"Start again," said El Directore with a put-upon sigh. "Uh, Macduff with 'I have no words.'"

Kostas had that look on his face: Doubtless he *had* no words. Luckily Shakespeare could speak for him. "'My voice is in my sword, thou bloodier villain Than terms can give thee out!'"

They fight.

Kostas restrained himself admirably, even when Bax again deviated from Yu-Sun's blocking and this time slapped Kostas with the flat of his blade hard on the abdomen. We finally gave up watching, because it was too painful, for Kostas personally and for us as artists. Rehearsal is always tedious when an actor refuses to discover his role and instead attempts to cram it into a pre-formed shape.

We had to take off the next day while the Squats put the atmospheric shield in place. At the hostel, Cheri suggested strip poker. We settled on whist.

The shield rose like a clear glass wall from the yard about one meter in front of the proscenium and bound us all the way back to the back galleries, snaking in to seal off the back rooms and the cellar as well. It felt like performing in a fish bowl. It felt, all at once, restrictive. Octavian and Emmi and I went and sat on the edge of the stage and gazed mournfully at the house, lost to us now. A single Squat walked the galleries, vanished, and then reappeared in the yard, pacing out the area with a stately tread.

Emmi smiled. "They seem more even-tempered," she said. "Don't you think?"

"How can you tell?" asked Octavian. "It isn't as if we've had any real contact with them."

Emmi shrugged. "Oh, I don't know. Just a feeling I get. They feel more serene."

Octavian lifted one eyebrow, looking skeptical. "Emmi, my dear, you're becoming positively spiritual these days."

She laughed, and as if at the sound the Squat lifted its fern ears and wiggled its turnip nose and turned to regard us with the same intent curiosity as we regarded it. Or at least, so we assumed.

Daringly, Emmi lifted a hand and waved to it.

And it lifted one of its legs and copied the gesture.

Emmi broke out into a wide grin. Even Octavian smiled.

"First contact," I said.

"Only for me," said Emmi. "The first was that little one that came up to Peng-Hsin."

The Squat lowered the leg and ambled back into the galleries and disappeared.

"Maybe they're not standoffish," said Octavian in a tone trembling with revelation. "Maybe they're just polite."

"Octavian," I said, "they did ask us to come here, after all. Why wouldn't they be polite?"

"They're just so—reserved."

"Maybe they just don't want to offend us," said Emmi.

"Or us to offend them," I added, thinking of Bax. And, like the devil, he appeared stage left and shuffled over to us. He looked hungover.

"Hey you, uh—" He faltered, running a hand through the tangled black frizz of his hair. "—uh, Witch, you. Can you get me something to drink?"

Emmi got that set look on her face. "Sorry," she said, hunching a shoulder up against him. "I'm working on my lines."

He began to say something more, but then unlucky Patrick came in stage left. "I need something to drink," said Bax, and burped loudly, and Patrick spun on his heel and went out again. Mercifully, Bax followed him.

It was a bad day for a run-through. Feeling caged-in got on everybody's nerves. We either had to stay locked into the warren of rooms behind the stage or else watch the action through the one-way curtain in the musician's gallery, and tempers ran shorter than usual, which is saying something. Bax couldn't keep his hands off the witches, and he kept ignoring his blocking and getting in front of the king. The ambient emotional temperature went up about fifty degrees. Except Peng-Hsin, who evidently had huge reserves of calm to draw from. She wore her silver leaf necklace like a badge of courage and grace, and even in her love scenes with Bax managed to steer away from his groping hands without seeming to avoid him.

Watching them act together was a study in contrasts. The true test, we had long since decided, of Peng-Hsin's professionalism was the way she could play a loving Lady Macbeth to Bax's Macbeth. "'And I feel now the future in the instant,'" she says in Act I Scene V.

"'My dearest love,'" he said—and bit her.

And I mean really bit her.

Peng-Hsin let out a startled and most unprofessional shriek. She jerked away from him, slapping a hand up over her cheek. A drop of blood leaked out from between her fingers, then another, then a third. She lowered her hand to reveal her cheek; his teeth marks showed clearly, as well as the blood welling up in a rough semicircle, where his bite had broken her skin.

All hell broke loose. Cheri gasped so loudly she might as well have shouted, and we all began talking and shouting at once. Peng-Hsin spun and ran off the stage. Patrick hurriedly called for a break, and Cheri and Emmi ran downstairs to minister to Peng-Hsin. El Directore laid his head down on the edge of the stage. For an instant, I thought he was hiding tears of sheer frustration.

Bax licked his lips. "Hey, what about the rest of my scene?" he demanded.

El Directore lifted his face—dry-eyed, I noted—and lifted a hand to signal to Patrick, sealed into the control booth in the back of the house. "Cast meeting on stage in thirty minutes," he said. He circled the stage and vanished into his office. Bax left for his dressing room.

In thirty minutes, we gathered like vultures, all of us. Peng-Hsin, flanked by Emmi and a militant-looking Cheri, had a patch of skin-meld covering the wound on her cheek. Patrick and El Directore arrived. Then we waited for another five minutes. Bax ambled out finally, looking bored.

"I think," said El Directore in a low, irresolute voice, "that you owe an apology."

Bax sighed, looking put-upon. "All right, all right," he said briskly. "I'm sorry I brought the girls with me. It was a little tasteless, I know, since we're stuck here and you guys and gals can't possibly be getting the same quality of sex as I am, but hey, we're all professionals here, and this is one of the things you have to go through to do this kind of work."

Struck dumb, we merely stared at him.

El Directore, surprisingly enough, spoke first. "Er, ah," he said forcefully. "Well, then, I'll make this short. We have our premiere performance in seven days. Tomorrow we do a full tech run-through and the day after we go to dress."

And so we did. Bax restrained himself to minor and individual acts of cruelty, like twisting arms and hitting people with his sword and the usual groping. And of course we couldn't say anything. He *had* apologized, after all, or so El Directore reminded us. And he was a Star.

Bruised and battered we got ready for the premiere.

Still, it was hard not to get excited, especially as the galleries and the yard filled up with hooting Squats. Against all rules, I snuck up to the musician's gallery to catch a glimpse, and found Emmi and—mark my soul!—Peng-Hsin there, gazing wide-eyed out at our audience.

"Gee," said Emmi on an exhalation. "Wow."

The shield was marvelously transparent and gave us a clear view of the house and the two thousand aliens. Ivory fern ears furled and unfurled to some unknown rhythm and the Squats almost seemed to be bobbing, like a swelling sea, as they waited. For an instant, I felt their excitement as much as my own.

"I can't believe I'm doing this," Peng-Hsin said, and then covered her mouth with a hand and laughed the kind of laugh a child gives on Christmas Eve when she sees the lit tree and all the presents for the first time.

"Places," said Patrick through the inner-mike system. As we went down the stairs, we met M. Caraglio coming up, to watch from this hidden vantage point.

"Good luck," he said, and we all winced in horror, and like a good diplomat he caught our reaction and added, stumbling, "Oh, ah, break a leg." We retreated in some disorder back to our rightful places.

House lights down. Stage lights up. A desert Heath. Thunder and lightning. Enter three Witches.

It went well. Our audience was attentive; even through the shield we heard their taut silence. And we had come together as a cast over the last five weeks, especially since we all felt the same way about one person in particular. There is nothing like shared disgust to bring focus to a play, especially the Scottish play with its bloody villain.

He was the villain, and we made him so.

Birnam Wood did come toward Dunsinane, and Macbeth met, at long last, the man who was of no woman born. They fight.

We watched through the door plackets set up, like the gallery curtain, to be a one-way view port. Was it possible that we would finish as we were meant to, that we wouldn't be embarrassed in front of these intent aliens, that we, the first human artists they had encountered, could give a command performance and prove ourselves worthy of the title of artists?

Octavian gave a little groan. Of course not. Even here, in the actual performance, Bax had to ruin it. The two men lock swords corps-a-corps; it was supposed to come to naught—they break away from each other and the fight continues to its inevitable end. But Bax, damn him, had to throw it. With Kostas unsuspecting, it was possible for Bax to throw and twist and wrench Macduff's sword out of his grip. The sword clattered to the stage with awful finality.

There was a terrible pause. Macbeth holds Macduff at his mercy.

Like an animal cornered by a cobra, we were too paralyzed with fear and—yes, with sheer hatred—to close our eyes.

And Bax stepped back, allowing Kostas to pick up his lost sword. Bax opened his arms to receive the death blow. And then he added the crowning insult of adding a line to Shakespeare.

"Oh, my God," he said. His eyes widened. Kostas, no fool, ran him through between the body and the arm.

Bax fell and lay as still as death. It was the best acting he'd done the whole time. Entering with the other lords, I was impressed despite myself.

Meanwhile, Macduff had, as we staged it, staggered off and collapsed where we could conveniently overlook him until Siward sees him.

The final lines passed smoothly. They had never run quite so strongly before. "'Hail, King of Scotland!'" we cry, and Malcolm makes his final speech. Curtain.

The shield dimmed until it was opaque. Through it, we heard the muted hooting of the Squats. We panted, waiting for the rest of the cast to come out for the curtain call. Bax didn't move.

"Sulking," muttered Octavian.

Jon-Jon, who'd been too long in the business to let a grudge mar the professionalism of the moment, hurried over to help him up. He bent. He shook Bax. He shook him again. He gave a little cry and straightened up.

"I think he's dead."

He *was* dead.

M. Caraglio burst onto the stage, took one look at the situation, and barked, "No curtain call! Where's—"

El Directore stumbled out from the back as well. He wrung his hands together. "What will we do? What will we do? What if the studio withdraws their funding? This is terrible. How did this happen? He had no heart condition listed on his health records."

"We must go apologize at once to the Squanishta," said Caraglio. "Can you imagine the kind of misunderstandings this could foster?"

All at once I recalled that if the Squats really were empathic, then our audience was absorbing an entire second performance here and now, despite the curtain being nominally closed.

Finally, thank goodness, Patrick appeared and took everything in hand. "Yu-Sun, you and Octavian carry off—ah—" Even his aplomb was shaken by the sight of Bax lying there dead. "Move him back to his dressing room. And for the Goddess' sake, get the three good-time girls out of there."

"If you'll come with me," said Caraglio to El Directore. "And perhaps a representative from the actors as well."

They all looked at me. Ah well, once a go-between, always a go-between. I walked in a daze with the other two around front to the communications lock. I was not surprised to find that three Squanishtas had arrived before us, fern ears unfurled, their bodies otherwise motionless as they hunkered down on the other side of the lock wall.

Both sides spoke at the same time. "We beg your pardon—"

Both sides stopped.

After a moment of polite silence, Caraglio began again. "Please, your excellencies, be assured that the tragedy that has happened here today is a complete mystery to us. I must beg your pardon for this terrible disruption. We hope you will forgive us and allow us a suitable time to—ah—recover and explain."

They hooted. The translation crackled through the screen. "It was a wise and well-thought play. Please do not think we did not appreciate it, or think that it failed in any way although there was this slight mishap. One has only to hear the words to understand their meaning."

The middle one shifted forward—somewhat rashly, I thought, given what I'd seen of them—and pressed its turnip nose up against the cloudy lock wall as if to make sure we understood how important the next remark was. As if to make sure that we understood that it understood. "My voice is in my sword."

There was a pause while the three jockeyed for position, and the rash one was shouldered to the back as if the other two were aghast at its rudeness.

"We hope," continued one of the other two—I couldn't be sure which—"that in this small way we have spared you the distress of failing to complete your work of art."

"Oh, my God," said Caraglio, an eerie echo of Bax's last words. "I've got to get back to the office."

"I don't understand," said El Directore. But *I* did.

Caraglio made polite farewells, and we exited the lock. We wound our way back through the protected corridor. Caraglio left at once. I went back to the stage.

Bax was still lying there, dead. Through the tiring house doors, thrown open, I could hear shrieking and wailing from the back: The lamias were objecting to being thrown out of the dressing room—I couldn't tell if they were also mourning for their lost patron, or only their privileges—and Yu-Sun and Octavian didn't want to touch the body until they had somewhere to take it.

"But what happened?" demanded Cheri. Emmi wiped tears—not, I think, for Bax personally, but for the shock of it all—from her cheeks. Peng-Hsin stood with regal dignity. The others crowded together for comfort.

"The Squats did it," I said. "I'd guess that they sort of used their empathic powers to make his heart seize up, or something."

"But why?" asked Peng-Hsin quietly.

"Isn't it obvious what the outcome of the play is? Isn't it almost a ritualistic act, the entire thing? And they wouldn't have built this—" I waved at the theater, "—if they didn't care about us doing well. If they didn't want us to succeed. And they read, from us, the object of the play was for Macbeth to die. How embarrassing for us if we failed to accomplish that act, in our first performance for them."

Mercenary Cheri suddenly stifled a giggle behind a hand.

I shrugged. What else was there to say? The real cleanup would be left for the diplomats. And it was funny, in a black kind of way.

I looked over at Bax. The rest of them did, too. It's hard not to look at a corpse, especially when he's the one person in the room that everyone was wishing dead just half an hour before.

"They were just trying to be helpful."

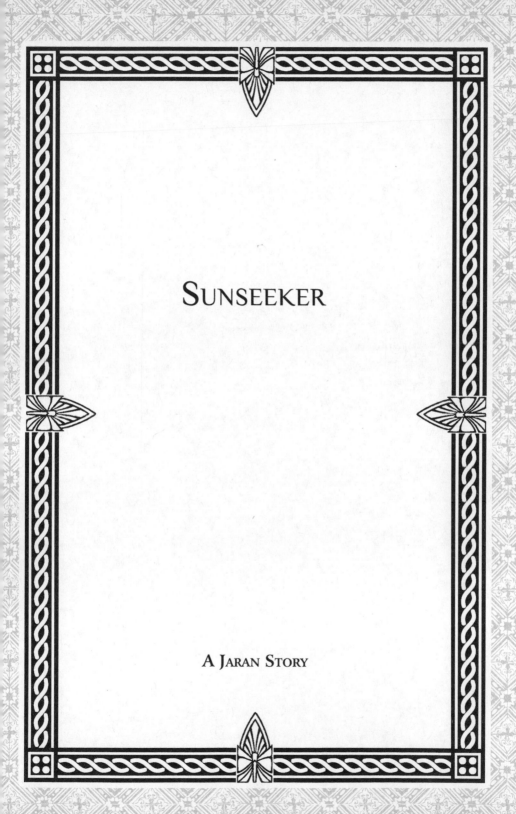

SUNSEEKER

A JARAN STORY

They gave her a berth on the *Ra* because her father was famous, not because he was rich. Wealth was no guarantor of admittance to the ranks of the fabled Sunseekers; their sponsors didn't need the money. But there was always a price to be paid, due at unforeseen intervals decided upon by the caprice of the self-appointed leaders of their intrepid little band of a dozen or so sunseeking souls.

Right now, they had started in on Eleanor, an elegant girl of Bantu ancestry whose great-grands had made their fortune gunrunning along the Horn of Africa (so it was rumored) and parlayed that wealth into a multisystem import/export business.

"Sweetkins, I'm not sure I can stand to look at much more of that vegetable fiber. Cotton!"

"Algodón!" Akvir mimicked Zenobia's horrified tone. "I thought we'd agreed to wear only animal products."

"If we don't hold to standards," continued Zenobia, "it'll be soybric next. Or, Goddess forbid, nylon."

Eleanor met this sally with her usual dignified silence. She did not even smooth a hand over her gold and brown robe and trousers, as any of the others would have, self-conscious under scrutiny. Rose suspected her of having designs both on Akvir—self-styled priest of the Sunseekers—and on the coveted position of priestess. Of course it went without saying that the priestess and the priest had their own intimate rites, so after all, if one was priestess, one got Akvir—at least for as long as his sway over the group held.

"That a tattoo?" Eun-soo plopped down beside Rose. The seat cushion exhaled sharply under the pressure of his rump. He was new on board, and already bored.

"What?" Self-consciously, remembering—how could she ever, ever forget?—she touched the blemish on her cheek.

"Brillianté, mon," he said, although the slang sounded forced. He was too clean-cut to look comfortable in the leather trousers and vest he sported. He looked made up, a rich-kid doll sold in the marketplace for poor kids to play pretend with. "Makes a nice statement, cutting up the facial lines with a big blotch like that. It's not even an image tattoo, like a tigre or something, just a—" He paused, searching for words.

She already knew the words.

Blot. Eyesore. Flaw. Birth defect.

She was irrevocably marred. Disfigured. Stained.

These words proclaimed by that famous voice which most every soul on this planet and in most of the other human systems would recognize. Golden-tongued and golden-haired. Chrysostom. Sun-struck. El Sol. There were many epithets for him, almost all of them flattering.

"Ya se ve!" Eun-soo clapped himself on the head with an open hand, a theatrical display of sudden insight. "You're the actor's kid, no? You look like him—"

"If never so handsome," said Akvir, who had bored of his pursuit of Eleanor.

"No one is as handsome as my father," snapped Rose, for that was both her pride and her shame.

"I thought there were operations, lasers, that kind of thing." Eun-soo stared at her with intense curiosity.

To see a blemished person was rare. To see one anywhere outside the ranks of the great lost, the poor who are always with us in their shacks and hovels and rags even in this day of medical clinics in every piss-poor village and education for every forlorn or unwanted child, was unheard of.

"Yeah, there are," she said, standing to walk over to Eleanor's seat. She stared out the tinted window of the ship. The Surbrent-Xia solar array that powered the engines made the stubby wings shimmer as light played across them. Here, above the cloud cover that shrouded the western Caribbean, the sun blazed in all its glory. Ever bright. Up here, following the sunside of the Earth, it was always day.

"You going to see the big head?" asked Eleanor in her lean, cultured voice. "The archaeological site is called after a saint. San Lorenzo."

"Yah." She put on the bored, supercilious tone used by the others. "Sounds very slummy, a little Meshko village and all."

"Quaint," said Eleanor. "The right word is *quaint*. It's gauche and rude to say *slummy*. Saint Lorenzo was one of the seven deacons of the Church of Rome, this would be back, oh, way back during the actual Roman Empire when the old Christian—" She said it like a girl's name, Kristie-Anne. "—Church was just getting a toehold in the world. Like all of them, he was made a martyr, but in this case he was roasted over a gridiron."

"Over a football field?"

"No." Eleanor laughed but not in a mocking way. She never used her knowledge to mock people. "No, it's like a thing with bars you grill fish on. But the thing is, that he was burned, roasted, so you see perhaps he was in a prior incarnation related to some form of sun worship. The fire is a metaphor for the sun."

"Oh. I guess it could be."

Eleanor shrugged. Rose could never understand why someone like *her* ran with the Sunseekers. Only except they were, so everyone said, the jettest black of all social sets, the crème de la crème, the egg in the basket, the two unobtainable birds in the bush. That was why her father never came running after her after she ran away to them.

Wasn't it?

She had seen a clip about two months ago as the night-bound told time, for up here in the constant glare of the sun there was only one long, long day. He had referred to her in passing, with that charmingly deprecatory smile.

"Ah, yes, my daughter Rosie, she's on a bit of a vacation with that Sunseeker crowd. That's true, most of them are older, finished with their A-levels or gymnasium or high school. But. Well. She's a high-spirited girl. Fifteen-year-olds always know just what they want, don't they? She wanted the Sunseekers." The rest went without saying: The very most exclusive social set, don't you know. Of *course* my child would be admitted into their august ranks.

He had only to quirk his lips and shift his elbow on the settee to reveal these confidences without any additional words passing his lips. His gift consisted, as so many, many, many people had assured her as she grew up and old enough to understand what their praise meant, of the ability to suggest much with very little.

But her elder siblings—long since estranged from the family—called it something else: the ability to blind.

The engines thrummed. Rose set a hand against the pane that separated them from the air and felt the shudder and shift that meant they were descending. In the lounge, Eun-soo flipped through the music files. The mournful cadences of an old Lennon-McCartney aria, "I'll Follow the Sun," filled the cabin. Eleanor uncoiled herself from her seat and walked, not without a few jerks to keep her balance as the pitch of the *Ra* steepened, back to the dressing and shower room, shared indiscriminately by the almost two dozen inhabitants of the ship. She did dress, stubbornly, in fabrics woven from vegetable forebears. Rose admired her intransigence but more than that the drape of the cloth itself, something leather cured in the sun or *spinsil* extruded and spun and woven in the airless vaults of space stations could not duplicate. Style, her father always said, sets apart those who are watchable from those fated only to watch. It puzzled and irritated him that his daughter had no sense of style, but she had only ever seen him actually lose his temper once in her entire life: that day in the hospital when her mother had finally backed her up after she stubbornly refused, once again and for all, to undergo the simple laser operation that would remove the port-wine stain.

He wanted to be surrounded by handsome things.

The ship turned as it always did before landing, going down rump first, as some of the Sunseekers liked to say. Her hand on the pane warmed as the rising sun's rays melted into her palm. They cut down through the clouds and the sun vanished. She shivered. Gray boiled up past her, receded into the sky as they came down below the clouds and could see the ground at last.

Rugged mountains rose close beside the shore of the sea, receding behind them. The lowlands were cut by ribbons of muddy water beside which sprawled the brown and white scars of human habitation, a village. The old ruined Zona Arqueológica lay on higher ground, the centerpiece of a significant plateau.

It had been a week since they'd last landed. The texture of the earth, the lush green carpet of vegetation, amazed her anew. She blinked on her computer implant to get an identification of the river. A map of the region came up on the screen, not a real screen, of course, but the simulation of a screen that according to her tekhnē class was necessary for the human eye to register information in this medium. Sim-screens for primates, they would shout when they were younger, but it was only funny when you were young enough to find the parallel between simulation and simian amusing, like being six years old and getting your first pun. But like a bad pun or a particularly obnoxious advert balloon, the phrase had stuck with her.

The lacy mat of tributaries and rivers floated in front of her eyes on the sim-screen, spidery lines that thickened and took on weight and texture, finally moving and melding into the landscape until they seemed to become one. Disoriented, she blinked the screen off and staggered back to find a couch for the final deceleration. The couch snaked a pressure net across her, calibrated to her weight, and she tilted her head back, closed her eyes, and waited for landing. Aria segued into gospel hymn, "Where the Sun Will Never Go Down." Eun-soo hummed along in a tuneless tenor until Zenobia told him to shut up. Finally, they came to rest; the altosphere shades lightened away and everything went quiet. She felt giddy. When she stood up, her feet hummed with the memory of engines and she swayed as she walked, following the others to the 'lock and out onto the plank that led down to the variegated earth of the night-bound, the lost souls—all fourteen billion of them—who must suffer the sad cyclic subjugation to the endless and cruel celestial reminder of our human mortality, night following day following night. Or so Akvir put it. He had not seen night for nine months.

The village itself was so small, so pathetic, and so obviously isolated that at first Rose thought they had inadvertently stumbled across the set for an actie, the kind of thing her father would star in: *Knight in the Jungle*, in which the liberation priest, Father Ignatius Knight, gives his life to bring literacy and the World Wide Web to a village under the censorious thumb of a Machine Age dictator, or *Dublo Seven, Heritage Hunter*, in which the legendary M. Seven seeks out and recovers artifacts hidden away by greedy capitalists so that he can turn them over to the Human Heritage Foundation, whose purpose is to preserve human culture for the all, not the few.

The air was so hot and humid that even her eyelids began to sweat. It stank of mud and cow dung. A pair of skeletally thin reddish dogs slunk along the tree line. Curious villagers emerged from houses and from the outlying fields and trees to converge on the landing spot, a cleared strip beside a broad concrete plaza marked by a flagpole and a school building. There were sure a lot of villagers, more than she had expected. A dilapidated museum stood by the river at one end of the road. The great Olmec head Akvir wanted to see rested in the central courtyard, glimpsed from here as a rounded bulk behind wrought-iron gates. Right now Akvir was head-hunting, as he called it. In the last month they had stopped at Easter Island, Mount Rushmore, Angkor Thom, and the Altai Mountains.

A bird called from the trees. Eleanor stepped out in front of Akvir and raised a hand, shading her eyes against the early morning sunlight. But she was looking west, not east into the rising sun.

Rose felt more than heard the cough of an antiquated pulse gun. Dogs yipped frantically, yelping and bolting, but the sound that bit into their hearing was too high for humans to make out.

"Effing hells!" swore Eun-soo behind her. "My transmitter's gone dead."

Who used pulse guns these days? They were part of the lore of her dad's acties, like in *Evil Empire* where he played a heroic West Berliner.

Eleanor shouted a warning as a dozen of the villagers circled in on them. Were the natives carrying rifles? For a second, Rose stared stupidly, thoughts scattering. What was going on?

Akvir started yelling. "Back on board! Back on board! Everyone back on board!"

Voices raised in alarm as the Sunseekers blundered toward the ramp, but their escape was cut short by the unexpected barking stutter of a scatter gun. A swarm of chitters lit on her skin. She dropped to her knees, swatting at her face and bare arms.

The crash of a riot cannon—she knew the sound because her father had just premiered in a serial actie about the Eleven Cities labor riots of fifty years ago—boomed in her ears. A blast of smoke and heat passed right over her. As people yelled and screamed, she lost track of everything except the stink of skunk gas settling onto her shoulders and the prickles of irritant darts in the crooks of her elbows and the whorls of her ears.

Someone grabbed her wrist and yanked her up into the cloud. Her eyes teared madly, melding with sweat; the smoke blinded her. But the grip on her arm was authoritative. She stumbled along behind, gulping air and trying to bite the stinging sour nasty taste of skunk gas from her lips. The rough dead earth of the lander clearing transformed between one step and the next into the soggy mat of jungle; an instant later they were out of the smoke and running along a sheltered path through the trees.

Eleanor held her by the wrist and showed no sign of letting go. She didn't even look back, just tugged Rose along. Rose blinked back tears and ran, hiccuping, half terrified and half ready to laugh because the whole thing was so absurd, something out of one of her father's dramas.

Instead of elegant gold-and-brown robe and trousers, Eleanor now wore a plain but serviceable ice-green utility suit, the kind of clothes every and any person wore when they did their yearly garbage stint. Woven of soybric, it was the kind of thing fashionable Sunseekers wouldn't be caught dead in.

What had happened to the others?

She tried to speak but could only cough out a few hacking syllables that meant nothing. The skunk gas burned in her lungs, and the awful sodden heat kept trying to melt her into a puddle on the dirt path, but still Eleanor dragged her on at a steady lope while Rose gasped for air—such as it was, so thick you could practically spoon it into a cup—and fought to stop the stitch in her side from growing into a red dagger of pain. Her ears itched wildly.

They hit a steep section, and got about halfway up the slope before her legs started to cramp.

"Got . . . to . . . stop . . . ," she gasped finally and went limp, dropping to her knees on the path. Her weight dragged Eleanor to a halt.

"Shit," swore the woman. "Damn, you *have* been spending too long with the do-nothing rich kids. I thought you weren't like them. Don't you ever get any exercise?"

"Sorry." It was all she could manage with her lungs burning from exertion and skunk gas and her elbows and knees itching as badly as her ears from the irritant darts, but she knew better than to scratch at them because that only spread the allergens, and meanwhile she had to bite her lip hard and dig her nails into her palms to stop herself from scratching. The skunk gas and the pain made her eyes tear, and suddenly she wanted nothing more than for her mother to be there to make it all better.

That made her cry more.

"Aw, fuck," said Eleanor. "I should have left you back with the others. Now *come on*."

She jerked Rose upright. Rose had enough wind back that it was easier to go than to stay and deal with the itching and the burning lungs and the pain again, the memory of watching her mother die of a treatable medical condition which she was too stubborn to get treatment for because it went against the traditional ways she adhered to. Rose touched her blemished cheek, the habitual gesture that annoyed her father so much because it drew attention to the blemish and thereby reminded them both of those last angry weeks of her mother's dying.

Sometimes stubbornness was the only thing that kept you going.

Eleanor settled into a trot. Rose gritted her teeth and managed to shuffle-jog along behind her, up the ghastly steep path until it finally, mercifully, leveled off onto the plateau. The jungle smelled rank with life but it was hard enough to keep going without trying to look around her to see. Wiry little dappled pigs, sleek as missiles, scattered away into the underbrush.

By the time they came out into the clearing—the Zona Arqueológica—Rose's shift was plastered to her body with sweat. Eleanor, of course, looked cool, her utility suit—wired to adjust for temperature and other external conditions—uncreased and without any of the dark splotches that discolored Rose's shift. At the tuft of hairline, on the back of the woman's neck, Rose detected a thin sheen of sweat, but Eleanor brushed it away with a swipe of her long fingers.

They stepped out from under the cover of jungle onto a broad, grassy clearing, and at once an automated nesh-recorded welcome program materialized and began its preprogrammed run.

"Buenos días!" it sang as outrageously bedecked Olmec natives danced while recorded pre-Hispanic musicians played clay flutes, ocarinas, and turtle shells, and shook rain sticks, beating out rhythms on clay water pots. Fat, flat-faced babies sat forward, leaning onto their knuckles like so many leering prize fighters trying to stare down their opponents, and jaguars growled and writhed and morphed into human form in the interstices of the background projections. "Bienvenidos al Parque Arqueológico Olmeca! Aquí es San Lorenzo, la casa de las cabezas colosales y el lugar de la cultura Madre de las civilizaciónes Mexicanas! Que idioma prefieren? Español. Nahuatl. Inglés. Japonés. Mandarín. Cantonés. Swahili." The chirpy voice ran down a cornucopia of translation possibilities.

The place looked like a ruin, two reasonably modern whitewashed buildings stuck on the edge of the clearing with doors hanging ajar and windows shattered, three thatched palapas fallen into disrepair. A herd of cattle grazed among the mounds, which were themselves nothing much to look at, nothing like what she expected of the ancient and magnificent home of the mother culture of the Mexican civilizations.

But the technology worked just fine.

Eleanor gave her a tug. They followed a path across the ruins toward the larger of the two whitewashed buildings. Every few meters 3-D nesh projections flashed on and began their fixed lecture-and-display: The old ruins came to life, if nesh could be called life or perhaps more correctly only the simulation of life.

Poles stuck in the ground were the storehouses for the treasure— the knowledge, the reconstruction of the past. Between them, quartered, angled, huge image displays whirled into being: here, a high plaza topped with a palace built of clay with a stone stele set upright in front; there, one of the great stone heads watching out across a reconstructed plaza with the quiet benevolence of a ruler whose authority rests on his unquestioned divinity; suddenly and all of a piece, the entire huge clearing flowering into being to reveal the huge complex, plaza, steps, temples, and courtyards paved with green stone, as it might have looked three thousand years before during the fluorescence of this earliest of the great Mesoamerican civilizations.

Eleanor yanked her inside the building. Rose stumbled over the concrete threshold and found herself in a dilapidated museum, long since gone to seed with the collapse of the tourist trade in nesh reconstructions of ancient sites. All that investment, in vain once the novelty had worn off and people stopped coming. Most tourists took their vacations upstairs, these days. Mere human history couldn't compete with the wonders of the solar system and the adventure promised by the great net, and affordable prices, that opened out into human and Chapelli space.

The museum had been abandoned, maybe even looted. Empty cases sat on granite pedestals; tarantulas crowded along the ceiling; a snake slithered away through a hole in the floor.

"Shit," swore Eleanor again. "Did it have bands? Did you notice?"

"Did what have bands?"

"The snake. Goddess above, you ever taken any eco courses? There are poisonous snakes here. *Real* poisonous snakes." Dropping Rose's wrist, she stuck two fingers in her mouth and blew a piercing whistle. Rose clapped hands over her ears, but Eleanor did not repeat the whistle. Her ears still itched and with her fingers there in such proximity, Rose could not help but scratch them but it only made them sting more. She yanked her hands away and clutched the damp hem of her shift, curling the loose spinsil fabric around her fingers, gripping hard.

A trap in the floor opened, sliding aside, and a ladder unfolded itself upward out of the hole. Moments later a head emerged which resolved itself into a woman dressed in an expensive business suit, solar gold knee-length tunic over plaid trousers; the tunic boasted four narrow capelets along its shoulders. She also wore tricolor hair, shoulder length, all of it in thin braids of alternating red, black, and gold—the team colors of the most recent Solar Cup champions. Rose knew her fashionable styles, since in her father's set fashion was everything, and to wear a style six months out of date was to invite amused pity and lose all one's invitations to the best and most sunny parties. This woman was fashionable.

Two men, dressed in utility suits, followed the woman up from the depths. Both carried tool cases.

"Eleanor," said the businesswoman. They touched palms, flesh to flesh, by which Rose saw—though it already seemed likely given her entrance—that this was the real woman and not her nesh analogue. "All has gone as planned?"

"I'm afraid not. The *Ra* is disabled, but we seem to have run into some competition." She gestured toward the two men. "Go quickly. We'll need to transfer the array to our hover before they can call in reinforcements." They hurried out the door.

"And this one?" asked the businesswoman. "Is this another of your ugly puppies?"

Rose wanted desperately to ask, *What are you going to do with me?* but the phrase stuck in her throat because it sounded so horribly like a line in one of her dad's acties. Maybe she sweated more, because of nerves, but who could tell in this heat?

"When the operation is over, we can let her go." Eleanor spoke almost apologetically. "I just wanted her out of the way in case there are complications. And she's a good rabbit to keep in the hat, in case there *are* complications. She's the daughter of the actor."

"Oh!" the businesswoman crooked one eyebrow in surprised admiration. "Oh! Well, I mean, there was so much publicity about it. She's not nearly as pretty. And that—" She stopped herself, although her hand brushed her own cheek in the place the mark stood on Rose's face. She lowered the hand self-consciously. "Vasil Veselov is your *father?*"

Rose didn't know what to say. She nodded.

The businesswoman waved invitingly toward the trap. "Put her in the basement."

Eleanor took hold of Rose's wrist again and pulled her toward the extruded ladder.

"Go on."

A touch of cool air drifted up from the hole, quickly subsumed in the heat. Rose glanced toward the businesswoman, now making calculations on a slate; she had apparently forgotten about her partner and Rose, much less the great actor.

"Go on." Eleanor snapped her fingers. "Go."

Rose climbed down. Beneath lay a basement consisting of a corridor and six storerooms. Water beads like the sweat of the earth trickled down the concrete walls. Eleanor shoved her along to the end of the row where a door stood ajar. Waving Rose in, she began to push the door shut.

"What are you going to do with me?" Rose demanded, finally succumbing to the cliché.

"Nothing with you. You're a nice kid, Rose, unlike those obnoxious spoiled brats who have nothing better to do with their time than waste it circling the Earth as if that somehow makes them more especial than the rest of humanity. Like they're paying for it! What a sick advertising stunt! I didn't want you to get hurt."

"What did you mean about keeping a rabbit in the hat?"

"Planning for contingencies. It doesn't matter. Anyway, I really admire your father. *Sheh.*" She gave a breathy whistle. "I had a holo of him in my room when I was younger. You'll be free to go in an hour or so."

"What's going on?" This request, Rose knew, would be followed by the Bad Guy telling all, because Bad Guys always told all. They could never resist the urge to reveal their diabolical plans.

Eleanor slammed the door shut—not because of anger but because the door wasn't hung true and was besides swollen from moisture and heat and that was the only way to get it to shut. Left alone in the room, Rose tested the door at once, but it didn't budge. She stuck her ear to the keyhole but heard nothing, not even footsteps. At least the itching had begun to subside. Finally, she turned and surveyed her prison.

It was an ugly room with concrete rebar walls, a molding ceiling sheltering two timid tarantulas in one corner, and a floor made up of peeling rectangles of some mottled beige substance. The tarantulas made her leery, but she didn't fear them; she knew quite a bit about their behavior after living on the set of *Curse of the Tarantula*. The rest of the room disquieted her more. The floor wasn't level, and the tiles hadn't been well laid, leaving gaps limned with a powdery white dust. Two old cots made up of splintery wood supports with sun-faded, coarse burlap stretched between stood side by side.

Ugly puppies.

She winced, remembering the businesswoman's casual words. In one corner someone had set up a shrine on an old plastic table, one of whose legs had been repaired with duct tape. Two weedy-looking bouquets of tiny yellow-and-white flowers resting crookedly in tin pots sat one on either side of a plastic baby doll with brown hair, brown eyes, and painted red lips. The doll was dressed in a lacy robe, frayed at the hem and dirty along the right sleeve, as though it had been dragged through dirt. A framed picture of the same doll, or one just like it, lay at its feet, showing the doll sitting on a similar surface but almost smothered by offerings of flowers and faded photographs of real children, some smiling, some obviously ill, one apparently dead. Someone had written at the bottom of the picture, in black marker in crude block letters, *El Niño Doctor*. Doctor Baby Jesus.

Rose knew something about the Kristie-Anne religion. Jesus was the god-person-man they prayed to, although she had never quite understood how you could be both a god and a mortal human being, more or less, at the same time. "The gods are everywhere," her mother used to say. "They are what surround us, Mother Sun and Father Wind, Aunt Cloud and Uncle Moon, Sister Tent and Brother Sky, Daughter Earth and Son River, Cousin Grass and Cousin Rain. Gods are not people."

Yet some people thought they could be. Rose sniffled. She wanted to cry, but because crying made her eyes red and puffy, unattractive, she had learned to choke down tears. But she was still frightened and alone.

She tongued the emergency transponder implanted in her jaw, but it was dead, killed by the crude blast of the pulse gun. Everything else she had left on the *Ra*.

"I want my daddy," she whispered.

A flash of light winked in the staring eyes of the baby doll. It began to talk in a creaky, squeaky, distorted voice, stretched, tenuous, and broken with skips and jerks.

"Si habla Español diga, 'si.' Nahuatocatzitziné, amehuantzitzin in anquimocaquilia, in anquimomatilia inin tlatolli, ximotlatoltican. If you speak English, say 'yes.'"

Startled, she took a step back just as she said, scarcely meaning to, "Yes."

"Please wait while I connect you. A medical technician will be with you in a moment. Catholic Medical Services provides sponsored medical advice free of charge to you, at any hour of the day or night. Help will be given whatever your circumstance. Please wait. When the doctor comes on line, state your location and your—"

A fluttering whir scattered the words. After a pause, a barely audible squeal cut at her hearing. The doll spoke again, channeling a real person's voice.

"Please state your location and need. I am M. de Roepstorff, a medical technician. I am here to help you. Are you there?"

She was so stunned she forgot how to speak.

Patiently, the voice repeated itself. "Are you there?"

"I am. I am! I'm a prisoner—"

"Stay calm. Please state your location and we'll send a team out—"

Static broke the connection.

There was silence, stillness; one of the tarantulas shifted, moving a few centimeters before halting, suspended, to crowd beside its fellow.

"Are you still there?" Rose whispered. "Are you there? Yes. Yes, I speak English."

"Please wait while I connect you. The medical technician will be with you in a moment. Catholic Medical Services. . . ."

The doll's recorded voice squealed to a bruising pitch, ratcheted like gears stripping, and failed.

A grinding, grating noise startled her just as the kiss of cooler air brushed her face. The table rocked, tilted to the right, teetered, and crashed sideways to the ground, spilling pots, flowers, picture, and doll onto the concrete floor. Nothing broke, except the floor. One of the rectangular tiles wobbled, juddered, and jumped straight up. Rose leaped back, stumbled against a cot, and sat down hard as a man dressed in dark coveralls with a crude burlap mask concealing most of his face emerged from a hole in the floor, climbing as if going up a steep staircase. All she could see was his mouth, undistinguished, and his eyes, the iris dark and the white bloodshot with fatigue or, maybe, some barbaric drug intoxication.

"Quién eres?" he demanded. He carried a scatter gun. With it trained on her, he called down into the hole. "Esperabas un prisionero? Es una muchacha."

Be cool and collected. That's what her father always did in the acties.

"Eleanor put me here," she said aloud as calmly as she could, hoping Eleanor was on their side. She was so scared her knees actually knocked together. "I don't know what's going on. Please don't hurt me. I'm only fifteen. I can't identify you because you're wearing that mask, so I'm no threat to you."

The man climbed out of the hole, crossed to the door, and tested it.

"It's locked," she said helpfully. "I'm a prisoner. I'm not a threat to you."

He cursed, trying the handle a second time. A nasty-looking knife was thrust between belt and coveralls, blade gleaming.

A second figure—head and shoulders—popped up in the hole. This one wore an old com-cap, with a brim, the kind of thing people wore before implants and sim-screens rendered such bulky equipment unnecessary. She was also holding an even more ancient rifle, the kind of thing you only saw in museums next to bazookas, halberds, and atlatls under the label *Primitive But Deadly*.

Had the pulse gun killed her implant? She didn't think so; it was technologically far more sophisticated than plain jane location/communication transponders and phones. She blinked to trigger it, caught a sigh of relief as the screen wavered on. Sotto voce, she whispered, "Spanish translator, text only. Cue to voice."

The one with the rifle, dark eyes unwinking as she studied her captive, lifted her chin dismissively.

"Termina ya." A woman's voice, hard and impatient. Words scrolled across the sim-screen as Rose pretended she couldn't understand them. "No podemos dejarla aquí ... *cannot leave her here. She will go and tell of our hiding place.*"

Adrenaline made her babble, that and her father's maxim: Keep them talking. How successfully he'd used that ploy in *Evil Empire!* "Is that an AK-47? I've seen one in nesh but never in the flesh before. Is that a thirty-round magazine?"

"No puedo hacerlo ... *I cannot do it,*" said the first terrorist. "*She is too young. She is too innocent.*"

"*No [untranslatable] is innocent.*"

The itch on her ears returned until she thought it would burn the lobes right off, but she clutched the side of the cot hard and the pain of the wood digging into her hands helped keep her mind off the itching and the fear.

Don't give in to it. Once you gave in, the itching—or the fear—would consume you.

"*Look at the mark on her face. It is real. It is not a tattoo of a rich child. No one with this type of mark on the face can be our enemy.*" He took three steps, close enough to hit her or stab her, but his touch—fingers brushing the blemish—was oddly gentle.

"*I shoot the street dogs,*" said his companion. "*Things like this will be the death of you.*"

"*Then how will the outcome change? I do not like to kill. And I question what this locked door signifies. It should have been left open.*"

"*We've been outmaneuvered. There's another party involved who wants the same thing we want.*"

He nodded decisively, the kind of man used to being obeyed. She knew that look, that stance, that moment when the choice was made. She had seen her father play this role a hundred times: the charismatic leader, powerful, strong, ruthless but never quite cruel. "*I thought we could use this as a base for storage, but it is compromised. Let us go. They will not take our prize so easily.*"

"*The girl will make a good hostage.*"

"*You believe so? I do not believe that anyone preoccupies themselves over her.*" He turned to Rose and, for the first time, spoke in the Standard she knew. "Does any person care for you? Will any person pay a ransom for your rescue?"

Was it fear that made her tremble convulsively? She snorfled and hiccuped as she tried to choke down her sobs. Never let them see you cry. Never let them see how unattractive you are. How scared you are.

Beautiful people were less likely to die.

He gestured with the scatter gun, the universal sign: *Get up.* She got up, shakily, followed them down a short wooden ladder into a low tunnel weeping dirt, hewn out of rock and shored up by a brace work of boards nailed together and old rebar tied tightly with wire. Down here they paused, she crouching behind the fearsome woman while above she heard the man moving things before he climbed back down into the tunnel and levered the tile into place. The woman spoke a command to make a hazy beam of light shine from her cap.

Rose blinked down through menus, seeking information on San Lorenzo. It ran across the lower portion of the sim-screen as the man poked her in the back with his gun.

Miocene sedimentary formations . . . salt domes . . . the entire San Lorenzo site is a great mound in itself, largely artificial in construction.

"Ándale," he said.

The screen read: *Move now. Imperative!*

They crawled until her hands were scraped raw and her knees were scuffed, reddened, and bleeding in spots. Neither of them spoke again, and she dared not speak until spoken to. Not soon enough, gray light filtered in. They pushed out through undergrowth into a ravine where a pair of young people waited, their faces concealed by bandannas tied across nose and mouth, their bodies rendered shapeless by loose tunics worn over baggy trousers. They each carried a rifle, the wood stock pitted and the curved magazine scarred but otherwise a weapon well oiled and clean. The man spoke to them so softly that Rose could not hear him, and as she and her captors hiked away, she glanced back to see the other pair disappear into the tunnel.

They followed the rugged ground of the ravine through dry grass and scrub and past stands of trees on the ridgeline above, Rose stumbling but never getting a hand up from her captors. The sun stood at zenith, so hot and dry beating down on them that she began to think she was going to faint, but they finally stopped under the shade of a ceiba and she was allowed to drink from a jug of water stashed there. The ceramic had kept the water lukewarm, although it stank of chlorine. Probably she would get some awful stomach parasite, and the runs, like the diamond smuggler had in *Desert Storm*, but she knew she had to drink or she would expire of heat exhaustion just like the secondary villain (the stupid, greedy one) had in *Knight in the Jungle*, despite the efforts of Monseigneur Knight to save him from his own short-sighted planning.

The man had brought Doctor Baby Jesus with him, bound against his body in a sling fashioned from several bandannas so that his hands remained free to hold the scatter gun. The bland doll face stared out at her, eyes unblinking, voice silent. As her captors drank, they talked, and Rose followed the conversation on the screen that was, of course, invisible to them.

"We have to fight them," he said wearily.

"I knew others would be after the same thing," she said. "Bandits. Profiteers. Technology pirates."

He chuckled. "And we are not, Esperanza? We are better?"

"Of course we are better. We want justice."

"So it may be, but profit makes justice sweeter. It has been a long fight."

Distant pops, like champagne uncorked in a faraway room heard down a long hall, made the birds fall silent.

"Trouble," Esperanza said.

Rose had hoped they might forget her if she hung back, pretending not to be there, but although Esperanza bolted out at a jog, the man gestured with his gun for Rose to fall in behind his comrade while he took up the rear. The pops sounded intermittently, and as they wound their way through jungle, she tried to get her bearings but could make no sense of their position. After a while, they hunkered down where the jungle broke away into the grassy clearing she had seen before, the Zona, but now a running battle unfolded across it, figures running or crouching, sprinting and rolling. A single small-craft open cargo hover veered from side to side as the person remote-controlling it—was that him in the technician's coveralls?—tried to avoid getting shot. All the cattle were gone, scared away by the firefight, but there were prisoners, a stumbling herd of them looking remarkably like Akvir and the other Sunseekers, shrieking and wailing as they were forced at gunpoint to jog across the Zona. The nesh-reenactments had spun into life; from this angle and distance she caught flashes, a jaguar skin draped over a man's shoulders as a cape, a sneering baby, a gaggle of priests dressed in loincloths and feather headdresses.

The firefight streamed across the meadow so like one of her dad's acties that it was uncanny. Unreal. Shots spat out from the circling jungle, from behind low mounds. A man in technician's coveralls—not the one controlling the cargo hover—toppled, tumbled, and lay twitching on the ground. She couldn't tell who was shooting at whom, only that Eun-soo was limping and Zenobia's shift was torn, revealing her pale, voluptuous body, and Akvir was doubled over as though he had been kicked in the stomach, by force or by fear. She didn't see Eleanor or the woman in business clothes. A riot cannon boomed. Sparks flashed fitfully in the air, showering down over treetops. It boomed again, closer, and she flattened herself on the ground, shielding her face and ears. Esperanza shouted right behind her, but without her eyes open she couldn't see the sim-screen. A roaring blast of heat pulsed across her back as, in the distance, people screamed.

Now the cavalry would ride in.

Wouldn't they?

The screams cut off, leaving a silence that was worse than pain. She could not even hear any birds. The jungle was hushed. A footfall scuffed the ground beside her just before a cold barrel poked her in the back.

"Get up," said the man.

She staggered as she got to her feet. No hand steadied her, so she stumbled along in front of him as he strode out into the Zona. Esperanza had vanished.

The cargo hover was tilted sideways, nose up, stern rammed into the ground so hard that it had carved a gash in the dirt. Bugs swarmed in the upturned soil. The technician still clutched the remote, but he was quite still. A youth wearing trousers, sneakers, and no shirt stood splay-legged over the dead man. The boy's mouth and nose were concealed by a bandanna, black hair mostly caught under a knit cap pushed crookedly up on his head. He had the skinny frame of a teenager who hasn't eaten enough, each rib showing, but his stance was cocky, even arrogant. He stared at Rose as she approached. Her sim-screen had gone down, and his gaze on her was so like the pinprick of a laser sight, targeting its next victim, that she was afraid to blink. He said something to the man, who replied, but she couldn't understand them.

The Sunseekers lay flat on their stomachs on the ground a short ways away, hands behind their heads. Three more bandanna-wearing men waited with their ancient rifles and one shotgun held ready as six newcomers jogged toward them across the clearing, but the newcomers paid no attention to the prisoners. Like the bugs in moist dirt, they swarmed the hover.

"March," said the commander, gesturing with his scatter gun.

No one complained as their captors prodded the Sunseekers upright and started them walking, but not back the way they had come.

Akvir sidled up beside Rose. "Where'd you go? What's going on?"

The boy slammed him upside the head with the butt of the rifle. Akvir screamed, stumbled, and Rose grabbed his arm before he could fall.

"Keep going," she whispered harshly. "They killed some of those people."

The youth stepped up, ready to hit her as well, but when she turned to stare at him defiantly, he seemed for the first time really to see the blemish that stained her face. She actually saw him take it in, the widening of the eyes, and heard him murmur a curse, or blessing. She had seen so many people react to her face that she could read their expressions instantly now.

He stepped back, let her help up Akvir, and moved on.

"No talking," said the commander. "No talking."

No one talked. Soon enough they passed into such shelter as the jungle afforded, but shade gave little respite. They walked on and on, mostly downhill or into, out of, and along the little ravines, sweating, crying silently, holding hands, those who dared, staggering as the heat drained them dry. After forever, they were shepherded brusquely into a straggle of small houses with sawed plank walls and thatched roofs strung alongside a tributary river brown with silt, banks densely grown with vegetation. An ancient paved road that was losing the battle to cracks and weeds linked the buildings. Someone still drove on it: At least four frogs caught while crossing the road had been flattened by tires and their carcasses desiccated by the blast of the sun into cartoon shapes. Half covered by vines, an antique, rusting pickup truck listed awkwardly, two tires missing. Three of the houses had sprouted satellite dishes on their roofs, curved shadows looming over scratching chickens and the ever-present dogs. A few little children stared at them from open doorways, but otherwise the hamlet seemed empty.

A single, squat building constructed of cement rebar anchored the line of habitation. It had a single door, through which they were herded to find themselves in a dimly lit and radically old-fashioned Kristie-Anne church.

A row of warped folding chairs faced the altar and a large cross on which hung a statue of a twisted and agonized man, crowned with a halo of plastic thorns. None of the chairs sat true with all four legs equally on the floor, but she couldn't tell if the chairs were warped or if the concrete floor was uneven. It was certainly cracked with age, stained with moisture, but swept scrupulously clean. A bent, elderly woman wearing a black dress and black shawl stood by the cross, dusting the statue's feet, which were, gruesomely, pierced by nails and weeping painted blood.

The old woman hobbled over to them, calling out a hosanna of praise when the commander deposited Doctor Baby Jesus into her arms. As the Sunseekers sank down onto the chairs, dejected, frightened, and exhausted, the caretaker cheerfully placed the baby doll up on the altar and fussed over it, straightening its lacy skirts, positioning the plump arms, dusting each sausagelike finger.

"What kind of place *is* this?" whispered Eun-soo. "I didn't know anyone lived like this anymore. Why don't they go to the cities and get a job?"

"Maybe it's not that easy," muttered Rose, but no one was listening to her.

The commander was pacing out the perimeter of the church, but at Rose's words he circled back to stand before them. "You don't talk. You don't fight. We don't kill you."

Zenobia jumped up from the chair she had commandeered. "Do you know who we are?" Her coiffure had come undone, the careful sculpture of bleached hair all in disarray over her shoulders, strands swinging in front of her pale eyes. "We're important people! They'll be looking for us! You can't just—! You can't just—!"

He hit her across the face, and she shrieked, as much in outrage and fear as in pain, remembered her torn clothing, and sank to the ground moaning and wailing.

"I know who you are. I know what you are. The great lost, who have nothing to want because you have everything. So you circle the world, most brave of you, I think, while the corporation gets free publicity for their new technology. Very expensive, such technology. Research and development takes years, and years longer to earn back the work put into it. Why would I be here if I didn't know who you are and what you have with you?"

"What do you want from us?" asked Akvir bravely, dark chin quivering, although he glanced anxiously at the young toughs waiting by the door. For all that he was their leader, he was scarcely older than these teens. Behind, the old woman grabbed Doctor Baby Jesus and vanished with the doll into the shadows to the right of the altar.

The commander smiled. "The solar array, of course. That's what that other group wanted as well, but I expect they were only criminals."

"You'll never get away with this!" cried Zenobia as she clutched her ragged shift against her.

Rose winced.

The commander lifted his chin, indicating Rose. He had seen. "You don't think so either, muchacha?"

"No," she whispered, embarrassed. Afraid. But he hadn't killed her because she had, in his eyes, a kind of immunity. "I mean, yes. You probably won't get away with it. I don't know how you can escape surveillance and a corporate investigation. Even if the Constabulary can't find you, Surbrent-Xia's agents will hunt you down in the end, I guess." She finished passionately. "It's just that I hate that line!"

"That *line?*" He shrugged, not understanding her idiom.

"That line. That phrase. 'You'll never get away with this.' It's such a cliché."

"Oh! Oh! Oh! You—you—you—*defect!*" Zenobia raked at her with those lovely, long tricolor fingernails. Rose twisted away as Akvir grabbed Zenobia by the shoulders and dragged her back, but Zenobia was at least his height and certainly as heavy. Chairs tipped over; the Sunseekers screamed and scattered as the toughs took the opening to charge in and beat indiscriminately. Eun-soo ran for the door but was pulled down before he got there. What envy or frustration fueled the anger of their captors? Poverty? Abandonment? Political grievance? She didn't know, but sliding up against one wall she saw her chance: an open path to the altar.

She sprinted, saw a curtained opening, and tumbled through as shouts rang out behind her, but the ground fell out beneath her feet and she tripped down three weathered, cracked wooden steps and fell hard on her knees in the center of a tiny room whose only light came from a flickering fluorescent fixture so old that it looked positively prehistoric, a relic from the Stone Age.

A cot, a bench, a small table with a single burner gas stove. A discolored chest with a painted lid depicting faded flowers and butterflies, once bright. The startled caretaker, who was standing at the table tinkering with Doctor Baby Jesus, turned around, holding a screwdriver in one hand. A chipped porcelain sink was shoved up against the wall opposite the curtain, flanked by a shelf—a wood plank set across concrete blocks—laden with bright red-and-blue plastic dishes: a stack of plates, bowls, and three cups. There was no other door. It was a blind alley.

The light alternately buzzed and whined as it flickered. It might snap off at any moment, leaving them in darkness as, behind, the sound of screams, sobs, and broken pleas carried in past the woven curtain.

What if the light went out? Rose bit a hand, stifling a scream. She hadn't been in darkness for months.

This was how the night-bound lived, shrouded in twilight. Or at least that's what Akvir said. That's what they were escaping.

Saying nothing, the old woman closed up the back of Doctor Baby Jesus and dropped the screwdriver into a pocket in her faded skirt. She examined Rose as might a clinician. Rose stared back as tears welled in her eyes and spilled because of the pain in her knees, but she didn't cry out. She kept biting her hand. Maybe, possibly, they hadn't noticed her run in here. Maybe.

In this drawn-out pause, the shadowy depths of the tiny chamber came slowly clear, walls revealed, holding a few treasures: a photo of Doctor Baby Jesus stuck to one wall next to a larger photo showing a small girl lying in a sick bed clutching the doll itself, or a different doll that looked exactly the same. A cross with a man nailed to it, a far smaller version of the one in the church, was affixed to the wall above the cot. Half the wall between shelf and corner was taken up by a huge, gaudy low-tech publicity poster. Its 3-D and sense-sound properties were obviously long since defunct, but the depth-enhanced color images still dazzled, even in such a dim room.

Especially in such a dim room.

Her father's face stared at her, bearing the famous ironic, iconic half smile from the role that had made him famous across ten star systems: the ill-fated romantic lead in *Empire of Grass*. He had ripped a hole in the heart of the universe—handsome, commanding, sensitive, strong, driven, passionate. Doomed but never defeated. Glorious. Blazing.

"Daddy," she whimpered, staring up at him. He would save her, if he knew. She blinked hard. The sim-screen wavered and, after a snowy pause, snapped into clear focus.

The curtain swept aside and the commander clattered down the three wooden steps. One creaked at his weight. He slid the barrel up her spine and allowed it to rest against her right shoulder blade.

"Ya lo veo!" cried the old woman, looking from Rose to the poster and back to Rose. She began to talk rapidly, gesticulating. When the commander said nothing, did not even move his gun from against Rose's back, she clucked like a hen shooing feckless chicks out of the way and scurried over to take Rose's hands in hers.

"Su padre? Si, menina?" *Your father? Yes?*

Then she turned on him again with a flood of scolding. The rapid-fire lecture continued as the commander slowly backed up the stairs like a man retreating from a rabid dog.

"What kind of fool are you, Marcos, not to recognize this girl as the child of El Sol? Have you no kind of intelligence in your grand organization, that it comes to an imprisoned old woman like me—" She spoke so quickly that the translation program had trouble keeping up. *". . . que ve las telenovelas y los canales de chismes . . . who watches the soap operas and the channels of gossip [alternate option] entertainment channels to tell you that you should have known that more people would be on that ship than the children of businessmen?"*

The old woman finished with a dignified glare at her compatriot. *"This girl will not be harmed."*

"That one?" He indicated the actor, then Rose. *"This child? How is it possible?"* He touched his own cheek, as if in echo of the stain on hers. *"The children of the rich do not have these things."*

"God's will is not ours to question," she answered.

He shrugged the strap of his scatter gun to settle it more comfortably on his shoulders. *"Look at her. Even to look past the mark, she is not so handsome as El Sol."*

"No one is as handsome as my father," retorted Rose fiercely, although it was difficult to focus on the poster since the image blended with the words scrolling across the bottom of her sim-screen.

They both looked at her.

"Ah." Señora Maria waved a hand in front of Rose's face. Her seamed and spotted palm cut back and forth through the sim-screen. Swallowing bile, reeling from the disrupted image, Rose blinked off the screen.

"Imbécil! Que estabas pensando? Esta niña, de semejante familia! Por supuesto que lleva implantada la pantalla de simulación. Ahora ya ha entendido cada palabra que has dicho, tu y los otros brutos!"

Without effort, she turned her anger off, as with a switch, and presented a kindly face to Rose, speaking Standard. "Por favor, no use the seem . . . what it is you call this thing?"

"Sim-screen."

"Sí. Gracias."

The señora looked up at the commander and let loose such a stream of invective that he shrank back against the curtain momentarily, but only to gather strength before he began arguing with her. Their voices filled the chamber; Rose covered her ears with her hands. Mercifully, the itching had subsided completely. She dared not blink the screen back on, so she cowered between them as they argued fiercely over her head. One of the young toughs stuck his head in but retreated as the señora turned her scolding on him.

Through it all, her father watched, half amused, half ready to take action, but frozen. It was only his image, and his image could not help her.

In the church, the screaming had subsided and now Rose heard whimpering and weeping as orders were given.

"Go! Go!"

"But where—!" The slap of a gun against flesh was followed by a bruised yelp, a gasp, a sob, a curse—four different voices.

"Go!"

Shuffling, sobs, a crack of laughter from one of the guards; these noises receded until they were lost to her ears. The Sunseekers had been taken away.

"Are you going to kill them?" she whispered.

They broke off their argument, the commander frowning at her, the señora sighing.

"We no kill—we do not kill." The señora spoke deliberately, careful over her choice of words. "They bring us better money if the parents buy them from us."

"But kidnappers always get caught in the end."

The commander laughed. "Fatalism is the only rational worldview," he agreed.

"In the stories, it may be so, that these ones are always caught," continued the señora. "We take a lesson, a borrowing, from our own history, but this thing called ransom we use for a different purpose than the ones who stole the children."

"What purpose?" Rose demanded. She had gone beyond worrying

about clichés. "I see the poverty you live in. Are you revolting against the inequality of League economics? Is this a protest? Will you use the array to help poor people?"

The commander's sarcastic laugh humiliated her, but the señora smiled in such a gentle, world-weary way that Rose suddenly felt lower than a worm.

"Hija, I am the inventor of one of the protocols used in this solar array that powers the ship you children voyage on. These protocols were stolen from me and my company by operatives of Surbrent-Xia. In much this same way as we steal it back, but perhaps not with such drama." She gestured toward the poster and the stunningly handsome blond man who stared out at them, promising dreams, justice, excitement, violence, and fulfillment. "No beautiful hero comes to save me. The law listens not to my protests. Surbrent-Xia falsifies their trail. They lay certain traps for me, and so the corporation and patent laws convict me, and I am dropped into the prison. There I sit many years while they profit from what I helped create. All these years I plot my revenge, just like in this story, *The Count of Monte Cristo*, no? Was not your father starring in this role a few years ago? So now we have the array in our hands. I leave—have left—markers in my work. Like this stain upon your cheek, those markers identify what is mine. With these markers, no one can mistake it otherwise. With this proof—"

"And the children to draw attention to us," added Marcos.

"—we will get attention to this matter."

"But you'll be prosecuted for kidnapping!"

"Perhaps. If we get publicity, if a light is shined onto these criminal actions made by Surbrent-Xia ten years ago, then we are protected by exposing them. Do you see? Surbrent-Xia 'got away with it'—they say this in the telenovelas and the acties, do they not?—they got away with it last time because it was hushed."

"They kept it quiet," said Marcos. "No one knew what they had done."

"But why did you have everyone beat up? What did Akvir and Zenobia and Eun-soo and the others have to do with anything or what anyone did ten years ago?"

The old woman nodded, taking the question without defensiveness.

She seemed a logical soul, not an emotional revolutionary at all. "We have not harmed them, only bruised them. It is in answer to—it is in—"

"—retaliation—" said Marcos.

"That is right. Excuse my speech. I have been many years in isolation on these false charges. The world, and my enemies, did not play nice with my relatives in the old days. We are not the only ones who play hardball. An eye for an eye."

"But they're innocent!"

"They are all the children of shareholders. That is why they come to ride on the beautiful ship, to be made much of. You do not know this?"

"I just thought—" She faltered, knowing how unbelievably stupid anything she said now would sound.

I didn't know.

Hadn't her father talked and talked and talked about the Sunseekers, how very sunny and fashionable they were? Hadn't she run away to get his attention, so he would be surprised she had gotten into some group so very jet, so very now, even with her disfigurement?

"They are lucky you came to them," continued the señora. "Of what interest are the children of shareholders, except to themselves and their parents and their rivals? But you are the child of El Sol. When you came aboard, everyone is watching."

"Good publicity is good advertising," added Marcos sardonically. "This is what we all want."

Right now, she just wanted her daddy.

"It still doesn't seem right." They hadn't bitten her yet. They hadn't bruised her, not more than incidentally. "To hurt them. They aren't bad, just—" *Just pointless.* "And what about Eleanor? I mean, the other ones."

"The other ones?" asked Señora Maria.

"The competition," said Marcos. "We don't have a positive ID on them yet, but I presume they are working for Horn Enterprises. Horn wants the array, too."

"Horn filed a wrongful-use claim against Surbrent-Xia for theft of their cell-transduction protocol."

"Which came to nothing. But they had a grievance, too, and plenty of markets out-system who won't ask too many questions about whether they have patent rights. This is so much useless speculation, now. We got the array. They did not."

How could they analyze the day's nasty work so dispassionately, as though it were the script of an actie in development?

"You killed two men! Eleanor was really nice to me!" Another second and she would be blubbering, but she held it in, sniffing hard, choking down the lump in her throat.

"We killed no one," said Marcos angrily. "Just two hurt, in the Zona, but they are only stunned."

"There was blood."

"There is always blood. This other, this Eleanor—no sé. There was a hover that flew off once they saw they had lost."

"What about me?"

Señora Maria gestured.

Rose eased up to her feet, wincing with pain as her knees unbent. "Ow."

"We should let this pauvre go home. She can use the call-up in Anselmo's house."

"The Constabulary will come," said Rose.

"Not soon," said Marcos. "Your flight plan registers a stop at San Lorenzo to visit the museum. They do not know otherwise. They will not be expecting you to leave for some hours. We have time."

"Ándale," said Señora Maria.

Marcos shrugged, sighed, and motioned with his gun for Rose to follow him. Perhaps he wasn't the commander after all, or perhaps he was just behaving as men ought—as her mother used to say: respectful toward the grandmother of his tribe.

The house belonging to Anselmo sat riverside, one door facing the road and a second overlooking the bank. A small receiver dish tilted precariously on the roof, fastened to the topmost beam. They had to walk up two steps made of stacked concrete blocks to get onto the elevated wood floor inside. Like the entire village, the little one-room hut was untenanted, except for a burlap cot without bedding, a table, and a bright yellow molded plastic bench pitted with pinprick holes. An old-fashioned all-in-one sat closed up on the table. Looking out through the other door, Rose watched as a loose branch drifted past on the water and snagged on a tree, while Marcos powered up the box and tilted up its view screen.

"Where did you take the others?" she asked. The driftwood tugged loose from its trap and spun away down the river.

He mulled over the controls, not looking up at her, although a hand remained cupped over the scatter gun's readouts. "They will be safe." He spoke to the box in his own language. Lights winked on the console. "Here. You may enter a number. Use the keypad."

She had a priority imavision code, of course, that identified her immediately to her father's secretary since her father never ever took incoming calls personally.

A whir. A beep.

"One moment, Miss Rose. Putting you through."

The secretary did not turn on his own imavision. Although the screen remained blank, Marcos stepped away and turned sideways to give her privacy and to keep an eye out the door. But even so he started when that famous golden voice spoke across the net in a tone richly affectionate and so precisely intimate, using the pet name for her that no other dared speak.

"Mouse?"

"D—d—daddy."

"I didn't expect you to call." He hadn't turned on the imavision. Maybe he was getting dressed or entertaining visitors. Maybe today he just didn't want to see her face. "It's been so long since we talked. I've missed your voice so much, here at home. All your little quiet noises in the background. It seems so empty here without you puttering around. How are you? Are you having fun up there in the eternal sunshine?"

"N—n—no, Daddy. I'm just—" She faltered, glancing toward Marcos, who still stared out the door at the sluggish river.

"You should be in—" A pause. A voice murmured in the background. "San Lorenzo Tenochtitlán. Some kind of a museum there, I see. Olmec civilization. Pride of the collection is a large stone head! What will you children think of next!"

"D—daddy." She wiped away a tear with the back of her hand.

"Are you crying, little mouse?"

"Daddy, I'm in trouble."

A pause.

A silence.

"Rosie, you *have* a contraceptive implant—"

"No, Daddy. No. I'm in *trouble*. Please come get me."

"Come get you?"

The screen flashed, a nova of light that spread, swirled with color, coalesced, and formed into an image of his face. The most famous face in the universe, so people said.

He looked put out.

"Come get you?" he repeated, as though she just told him he had turned purple. "I have three interviews today to support the opening of *Judge Not*. The ratings aren't as strong as they need to be. After this a meeting with the Fodera-Euler Consortium to sign the contract for the Alpha Trek 3-D."

He glanced back over his shoulder, speaking to a person not within the imavision's range. "What's the time frame?"

"Ten days," said his secretary, off screen.

"And the Consortium wants to begin recording—?"

"Fourteen days."

He turned his brilliant smile on her. He had the most glorious blue eyes, warming as he stared intently at her through the imavision, as though he were really right by her side, comforting her infant sobs on a stormy night. "Listen, Rosie. You hang in there for ten more days and I'll come get you. We'll make the most of it, father and daughter reunited, that kind of thing. Let Joseph know when your first landfall comes once the ten days are up. I'll be there to meet you. No need to mention you called now and arranged it in advance. Pretend you're surprised to see me."

"But, Daddy—"

"Are you in danger of being killed?"

Marcos had not shifted position, nor his grip on the scatter gun. "No. I don't think so, but—"

"Rosie. Mouse." His tone softened, lowered. "You know I will never let you down. But as long as your life or health isn't in danger, it can't be done for ten days. I made an arrangement with Surbrent-Xia that you would stick with the Sunseekers for three months. You weren't to know, but I trust you can see how important it is that I fulfill my contracts. You know how tight money is these days—"

"You 'made an arrangement' with Surbrent-Xia! I thought I ran away!"

"You did. You did. Fortunately, you picked the right place to run away to."

"But I want to come home, Daddy. Now. I need to. You don't understand—"

"It can't be done. If I break the contract, we get nothing. Just ten more days."

She hated that tone. "But, Daddy, the—the—" What was Marcos going to do? Shoot her with a nonlethal weapon while her father could see and hear? "I *am* in danger. An awful thing happened. We landed at San Lorenzo and then we were attacked by corporate raiders who wanted the solar array. And then we were caught in the crossfire when another group who had their technology stolen stole it back. I thought they were bandits, first, but it's all some kind of corporate espionage that goes back for years and years, like they're always stealing things, bits or patents from each other and stealing them back and selling them out-system—"

"Joseph! Joseph!" He turned away from her, showing his profile. Always aware of the camera's eye, he never lifted his chin because it distorted the angle of his nose. "Did you get that down? We need more information! This could be a gold mine if we get it into development first. I see it as a serial. A family saga about ruthless technology pirates!" His beautiful face loomed again, grinning at her. "What a good girl, Rosie! I knew I could count on you! Is there someone there I can talk to, who would be interested in a contract? Who has inside information?"

"A contract!" She recoiled from the table, sure she hadn't heard him right.

Marcos was already pushing past her. "What kind of contract? Is there money? Is there publicity? We'll need leverage. . . ." He leaned down in front of the view screen, introduced himself, and began bargaining.

"Daddy!"

"Love you, Rosie! Now, M. Marcos. First we'll need an all-hours contact number—"

"Daddy!"

Marcos ignored her, and her father had forgotten her. Amazingly, Marcos didn't even object, or seem to notice, as Rose left the hut and trudged down the dirt street back to the church, her only companions half a dozen chickens and two mangy dogs who circled warily, darting in to sniff at her heels until she kicked one. Yelping, they raced away.

The church remained empty, abandoned, six chairs overturned and one drying bloodstain, nothing serious.

Only bruised.

Señora Maria had departed from the little back chamber, but she had left Doctor Baby Jesus sitting upright on the shelf, plump arms spread in a welcoming gesture as Rose halted in front of him.

"I speak English," said Rose, her voice choked. Tears spilled, but she fought against them. "I need help."

A whirr. A squeal.

"Please wait while I connect you."

A different voice, this time. A woman. "Please state your location and need. I am M. Maldonado, medical technician. I am here to help you."

A pause.

"Are you there?" The voice deepened with concern.

She found her voice, lost beneath the streaming tears. "I just need your help. Can you connect me to my brother? His name is Anton Mikhailov. He's an advocate at—uh—" She traced down through her sim-screen. "This is his priority number."

"Are you in danger?"

"No. No. Kind of. Nobody's going to kill me. But I'm lost—I'm sorry. I know this isn't what you're here for. I know this isn't important. You must get thousands of life-and-death calls every hour."

The woman made a sound, like a swallowed chuckle. "This system was defunct twenty years ago, but we keep a few personnel on-line because of people who have no other access. It's all right. It's all right. What's your name?"

"Rose."

"Please stay on the line, Rose. I'll get a channel to your brother. If you want to talk, just say something. I'm here listening."

She had nothing to say. She fidgeted anxiously, swallowing compulsively, each time hoping to consume the lump that constricted her throat.

Dull, officious Anton, who worked as an advocate for troubled children or some other equally worthy and boring vocation. He had left the family fourteen years before, when she was only a baby. He had been raised by someone else, by traitors, thieves, defectives. He had rarely visited his parents and then only on supervised visitations, because the ones who had stolen him had poisoned his mind. Yet he always wrote to her four times a year on the quarter, chatty notes detailing the obscenely tedious details of his life. Each note repeated at the end the same tired cliché: Call me any time, Rosie. Any time.

She didn't really know him. He could as well have been a stranger. Why should he do anything for her if her father didn't even care enough to come when she asked? Wasn't this the only time she had ever asked anything of her father?

All these years she had never asked.

"Patching you through," said helpful M. Maldonado. "M. Mikhailov, I'll remain on stepped-back link if you need me."

"Thank you. Rose?" Anton had a reedy tenor, rising querulously. She didn't know him well enough to know if he was surprised, annoyed, or pleased.

"Anton, it's Rose."

I'm Rose, she thought, half astonished, hearing her own voice speak her own name: a small, isolated voice, lost in the dim room, in the old church, in the forgotten village, in the green jungle, on the common earth beneath clouds that covered the all-seeing eye of the sun. It was amazing anyone could hear her at all. She sobbed, choking on it, so it came out sounding halfway between a cough and a sneeze. She could barely squeeze out words.

"Please, come get me."

"Of course, Rose. Right away. Where are you?"

"I'm all alone."

The buzz of the fluorescent lamp accompanied her other companion: the solitude, not even a mouse or a roach. The world had emptied out around her. For an instant, she thought the connection had failed until Doctor Baby Jesus whirred and Anton spoke again, an odd tone in his suddenly very even, level all-on-the-same-note voice.

"Did you call Dad?"

She sobbed. She could get no word past her throat, no comprehensible sound, only this wrenching, gasping, ugly sound.

The baby doctor sighed with Anton's voice. "He'll never love you, Rosie. Never. He can't love anyone but himself."

Fury made her articulate. "He *does* love me. He says so."

"Love is just another commodity to him. Maybe you get something, but there's always a price to be paid. I'm so sorry."

"He does love me."

"I'll come get you. Stay where you are, Rosie. I'll come. Will you stay? Will you be there? Don't go running off anywhere? You're not going to change your mind and follow those damned Sunseekers?"

"But he doesn't want me." She began to sob again, torn in two. She heard Anton reply, faintly, only maybe his voice wasn't any fainter and it was just her own weeping that drowned him.

"I'm coming, Rosie. Just tell me where you are."

She couldn't speak. She could only cry as their voices filtered through the creaky stutter of the baby doll's speaker.

"M. Mikhailov, I'm attempting to triangulate, but the intercessor has been partially disabled so I can't get a lock on your sister's position."

"Do you have a position on the Sunseekers?"

"The Sunseekers?"

"That ship with the new solar array technology. That grotesque advertising ploy—'you need never set foot in darkness again,' something like that. I can't remember their idiot slogan. Maybe in your line of work you don't have to keep up on the gossip rags—"

"Oh!" said the voice of M. Maldonado. "Isn't that the ship that the actor Vasil Veselov's daughter ran away to—"

"That one," interrupted Anton. "Do you have any way to get a fix on it? Here, let me see, they've got a public relations site that tracks—yes. Here it is. I've got it touched down in a municipio called San Lorenzo Tenochtitlán."

"I'll get all transport information for that region, but if you're in—ah—London, it will take you at least eighteen hours with the most efficient connections, including ground transport or hovercab."

"I have access to a private 'car. Rose. Rose?"

"I'm here." Amazing how tiny and mouselike her voice sounded, barely audible, the merest squeak.

"Rose, now listen. It says here there's an old historic museum in San Lorenzo Tenochtitlán. Do you know where that is? Can you get there and wait there?"

Of course, maybe it wasn't more than open welts sown with salt, discovering the truth: Her father had wanted her with the Sunseekers all along. Had manipulated her to get her there. Surbrent-Xia had paid him to get his daughter onto the ship in the most publicly scandalous way possible. He had set it all up, used her to get the money and the publicity.

"Daddy doesn't want me," she said, voice all liquid as the horrible truth flooded over her, soaking her to the bones.

"I know, Rosie. But I love you. I'm coming. Just tell me where you are. Tell me if you can get to the museum."

"Okay," she said, to say something because she had forgotten what words meant. A chasm gaped; she knelt on the edge, scrabbling not to tumble into the awful yawning void. What would she do now, if no one wanted her? Why would anyone want her anyway? Blemished, disfigured, stained. Ugly.

"Okay," he repeated, sounding a little annoyed, but maybe he was just worried.

Maybe he was actually worried about her. The notion shocked her into paying attention.

"Okay," he repeated. "I will be there in no less than six hours. You must wait by the museum. Don't go off with the Sunseekers, Rosie. I will meet you there, no matter what. Okay?"

"Okay."

Doctor Baby Jesus fell silent, having done his work. The fluorescent light flickered. A roach scuttled across the shelf, and froze, sensing her shadow. Her tears stained the concrete floor, speckles of moisture evaporating around her feet. She just stood there, stunned, unable to think or act. She couldn't even remember what she had agreed to. The light hummed. The roach vanished under the safety of the baby doll's lacy robe.

"Hola! Hey! You in here, chica?" The voice, male and bossy, spoke perfectly indigenous Standard. The young shirtless tough who had hit Akvir upside the head and cursed at him in Spanish pushed aside the curtain and ducked in. "There you are. I'm taking you back to the village."

"The village?" she echoed stupidly, staring at the rifle he held. Staring at him. He had pulled the bandanna down and the ski mask off, revealing a pleasant face marred only by the half-cocked smirk on his lips. He sounded just like one of her friends from home, except for the Western Hemisphere flatness of his accent.

"The village," he agreed, rolling his eyes. He did not threaten her with the gun. "Those Sunseeker people, they're all there, waiting to get picked up. You're supposed to go with them. We got to go, pronto. You know. Fast."

"That's by the old museum, isn't it?"

"Si," he said, eyes squinted as he examined her. "You okay?"

She wiped her cheeks. Maybe the dim light hid the messy cry.

"We got to go," he repeated, shifting his feet, dancing up two steps and pressing the curtain aside with his rifle as he glanced out into the church. "They got some 'cars coming in to get all of you out of here before sunset. You got to get out before sunset, right?"

"The museum," she said. "Okay. Is it far?"

"Four or five kilometers. Not far. But we got to go now."

She nodded like a marionette, moving to the strings pulled by someone else. She got her feet to move, one before the next, and soon enough as they came out of the church she found her legs worked pretty well, just moving along like a normal person's legs would, nothing to it.

A group of little boys played soccer along the dirt track of the hamlet, shouting and laughing as the ball rolled toward the river but was captured just in time. They turned off into the ragged forest growth before they passed the house where she had talked to her father; she saw no sign of Marcos except the flash of the ceramic satellite dish wired to the roof.

The boy walked in front of her. He had a good stride, confident and even jaunty, and he glanced back at intervals to make sure she hadn't fallen behind or to warn her about an overhanging branch and, once, a snake that some earlier passerby had crushed with repeated blows. It had bright bands on what she could see of its body, a colorful, beautiful creature. Dead now. She sweated, but he had a canteen that he shared with her—not water but a sticky sweet orange drink. A rain shower passed over them, dense but brief, to leave a cooling haze in its wake. All the time they walked, he kept the big plateau to their left, although they did not ascend its slopes but rather cut around them along a maze of dirt trails.

"Who was that woman?" she asked after a while.

"My great-aunt? She's some kind of crazy inventor, a genius, but she got into trouble with corporate politics. She was in prison for a long time, so I never saw her but I heard all about her. She was a real, uh, cabrona. Now maybe she is more nice."

Rose could think of nothing to say to this; in a way, she was surprised at herself for asking anything at all. Just keeping track of her feet striking the dirt path one after the other and all over again amazed her, the steady rhythm, the cushioning earth, the leaf litter.

The forest opened into a milpa, a field of well-grown maize interspersed with manioc. A pair of teal ducks flew past. When they cut around the edge of the field they saw a stork feeding at an oxbow of muddy water, the remains of the summer's flooding. Lowlands extended beyond, some of it marshy, birds flocking in the waters.

Another kilometer or so through a mixture of milpas and forest brought them to San Lorenzo Tenochtitlán on the shore of El Río Chiquito. Here the houses had a more modern look; half a dozen had solar ceramic roofs. There was a fenced-off basketball court and a school with a satellite dish and a plaza with a flagpole where the Sunseekers sat in a distraught huddle on the broad concrete expanse, staring anxiously westward while a few onlookers, both adults and children, watched them watching the horizon.

It was late afternoon. The sun sank quickly toward the trees.

The *Ra* sat forlornly on the grassy field behind the school, within sight of the old museum. Its stubby wings looked abraded, pockmarked, where the solar array had been stripped off.

"Rose!" Akvir jumped to his feet and rushed to her, his hand a warm fit on her elbow. "We thought we'd lost you!" He was flushed and sweating and a bruise purpled on his cheek, but he looked otherwise intact. He dragged her toward the others, who swarmed like bees around her, enveloping her with cries of excitement and expansive greetings. "You're the hero, Rose! They said you begged for our lives to your dad and he asked them to let us go. And they did! All because of your father! They're all fans of your father! They've all seen his shows. Can you get over it?"

She stood among them, drowned by them. All she could do was stare past their chattering faces at the boy who had led her here. He had fallen back to stand with a pair of village women, his arms crossed across his bare chest and the rifle, let loose, slung low by his butt. One of the women handed him a shirt; she seemed to be scolding him.

"Look!" screamed Zenobia, still clutching her torn clothing. "There they are! There they are!"

A pair of sleek, glossy hovercars banked around a curve in the river and leveled off by the boat dock, but after a moment during which, surely, the navigators had seen the leaping, waving, shouting Sunseekers, they nosed up the road to settle, humming, on the grassy field beside the disabled *Ra*. Akvir and the others jumped up and down, clapping and cheering, as the ramp of the closer 'car opened and three utility-suited workers, each carrying a tool kit, walked down to the ground. They ignored the crying, laughing young people and went straight for the *Ra*. After about five breaths, the second 'car's ramp lowered and a woman dressed in a bright silver utility suit descended to the base where she raised both hands and beckoned for them to board.

The sun's rim touched the trees. Golden light lanced across the village, touching the half-hidden bulk of the great stone head beyond the museum gates.

With a collective shout rather like the ragged cry of a wounded, trapped beast who sees escape at long last, the Sunseekers bolted for the 'car. Halfway there, Akvir paused, turned, and stared back at Rose, who had not moved.

"Aren't you coming?" he shouted. "Hurry! Hurry! They're fixing the *Ra*, but meanwhile we're going on. You don't want the sun to set on you, do you?"

"I'm not coming."

Everyone scrambled on board, one or two shoving in their haste to get away. Akvir glanced back at them, shifting from foot to foot, as Zenobia paused on the ramp to wave frantically at him. The sun sank below the trees.

He took two steps back, toward the hover, sliding away as they were all sliding away, following the sun. "You don't want to stay here with the night-bound? With the great lost?"

"It's too late," she said.

She had always belonged to the great lost. Maybe everyone does, each in her own way, only they don't want to admit it. Because no matter how diligently, across what distance, you seek the sun, it will never be yours. The sun shines down on each person indifferently. That is why it is the sun.

His fear of being caught by the approaching dark overcame him. He gave up on her and sprinted for the ramp; as soon as he vanished inside, it sealed up and the second hover lifted off with a huff and a wheeze and a high-pitched, earsplitting whine that set all the dogs to barking and whimpering until at last the 'car receded away over the trees, westward. The first hover remained, powering down. The technicians had lamps and instruments out to examine the scarred wings of the *Ra*.

Rose stared at the lines the grass made growing up in the cracks between the sections of concrete pads poured down in rectangles to make the huge plaza. The eruption of grass and weeds created a blemish across the sterility of that otherwise smooth expanse. In the village, music started up over by the museum where someone had set up a board platform in front of the fence. Guitars strummed and one took up a melody, followed by a robust tenor. A couple of older men began dancing, bootheels drumming patterns on the wood while their partners swayed in counterpoint beside them, holding the edges of their skirts.

The boy approached across the plaza, torso now decently covered by a khaki-colored long-sleeved cotton shirt that was, not surprisingly, unbuttoned halfway to the waist. He no longer carried the rifle.

"Hey, chica. No hard feelings, no? You want to dance?"

"I'm waiting for my brother," she said stoutly. "He's coming to get me. He said to wait right here, by the museum."

"Bueno," agreed the boy. "You want a cola? There's a tienda at the museum. You can wait there and drink a cola. I'll buy it for you."

Shadows drowned the village, stretched long and long across houses and grass and the concrete plaza. The transition came rapidly in the tropical zone, day to night with scarcely anything like twilight in between. She had not seen night for almost three months. Was it possible to forget what it looked like, or had she always known even as she tried to outrun it? Had she always known that it was the monster creeping up on her, ready to overtake her? The daylit gleam of the *Ra*'s wings was already lost to theft and now its rounded nose and cylindrical body faded as shadows devoured it.

Laughter carried from the museum as a new tune started up. The smell of cooking chicken drifted on the breeze. Dogs hovered warily just beyond a stone's throw from the women grilling tortillas and shredded chicken on the upturned, heated flat bases of big canister barrels.

"You want a cola?" repeated the youth patiently. "I'll wait with you."

"I'll take a cola," she said, surprised to find that all her tears had dried. She set her back to the west and trudged with him toward the museum, where one by one lamps were lit and hung up to spill their glamour over the encroaching twilight. A woman's white dress flashed as she danced, turning beside her partner.

"Your dad's El Sol?" he asked, a little nervously. "En verdad? I mean, like, we all see all his shows. It's just amazing!"

"Yeah."

Inside she was as hollow as a drum, but down and down as deep as the very bottom of the abyss, there was still a spark, her spark. The spark that made her Rose, no matter who anyone else was. It was something to hold on to when there was no other light. It was the only thing to hold on to.

"Yeah," she said. "That's my dad."

The sun set.

Night came.

A Simple Act
of Kindness

A Crown of Stars Story

Clouds massed, black and brooding, over the hills and the great length of forest that bordered the village of Sant Laon. They sat, almost as if they were waiting, and the wind died down and tendrils of mist and spatterings of rain were all that came of them through the day. At evening Mass, at a twilight brought early by the lowering clouds, Deacon Joceran spoke solemnly of storms called up by unnatural means, and she warned all the villagers to bar their doors and shutters that night and to hang an iron knife or pot above the door and a sprig of rosemary above the window.

"No matter who knocks, invite no one in. May the Father and Mother of Life bless us all this night."

So it was that not one soul saw the woman ride into town just ahead of the first fierce lashings of the storm. No one but Daniella.

The back door to the inn slammed shut and set the baby to crying, again, but it was only Uncle Heldric. His cloak seemed to sparkle in the lantern light of the hearth room of the farmhouse.

"Lord and Lady have mercy," said Aunt Marguerite, signing the circle of unity above her breast. "It looks like snow and ice on your cloak."

"And this midway through summer," said Uncle as he brushed the stain of snow off his shoulders. "'Tisn't a natural storm, Deacon was right in that." He cast his gaze round the room and found Daniella, where she sat on a stool in one shadowed corner, trying not to be noticed while she spun a hank of wool into yarn. "Girl, you take Baby upstairs and send down your brother. Seven of the sheep have got out and we must get them in before we lose the beasts to whatever walks in this storm. Night's coming on soon."

With the shutters closed and only a thin line of light showing around the cracks of the door and the window, it seemed like night already. A wind howled, whistling along the roof. Smoke from the hearth curled up toward the smoke hole in the roof, and a few flakes of snow spun into view in the patch of sky visible through the hole, only to melt at once, vanishing into the heat.

"I'll go," said Daniella. Upstairs lurked many things, not least her cousin Robert, who had been pestering her for months now, ever since her first bleeding came on her, and anyway, unlike her brother Matthias, she wasn't scared of storms. She liked them. They had life in them, even if Deacon Joceran warned that some storms had demons and other ungodly life swirling in their winds and rain. Better outside in a storm than trapped in here.

"Ach, well," said Uncle, knowing her well enough to forgive her impertinence. And she was better with the sheep, and not afraid of her own shadow, the way Matthias was. "You come, then. Put on a tunic over that. It's bitter cold out. And the sheep clipped and likely to freeze."

"It won't last," said Aunt, but she drew the circle again, not wishing to tempt the Evil Ones.

Uncle merely grunted and Daniella was quick to abandon the baby, who had stopped wailing in any case and was now busily tearing the hank of wool to shreds and stuffing bits of wool into its mouth.

"Matthias!" Aunt called loudly, through into the common room, where the ladder that reached the loft rested against one bowed wall of the long house. "Come and mind the baby."

Daniella gave a last shuddering glance at the baby and hurried outside after her uncle. That's what came of simple acts of kindness, of hiring a landless man to work a season for them because he was fair-spoken and likable and down on his luck. He had stayed the summer, worked hard for the harvest and the slaughtering, and then gone on his way . . . but it had been her cousin Dhuoda who had died giving birth to the child he had gotten on her, and who knew where he might have been by then. Perhaps getting another pretty young woman with child, and going on his way. And with Dhuoda's death the life had gone out of the house.

That was the way of it, Deacon Joceran had said, that the Lord and

Lady gather to their breasts the best-loved and the sweetest, to sing as angels crowned by stars.

Outside, the slap of winter wind on her face shocked her. She stopped, staring at the dusting of snow and the long tendrils of fog that laced through the village longhouses, coating half-ripened apples with frost and withering the asperia blossoms where they grew in clumps by the back door. Then Uncle shouted at her, his words lost in a gust of wind. She hurried after him.

Four sheep had strayed out onto the commons, huddling together near the pond, and she herded them back toward the stables, carrying a half-grown lamb over her shoulders. A cloaked woman—Mistress Hilde—ran from the porch of the church toward her own house, hunched over an iron pot which she sheltered from the wind and the gentle fall of snow as if it were as precious as a casket containing the bones of a saint. Daniella smelled, like someone's breath brushing her face, a distant stench like a rotting carcass, but then the door into the stables banged open, caught by the wind, and she chivvied the sheep in under shelter. Her cousin Robert, closing the door behind her, brushed against her suggestively. She shook him off. The old sheepdog lay in the corner nearest the door into the kitchen, whining. He had urinated in the corner, so frightened that he wouldn't even move off the wet straw.

"Gruff," she said, coaxingly, "Gruff, come here, old boy." But he wouldn't come to her.

"Scared the piss out of him," said Robert, thinking it a great joke, but even so she could hear the shake in his voice. From the other side of the wall, she heard Aunt scolding Matthias, and that made her angry, too. It wasn't Matthias's fault that he was sickly, and that he'd been the one five years ago to find their Da's body in the slough after the spring rains where he had been caught in the branches and dragged under water, drowned by angry water nithies. Even Deacon Joceran had said so, that it was their revenge on Da for him building a dam and draining the south portion of the marsh for a new field. Matthias had been plagued by twitching and nerves ever since.

The door slammed open, shuddering in a new gust of wind, and Uncle Heldric kicked a sheep in before him and passed a bawling lamb to Robert. "Still one missing, the black," he said. "She got past me, tore off into the woods." He glanced back behind him, and Daniella saw by the taut lines of his mouth and the glint of white in his eyes that he, too, was afraid, of the storm, of venturing so far away from the house, which was protected by iron and rosemary. An iron knife hung above the stable door, rosemary over the shutters that opened onto the trough.

"I'll go," she said, because she knew he would let her, however reluctantly, however guiltily. The holding would go to Robert, with perhaps a field left over for Matthias, but there would be nothing for her except the kettle, knife, and wedding shawl that had been her mother's, together with the length of green bridal cloth that Dhuoda had been embroidering in expectation of her own betrothal, whenever that might have taken place, though it never would now. Nothing else could she expect to receive from Heldric and Marguerite's family, hard as times were and burdened now with three orphans, except for a necklace of amber beads that Dhuoda had, with her dying breath, left to her cousin.

As if it were a luck charm, Daniella brushed her fingers over the necklace of beads where it lay beneath her tunic, together with the Holy Circle she had inherited from her mother's mother. Uncle Heldric handed her his cloak. She wrapped it around her shoulders and went back outside. Hunched down against the tearing wind, she walked out toward the scattering of trees, not truly a wood because so many had been cut down for firewood, that marked the farthest edge of the great forest that lay to the east.

The black sheep was hard to find, for by now it was full twilight and the ewe's coat blended in to the fog and the dark lean curves of tree trunks. But Daniella listened and heard a frightened bleating. Her feet knew the paths in this wood better perhaps than her eyes did, and she knew where the sheep wandered . . . down by the stream that wound through the wood and emptied at last into the marsh. Only one branch stung her face as she made her way through the wood and came out on the bank of the stream where the little ewe was poised between the trees and the steep slope that led down to the trickle of water and reeds that was all that was left of the stream in the summer heat.

There was no point in chasing it home. It would run off again. She lunged for it, grabbed its hind legs just as it bolted, and brought it hard to the ground, both of them together. It bleated, terrified, and voided all over, luckily missing her, but she could smell excrement and piss. The trees whispered in the wind, calling names, one name, like an old name in a dream. She got to her knees and wrestled the sheep up and over her shoulders. Unaccountably, the ewe calmed. Daniella looked up.

There, on the opposite bank of the stream, were not trees, though she had with that first swift glance thought them trees, so well did they blend in with the wood beyond.

They were creatures.

She stood rooted to the ground with terror.

Like rushes grown thick and tall, they loomed above her, whispering, dark shapes leaning over the stream like gigantic reeds bent down in a strong wind. They were darker than the twilight and an odor like hot iron swelled out from them. Their stirring and rustling made a noise like the thousands of leaves in a forest blown in a stiff wind, anchored by the distant ringing toll of a bell, caught below, as if their bodies—if they truly had bodies—rang on the earth with each step. They had no hands she could see, no faces, and yet she knew instinctively that they could both grasp and see. She took a single step back, slowly, and then a second, the poor ewe draped over her shoulders.

A sharp wind blew a flurry of snow from the heights of the pines down on her. As if lifting themselves on that wind, the creatures leapt and crossed the stream, twelve of them, at least. They brushed past her, and she smelled the liquid iron of the forge hot and stinging against her nostrils, and their whispering voices spoke a name into the wind and the sound of that name tolled on the air, like bells rung to pass a dying soul up through the seven spheres to the Chamber of Light where it would come, at last, to rest.

"Liathano."

Then they passed her, oblivious to her, to the weakly bleating ewe, and were gone, on toward the village.

Toward the village!

Daniella, shorn abruptly of her fear, ran after them, but her feet followed the worn and familiar paths, and the creatures were gone, made invisible by the twilight and the tall length of trees or by their own arts, she could not know.

By now, the village was empty, every door shut, every shutter closed, only, here and there, the glint of light showing a fire or lantern within. Only, and alone in the huddle of buildings, the door to the church stood ajar. Perhaps, as Deacon Joceran had said, the Father and Mother of Life need fear no demons, no creatures sent by the Evil Ones. Perhaps Deacon dared not shut her doors, for fear of showing fear.

Then Daniella saw a horse, standing, head down, against the wall of the churchyard. Its coat was the gray of stone, and only the saddle and the saddle blanket, trimmed with silver, and the winking lure of the bridle gave it away. No one in Sant Laon owned such a horse or such fine tack. A moment later the right side door to the church opened a bit further and a strange hump-backed Thing scuttled out, took the reins of the horse, and coaxed it up the steps in toward the church.

To profane the church. . . .

But with that thought she recognized that the Thing led its horse in to safety, what safety the church might afford it. She smelled iron, borne on the wind, and she turned slowly and saw the tall, drifting shapes milling round the commons pond, as if they had lost their prey—lost the scent—there, by the water. The Thing vanished into the church, the horse behind it. Before Daniella realized she had made the decision, she settled the ewe, quiescent now, more firmly onto her shoulders and ran to the church, taking the steps two at a time. She pushed past the door just as the startled Thing reached to close the door.

Only, by the light of seven candles lit round the altar and protected by glass jars, Daniella saw it was no Thing at all but a young woman, dark-haired and dark-eyed, her skin dusky-colored like bread baked too long in the oven, her back misshapen. The horse was a fine beast, big-boned but not enormous, with an intelligent head—a nobleman's mount. Tied on beside the saddlebags were a tasselled bowcase of leather embossed with griffins and a quiver full of arrows. A small shield painted black hung from the saddle. The woman wore a sword at her belt. In all things, she looked like a normal woman, except for her misshapen back and the sun-blackened color of her skin.

She looked at Daniella and then at the ewe, and she removed her hand from her sword. Moving, she slammed the door shut, and barred it.

"It will do no good," she said, clearly enough, though her words bore the accent of other, foreign lands, "but only gives us respite. They do not fear the House of Our Lady and Lord."

"Who are you?" asked Daniella, who was unaccountably not afraid of this stranger, though the woman clearly knew and expected the creatures who hunted abroad this night to follow her here. "What are those creatures? Are they hunting—" She hesitated.

"Yes," said the woman calmly enough, turning to care for the horse. Rain began to pound on the roof above, so loud that Daniella could barely hear her words. "They are hunting me. If there is a door out beyond the altar, you should go, flee to your house. They do not know of you. They will not see you. You can find shelter in your own place, if your Deacon is wise and has told you all to protect yourselves with iron and herbs." She shifted her grotesque shoulders and with a casual gesture unhooked and shrugged off her cloak.

Daniella stared into the clear, cool green eyes of a baby.

It had a thatch of black hair and skin like burnished gold, and it stared at Daniella solemnly, like a great queen or king, marking her. It did not cry, though rain pounded loudly on the roof and a flash of lightning lit the glass windows, followed hard by the crack and roll of thunder. Daniella jumped, the thunder came so suddenly, when any natural storm would have given warning, rolling steadily toward them over the hills. The baby flinched not at all. Dhuoda's child cried at any loud noise.

The ewe bleated softly and struggled. Daniella knelt, eased it off her back, and held it tightly between her knees, gripping its neck with both hands.

Strange shadows played over the altar and the wooden benches that lined the nave. Outside, through the windows, Daniella saw lines of darkness, swaying under the rain. A bolt of lightning lit the commons, blazing, and there was a sharp snap and the smell of iron.

"Ah!" said the woman triumphantly.

But more lines of darkness crowded round the windows, seeking entrance, as if supple trees moved in on the church from the forest.

"They're getting stronger," said the woman. "Once this storm would have dissolved them. Now it barely hinders their approach." She turned her gaze on Daniella, a dark mirror of the child's gaze. "They know where I am. You must leave."

She drew from her bow quiver a staff, black wood polished to a sheen. With it in her right hand she circled the altar with measured steps, pressing her boot into the stone floor every fourth step, as if she was trying to engrain some substance into the stone. She stopped, kneeling at the point of north, and struck the staff against the stone four times, speaking words Daniella did not understand. Abruptly, the rain stopped pounding overhead and the thunder, instead of rumbling away west, simply ceased.

"Did you bring the storm?" whispered Daniella. "Are you a tempestari?"

Although the woman knelt too far away to have heard, she answered anyway, rising to her feet and shrugging the sling that held the baby down from her back and gently setting the child, still wrapped tight, in the center of the altar between the seven candles that marked the perimeter, as if this sanctity would protect it. The child watched with preternatural calm, although it was far too young to understand.

"No, I am not. I am much worse. I am a mathematici, a magi, you would call it, who draws power down from the stars and the moon and the sun."

"Then how is it you can stand on consecrated ground?"

"Beware," said the woman, and raised the ebony staff above her head.

Fear stabbed through Daniella, and she shied away from that expansive gesture. She lost hold of the ewe just as the door to the outside burst asunder. The ewe bolted for the commons.

"Catch!" cried the woman, throwing the staff up toward the roof. The wood winked, sparked, and as darkness shrouded the church and the ewe vanished into a pit of blackness, the staff blazed with light, sucking darkness into it.

With a crack as loud as thunder it splintered into shards. The air cleared, reeking of the tang of hot iron, as the remains of the staff fell to the floor in a hail. Then it was silent. The seven candles at the altar burned peaceably, and the baby watched without a sound. By the shattered door, the ewe lay still. Daniella crept over to it.

She gasped, gagging, and clapped a hand over her own mouth. The ewe was dead. It already stank like a carcass five days old.

Outside, it was still, but trees swayed in the wind, or were there more of these creatures? Daniella backed away from the door.

"What are they?" she asked, barely able to form the words.

"They are galla," the woman said, her voice hoarse on the "g" as if it had formed an unholy conjoining with a cough, rough and guttural, a suggestion of the creatures themselves.

"You said you are not a tempestari. Did they bring the storm, then?"

"I brought the storm. Water can dispel them, sometimes, but they are strong in numbers this day, and strong in this world. Wind and rain can hide a trail, but they know my scent too well by now."

Daniella's gaze caught on the woman's cloak where it had been left to lie on the floor. Odd traceries decorated the lining, as if signs or spells had been sewn into it. She shivered, but it was not only the strangeness of the cloak and the woman and the shards of the black staff that littered the floor. Now it had gone winter cold again, though the storm had vanished. She braced herself against a hard swell of chill air, feeling it like a wave coming in through the broken door.

The horse neighed suddenly and kicked out, overturning one of the benches.

"Blessing!" cried the woman, bolting toward the altar, toward the child.

A blast of wind gusted into the church and that fast, like the snap of fingers, the candles around the altar went out.

It was night, black and empty. Daniella dared not move for fear she would step into an abyss, for everywhere around her it was as black as the chasm of Hell. Cold darkness poured past her like water.

But the baby cried, once, sharply. The woman cursed. As black as the air now was, the stripes of the demons—the galla—were blacker still, and by their shadows Daniella saw them struggling with the woman, writhing as if to imprison her, as if to swallow her. From the altar rose a faint gleam, like a light shielded under cloth.

It was the child.

Daniella could not leave it to die. She clamped the cloak under one arm and dashed up the aisle. Her feet knew the way better than her eyes, from the many times she had come forward to taste of wine and bread at Mass.

She flung the cloak toward the woman, praying, hoping, that it might distract the galla, and grabbed the child off the altar, clutching it against her chest, tucking Uncle Heldric's cloak over it, knowing common wool could not truly shield it.

A sizzling, snapping sound, like the rain of pebbles, like water boiling onto stone, scorched the air around her. She smelled fire and the acrid scent of the blacksmith's forge. An arc of flame shot up toward the roof and the galla scattered with the tolling of bells. They scattered like grass blown on the wings of a firestorm. Heat warmed Daniella's face, then the slap of cold. Dark shapes curled around her, a ring of cold, twisting tighter, ever tighter. She felt their circle shrink. She felt their hidden eyes upon her, felt their hands grasp, reaching, touching her and insinuating their bodiless hands into her, inside her. She began to cry, soundlessly, from sheer terror. The baby did not—could not—stir, but its green eyes shone like emeralds.

"Blessing," their iron voices said. "Child born of fire and blood." And then, like Death calling her name, they spoke again: "Daniella, daughter of Leutgarda and Gerard."

And against the hard scent of iron, enveloping her, she smelled, as if it was coming from the baby, like a warding spell, the pungent, sweet scent of roses.

Fire scorched the church. The candles on the altar burst into flame, and the darkness retreated from it. But it drew back only halfway down the aisle. There the entwined galla crouched, waiting, stirring, poised to engulf their prey. Benches crashed and toppled and Daniella caught a glimpse, through the shadow of the galla, of the gray horse plunging out through the doors. It vanished into the night—only it was not entirely night. The first line of gray, heralding dawn, limned the height of the trees. It had begun to rain again outside, but softly. How could it be near dawn? How could time pass so swiftly? Yet the hint of light to come soothed Daniella's terror. Surely the sun would dispel these creatures? But the galla waited, murmuring, creeping closer and ever closer by slow degrees, their approach like the echo of drowned bells.

The woman rose from her knees with a soft moan. She was hurt. Her dark skin was scored with thin white scars, as if she had been burned by fingers of ice.

"You have my blessing," she said, and she limped over and took the baby from Daniella's arms. "I have no means by which to thank you for this kindness. You owed me nothing."

"We all owe kindness," said Daniella. "It is what the Lord and Lady grant us, to ease our pain."

To her surprise, the woman wiped tears from her scarred cheeks. "I can give you nothing that will repay you in full for what you have done. Guard my horse for me, in case I ever return and find you again. His name is Resuelto."

Daniella was too stunned to reply. The galla shifted, easing nearer, but slowly, as if they feared another blast of fire. Their voices whispered, naming, marking.

The woman ducked her head and with an efficient movement slipped a chain off from around her neck. She held it out, and the galla shrank back, the darkness retreating, bending backward, away. On the gold chain hung a medallion of beaten bronze embossed with three symbols which Daniella could not read.

"Take this, put it on. This alone will protect you."

"Protect me?" Daniella stammered.

"They have noticed you and will always mark you. You will never be entirely safe from them without this, nor will anyone nearby you. Forgive me for bringing this trouble on you, that is all of the gift I can give in exchange for your kindness."

Daniella thought of the darkness writhing around the woman,

thought of these creatures taking her and the baby, enclosing them, engulfing them, ripping life from them as they had from the black ewe, leaving a five days' dead carcass in their wake. She did not reach out for the amulet.

"Won't you need it?" she asked, thinking that no one needed her. At least this woman had a child she cared for, that was probably her own. And if she died, the child, too, would be another orphan, living on the sufferance, however kindly meant, of others.

"I must go elsewhere, where they can't follow." She hugged her child closer to her, with her free arm, and bent her head to kiss its cheek, by this small gesture revealing that she loved it, wept for it, fed it, and sheltered it. As Dhuoda would have loved and sheltered her baby, though it was fatherless, had she lived.

"Take it," said the woman, and Daniella saw that she was adamant, that she would not stir until Daniella accepted the gift, though the galla whispered, muttering like bells, like words in dreams, like the language of the forest at night and all the wild places that are haunted, that care not for human kindness or human love and show no favor because, like the wood and the wild places, they cannot know a good man from an evil one.

Daniella reached out and took the amulet. The galla sighed and massed, drawing together into a great dark column, a vast funnel of night. Outside, the first pink rim of dawn rose along the treeline. The village was utterly quiet. No person stirred. Not even a lamb bleated, nor dog barked. The rain had stopped, although the sky was still dark with clouds.

Calmly, the woman gathered the child closer against her and walked past the massing galla and out the shattered door and down the steps to the lane that fronted the church. In a daze, Daniella watched her, watched the dark shape of the galla shift and turn and glide along the stone floor of the church, following the woman, bells ringing hollowly as they moved. Above, the whitewashed ceiling of the church was scorched, blackened by flame. The candles round the altar burned steadily, without flickering.

Daniella's feet seemed to move of their own accord toward the door.

They echoed in the empty church, leaving the trailing sound of a second set of footsteps behind her. She emerged from the door, picked her way over the splintered wood, and halted on the steps.

The woman, cloak and bow and quiver slung over her back, still clutching her baby in one arm, knelt before a puddle of water in the lane. She passed a hand over it, palm down, and seemed to be speaking as she peered deeply into it. Behind her, the galla closed on her, spreading their cloak of darkness out to engulf her. And she was now unprotected.

Daniella opened her mouth to cry out, to warn her, but no sound came out. No sound but the scuffing of feet behind her. She turned her head to look behind her, only to see Deacon Joceran, blinking confusedly, pick her way across the entrance and halt, staring, at the black cloud that had expanded to cover most of the commons.

"They'll kill her," cried Daniella, and snapped her head back, starting down the steps.

Only to stop short, staring.

Dense fog smothered most of the commons except for a patch of clear ground around a smooth puddle. Daniella ran down the steps. The fog parted before her, and she crouched in the middle of the lane, beside the puddle, looking for remains. Surely the galla could not have utterly consumed both woman and child?

Though it rained softly, the puddle remained a still smooth surface, oddly unmarked by the raindrops Daniella felt on her head and arms and back and could see in other smaller puddles that filled the potholes in the lane. She stared into the water. There, in the clear pale blue water, she saw a reflection of the woman and the baby looking out at her, looking, peering, as if to see her, as if to say good-bye.

Then the image faded and the water turned muddy. Rain stirred its brown surface, spreading tiny ripples.

Slowly, the fog dissipated. The sun rose. Its edge cleared the trees and threw morning shadows long across the commons, striping the church.

"What has happened here this night?" Deacon Joceran asked, coming down the steps. Daniella rose. She ached everywhere, as if she had worked for hours, though it seemed no time at all had passed since she first saw the woman flee into the sanctuary of the church.

"I followed the black ewe into the woods," said Daniella, and told her the story. When she had finished, Deacon Joceran signed the circle of unity and asked to look at the medallion. She studied it for a long time. Daniella grew increasingly nervous. The church denounced magic and sorcery, all but those miracles granted to saints by the Lord and Lady and what healing magic that holy men and women of the church might use to succor the ill and dying. But magic roamed abroad nevertheless, everyone knew that, and some sought to tame it or wield it, and some sought to confine or destroy it, while the church demanded penance from those who touched it or who begged help from the magi and arioli and tempestari who practiced the forbidden arts despite the ban.

But Deacon Joceran had lived many years in Sant Laon and had never once in Daniella's memory spoken out against Mistress Hilde's potions for lovelorn lads or old Ado's reading of thunder and the flight of birds and the movement of the heavens in order to predict the weather for the farmers, especially since old Ado was always right. Once she had mildly rebuked the congregation for giving credence to a travelling mathematici who offered, for a price, to read a man's or woman's fate from the courses of the sun and moon and stars, but who Deacon said was a charlatan.

Now she simply handed the amulet back to Daniella.

"These are strange and dark times," she said. "You must wear this. What will you do with the horse? How feed it? Such a horse must have grain, and there are those, alas, who will envy you the having of it, and its fine bridle and saddle. Some gifts are as much of a curse as a blessing."

The gray gelding grazed out on the commons. Like an orphaned child, it suddenly appeared to Daniella as more burden than bounty. But she rose determinedly and walked over to the horse. He allowed her to approach, but with stiff arrogance, like a noble lord forced to allow the approach of a simple farmer. One of the saddlebags was filled with more coin, coppers and silver, than Daniella had ever seen in her life, some stamped with King Henry's seal, others with that of his father and father's father, the two Arnulfs. The other bag contained a book.

Deacon Joceran walked over carefully, favoring the leg that had suffered from an infection this last winter, and when Daniella handed her the book and she opened the plain leather cover and read what was inside, she blanched. Daniella had never seen Deacon at such a loss before.

"These are terrible things," she whispered. "You must let no one see this."

"You must keep it, then, Deacon."

But Deacon Joceran closed the book and with hands trembling not with age, as they well might have, but with something else, fear or passion or some old memory, she thrust it firmly back into the saddlebag. "Once," she said, shutting her eyes against memory, "I dedicated my life to the convent, before I was cast out from the life of contemplation and sent into the world, to atone for my misdeeds. I was curious, and the old books speaking of the forbidden arts tempted me. They tempt me still, though thirty years have passed since those days. Hide it. Let no one know you have it. If a trustworthy friar passes through here, we can send it on to the Convent of Sant Valeria or to Doardas Abbey."

"But who was she, then, Deacon?"

"A mathematici indeed, child, whom we would call one of the magi. She spoke truth to you. Great powers lie hidden in the earth and in the heavens, and not all believe that the Church ought to forbid their study. I have seen with my own eyes. . . ." But she trailed off, and Daniella thought that perhaps age lay heavily on the old woman as much from what she had seen as from the passing of years. "Now you have seen, and those who see are marked forever. Go then, child. Go back to your house. I will speak to the congregation of the storm and what it brought, but I pray that the Father and Mother of Life will forgive me for not telling them all that occurred in the night."

Daniella led Resuelto home and installed him in the stables next to the sheep, whom he deigned to ignore. He allowed her to unsaddle him and rub him down, but when Uncle Heldric and Aunt Marguerite ventured out, exclaiming over the dark storm that had swallowed the village for the night, he snorted dangerously and would not let them near him. Matthias was afraid to come into the stables at all, with the big horse there, and Robert, for once, was so in awe of Daniella, or so afraid of what she might have seen and what might have seen her, that he left her alone, not brushing against her hips at every chance, not groping at her budding breasts or whispering suggestions in her ear when no one was nearby to hear.

So the day passed, and the next day, and the one after that, except that strange accidents occurred in the village. Mistress Hilde's prize goat escaped and was found drowned in the pond. Uncle Heldric and Master Bertrand, their neighbor, were hit by a falling tree in the wood, crushing Bertrand's foot and breaking Uncle's left arm. Milk curdled and the hens stopped laying eggs. Churns were overturned, looms unraveled, and the candles at the altar blown out every night. Every person in Sant Laon was struck by misfortune, great or small, everyone except Daniella. Old Ado said the movements of the birds and the lizards warned of worse misfortune to come. Fog wrapped itself round the village at night and increasingly during the day, and out of that fog rose the whisper of bells and soft, guttural voices naming a name: "Daniella."

They have noticed you and will always mark you. You will never be entirely safe from them without this, nor will anyone nearby you. Forgive me for bringing this trouble on you, that is all of the gift I can give in exchange for your kindness.

At dawn on the fourth day since the storm, Daniella woke abruptly and realized that Dhuoda's child, called Blanche for her pale hair, was gone from the bed. She dressed quickly and climbed down from the loft. No one was awake yet; Uncle and Aunt snored softly from their bed by the kitchen fire, and even Gruff lay curled up asleep on the bricks that lined the hearth. She ran outside. And there . . .

There on the commons a dense blot of fog, as dark as the smoke from a blacksmith's forge, swirled round a crying, stumbling child, driving it toward the pond. Daniella cried out loud, and little Blanche, hearing her, bawled even louder and tried desperately to turn, to toddle back toward her aunt, but she could not. The galla forced her closer and ever closer toward the water.

Daniella ran. The fog parted before her, hissing, angry, and she grabbed Blanche just as the little girl teetered on the edge of the pond, her dirty dress wet along the hem.

"Begone!" Daniella shouted, forgetting to be frightened because she was so furious. She pulled the amulet out from under her tunic and held it forward, driving them away. "Begone! What right do you have to torment the innocent?"

But all they said in answer was to whisper her name: "Daniella."

The sun rose and the fog faded to patches, retreating to the wood, where it curled like snakes around the trunks of trees. Waiting. As it would continue to wait, forever, not knowing human time or human cares.

Daniella stood silently by the pond, soothing the weeping child, until Deacon Joceran came out of the church to discover what the shouting had been.

"I must leave," Daniella said, the knowledge hanging on her like a weight. She fought against tears, because she was afraid that if she wept now she would not have the courage to do what had to be done. "They will never leave the village, not until I am gone."

Deacon Joceran nodded, accepting what was necessary, what she could see was true.

Aunt Marguerite wept, when they held a council that morning in the church, Uncle and Aunt and the eldest in the village, those that had their wits about them still. Uncle Heldric offered Daniella his cloak, but he did not beg her to stay. He held little Blanche on his lap. She was smiling now, playing with his beard, and he even laughed a bit. He was fond of Dhuoda's child, what was left to him of his only daughter, favored child, the best-loved and the sweetest.

"You take my cloak," he said gruffly to her.

"You have nothing to replace it with," said Daniella. "Take my mother's wedding shawl in exchange."

"Nay, child," he replied, looking shamed by her generosity, "we have nothing else to give you. It is all you have left of her."

She gave Matthias four silver coins, which was all she could spare, knowing that she would need the rest for the care and feeding of the gelding, and Matthias sobbed as disconsolately as he had when their Da had been buried, and their Mother, dead bearing a child. He begged to come with her. Perhaps he even meant it, but with the coin he could buy himself a start on his own farm and get a wife, and like their Da he had the gift of understanding the land and the seasons, for all that he was scared of the wild lands surrounding the fields.

"You are meant to stay here," she said to him. To Blanche she left Dhuoda's bridal cloth, and to Robert, a single kiss of forgiveness.

"You must go to the Convent of Sant Valeria," said Deacon Joceran. "You must walk seven days east and ten days north, and there at the town known as Autun ask for further direction. At the convent you will find, if not protection, at least advice, for the Abbesses there are known for their wisdom and for their understanding of the forbidden arts. You must not linger too long in one place as you travel, or these creatures, these galla, may bring mischief onto the people among whom you stay, and you will be named as a witch or a malefici and driven out, or worse. Take this letter and give to the Abbess at the convent. They will take you in."

Daniella looked long and searchingly at the marks on the parchment, but they meant nothing to her, just as the book left behind in the saddlebags meant nothing.

"She will try to find me," said Daniella suddenly. "For the book, if nothing else."

"If she has the power, if she yet lives, she will find you," said Deacon, "but whether that would bode good or ill for you, I cannot say, child."

Daniella did not reply, but she felt in her heart that she left Sant Laon, the only place she had ever known, not just to spare her family, to spare the others, but to seek after that meeting, as if it was ordained whether she willed it or no.

Aunt Marguerite brought her bread and cheese, which she put in one of the saddlebags, and Uncle Heldric brought her mother's knife, which he had sharpened to a good edge. She tucked it in her belt, kissed Matthias one final time, and took the reins of Resuelto from Robert.

"Go with the Lord and Lady," said Deacon Joceran, signing a benediction over her.

"Go safely," said Aunt Marguerite. Little Blanche, caught up in her grandda's arms, began to cry, reaching her arms out for Daniella.

But Daniella turned quickly away from them and started down the lane, leading Resuelto, since she did not know how to ride. She did not want them to see the tears in her eyes. She did not want them to fear for her or grieve for her. It was bad enough that they must grieve for Dhuoda, for Da, for her Mother. Let them believe that she went with a light heart, that it was a fate she went to meet willingly. It was the only kindness she could show them, as she left them behind, probably forever.

The gelding walked with dignity beside her, ears forward, eager to explore the road ahead. She kept her eyes on the dirt lane and the wood, and as she passed under cover of the trees, she looked back once to see her village, free of any trailing mist or tendrils of fog, lying in the bright warmth of the noonday sun. The sky was clear above, as blue as she had ever seen it.

At last, with a wrench, she turned to face the road ahead once more, and she walked resolutely on toward unknown lands.

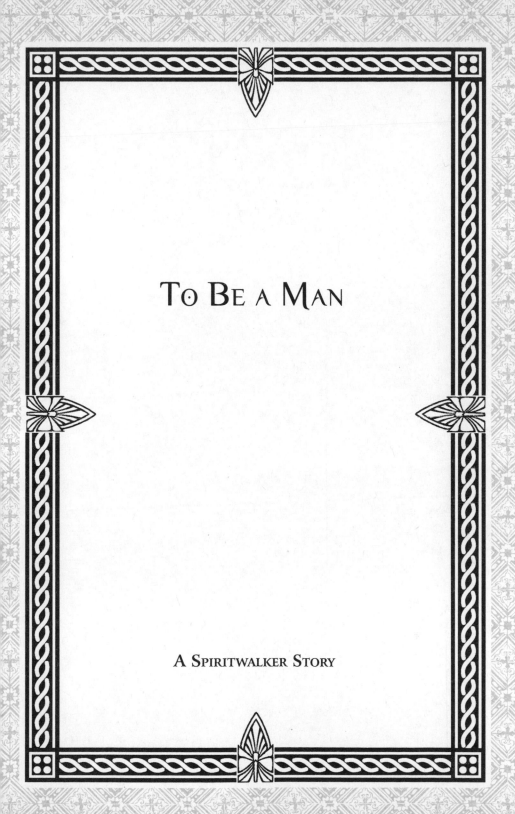

TO BE A MAN

A SPIRITWALKER STORY

It might have been the dog, or it might have been the woman. He wasn't sure.

When he had prowled into the garden from the enclosed parkland beyond, the little pug dog had been yapping in a skull-rattling fashion. His first instinct was to shut it up. He'd also wanted to cleanse his palate of those tickling feathers from the peahen he'd had so much fun chasing down in the parkland. So he'd bounded after the dog, snapped it up, and shaken it. The dog was small and fatty and sour-smelling, but at least it didn't have feathers.

Then a woman's voice tensely said, "Blessed Venus, step back out of sight, Felicia. A slow step. Don't startle it. Just back away and it will eat that hells-cursed pug and not you."

"But do you see what it is, Ami?"

"Yes, I see what it is. It is a very large and very hungry saber-toothed cat."

He raised his head just as the dog weakly wriggled, its blood dribbling down his dagger-like incisors.

"It's so beautiful."

A woman stood on marble steps lined by troughs of prickly winter shrubs that were dusted by snow. She was anything but prickly. She was delectably plump. She was wearing indoor clothes with a bodice laced tightly over a full bosom and white petticoats pulled up to keep their hems out of the snow. Her ankles were so shapely he wasn't sure whether he wanted to gnaw on them or lick them.

The pug gave a last little farting gasp.

Her ankles, or the pungent scent. Hard to say which triggered the sudden flowing river of change that cut through his lean cat's body like the tide of a dream changing him from one creature into another.

He shivered out of the skin of the cat in which he'd been born and lived in his natural home in the spirit world, and slipped into the skin of the man's body he wore here in the Deathlands.

Which meant he found himself sitting on his bare ass in cold, slimy snow.

He spat out a foul-tasting hairy mouthful of bloody skin. The pug plopped limply across his lap like an incongruous set of lumpy drawers. Scraps of the clothing he had been wearing when he'd changed earlier from man into cat shed onto the ground around him with a smattering of pats and thuds. A torn hank of boot leather was caught between toes. His long black hair, and the dead dog, were his only covering.

How on earth did creatures survive in this blistering cold?

"Oh! My!"

He looked up to see the woman the other one had called Ami venture onto the steps. She was tall, strong like a whip, much darker in skin than the first, and with a magnificent cloud of black hair surrounding her head. She also had a metal stick in her hand which she held as if she knew how to whack with it. She halted beside the paler, plumper one called Felicia. Together they stared at him.

"Yes, that was my thought, too," said Felicia. "He's gorgeous."

He wiped his blood-smeared mouth with the back of a hand before smiling at them, for he was sure his half sister Cat would have told him to use proper manners. "I have no clothes. They came off. My apologies."

The two women looked at each other. The wordless interchange reminded him of Catherine and her spoiled and irritating cousin Beatrice (no actual relation to him, he was glad to know!). Cat and Bee spoke a great deal without saying anything. Sometimes they did it when they rattled on with words to addle their listeners into thinking they hadn't even a pair of half thoughts to rub together into one. Other times they displayed the uncanny ability to look at each other and come to an unspoken agreement.

"And I'm cold," he added, aggrieved the two women hadn't already noticed that he would be cold because he had no garments. Cat would have noticed. "I'm very, very cold. And I'd like to wash out my mouth. I didn't mean to bite the pug," he added, for it abruptly occurred to him that the rules were different here and he could not just take what he wanted. "Perhaps it was a favorite of someone. However unlikely that may seem."

"That nasty little beast!" said Felicia, taking another step down as she looked him over. "It pisses on the couches and bites us as it wishes, and we are the ones who get slapped for it by the mistress."

Rory considered the dead dog. "My apologies, then, if there will be trouble for you because of what I did." He grasped it by the scruff and hoisted it with a sigh. "It is an unsightly creature. But I suppose it's dead now and can't be living again."

Ami gasped. "Blessed Mother, Felicia! Don't go any closer! You don't know what manner of creature he is. He could be anything, prowling about on Solstice Night!"

Felicia reached the base of the steps and halted on a strip of pavement swept free of snow. "What's your name?" she asked boldly. "How could you be a saber-toothed cat one moment and a . . . man the next?"

The tall one gave a snorting sort of sound like a choked-off laugh. She strode down the steps in an arrestingly commanding fashion, a woman who knew how to take charge. Halting beside Felicia, she brandished the metal stick, which he finally recognized as an implement with which you could poke fires.

"What is your name? Are you a cold mage? I don't think so, for I never heard that cold mages could change shape. It's only creatures from the spirit world who can change."

Still holding the pug, he stood. Their gazes took in the line of his body, and then they looked at each other again, and Felicia's brow raised in a deliciously charming way.

"Roderic Barr, at your service," he said, offering a smile to sweeten the introduction, "but you may call me Rory. That's my pet name. What shall I do with the dog? How can I help you? I wouldn't want you to be punished for me biting it. That doesn't seem fair."

"Little enough about life is fair," said the tall one, but Rory noted how she nudged Felicia with her hip, as if reminding her to not say anything. "How did you get in the garden?"

"There was a tree and a wall and another tree, easy to leap and climb if you know trees. Where I come from, I'm used to trees and walls. I'm very agile."

"I don't doubt that," murmured Felicia with a sensuous upward curve of her rich red lips.

"Hush," said the tall one. "Don't even think it, Fee. He's some kind of spirit man. My grandmother would tell you such creatures cross over from the spirit world to seduce women."

"And then?" asked Felicia. "What happens then?"

"Then everyone is pleased," said Rory. "Is there something wrong with that?"

A bell rang, shaken impatiently. Ami and Felicia winced.

"Where is my Coco?" cried a booming female voice from within. "Where is my little chub'ums? He'll take his death if you force him outdoors to do his widdle business! Really! Why you cannot let him do his business under your cots as he likes to do for it's safest and warmest there in these cold winter nights . . . girls? Girls? Where have those lazy sluts gone?"

"Hide!" said Felicia. "Behind the troughs."

"What about—?" He shook the limp body with a hand rather as he had earlier shaken its living self in his jaws.

"Hurry!" Ami leaped down to grab him by an elbow and drag him to the prickly shrubs.

He'd grown up in a pride of saber-toothed cats ruled by his mother's implacable will, so he simply never argued with females. With the oozing pug still in hand, he dashed behind the shrubs and crouched. The stone was like ice against his bare feet. The needles scratched him most painfully. But when a woman dressed in a robe of flowing gold swept out onto the patio at the top of the steps, bellowing about her chub'ums and her ungrateful servants, she did not see him. Another small dog was tucked in the angle of one of her arms. This one was even fatter and uglier than the corpse he held.

"Where is he?" she demanded.

For a moment he thought she had seen him, but then he realized her only thought was for the missing dog.

"We just saw him run inside through the parlor curtains, Your Highness," said Ami with a smile so false it would have curdled milk.

"My poor frightened Coco! You chased him! You heartless beasts!" The highness happened to be standing closest to plump Felicia. She slapped her. The pug on her arm snapped at Felicia, teeth catching on her sleeve. Felicia took a step back, and the highness grasped her sleeve and wrenched her back toward the growling dog. "Don't try to run away from your crime!"

A snarl escaped Rory, and he shifted forward to his toes and would have leaped up to pounce on her but Ami pounded the metal poker into the stone once in what he took as a warning to stay put. The pug began to huff out a wheezy cascade of barks. Its beady black eyes were fixed on the shrubbery, for it had clearly smelled Rory or the blood of its missing companion.

"We have not seen him, Your Highness," repeated Ami with a false smile.

Yes, yes, obviously they were lying to protect themselves; he could understand that. But that awful woman wasn't being fair to them at all. Yet by the flash of Ami's gaze toward the shrubbery, as if fearful he might spring out, he knew he had to stay hidden.

Felicia raised a hand to the red stain on her cheek. She spoke in a voice as smooth as cream. "Your bath is ready, mistress. We were just coming to tell you when we discovered that Coco had to do his business. Ami will be glad to take His Highness the Exalted Ramses inside, for the cold air has startled and discomforted him. I will escort you in to your bath."

"How can you think I can think of even having a bath at a time like this, with my little chub'ums so scared and likely shivering and cowering with fear! You are heartless and devoid of feeling, but no doubt you cannot help it being a bastard's bastard child. Only my devotion to your grandmother keeps you in my service."

"I cannot express my gratitude, Your Highness."

"Of course you cannot! It is inexpressible, what I have sacrificed for you!" She lifted a hand to the heavens as if exhorting some personage who lived in the clouds. The gold bracelets on her arms jangled as they slipped to her elbows. The pug in her arms nipped at the bracelets, clearly as ill-tempered as the highness and fortunately as distractible. "But the gods lay their claim on us to be generous. That is our princely lot in life."

The speech exhausted her reserves. She swayed as her lips pinched together as if to trap all the things she did not want to lose. She had an otherwise pleasant face soured by the expression of a person accustomed to slapping all underlings who did not accede quickly enough to her demands.

"I shall faint!" she decreed with the certainty of an oracle.

Felicia dabbed the woman's forehead with a scrap of fine linen, carefully avoiding the pug as it struggled to shift close enough to fasten its stubby muzzle around her fingers. "Take my arm, Your Highness. I shall help you inside to your couch."

"How can you think I would abandon my sweetling so! It is your flawed nature that twists your heart so cruelly. You must find Coco and bring him to me! I must lie down." She snorted out a copious sob, a sound similar to the honking of the big wild cows he with his mother's pride of saber-toothed cats sometimes hunted. "I haven't even the strength to feed poor Exalted Ramses his supper. You can see he is starving! But I do not doubt that you care nothing for his suffering!"

"Let me assist you into your chambers, Your Highness," said Ami.

"Aurea!" the highness bellowed.

A moment later a girl not yet full-grown scurried out onto the porch. She had the look of a mouse sure it is about to be gulped down, and she cringed as she made a clumsy courtesy.

The two serving woman again exchanged glances.

"I can help you in, Your Highness," repeated Ami. "Let me take the Exalted Ramses."

The highness shoved the growling pug into young Aurea's arms. It bit, mouth fixing over the girl's scarred fingers as its growl rose in pitch to a shrill frenzy.

The girl shrieked.

The highness slapped her. "How dare you abuse Ramses so!"

With a practiced swish of her sleeve, Ami got cloth in the way of the pug's next snap as she snatched the dog from the girl's arms. The beast squirmed impotently as Ami swept inside without a word, fabric muzzling its head.

"Come here, Aurea!" commanded the highness, holding out an arm. Blood dripping from her bitten finger, the girl scuttled under the outswept arm with its jangling bracelets. She physically sank as the highness settled her weight on her, but as the highness moaned, the girl staggered inside with her. A curtain swished down behind them.

Wind rattled through the branches. A crow swooped overhead as if to investigate the altercation. Ami returned, without the pug, shaking out a damp spot on her sleeve and carrying a shawl.

"I put him in his bed and took away the stairs so he can't get down," she said. "How I hate that foul stinking beast. He peed on my arm!"

Felicia hastily shut the glass-paned doors.

"The way she torments that child by pretending to favor her makes me want to smash her head in," added Ami with a flourish of the poker.

"That's a stabbing weapon, so it wouldn't do well for smashing," Rory said. "Can I stand up now? My right leg is falling asleep, and my feet are cold."

"You can't stand up until we're sure she won't come back. Put this on." She tossed the shawl over the shrubbery.

"Cat would make sure I had shoes," he muttered as he tugged the shawl around his shoulders.

Heartlessly, Ami turned away from the bushes to confront her companion. "We must do something or she'll kill poor Aurea. The girl has become nothing but bones and skin. And for her to prate on about her devotion to your grandmother, Fee! That nasty bitch bought your family's debt purely to hold it over a woman who was prettier than her when they were young. Not that your sweet old grandma would have ever shoved it in her face back in those days."

"You don't know my sweet old grandmother very well, do you?" Felicia's smile, as sumptuous as gravy, distracted him from his cold feet. He licked his lips, wishing he could be licking hers instead. "They still hate each other. Every morning when I wake up I think of why I'm stuck here for seven years and I know that every time Her

Royal Bitch sees me, she has to remember my gorgeous granddam. Let her stew in her own juices until she dries up! Rory? You can come out now."

Ami's hard glare softened as Rory cautiously rose to his feet. He held out the pug.

"What in the hells are we going to do with the cursed dog?" Ami muttered.

"Bury it?" Felicia studied the limp canine with a frown.

Ami shook her head. "The gardeners will find it. You know how the prince hates anything disturbed except what he has given permission for. This time of year, any digging will be quite obvious, even if we try to hide it behind a shrubbery."

"Throw the corpse in the privy?"

"She'll have it raked. You know she will. One of the stablehands will be made to do it."

"What will happen to you if the highness finds the dead dog?" Rory asked.

Felicia blanched, her magnificent bosom quivering.

Ami shrugged. "Fee will be whipped. So will Aurea, just for the pleasure the old cow gets in knowing she can command it."

"Whipped!" If he could have laid his ears back, he would have. "Will you be whipped, too?"

"No. I'll be sent home in disgrace. She dares not lay a hand on me for my family is too important. But one of my poor cousins will be sent to take my place. I don't mind serving the bitch. Keeps me free from a marriage I don't want. You must be freezing. We've got to sneak you inside."

He was shivering, but his honor was on the line: He had created the problem that would cause them to be harmed. So it was up to him to solve it.

"I could eat the dog," he said.

Ami looked thoughtful. "The whole body?"

"Not the bones and skin. But the flesh and insides."

Felicia was clearly a tenderer soul. She pressed a hand to her mouth. "How could you do that? Wouldn't it be nasty?"

"I would have to change back. Then I could eat it. You'd have less to get rid of."

"Are you experienced at that sort of thing?" demanded Ami.

He considered the pug with a frown. "I've never eaten this sort of creature exactly . . ." Her eyebrows had drawn down, so he paused.

"Changing back and forth at your own will, I mean," she said.

"It's something I didn't know I could do until recently," he temporized, for he wasn't sure how much he ought to tell them. But he liked the way they were looking at him with hopeful, interested expressions. A man who did a good deed to make up for his bad deed would surely be rewarded. He might even hint at the sort of reward he would like most. "You would have to help me. You'd have to be very brave. I would have to become a cat and eat as much of the dog as I can. Then you'd have to persuade me back, to remind me how much I would rather be a man than a cat."

"You wouldn't just eat us?" Ami asked, but she was biting her lower lip as she considered.

He smiled, flashing a gaze at Felicia. "Not in that way, anyway."

Felicia gave a most gratifying gasp and blushed bright red.

The music of Ami's answering laugh was so seductive that his man part stirred alarmingly, even in this tremendous cold.

"Oh!" said Felicia. "My!"

"You think we might coax you back from cat to man?" murmured Ami.

"I think you've already had your answer," he said, not bothering to hide because even though Cat would likely have told him it was very rude to stand naked in public in such a state, his two new friends were not troubled by it. "But my feet are very cold. Could we make a decision quickly?"

The two women looked at each other. If his feet hadn't been quite so cold he would have enjoyed the way their expressions spoke in emotions instead of words. Ami's lips quirked up in a half smile as her eyebrows rose as if with a question. Felicia's mouth parted as she exhaled, and she ran white teeth over her lower lip in a way that made him want to nibble that luscious mouth right there.

"All right," said Ami, turning back to him with the poker slightly raised and slightly trembling, rather as he was. "We'll do it."

He set down the pug on the stone. Hands at his side, he considered his man body and the memory of his cat body and how the two things were the same body but different in texture and movement. Deep inside himself there flowed a current like the stream of a river. He let his awareness sink into the current; he dropped into the flow where his cat body waited, ready to pour back into his flesh. He let the cat out and put the man in the river.

He changed.

A shiver flew through him. His body curled forward as it bristled with fur and claws and teeth. He huffed out a breath and brushed his whiskers along the pug's body. It smelled better than he had been thinking it had smelled. Lots of nourishing fat! But not much time!

He pinned the body with a paw and carefully opened up the belly with a sideways tear. Blood oozed. He licked it up and pulled out flesh and liver and the fatty heart, leaving aside the intestines, working around the bones and spine. It was a pleasant morsel coming after the less-appetizing peahen, which had been scrawny and dry. Sour blood and bits and scraps of fat and liver dribbled from his mouth. He settled onto his haunches and began cleaning himself. Then felt the sting of cold snow on his hindquarters, and wondered if there might be a more sheltered place to settle down.

Suddenly two larger morsels slipped in on either side of him. He sniffed. They smelled very tasty in a way he could not quite identify. He didn't want to devour them, precisely; he wasn't hungry, or at least, not in that way. A hand brushed his neck, then kneaded down the line of his spine. He rumbled, then began to purr.

"He's so tame," whispered the plumper one to the more muscled one.

The muscled one with the cloud of hair bent so close her breath misted along his muzzle and caressed his nose. The tips of her hair mingled with his whiskers, making him shiver with delight. "I don't think he's as tame as all that. If he would just change back into a man, we could find out."

A man? What was a man? A man was shaped something like them, wasn't it? Upright, a fast runner, but with flesh that was not very appetizing when it came down to it. He could be a man if he could just remember the way the river flowed and dive into it, even though water was not really to his liking. But their thighs brushing against his flanks made him think a swim might be worth it. Their hands petted him, and their voices murmured with crooning promises.

Anyway, he liked this new skill that was a sort of freedom. As a cub, he had learned to hunt. Hunting made him useful and gave him pleasure. Not being trapped in a single form gave him a weapon the poor creatures here in the Deathlands did not have, for they were confined into one form from birth until death. All they could do was grow, and die.

He twisted his thoughts inward and plunged into the current. The flow poured around him and through him and into him, and he made his thoughts take a man form. The change shuddered through him, and he became a man.

"That wasn't too hard!" he said, rather delighted at himself for managing it so easily.

Think of what Cat would say! She would praise him, wouldn't she? He was less sure of his mother's opinion, as she was always apt to give him a long reproachful look when he attempted to impress her as if to say, "Why are you bothering me with these trivialities?" He frowned. An unpleasant taste rimed his lips, and his paws—his hands—were streaked with blood and other more unsavory substances. He was sitting right by the ripped apart carcass of what had once been a small, fat, squashed-face dog. The intestines simply reeked, for although he had been careful not to puncture them, they had spilled anyway and the dog had voided in its last moments. His feet slipped in the mess.

He wrinkled up his nose, lifted a hand to his lips, and licked at it, but the taste made him gag.

"Hurry," said Ami briskly, throwing the long shawl around him. "We have to get you inside before anyone sees you. But the dog...."

Felicia reached under her own skirts and pulled off her drawers. "I'll wrap them up in these until we figure out how to hide them. The laundresses will just think I'm having my bleeding."

He sniffed. "You aren't bleeding, though. You're not even in your fertile passage. Won't people know it for a lie, if you say the blood is yours?"

She flushed. "How can you tell?"

"Can't people smell here?" he asked, astonished.

"That's very rude to talk about people smelling," said Ami in a kindly way meant, he supposed, to gently correct him. "But what did you mean, that she's not in her fertile passage?"

Standing, he bent closer, pulling back his lips and brushing his cheek alongside Ami's. She was attracted to him, that was obvious by her smell. "You're not fertile at the moment either," he said.

She drew back so sharply he thought he might have offended her, but when he examined her wide eyes and lifted chin, he thought instead she was merely startled.

"Did you want to be bred?" he asked. "If you're not fertile, I can't manage any breeding."

"No, no, all the better," she said with an arched eyebrow and a quizzical smile as she studied him. "Women would pay a lot to a man who could tell when they weren't fertile. Especially one as attractive as you are."

He almost said, "Am I?" but decided that since he knew he was and since he knew they thought he was, it might be unseemly to say so. So he merely smiled, to acknowledge what they all were happy was true.

Her smile sharpened, lips twitching up. "But I warn you, you're a bit forward to say so, so bluntly, to two women you barely know."

He coughed out a curt laugh. "Now you're just teasing me. I can tell what your body is saying. But my apologies if I'm not to say so. I haven't quite figured that out yet. My sister Cat is always correcting me. I have a lot to learn. As long as we don't get caught with the corpse."

Ami broke off to turn in the direction of voices sounding from inside.

He stepped back behind the row of potted shrubs as Fee bent to roll up the bloody skin and bones in her spotless white linen. The voices moved on, footsteps tap-tapping on wood flooring. No one came outside into the cold after all, like sensible people remaining indoors where there was warmth.

He was starting to shiver again. Out of the darkness, a voice called out a bellowing "halloo" and was echoed by a second, then a third, from farther out. A light swayed on the distant wall, a lantern being carried.

"Bright Venus," said Fee, "you're cold, you poor naked man. We've got a hot bath that the princess has rejected. Do you think we can sneak him in? She went to lie down, and she'll want freshly heated water when she wakes."

Ami pushed a hand over her hair, a gesture that looked habitual. "If we're discovered with a man in the women's quarters, we will certainly both be turned out bare-ass naked in the snow. The sensible thing to do would be to have him turn into a cat and jump back out over the wall."

"Darling," said Fee in a coaxing voice like a child begging for one more piece of cake, "you can hear that the watch is changing, so he can't go right now in any case lest the soldiers spot him. Anyway, there's no telling if he can get back out the way he came in. Let's get him clean, and sort it out after."

"I like to be clean," said Rory with what he hoped was a grateful smile that wasn't too begging nor too eager. "It's especially nice when others lick me."

The two women exchanged a glance fraught with an emotion he felt as a hand caressing his skin. His body reacted predictably, even though his feet were terribly, terribly cold.

"After heating and hauling that bathwater," added Felicia suddenly, "I should hate to see it go to waste."

"Yes," said Ami decisively, and to his surprise, both she and Fee giggled in a girlish way that made his loins grow hotter and his ears burn as with whispered promises.

"I'll carry the dog," he added, thinking it a polite gesture that they might appreciate. "I'm already bloody."

He picked up the flaccid leavings. Fluids mottled the linen. Ami swept the stone with a branch broken off from an evergreen shrub, then wiped up the last of the spume with her sleeve. Rory followed Felicia inside, as quiet as if he were stalking unsuspecting prey. In a way he was.

Inside and up the steps, the floor was remarkably warm, oozing pleasure into the soles of his feet.

"Ahh, it's so much better to be inside than outside!" He brushed a shoulder along Fee's.

The touch brought her to a halt as she looked at him sidelong in a marvelously delicious way. Fee blushed, and chewed on her lower lip as if she were chewing on him. He sniffed. Dog scent drenched the chambers. Streaks of dried urine stained chair legs, table legs, and the lowest span of the brightly painted wallpaper where the dogs had marked where they wished. Their dribblings spotted the fine carpets like a series of tiny ponds long since dried into rancid swales. The highness's fraught moans echoed through the linked chambers like labored grunts. Her bedchamber lay to the left through a series of closed doors. He smelled blessedly hot water in the opposite direction.

Fee's hand brushed his elbow. She pulled it back nervously, then with a delightfully skittish grin let her wonderfully plump fingers tickle on his forearm. His hair tingled at the touch, and she inhaled in a way that made him quite amorously inclined.

"Come with me," she whispered.

He dipped his head down to brush his cheek against her soft one. "I'd like that."

She let go of him so fast he thought he had offended her. Yet with a teasing backward glance and a provocative swish of her lushly rounded hips, she hurried off toward the bathing chamber.

From behind a curtained alcove, a dog whined with thwarted anger. Rory pulled the curtain back and glanced into the chamber beyond, a spacious room furnished with gold-painted wallpaper and two gilded beds covered with dog hair. In dimness, the noble Ramses huffed indignantly. Ami had indeed deposited Ramses on his bed and pulled away the steps so the ungainly creature could not descend unless it leaped. Rory was pretty sure it was too fat to leap, and in any case too accustomed to its privileges to make the attempt.

Cornered and trapped, the little thing growled shrilly at him, quivering all over.

Ami slipped up beside Rory and slapped him on the ass.

"If he starts barking, we're all in," said Ami. With her free hand she tossed a hank of bread that landed neatly right in front of Ramses. His growls turned into slobbering as he set to gnawing on the crust with the sort of gluttonous lack of fastidiousness common to dogs. Meanwhile, Ami's fingers strayed along the curve of his ass before darting up to grasp his elbow. "Come along, Rory."

He followed obediently through a set of linked sitting chambers lit by handsome gold lamps molded in the shapes of overly fed hounds so unlike the lean, cruel beasts he knew in the spirit world that at first he thought they were meant to be cows. Behind a pair of carved doors lay a small stone room painted with a mural of cavorting mermaids and dolphins engaged in unexpectedly acrobatic water games and fitted out with a large brass tub brimful with hot water. Six full buckets and two large brass pitchers suitable for pouring sat on a stone bench alongside. There was also a rack to hang a robe or dress or other clothing, and a closed wardrobe. At a side table with a basin, he washed the blood off his hands.

"These aren't the real baths," said Fee, who was waiting beside the tub with her gaze fixed shyly on the floor. "The maidservants wash here. But the highness likes us to bathe her here. She likes to pretend sometimes she's a lowly servant cavorting among her friends."

"You just bet she does," remarked Ami. "Since the prince never touches her, we're the only ones except her hired lovers from whom she ever gets a stroke. We do it to keep her temper under control. If she weren't such a misbegotten tyrant, I would almost feel sorry for her. But she is, so I don't."

She began to strip off her clothes.

"Ami!" breathed Fee, turning pink.

"You know what I think of her!"

Fee gestured to a now mostly naked Ami. "Not that. Your clothes. . . ."

"Oh! Well! He can't be expected to wash himself, after everything he's gone through, can he?"

"He can't!" agreed Rory. "After everything he's gone through? Certainly not! What do I do with—?" He held up the damp cloth that veiled the oozing corpse. He was so distracted by Ami's long, dark limbs and firm breasts that he took a step back and set the dead dog beside the door, to one side, before turning back to the women with his slyest smile. The shawl slipped off his body. "Where do I get in?"

"Do you say such things for their double meaning, or are you just that charming?" asked Ami with a laugh.

"I like to let people wonder how tame I am. Until I eat them up."

"You are the worst flirt I've ever met," said Ami appreciatively as she slipped out of her drawers.

Such soft pleasing undergarments they were, too. He took them from her before she could drape them over the bench and held them over his hips.

"Do you think they would fit? My sister says I'm not to wear women's undergarments because I'm male, but I think that's not fair. What do you think?"

Ami was as bold as Fee was shy. She pressed herself against him, naked chest to naked chest, and looked him right in the eye, for she was quite tall. She spanned his hips with strong hands. "I think they would fit you, but you'll look oh so much better handsomely clad in a dash jacket and well-fitting trousers, don't you think?"

"Whatever you think is what I think," he murmured into her ear, and then he nibbled at the lobe.

She had such an air of command that the way her breathing grew unsteady made him most pleasantly excited.

She steered him toward the tub. "Now you've gotten me dirty, too, you wicked beast. We'll have to both go in the tub. Darling Fee, what are you waiting for? I know you've seen naked men before. And Bright Venus knows we've been in that tub together before."

His ass came into contact with the tub.

"In you go," said Ami, wrapping an arm around him and tipping him backward.

He grasped her just as tightly, and together they fell in with a huge splash that soaked the front of Fee's gown. The wet fabric clung to her generous curves, and displayed the rounded curve of her breasts and her erect nipples in a most marvelous way.

"Now I'm wet," said Fee in a tone whose astonishment made Ami laugh.

"Milady Aminata?" A mouselike girlish voice murmured from outside the closed doors. "Milady Felicia? I don't—I mustn't—I'm sorry—"

"Angry Jupiter," muttered Ami, sitting up in the bath and pushing Rory behind her. He found that he could curl his naked body around hers in a very amorous way and keep his head hidden by pressing kisses between her shoulder blades. "What is it—? Ah! Mmm. What is it, Aurea? Aren't you attending Her Highness?"

"She sent me to look for Coco," came the plaintive voice. "The mistress is wanting him."

"Is she up?"

"No, she is sleeping."

"Well, then, child, we'll sort it out later. We're just warming up in here. We were so cold searching outside that I thought our toes would—Stop that!—freeze off. You had best go to the kitchens and try the yam pudding to make sure it is fit for when Her Highness wakes up. And the biscuits and the rabbit, too, for you know how Her Highness likes her food just so. Make sure you try everything, and not just a spoonful, either, enough so you—Ah!—so you can make sure it will be to her liking. Go on. She won't wake for another hour."

"But I can't. Her Highness ordered me to look for Coco."

"Felicia and I will look for him, I promise you. As for the other, I command you, for I am senior to you, so you must obey me."

"But I'm not allowed—"

"I'll obey you," murmured Rory at the same time, exploring the part of her that rested under the water.

"Ah! Stop that, you beast!"

The little voice quavered. "Milady, did I displease you?"

"Yes! You displease me by not eating enough to keep up your strength and feed your appetite. I have changed my mind. You must eat two bowls of yam pudding first, at my order, and then try all the other foods. Is that clear, Aurea?"

"Two bowls?"

Rory discovered how well his two hands could fondle Ami's two breasts. Her head sagged back against his, her hair caressing his two lips.

Fee had been standing mute and damp, looking from tub to door and back to tub. "Yes, you must eat two bowls of yam pudding for supper every night, Aurea," she said with unexpected decisiveness. "Besides the rest of your meal. That is an order. Go right away, so you can eat as much as you wish while the highness sleeps. And then take a nap until we call for you. Go!"

The scuttling footfalls of the girl faded.

"You're feeling frisky," said Rory with a laugh.

"So I am," she said as she stripped off her gown and gathered up a thick bar of soap and a sachet of herbs and leaned over the tub.

So she was, and Ami, too. They frisked quite delightfully and energetically in a way that splashed a great deal of water over the floor. Eventually, they ended up on the floor on a pile of lovely thick towels. They took their time, indeed they did.

But really, considered in the greater scheme of things, it was all over far too quickly. He was granted the merest scant interval of lying, spent and satisfied, with a woman on each side nestled cooingly against him, before a high light bell sounded.

Ami sat up. "Curse the old bitch with boils and an itching arse."

A great deal of shouting and bellowing rose from the princess's rooms. A bird-like scratch scraped the door.

"Lady Aminata. Lady Felicia. Her Highness is awake and looking for you. She's rousted the gardeners to search the ground. I didn't tell her yet where you were, but. . . ."

The one truly impressive thing about the highness was her voice. "Aurea! Where is that useless bit? Why is she not here by my bedside?"

Although Rory could tell she was nowhere near, her shout carried marvelously, like warning of a distant storm that would break over them at any moment.

Ami went to the door and cracked it open. "Aurea. Go tell Her Highness we're outdoors looking still. That will give us time to make sure she doesn't find us here. Hurry."

The girl scuttled off as Ami closed the door and turned to regard first her naked companions and then the messy linen that wrapped the remains of darling Coco. "We have to get you out of here," she said to Rory. "The problem is that men are not allowed in this wing. The moment you're seen, they'll know something is up."

"Will you be punished?" he asked.

Her frown had a grim cast that chased all thoughts of dalliance out of his mind. His lazy languor burned off at the thought of these delectable females being punished, especially because he would have been responsible and they left to accept the blame. His mother always told him that if there was anything she hated, it was males who let the women do all the work. "I would rather give myself up to spare you that. If I become a cat again and run back through the garden, they'll never know you were involved."

"The soldiers will shoot you!" exclaimed Ami with a look of real alarm.

Fee planted a firm kiss on Rory's lips, but then rose. "I know exactly what to do."

She flung open the wardrobe and rummaged around until she found what she wanted. "Here." She dropped men's trousers, shift, waistcoat, and a sober green dash jacket onto Rory's lap. "Get into these."

"But Fee—?" Ami's protest died as Fee tossed a clean gown at her and shook out a second gown, one cut to fit Fee's more generous figure.

"He's got no beard. We'll dress him in a gown, veil his face in a shawl, and tell the guards at the gate that he's my cousin come to visit me for the day and leaving now for home. His hair is long and beautiful enough to be a woman's. Once he's outside he can take off the gown and go about as a man, although it will be cold without a coat."

"My sister will find me a coat," he said, much taken with this idea as he swiped Ami's drawers from the bench and pulled them on, covering them quickly with the trousers so she wouldn't notice and thus object to his stealing them. So soft!

"You're brilliant, Fee!" breathed Ami in a voice so tender and admiring that he paused while buttoning up the front flap of the trousers. They were gazing at each other as if they wanted nothing more than to lick each other, and he abruptly felt that while this had been a pleasing dessert for them, he wasn't truly necessary to their repast.

After all, he was leaving, wasn't he? He had to return to his family, and they naturally would make their own little pride in the territory where they roamed. A sigh escaped him nonetheless.

"Dearest Rory!" said Fee at once, rushing over to him. "You're so honorable and good."

"Am I?" he asked, not to demand their agreement but because he wanted to be honorable and good. That was what males were meant to be, wasn't it?

"You are," she assured him. "Let me help you with those buttons."

Ami dressed also. "I still don't know what we're going to do with darling Coco," she said as they all finished dressing and the women helped sort out the gown so the drape and flow did not reveal the men's clothing beneath.

"I have an idea," said Rory as they wrapped the shawl around his head in way that made him seem a modest woman who did not wish to be stared at on the street. "A very cunning and devious idea. But you can't know, and you mustn't watch. Wait here."

"You can't let anyone see you!"

"There's no one outside right now. The highness is wailing in her bedchamber and the servants are either waiting on her or shivering about out in the cold." He gave them his sternest look, the one he reserved for moments of extreme danger or when he really had to convince his mother not to swat him after he had played a trick on his spoiled and obnoxious little sister, the other one, not Cat. To his surprise, they opened the door enough for him to slip through. He picked up the stinking remains and sneaked out.

Stealthy as only a cat can be, he sought the den of the foul beast, behind the curtained alcove.

Then he returned to the women.

"It's taken care of," he said with a smile. "Trust me."

The voice shook the walls. "Where are those sluts? Where is my darling Coco?"

"Hurry." Ami dragged him out of the bath chamber and along a servants' narrow hall by the light of the lamp Fee carried. A pair of lamps marked a door barred from the inside. Ami pulled open a square view hole and peered out.

"Who's out there? Ah, Captain Gaius, it's you. Open up. Lady Felicia's cousin has to get home. She was visiting, but Her Royal Highness is in a pet."

The soldier standing at guard laughed. "Are you telling me that's something new today? I reckon I'm glad I'm out here and you're in there tending to her fits and starts. Stand back, girls."

Ami slid shut the view hole and then gave Rory a sound kiss. On the other side, the guard fiddled to unlock a mechanism, for evidently the door was barred on both sides. Fee unbarred the door. As it swung in, the captain raised his lamp to take a good look at them with a proprietary air that made Rory want to claw him. But he knew better than to pick a fight and draw attention. So he smiled winningly instead. The man was rather good-looking, with the bluff, muscular build of a fellow who spends a lot of time wrestling and running and hacking at helpless objects. His broad hands looked as if they might be very adept at squeezing and kneading. His gaze was certainly probing.

"Who is this lovely? I've not seen her before, and I know all you girls by sight and by that lovely sway of your ass, Lady Felicia."

Lady Felicia was not, perhaps, as enamored of Captain Gaius as Rory thought he could be, given the chance.

"This is Rory," she said in a cool voice far removed from her passionate utterances not long ago. "She's not a serving woman to the princess, Captain, so you must show her respect."

Ami added, "She's really a saber-toothed cat dressed in a man's skin and wearing a woman's clothes."

"I have very nice man's skin," said Rory helpfully. "Do you want to see it?"

Captain Gaius laughed, slapped Rory on the ass in a most gratifying way, and then, unfortunately, stepped back. "You women and your jests. Go on. There's a commotion brewing, for I heard the wall captain call up half the men. If the old bitch finds me chatting up you lot, she'll have my balls. Get out of here."

A male voice shouted for the captain. With a frown he signaled to them to stay put as he stepped away around a corner and into a guardhouse. Across a courtyard, a closed gate in a high wall promised access to the city beyond.

"I can't believe you told the truth, Ami," said Felicia under her breath. She was still holding Rory's hand, and with obvious reluctance she released him. "About Rory, I mean."

"The benefit of telling the truth is that so few people believe you. You must go, Rory. Though I'm sorry to lose you so soon after finding you."

"All will be well," he assured them. "The highness will never suspect you."

At that moment, out of the depths of the princess's wing, a mighty shriek cleft the night like the anguished howl of a wounded monster.

"My chub'ums! My Coco! Aieeee! Ramses! HOW COULD YOU?"

Rory smiled smugly, imagining how sour Ramses must look with his nose smeared in blood and his paws dabbling in the moist remains. The two women looked at him with wide eyes. He kissed each one on her warm, willing lips, and stepped away as the captain returned, looking grumpy.

"Hurry, lass. Get out of here, as the lord general is bound to make his rounds with all this fuss. Cursed women! Either scolding or wailing."

One last glance was all he was permitted as the captain hustled him to the servants' gate and thrust him out into the cold night. The captain shut the gate.

Rory stood on the cobblestone street, savoring the adventure. That had felt good! And he had learned something important about himself, just as Cat would have urged him to do: By understanding what it meant to flow and change, he could now shift from cat to man and back again whenever he wished. Sadly, he knew he would never be able to tell Cat about all the best parts of the night, because she would no doubt be affronted and embarrassed.

A curious watchman paused to eye him and, when Rory snarled, hurried on. He stripped off the gown and shawl and folded them up to carry. He took in a draught of air. Beneath the many heated smells of the city, he sought his sister's distinctive scent, blended of both worlds.

Dressed in his man's clothes with his soft woman's drawers beneath, he sauntered off in search of her. Sometimes things did work out. He had righted a tiny wrong, done some good in the world, maintained his honor, and been well petted in reward.

It was good to be a man.

MAKING THE WORLD
LIVE AGAIN

Like a creature out of the old stories, caught between earth and sky, Eili stood with mud coating her feet and the sun rising at her back over the endless tidal flats and marshlands.

"'Hiai! Hiai!'" she sang. "'Before the first grass grew out of the mud, before the first tree grew from the ground, before people sprouted from the earth, before the first house was built, before the first village came to be, before the first city was made, the sea existed, nothing else. Then Eridu was built.'" Mud splashed her ankles as she danced. "When I'm a woman, I'm going to travel to Eridu and see the big temple for myself!"

"If you don't get back in the boat," said her brother, "we'll get home late. Then the only place *you'll* be going is to dredge the old canal with the slaves."

"And I'll take the dates with me!" she retorted, laughing.

"Not if you don't get in the boat!"

Eili swung a leg over the side, balanced the basket of dates against her hip, then slid in as her brother poled off. Thick with reeds on its shoreline, the low island hillock was crowned with a cluster of date palms whose bounty they had just harvested. The palms broke the flat expanse of water that glittered under Anu's morning rays.

"Look!" said Indu as his eyes swept the shore where Eili had danced and sung. "Some animal's been hurt. Do you see the blood?" He pointed with the pole as the boat slewed round in the water. A few drops of bright red blood spattered the muddy verge. "Hiai!" he muttered. "What kind of sign is that? Should we tell the priest?"

As they stared, a swell of water eased over the tracks Eili had left, obliterating all trace of her passing as well as the mysterious blood.

"Huh." Eili grunted, dismissing it. "It's nothing to do with me." She set down the little basket of dates and settled her feet on a pile of rushes left by the last occupant. "A whole city built all of bricks! What do you think of that, lazy Indu?"

He grinned, teeth a bright flash against his face. Indu had been blessed by the gods with an endless capacity to be cheerful. "I think it would take some poor artisan many long days to make so many bricks, and some other poor sore-backed laborer would have to lift them all up into place!"

She snorted. "You're always going to stay in the village if that's all you can think about!"

"I can think of things much more interesting than the big temple at Eridu which such as us will never see the inside of, no matter what we do."

Her breechclout had caught under her thigh; she hitched herself up and tugged it free. Like all girls, she wore a bare leather cord around her waist. She ran her fingers along it now, tracing it. When she became a woman, she would get to decorate it with beads, shells, and feathers to show she was of marriageable age. Indu had become a man last year at the New Year Festival, so he could wear a man's kilt over his breechclout: a length of cloth wrapped at the waist and reaching to his knees.

"Hiai!" she exclaimed as the marshflies swarmed round them. Not even a breechclout could protect against stinging flies and all the other voracious bugs that loved the marshlands and tidal flats. "Can't you move us any faster? These flies will eat me down to the bone."

"Rain's coming." Indu shielded his eyes from the sun as he peered eastward.

"Rain comes almost every day in the winter, Master Wisdom!"

He only laughed and lowered a hand to trail it in the water. Expression brightening, he shoved the pole into her hands, then touched a finger to his lips for silence. She poled while he fished. His hand trailed in the water as the boat skimmed along almost noiselessly. Reeds brushed its wood belly. In her hands, the pole dipped and rippled through the water as quietly as a heron's stalking. This boat, made of wood floated down from the faraway place called "Upriver," was the visible mark of their family's prosperity.

Indu darted forward, hands clapping together under the water. He twisted and silvery perch flew through the air to land in the belly of the boat. It flopped around until Eili took a clay net weight and clubbed it on the head.

Indu smiled triumphantly, and they poled on while he trailed a hand again through the water. Birds sang among the rushes or called to each other. She knew their voices: the harsh crow, the cheerful ducks, the croaks of night herons settling in to their daylight nest. A cormorant stood on a sand bank, wings outspread.

Indu darted again, twisted, and flipped another fish into the boat. In this manner he caught five seaperch before the shoreline came into view. Reed houses, their entries framed by thick pillars woven of reeds, marked the farthest limit of the village, which was set on the high ground above. Beyond them, under the shade of date palms, Eili could see the square block of the mud-brick village shrine set below the levee just outside the village. A stand of pines grew along the banks of the big canal and several small plots of cultivated land lay between the village and the marshlands: lentils, flax, and herb gardens.

Her mother squatted in the garden, thinning the onions. In the village, women sat before their houses. Some wove reeds into baskets and mats. Others painted pots or hunched over a grinding stone while their young daughters laughed and chatted behind them, spinning flax to thread and watching over the smallest children. The men would be dredging the canal against the spring floods, or weeding in the grain fields out in the irrigated lands, or watching over their sheep. Day in, day out, year in, year out, Eili watched them plant and harvest, bake pots over fires and paint them and then bake more, cook, fish, bury those who died, birth babies, and take offerings to the temple. It was always the same.

"There's nothing new!" exclaimed Eili. "Same old village! Same old work! Same old people! How can you be so cheerful?"

"Nothing new! The sun is new each day! New water flows down the river each day! Every year we grow new crops!"

"Same old crops! I want to see the world!"

Indu grinned and gestured toward the sky, where clouds moved in from the east like sheep headed homeward, then at the marsh behind and the village ahead. "The world is here! The world is where you and I are."

"Oh, you'll never understand." Disgusted, she stood in order to pole the boat precisely in against the earth jetty.

"Hiai!" Indu leaped out of the boat and into water that lapped his knees. The boat rocked wildly under Eili, but she steadied it quickly as she stared at her brother, now gone crazy. He splashed up to the shore and ran toward their mother. "Nin-Imah! Nin-Imah! Come quickly!"

Two pigs, foraging on the verge of marsh and land, ambled over to investigate. Ahead, her brother was gesticulating, talking to their mother with wide, sweeping gestures of his hands yet careful in his excitement not to touch her. It was only when Eili had settled the boat and brought it up beside the jetty that she looked down to see what had so startled Indu. Blood stained the wood bench where she had sat.

It had not been an animal's blood at all, on the marsh hillock where they'd gathered dates. It had been hers.

Nin-Imah sent Indu off to the little temple house to warn the priestess and then came over to Eili. She chased off the pigs, then helped the girl out of the boat, and leaned in after to touch her finger to the smear of blood on the bench. Touching the blood to her tongue, she considered its taste with great seriousness while Eili watched her apprehensively.

Nin-Imah was very old, so old she had a living grandchild who could already walk and talk, and Eili was her youngest child. But to Eili's eyes the white ringlets in her mother's coarse black hair represented just another sign of her great strength and wisdom. Stout of body, she had sharp, black eyes in a face wrinkled from endless hours working under Anu's bright rays. Eili couldn't remember her looking any other way. Maybe one day she'd look like that, but she couldn't imagine being so old.

Nin-Imah smacked her lips and nodded. "First blood," she said with satisfaction. "Your time is come, Eili. Now you'll be a woman and we can accept that offer of six sheep and the brindled ox from Natum's family as your bride-price."

"Hiai!" Eili jumped out of the boat. "Marry Natum!"

"Natum is a good boy," scolded Nin-Imah.

Eili made a face, but since it was true, she couldn't disagree. "Why can't I go to the big temple in Eridu?"

Nin-Imah snorted. "You and your talk of the big temple in Eridu! I know what you dream about, but your father can't afford that kind of dowry nor your brothers the upkeep it would cost every year."

She had practiced this response for a long time now, ever since her father and Natum's father had first spoken of a marriage contract between her and the young man. "You've no one to marry after me, Nin-Imah. Think of what a fine honor to our family it would be to send me to be a servant of the goddess at the temple in Eridu."

Nin-Imah only grunted, but that was enough for Eili.

"I know you'll convince Father."

"Huh. Don't pester me. You walking all the way to Eridu!" But she had that secret little half-smile on her face. She had some things of her own, did Nin-Imah, certain beads and precious shells, a copper knife, and even a few rods of silver tucked away, that could be added to her husband's wealth to make up a dowry for the temple. "At least it would relieve me of all your questions, day in and day out. But you must go to the priestess now. I'll speak to her of this. There'll be some kind of test, to see if you're suitable."

Eili wasn't afraid of any test, but she knew better than to say so out loud. After all, the demons might be listening and hatch a plan to ruin all her hopes.

Her mother tossed the fish into her basket with her thinned onions, then set the smaller basket of dates on top of them with a frown. With an efficiency that betrayed long years of practice, she bundled up the rushes that lay in the bottom of the boat. "Come, girl. All this you've gathered today will have to be offered to the goddess."

"Even the fish? Indu caught the fish."

"That fish could poison the men if they ate it. A girl's first blood is very powerful, almost as powerful as birthing blood. So you come with me and don't touch anything or look at any men! I'll have to scrub down the boat and even then the priestess will have to purify it before your brothers or father can go out again in it." She clucked her tongue between her teeth, thinking no doubt of the gifts they'd have to lay on the offering table so that the priestess could do all this work. Any change in life brought a great deal of trouble with it; *everyone* knew that. Demons hovered round all the time, though no mortal person could see them, and waited for people to do something wrong. That was where they got their power from.

She and her mother gathered up everything that had been in the boat, even the old rushes, and carried them together to the temple. Nin-Imah announced loudly to every passerby that Eili had started with her first blood so men would know not to look at her and possibly get themselves hurt. Eili had to keep her gaze on the dirt, once colliding with a pig, but it was better once they arrived in the temple precincts. Here she didn't have to stare at the ground. The priestess was very holy and the old priest powerful enough that women's blood wouldn't burn him as it might an ordinary man.

At the gate that led into the courtyard, the priestess met them. A fringed skirt and a woven winter shawl with shells and beads sewn into it draped over her arms. Silent, she dressed Eili in these garments, then permitted the girl to enter the temple precincts carrying the offerings. While Eili hesitantly walked into the empty courtyard, the priestess remained at the gate to speak with her mother. Eili waited until the old priest emerged from the temple itself and beckoned her inside.

Eili had never been in the temple before. Like any house it had a packed dirt floor, but there the resemblance ended. It reeked of incense: juniper, and myrtle. The walls had been whitewashed, and in each niche a bright painting flared like an animal caught in life: a lion, a bull, a twining scorpion, an ibex with its curling horns. There, in the center, stood the offering table, and at the far end, illuminated by a high, open niche in the wall, rested the altar with a number of small clay figures sitting on it. She tried not to look too closely. What if she wasn't strong enough to see such things? What if the goddess' power struck her down? She tried to keep her gaze on the dirt floor but couldn't help sneaking peeks.

The priestess returned, looking grave. She indicated to Eili that she was to set the offerings on the table. The girl set them down carefully, the dates, the basket of seaperch and onions, and the rushes bundled into a sheaf.

Then the priestess led her outside to the back portion of the courtyard, enclosed by the same man-high mud-brick wall. Here stood three small reed huts as well as a hearth fire ringed by stones, a small earth platform with a grindstone and clay pestles, and a flat stretch of ground patterned with small holes where, in the dry season, a ground loom would be pegged out.

One reed structure, more of a lean-to, rested up against the wall. The priestess gestured to her to go in, and Eili ducked under the low threshold. Inside it was dank and musty, strong-smelling with the scent of women's magic. She hesitated, wanting to ask what was expected of her, but the priestess' footsteps whispered away over the dirt. She was alone.

There wasn't much to look at. Even a poor man and his family lived in a better house than this, a big mat of palm leaves and sticks woven together and leaned against the mud-brick wall to form a shelter. A few narrow holes had been drilled through the thick wall. Peeking through them, she saw slivers of the village beyond, just enough that with her knowledge of the buildings she could piece together the whole in her mind's eye. She heard pigs grunting as they rooted through a midden, and the laughter of children.

A hush like pattering feet rose up from the marsh: The rains had come. They swept over the village, drumming on the dirt. Rain leaked through the reed canopy above her to drip on her bare shoulders. It was cool and she shivered, crouched down to wrap arms around knees and tighten the shawl over her shoulders and hair. Her belly ached. Blood dripped from between her legs to dampen and blend with the musky earth.

The rain moved off. No one came. She heard the ordinary sounds of life around her, but nothing else. Nothing unusual—nothing new at all. It was a long day, waiting, and when dusk shuttered down with its quick hand and Anu sank westward into the underworld, she even got a little scared: she, Eili, who was scared of nothing and wanted to know everything.

Maybe being a priestess wasn't such a good thing after all if it meant sitting alone in huts all day and night. Maybe it would be better to marry Natum.

"Eili!"

The whisper came to her through the drill holes. She squinted out through them but it was too dark to make out more than shadows.

"What is that? Who are you?" Could it be a demon, speaking in a voice meant to sound human? She didn't recognize the voice, and couldn't even tell if it was man or woman, muffled as it was.

"The Great Serpent is out tonight."

"Hiai! You're scaring me."

"You're safe, you're safe, woman," the voice replied and then laughed softly, a pleasant sound that made her feel easier. "You're on the island, the first island, the old island. You're protected by its magics and the power of your first blood. You belong to the goddess while you stand on her sacred ground. Go outside and tell me what you see."

She rose, groaning with the stiffness in her legs, and ducked out under the threshold. Outside, she looked around. It was hard to see anything but shadows though she could easily make out the square temple walls that loomed beside her. Then she looked up and gasped. Above, a winter shawl of brightness cloaked the night sky. She didn't look at the stars much. Usually she was asleep by now.

"I see the stars. And there! There's the moon." It was thin and curved, like a clay sickle.

"What are the stars?"

Eili opened her mouth, then stood there, gaping up at the stars. "I don't know. They're stars. They're the light by which the gods feast in the temple up in heaven."

"Watch the stars," said the voice, and nothing more.

Eili hissed between her teeth, angry at these riddles. She heard nothing, not even footsteps rustling away—but the voice did not speak again.

And now, as her irritation faded, she became curious. What *were* the stars? She watched for as long as she could keep awake, shivering in the cold night air. Like Anu, the stars rose in the east and set westward, rolling down into the underworld.

Finally she returned to the hut to curl up in a dry corner and sleep. In the morning the priestess brought her water to wash and a bundle of leaves to soak up the blood, though there wasn't much. She brought bread as well, served on a plate with dates and freshly baked seaperch.

"How long will I stay here?" Eili asked, but the priestess only smiled in her grave manner and handed her a spindle and flax so that she could spin.

In this manner she passed a tedious day in solitude.

That night, the voice came again.

"What are the *mes?*" it asked her.

"The *mes* are the spirits that govern the decrees the gods make. Everyone knows that!" Her belly ached a lot right now. That, and these stupid questions, made her grumpy.

If the voice could hear her bad mood, it took no notice but went on. "The Great Serpent troubles the world, wanting to return everything to the old sea which was all and everywhere before the first creatures came to be. But the *mes* keep order. The stars keep order."

"Hiai!" She forgot about her aching belly as a flood of questions came to her tongue. "How do the stars keep order? Are they *mes?* Are they also spirits?"

"Watch the stars, curious one. Watch the stars, you who know everything there is." Now the voice sounded amused, and Eili knew it could not be a demon. Demons didn't know how to be happy.

She crawled out of the hut and watched the stars. To her amazement, she recognized some of the patterns. At least some, then, were the same as they had been last night, bright torches flung up into the heavens: a sicklelike head traced in stars; a cluster of six bright stars like a handful of shining pearls just above a pair of horns; a wagon and curved shaft; two bright stars standing close together as might a sister and brother, she and Indu. The moon, like Indu, had been eating and had gotten a little fatter.

The next day the priestess brought food again, bread, fish cakes, and beer, and graciously allowed her to spend the day grinding emmer into meal.

The next night she waited and waited, but the voice didn't come. At last she curled up and fell asleep . . . only to be woken suddenly by a low chuckle and a hissing, like a snake. She jumped up, horrified. With the wood plate as a weapon she slapped the floor around her to kill any snake or scorpion that might have snuck in and curled up under her mat. But the hiss came from neither snake nor scorpion.

"When comes the New Year?"

The question startled her, and she stood, flatfooted, wood plate dangling from her fingers, and considered. She had never before given much thought to when the New Year came, only that the priestess always told them when the time was right to celebrate. But she wasn't willing to reveal her ignorance so easily. "Soon. It comes soon."

"When?"

Maybe it *was* a demon questioning her. Only demons would be so persistent. "Right before the floods come."

"When will the floods come?"

Did this voice know how to speak at all except to ask her questions she couldn't answer? "Soon, I said!"

"When?" the voice repeated without changing its patient tone. "How does the farmer know when to harvest?"

"When the grain is ripe, of course!"

"In this same way the stars tell us when it is time to make the world live again, to bury the old year and give birth to the new one."

This was a long way from ripening grain. She had to set down the plate in order to think about it. "How can the stars tell us that?"

It was very late. She saw now that the first faint lightening had come, the waking breath of Anu, the sun. Peering out through the drill holes, she tried to see who was talking to her, but she could see only shadows.

When she ducked outside, the priestess came to meet her in the gray light of dawn, carrying a bundle of rushes. Hiai! She did not need to ask what today's work would be. But she had never minded weaving mats: she liked the way the single strands wove together to make a solid whole whose pattern she could read and trace with her fingers.

When dusk came, the priestess led her up the stairs set against the temple wall. Several mats lay on the flat roof, and with some apprehension Eili followed the priestess over to them and gingerly sat down cross-legged, imitating the woman.

"Look there," said the priestess, pointing to the zenith—the sky directly above them—and at once Eili knew who had questioned her the past three nights. Overhead shone a sickle of stars. "That is the Lion's head," said the priestess.

"A Lion's head!" Eili could see it now, traced for her: the proud neck and head of the fearsome king who prowls the heavens unafraid.

"The Lion rules this sky. You see, there, the Lion has defeated the Bull, who sinks into the underworld together with Anu." Pointing to the western horizon, the priestess traced another pattern of stars just below the waxing sickle of the moon. "There lies the Sevenfold One and the horns of the Bull. See how they die now, with Anu?"

"But won't they rise again tomorrow night?" As the deep twilight darkened into full night, the horns of the Bull sank beneath the horizon, lost to her view.

"No, the Bull has died, killed by the Lion." The priestess pointed overhead again, then to the horizon, the gateway to the underworld.

Eili could not contain a gulping gasp, a sudden tremor of fear. Suddenly those questions about the Great Serpent devouring the world and returning everything to the all-encompassing sea seemed much more frightening. If the stars could die, then perhaps the world was about to come to an end. "Is the Bull gone forever, then?"

The priestess smiled. "Only to rest until the New Year."

"Until the New Year? But how do you know when the New Year comes?"

The priestess did not speak at once. Eili stared, gape-mouthed, at the stars. "In about forty days the Bull will rise in the east at dawn. That is how we know to celebrate the birth of a new year. The Bull brings the new year. Our duty as servant to the gods is to maintain the order of the world, to celebrate *a-ki-til* at the proper time, the power of making the world live again."

"What would happen if we didn't celebrate it?"

It was very dark now. Below the sickle head of the Lion Eili could see its bright heart, brightest of the stars in its body. A cold wind blew up from the marshes, soughing through the palms. The deep, croaking call of the night heron sounded from the canal.

"The Great Serpent waits for us to make a mistake. It is also our crimes, our faults, our *errors* which let loose the Great Serpent. That is why the gods have set the four corners of the year, as pillars so that we may help defend the world against chaos."

The four corners of the year. With a flash of insight, Eili remembered the four animals painted on the niches within the temple. "The Lion, the Bull, the Scorpion, and the Ibex."

"Ah," said the priestess, with approval.

"But how do we make the world live again at *a-ki-til?*"

"What? You don't know everything, Eili? I thought everything was old for you, nothing new at all in this old place. Isn't that what you tell your mother every day?"

Eili wiggled on the mat, trying not to bounce up and down in her impatience and her excitement. "I didn't know about all this!"

The priestess chuckled. "Do you want to learn?"

"Yes! Yes!"

"But I warn you, you'll have to be attentive. There's much to know you haven't discovered yet. And more to learn than you can learn this year—or perhaps in your entire life."

The priestess spoke with laughter in her voice, but Eili ignored it. "Are all the four corners of the year set in the stars? Then where is the Scorpion, and the Ibex?"

"Only wait, child. Only wait. You have learned a great deal for one night. I am an old woman and easily tired, and it will rain soon. You may escort me to my bed, and sleep on a pallet beside me, if you wish."

"Then I may stay here, in the temple?" The question caught in her throat, and as soon as she uttered the words, she was sorry to have said them. Hiai! How brash of her to presume so much, to ask such a thing of the priestess!

But the priestess only wrapped a corner of her shawl more tightly around her as the wind brought a spattering of rain over them, on their silent perch. "Of course. Who else would answer all your questions? I have already spoken to your mother about your dowry."

With that, they picked their way along the spine of the roof and climbed carefully down the stairs to the silent temple yard. The priestess made her bed in one of the stout reed huts.

But Eili could barely sleep for excitement. The wash of a late rain over the village woke her. She listened to the night calls of birds, to the honking of geese, and the barking of dogs. Each insect click, each drip of water startled her back awake, her mind tumbling all its new thoughts over and over. If only she could weave them into a pattern. . . .

In the morning, as soon as the dawn washed to pink and the first herons glided over the marshlands to stalk their prey, she was up and outside. With a stick she drew lines in the dirt, a picture of a lion grappling with and defeating a bull.

She glanced up at the sky, but Anu had washed it clean of stars. Clouds moved in from the east.

She sat back on her haunches, thinking about the four corners of the year. With a palm leaf she swept clear a patch of dirt and then drew a square with four corners and in each square, as in the niches in the temple, traced the rough outline of an animal: here, at the New Year, the Bull; here, for the high, hot summer, the Lion; for the late dry spell, the Scorpion; for the winter rains, the Ibex. A shadow eased across the dirt, shading her, and she turned to see the priestess standing behind her with a slight smile on her ageless face.

"Hiai, restless one! Is your heart now content?"

"No, not at all!" cried Eili without thinking. "Do all the stars have names?"

"Ah," said the priestess in the tone of a woman who has opened a box and found the finest pure lapis lazuli shining within. "The gods have many decrees set upon the world so that we can maintain order against the Great Serpent. Can you remember them all?"

Eili nodded, but her attention had already wandered back to her picture. "It isn't quite right," she muttered as she thought about the Bull sinking into the underworld, only to appear again in the east forty days later—as it would every year.

The priestess squatted beside her and gently took the stick from her hand. The woman drew a straight line from Bull to Scorpion and Lion to Ibex, then a curved line that linked them all in a circle.

"It's a wheel!" murmured Eili. She touched each animal in turn. "The four corners of the year are a wheel that turns around each year. It always comes back to its beginning."

"Making the world live again." The priestess was smiling as Anu's light spread over them in a wash of brightness, bringing a new day. "What, no questions, restless one?"

But for this once Eili was too filled with wonder to reply. After all, there would be many more days, and nights, in which to ask questions.

Four Essays

INTRODUCTION

We included these four essays (all originally posted online) because they felt integral to the issues and themes discussed in the introduction. I wrote "The Omniscient Breasts" as a teaching tool, with the hope it might help people see with fresh eyes how women are too often portrayed in an objectifying way and then offer the idea that, by being conscious of this gaze, writers can change their own writing if they wish to. "The Narrative of Women in Fear and Pain" expresses my anger at narrative forms that use suffering and pain to entertain while mostly ignoring the consequences of suffering. "And Pharaoh's Heart Hardened" specifically addresses the topic of immigration and race and prejudice in the USA, from the perspective of a child of immigrants; it was written during a particularly contentious discussion of immigration in the USA within the science fiction and fantasy online community. "The Status Quo Does Not Need World Building" calls into question the idea that a world can be created out of a contextless space of "pure imagination."

THE OMNISCIENT BREASTS:
THE MALE GAZE THROUGH FEMALE EYES

My reading experience of fantasy and science fiction over forty years is that it is mostly written with the male gaze. By this I don't mean it is written from the point of view of a male character, although that is often the case. Nor am I speaking about the gender of the writer: a male writer does not automatically write every line of every book with a male gaze just because he is a man; in fact, a male writer can write with a female gaze, and women can (and often do) write with a male gaze.

How am I using the terms "male gaze" and "female gaze"?

In fiction it is easy to simplistically understand the male gaze as, for instance, the gaze of a male author reflected across the entirety of his story; he's a man so therefore he has a male gaze. It's easy to understand it as that of the male reader reading the story. I have heard people say, "But if it is a male character, then of course the character is seeing with a male gaze."

The idea of "the gaze" is a theoretical concept about how we look at things, especially in visual culture. Who is presumed to be the viewer, and how does the viewer view the people in the frame? For the purposes of this essay I will use two short definitions.

Film critic Laura Mulvey writes that "the male gaze occurs when the audience, or viewer, is put into the perspective of a heterosexual male."

An example of the male gaze in film would be when the camera lingers on a partially clad or fully naked female body (rather than on a male body) or when, in film or advertising, women are photographed in more sexual poses and wearing fewer clothes than men.

When I asked on social media how people might briefly define the concept in its broadest terms, graduate student Liamog Drislane (@AnotherWord on Twitter) said, "The 'male gaze' is shorthand for a story being tailored to the perceived knowledge, interests, and prejudices of men."

I think it matters for fiction writers to recognize if, when, and how they are using an unexamined default "male gaze" in this broader sense as they write. But here is what I want to talk about in this post:

YOU CAN WRITE FROM THE POINT OF VIEW OF A FEMALE CHARACTER AND STILL BE WRITING WITH THE MALE GAZE.

A female point-of-view (pov) character is not necessarily written from the perspective of a female gaze. Everything about her might be male defined. By that I do not mean "defined within the cultural context of the narrative," as in "culturally in this society she is defined as the daughter of Lord John." I mean defined unconsciously by the writer who is not aware of writing a female character through a male gaze—that is, one that "tailors" her to the preconceived tastes and prejudices of (heterosexual) men.

One day on Twitter I exchanged comments about female characters and their often problematic depiction in fantasy novels with @Halfrican_One, aka TJ Tallie, a PhD student in history at the University of Illinois.

Reflecting on an epic fantasy novel he had recently been reading with several female point-of-view characters, he tweeted: "At one point I think one of the POV characters is having her breasts described omnisciently to the reader."

A pov character is a character through whose eyes and perspective we follow the action of the story.

OMNISCIENT BREASTS

Briefly, just to clarify my terms, first person is "I saw the child vanish around the corner" (and then nothing else because "I" can't see around the corner), third person is "She saw the child vanish around the corner" (and then nothing else because she can't see around the corner), and omniscient is "She saw the child vanish around the corner. The child ran into the candy store" because the omniscient narrator stands above and thus outside the action and can therefore See All.

Imagine a female pov character is going along about her protagonist adventure, seeing things from her perspective of the world as written in third person. She hears, sees, considers, and makes decisions and reacts based on her view of the world and what she is aware of and encounters. Abruptly, a description is dropped into the text of her secondary sexual characteristics usually in the form of soft-focus *Playboy*-magazine-style sexualized kitten-bunny-I-would-fuck-her-in-a-heartbeat lustrous-eyes-and-nipples phrases. Her breasts have just become omniscient breasts.

This is what I mean when I speak of the male gaze. The breasts are no longer her breasts, they have become the breasts as described by the omniscient heterosexual male narrator (in the person of the writer) who is usually not even aware that he has just dropped out of third person and into omniscient to describe her sexual attractiveness in a way that caters to a heterosexual male audience.

Listen, I like to read about positive, consensual sexual relations in stories. I am all good with descriptions of people's sexual attractiveness as an aspect of their person, whatever their sexual and gender identity, as long as it is not the only thing about them that matters.

One way a writer might describe a woman's sexual attractiveness is through the direct specific lens of another character examining her because that other character is attracted to her. "JJ checked out the woman as she walked into the room. Etc."

Another way could be a character deliberately measuring the female character for her sexual attractiveness because of a specific defined plot point. "JJ checked out the three women, trying to figure out which one had been down at the swimming pool when the painting was stolen. Etc."

If there is no specific reason to describe her sexual attractiveness for a defined plot or character reason, then the writer is deferring to the male gaze and objectifying the character even if the writer didn't intend to do that. The writer is dropping out of third into omniscient to package the character for a male reader who enjoys the titillation in large part because our culture so heavily exposes the female body to sexual objectification in our visual imagery, advertising, film, TV, games, and fiction.

If a female point-of-view character is constantly describing herself in sexual ways, ogling her breasts as if she is part of a *GQ* photo-shoot, or being placed in sexual situations that cater to heterosexual male "fantasies"—all too often defined by lubricious physical description and/or the use of "titillating" sexualized violence—she is probably being written with a heterosexual male gaze.

Female characters in science fiction and fantasy who are sex toys or sex workers are almost always being written from the male gaze regardless if they are the ones speaking, because the view of sex as being that of the male objectifying the female as his object of pleasure is so pervasive in our culture.

Is the character a lesbian or bisexual? Chances are good that her lesbianism or bisexuality is still being written through the veil of a male gaze if the way sexual attributes are being described leaps from the personal attraction to the omniscient breasts. [Note: I would guess that transgendered individuals are least commonly depicted in positive sexual ways via a male gaze. I'm hard pressed to come up with examples.]

Most problematically, descriptions of rape can be deeply offensive when they are purportedly being told from the point of the view of a woman being raped but when in fact everything about the description and situation is being seen through a male gaze.

Furthermore, the expectations of who a woman is, what she wants, how she reacts, much less how she is physically described differ wildly dependent on the assumptions wielded by the writer.

A problem arises when people write and/or read without knowing or realizing they are writing and reading exclusively from the perspective of a male gaze. When this perspective has been internalized as the most authentic or real perspective, it can subsume and devour all other perspectives because it is treated as the truest or only one.

Let me tell a story.

Many years ago, I was accused by a reader/reviewer of having a "homosexual agenda," a comment which puzzled me. I certainly do have such an agenda if by that one means I support QUILTBAG rights (as well as marriage equality). However, the reader meant a deliberate hidden agenda inserted into the books to warp young minds, perhaps as a form of semantic contagion. I usually don't argue with reviewers (except sometimes in my thoughts), but the way the statement was phrased really did make me wonder what in my work could possibly have triggered this particular interpretation.

In fact, I wondered so much that I did the thing I know better than to do: I emailed him.

He wrote back, and was polite but insistent that I had this agenda. We argued back and forth for a while until a lightbulb went on in my head.

The reader was reacting without understanding why to the fact that I often write men from a heterosexual female gaze. When I write female characters, I describe them sexually only if they're being observed from the point of view of a character who is sexually interested in them. Those of my female characters who are heterosexual, however, will see and describe male characters through a sexual gaze directed onto the men.

As an astute reader, this person was picking up on this (not particularly graphic) sexual description of men. Because virtually all the fiction he had read had been written from the heterosexual male gaze, to him a sexual gaze was by default a male gaze. I the writer was causing this reader to "see" male characters through a sexual gaze. Therefore, he interpreted my narrative gaze as a homosexual male gaze since "the gaze" and "the sexual gaze" by definition had to be male; thus he identified this as a homosexual agenda.

It's been my observation that in our culture women can read comfortably about men's sexual interest in women because it is considered normal and expected and acceptable, but men cannot always read comfortably about women's sexual interest in men. In the US in particular, I perceive that we have a cultural comfort in looking at women sexually and (although this is changing) a discomfort in looking at men sexually.

This reader hadn't thought to consider there might be another "gaze" possible in this story. The concept of a female sexual gaze as something that could be present in fiction had never occurred to him. To give him credit, when I pointed this out, he immediately got it.

Here's my theory:

We will never get past the supposed disjunction between male and female gazes and viewpoints until men think nothing of reading and writing through the female gaze because it seems ordinary, plausible, and interesting to them. Writers will stop writing about omniscient breasts once they pause to ask themselves whose gaze they are really writing from when they are ostensibly writing from a female point of view.

However, this is not the only way the male gaze permeates everything. In the examples I use above, I describe male writers writing a male heterosexual point of view through a female character's eyes as well as a male reader's reaction to a female gaze.

Women also have to struggle against this pervasive idea that the male gaze is the most real and most authentic view of the "world." Women can view their own stories through the lens of a male gaze, or can feel most comfortable in stories that reinforce these norms.

Women can read comfortably about men's sexual interest in women. Women can watch and observe visual representations of sexually objectified women seen through a male gaze and think it is not only normal but the way things always have been, are, and will be. Women can enjoy shows and books in which the female characters are unclothed and sexualized and the men are clothed and sexual or just active doers, and not necessarily think about the disjunction in how women are portrayed compared to men because it is so common that it is seen as right. To see in some other way, through a different lens, then seems not right but rather false and wrong.

So here it is: Stories told through a female gaze are just as valid, just as true, just as authentic and universal. And they are just as necessary, not just for women but for men, too.

ALL OF THE STORIES ARE NECESSARY.

This essay has focused specifically on gender, and on a binary view of gender at that, but I want to suggest what most of you already know: that the issue of "gaze" expands exponentially and intersectionally outward from here through gender identity, race, ethnicity, religion, age, nationality, class, and multiple other vectors.

Listen, there's nothing wrong in writing through a male gaze if that's the story you have to tell.

The problem lies in not being aware that the male gaze is a gaze. When readers don't realize how the male gaze pervades so much of our storytelling, they can't assess with what root assumptions the story is being told and how the default defines our expectations and our responses to how stories are told and how we read them. When writers don't even realize they are writing through the male gaze, then they can't possibly assess how that default male gaze influences the stories they tell and how they tell them.

THE NARRATIVE OF WOMEN
IN FEAR AND PAIN

My spouse and I started watching the television series *Fringe* to see if we would like it. The first episode was cool except for the clichéd and unnecessary "put the female lead in her underwear" scene. Undressed scenes are what killed my interest in watching the US remake of *Nikita* with Maggie Q because I could not get past the gratuitous bikini and lingerie scenes in the pilot, which were evidently needed to undercut the fact that she is meant to be a dangerous and out-of-control assassin and perhaps to attract a male viewership evidently deemed (by the producers and writers) too sexist to be willing to watch a show with a woman lead unless she is undressed for them. I don't know, maybe some other reason. What I do know is that the plot did not need the undressing for the scenes to work.

But then in the second episode of *Fringe* they went right for a "serial killer of young attractive women" plot for no reason other than there is evidently something in Hollywood or maybe our culture that gets off on these scenes of young women in poses of sexual passivity being terrified and mutilated and screaming screaming screaming. I had to walk out of the room because not only am I sick of it but it creeps me out.

I'm not creeped out by the knowledge that terrible things happen to young women (and old women, and children and men and all manner of people, especially those who are vulnerable and unprotected). I'm outraged and saddened by that knowledge, and I honestly think there is an important and even vital place in our literature (books, film, etc.) for strong, fearless depictions of suffering and injustice, so we don't lose sight of what we must strive to change. The people who suffer must not be silenced because of the discomfort of others who don't want to be forced to acknowledge, to see, that suffering and injustice exist.

But I *am* creeped out that images and portrayals of young women in positions of sexualized passivity who are in fear and in pain are used over and over again AS ENTERTAINMENT, to give us a thrill, to make our hearts pound.

I remember the time a couple of years ago I went with my daughter, then twenty, to a video store (remember those?) to get a movie to watch for the night.

After about five minutes she said, "Mom, I can't stand to look at all these DVD covers because so many of them show women in poses of fear or pain and it really disturbs me, like it is telling me that this is the story I have to internalize about becoming a woman."

I realized I had gotten so used to it—had gotten myself used to it—that when I browsed through a video store looking at film posters and DVD covers filled with shocking images of objectified and sexualized women in fear and pain, I just skipped my gaze right over it like it was ordinary and nothing to remark on. I had learned to stop seeing it as much as possible. It had become ordinary and nothing to remark on.

That brought me up short. I had hardened myself to it, and I had just assumed that my daughter would grow up learning to harden herself to it. But she couldn't, or maybe she didn't want to. Maybe she thought she shouldn't have to.

It made me think about how when I write I have to struggle against the idea, sunk down deep inside me, that when I write about women they have to be afraid or they have to be in pain.

Too often when the stories of women in fear and pain are told, we are seeing them in pain, we are being pushed into the perspective not of the woman who is suffering pain but into the perspective of the person inflicting the pain.

We are constantly being asked to identify with inflicting pain on others.

Of course we are. You don't just take over the other person's life and body; you also take their voice, their dreams, their perspective. You take their right to speak and leave them with only the power to suffer, a suffering that can be lifted from them by death or by rescue but always by an agency outside themselves. You take their eyes and turn them into your eyes, your gaze, your way of looking at the world. When such stories are told in this way, they reinforce the perspective of the person who is watching the voiceless have no voice.

But while it is important to say, "Let's stop telling those stories then because they exploit women and furthermore perpetuate the view of women as victims whose only role is to suffer fear and pain," I would go on to suggest that it is not quite that simple. It isn't binary; it's not either/or. All stories of women's fear and pain are not the same because it does make a difference from what perspective we see.

In her memoir *Mighty Be Our Powers* (written with Carol Mithers), Nobel Peace Prize winner Leymah Gbowee of Liberia talks about discovering the need to find spaces in which women could share their stories. Some of the stories she heard were stories that came out of the civil wars that wracked Liberia, the Ivory Coast, and Sierra Leone; others were stories that had to do with untold experiences within families, the kind of thing no one wants to talk about no matter where it happens. She writes:

Each speaker wept with relief when she finished; each spoke the same words: "This is the first time I have ever told this story. . . ."

Does it sound like a small thing that the women I met were able to talk openly? It was not small; it was groundbreaking. . . . Everyone was alone with her pain.

Everyone was alone with her pain.

That line stabs me in the heart. I do not want me, or you, or anyone to be alone with the pain.

Yes, I get angry and creeped out when I see and read stories about women in fear and pain, seen from the outside, looking down on them, inflicting pain on them through the gaze of the story.

I get especially angry when I'm told that these are the only or the most realistic stories, that they trump any other way of looking at the lives of women. Because they don't. This perspective looks in only one direction; that makes it an incomplete, biased, subjective, and even warped perspective.

You see, I worry that it is another form of silencing when women's stories of fear and pain are not given voice when the voice is theirs or when an incident of violence or fear is told from the perspective of the person who undergoes that experience, who must live with it, be changed by it, internalize it, fight against the injury it has done to her, build or continue her life, live defined by herself and not by her injury.

I worry that it is another form of silencing when all such stories are seen as the same without considering from whose perspective they're being told. It is not a small thing to speak up. It is not a small thing to hear stories and voices that have long been silenced.

There are indeed too many stories that fixate on women's fear and pain, and more than that, in my opinion, too often it is the wrong stories that get the attention, the wrong stories that are held up as the right ones, the only ones, the most authentic ones. The truth is usually difficult and complex and often so painful that it is easier to look away. All too often, silence is the ally of the powerful.

So, yes, I will rage against the exploitative portrayals of sexualized violence, of women in fear and pain. But I will also remember the women who never told their story because there was no one to listen.

And Pharaoh's Heart Hardened

I have never told this story to anyone except my father. I may have told my spouse at the time it happened, but I don't recall. My children were there, they were the reason it happened, but I doubt they remember.

In the mid '90s my spouse was attending graduate school at The Pennsylvania State University, in State College, Pennsylvania. He and I and our three then-small children lived in graduate student housing, on campus, in an old World War II–era duplex of 625 square feet. It got a bit close at times, to say the least, and in addition I worked at home writing, so I made every effort to get the kids out to do something, anything, when I had the chance and when the activity was age appropriate for small children.

A traveling photo exhibit came to the student union. I noted the photographer's name first because early in his career he had worked at the local newspaper in the area where I grew up. Brian Lanker had since expanded his journalistic photography; this exhibit contained a series of portraits of African-American women, specifically women who had contributed to the nation as artists, writers, activists, community organizers, business women, singers, what have you, that were collected into the book *I Dream a World: Portraits of Black Women Who Changed America* (Stewart, Tabori & Chang).

That looked promising!

One afternoon I walked the children over. I suspect that my daughter was seven and the twins were five.

The photos were all I could have hoped for, beautifully shot, large and imposing, opening a tiny window onto these magnificent women of strength and purpose. Many of the women were, at the time the photographs were taken, elders; maybe most were. They were a testament to the power and importance of age as a weight that anchors and balances a society when storm winds batter it, yet you could also see in their faces the hard work they had done when they were younger.

Some I had heard of; some were names I'd seen although I knew little enough of them; some I had never heard of. The children were as patient as children can be at that age and I knew better than to drag out our little expedition beyond their ability to enjoy the outing and the novelty. We didn't linger over any of the portraits until we came to Rosa Parks.

Like so many, I have a soft spot for Rosa Parks.

I thought it worthwhile to give my children an early lesson in citizenship.

I had to choose my words to work for the level at which they could understand, overly simplified and yet truthful. I said something like this (reconstructed from faulty memory):

"This is Rosa Parks. She is a great American hero. When she was younger, there was a law in some parts of the country that people who have black skin, as you can see she does, had to sit in the backs of public buses. People who had white skin, as you can see we do, could sit in the front. Isn't that a strange law? Just because people's skins are different colors? Of course, it was wrong to have a law like that. And she knew that, so she with the help of some other people decided to protest the law. She got on the bus one day after work and refused to sit in the back of the bus, and then she was arrested, but then many more people began to say that that law was wrong, and then the government got rid of that law. So she is a hero. She is a hero for the people who could now sit wherever they wanted on the bus. But she is also a hero for all America, because a law like that hurts all Americans, because a bad law like that hurts the spirit and heart of America."

They listened attentively, perhaps drawn by the fact that I got a bit of a tear in my voice, but by this time it was clear we had reached the limit of our visit to the exhibit, so I steered them toward the exit door.

As I herded them forward, a woman, also exiting, had paused at the door and turned back to look at me. She was an African-American woman about my age, maybe a bit older.

She caught my gaze, and she said, "I want to thank you for what you said to your children."

My first reaction was surprise, succeeded almost immediately by embarrassment. I said something in reply; I have no recollection what. She went on her way; we went on ours, and my embarrassment subsided to be replaced by a sudden and very sweeping sense of shame.

Not at myself. I try to live a decent life (as do most people, I truly believe).

It is difficult for me to express how deep the chasm is, this exposure of the pervasive racism that afflicts the USA.

My father taught American history. He taught his children that "if you grow up in a racist society, you are a racist," by which he meant not that you burn crosses on lawns but that you have absorbed unexamined assumptions about the way things are and that it is therefore incumbent upon you (I am using the generic "you" here, as he was) to honestly reflect and examine where you stand and what is going on around you as often as you can.

The presence of racism is not news to me, therefore. But I am white, and while I have intersectionally dealt with forms of prejudice directed at me personally or family members or friends or as part of the body politic, for someone like me it can still take a moment like this one to really expose that particular chasm, however briefly, in its full and terrible darkness.

She thanked *me*.

I have no idea what prejudice that woman had faced in her life, what moments of anger, hatred, denial, insult, grief, rudeness, and perhaps outright physical danger she might have experienced because she was black. That made her—the one afflicted by racism—take notice of a solitary woman and her three children, *and thank me* for such a small act. I felt shame, among so many other reasons, that what I said to my children was even worthy of comment. Because in a better world it shouldn't be. It should be ordinary. It should be unremarkable.

Never think this story is about me, because even though I naturally tell it from my perspective, it is a story about the way in which racism and prejudice harm our country in the most deep-seated ways imaginable.

Think instead that it might be the story of Pharaoh hardening his heart each time Moses asks him to "let my people go." He hardens his heart (or God hardens it for him, but that's another layer to a story that has many layers of meaning) in order to bring himself to say "NO."

To harden our heart means to turn away from our connection to others, to deny compassion, to refuse to change. Psychologist Erich Fromm says that "every evil act tends to harden man's heart, to deaden it. Every good act tends to soften it, to make it more alive."

Every time Pharaoh hardens his heart, he makes it easier to harden his heart again, the next time. Surely this is true for all of us. Every time we turn away from our connection to others, we imprison ourselves a little more. In the end we can so accustom ourselves to this condition that we cease to notice it is going on.

The question of the systemic racism threaded through American history, as well as the question of the extermination of so many of the original indigenous inhabitants of this continent as the destiny and dream of a mighty empire (for that is what we are, speaking in the context of history) was being established, cannot be dealt with in a brief piece of writing like this one. So I won't try.

This is what I will say:

Prejudice is a form of hardening the heart. Prejudice, as we unfortunately know, comes in many forms. Just as human beings show a propensity to be tolerant and inclusive, so also, often at the same time, and sometimes in the same person, they show a propensity to be intolerant and exclusive. Human beings are such forces for good, and yet such forces for bad, and sometimes in the same person. The contradiction makes one dizzy. I am not immune.

Prejudice harms and hardens each of us as individuals. It also harms and hardens that thing which those of us who are Americans like to call

"America," which is a dream and an ideal and, in some ways and at some times, a reality.

For those of you who are not Americans (USAians, to be precise), if you are still reading (and frankly, were I not American, I am sure I would get sick and tired of all the maundering Americans do about the Dream of America), I do not apologize but simply explain that this is specifically written from the perspective of an American speaking of America.

The USA has always had a contentious love affair with immigration, which may be inevitable in a country founded on the three-legged stool of genocide, slavery, and liberty.

In the nineteenth century, Jewish immigrants were considered, as a group, ineducable; in the twentieth century, some universities (more than I care to think about) maintained quotas for how many persons of Jewish background they would admit, because so many (i.e., "too many") qualified. Similarly, plantation workers brought in from different countries and regions of Asia in the nineteenth century to settle in Hawaii were considered not smart enough to succeed in Western-style schools. Of course this makes me laugh now—in a sardonic way, I suppose, the joke being on those self-righteous missionaries—given that perhaps three-quarters of the students in my sons' high school honors classes were, of course, girls who were Americans of Japanese ancestry.

In World War II, as I need not remind you, citizens of Japanese ancestry were forced into internment camps on the Mainland because they were considered threats, people who would "by nature" feel more loyalty to the place of their parents' or grandparents' birth than the place those same forebears had chosen to immigrate to, to make a new life, presumably because they sought greater opportunity here than what was available to them there. They were considered threats even though this was the country most of them had been born in and identified with.

My father's grandparents came to this country because it offered them more than the old country did. My mother, an immigrant, did the same, I believe. Why should I not assume that others came likewise when I see the evidence all around me that it is so?

Now, of course, Americans of Japanese ancestry are seen as a "model minority." These days if a child goes after school to, say, "Mandarin school" (as my father, back in the day, went to "Dane school" or my children attended "Hebrew school") to learn the language of his/her grandparents and the culture of her/his heritage or the religion of their ancestors, then we call that a fine thing. Or many of us do anyway. Or some of us, at any rate.

For the whole point of the USA is not that it is homogenous but that it is a greater whole woven from diverse strands. It has never been truly homogenous; the social fabric has always been influenced and altered by each latest wave of incoming immigrants. For me it is a truism that immigration is what makes this country strong, and that specifically the diversity of immigration does so.

When I grew up, we were taught that the USA was built from those who had the courage to leave the safety of the known to build a better life elsewhere. This story, of course, rarely took into account those who had no choice but to come, shackled by the slave trade, and the indigenous peoples who were already here. Part of the mythology of America is that the brave and the bold and the desperate and the ambitious come here to make a better life because America is the land of opportunity.

Yet a cycle repeats itself. Every generation seems to fixate on some "new" immigrant group as a threat that can't or won't assimilate itself properly, that is stubborn or ineducable or secretly under the thrall of the Pope or or or. You can fill in the blanks. It happens over and over again as, meanwhile, people who want to build a good life for themselves and their children, and their children who can conceive of nothing other than being Americans because that is what they are—they are Americans just as I am, or you over there, or you, or you—get on with living a decent life . . . if they can, if they aren't locked into internment camps or having their places of worship burned because they are this decade's or this generation's Threat to Our Way of Life.

But that's the thing. Our way of life is predicated on change. Change is embedded in the Constitution, in that codicil called the Bill of Rights. Change is embedded in life itself. Judaism survived as a religion because it changed from a religion based around a single temple to one based on community centers, although we call them synagogues. Societies that do not change will ossify and die. I guarantee it.

So is that not the beauty of the USA? That our institution, our mode of citizenship, creates the constant possibility of change? That change is not just a possibility but a necessity? Not often radical change but usually incremental change driven in part by reversals and resurgences?

Somewhere out there in the USA today a citizen of Indonesian-American descent who happens to also be Muslim is going about the ordinary business of life. So are you. So am I.

This should be unremarkable.

We do not become stronger through prejudice. We become weaker. Those against whom the prejudice is directed are hurt most, of course, but in the end, we all lose.

THE STATUS QUO DOES
NOT NEED WORLD-BUILDING

The imagination is not contextless.

The words and conceptual markers a writer puts on the page arise from thoughts and perceptions and interpretations rooted in our experiences and knowledge and assumptions. Writers write what they know, what they think is important, what they think is entertaining, what they are aware or take notice of. They structure stories in patterns that make sense to them. A writer's way of thinking, and the forms and content of what and how they imagine story, will be rooted in their existing cultural and social world.

Now consider the genre of science fiction and fantasy. Creators place a story within a setting. In the literature of the fantastic, this landscape must be explained to some degree so readers can situate themselves.

Some writers describe this landscape in extensive detail while others use a minimalist approach. To quote fantasy writer Saladin Ahmed:[1] "Some readers/writers want scrupulous mimesis of an otherworld. Some want impressionistic wonder. No inherent right/wrong/better/ worse there."

Complaints now and again arise about obsessive world-building and how such dorkery has ruined modern fantasy. Recently on Twitter, Damien Walter (writer and critic who, among other things,

1. https://storify.com/jennygadget/some-thought-by-kate-elliott-on-worldbuilding

writes about the SFF genre for *The Guardian*), stated, "Obsessive world-building is [a] common cause of crap books. . . . Like some other acts pleasurable to the individual, it shouldn't be done in public. Or in a book."[2]

Too much detail, too clumsily employed, is an issue of bad writing and should be addressed as such.

But complaints about depicting a detailed world in fantasy have potential sexist, colonialist, and racist implications. These implications are more damaging and pernicious than the alleged disadvantages imposed on literature by detailed world-building.

Why?

Let me explain.

The status quo does not need world-building.

It is implied in every detail that is left out as "understood by everyone," in every action or reaction considered unimportant for whatever reason, in every activity or description ignored because it is seen as not worthy of the doughty thews of real literature.

There are many ways to discuss elaborated world-building. This post will focus on material culture and social space.

Material culture can be defined narrowly as any assemblage of artifacts in the archaeological record, but here I am thinking of it more as the relationship between people and the physical objects used in life by those people and their culture(s).

Social space refers to the ways in which people interact in social spaces and how these interactions enforce and reinforce custom, authority, and social patterns and kinship.

What follows is an obvious statement that I am going to make anyway: Different cultures have different material cultures and different understandings of social space, just as they have different languages and language variants, different religious beliefs, different kinship patterns and household formations, different aesthetic preferences, and so on.

As well, every culture tells stories about itself and its past. These

2. Ibid.

stories work their way into that culture's understanding of the cosmos and its place in it.

Just to complicate matters further, cultures are not themselves purely discrete things. There can be cultures that live between and woven into or half outside of other larger and more dominant cultures so that they partake of elements of both (or more). I know this in part because I am the child of an immigrant and grew up in a household that was both part of and in some ways separate from the dominant culture.

The more minimal the world-building, the more the status quo is highlighted without anything needed to be said. This doesn't mean that minimal world-building can't work in narrative: Of course it can.

But minimal world-building championed as a stance against "obsessive world-building" veers dangerously into the territory of perpetuating sexist, racist, and colonialist attitudes. It does so by ignoring the very details and concerns that would make a narrative less status quo in terms of how it deals with social space and material culture as well as other aspects of the human experience.

When people write without considering the implications of material culture and social space in the story they are writing, they often unwittingly default to an expression of how they believe the past worked. This is especially true if they are not thinking about how the material and the social differ from culture to culture, across both space and time, or how it might change in the future.

Which details a writer considers too unimportant to include may often default to the status quo of the writer's own setting and situation, the writer's lived experience of social space, because the status quo does not need to be described by those who live at the center of a dominant culture.

For example, consider how many a near- or far-future SF story uses social space that is modern, Western, and in some cases very suburban American—and how this element of the world-building is rarely interrogated by writer or critic or readers when, meanwhile, other elements of a story may be praised for being bold, edgy, ground-breaking, or brilliant. Compare how deliberately Aliette de Bodard uses social space in *On a Red Station, Drifting*,[3] an example of far-future SF not focused on a Western paradigm and which needs—and relishes—the elaborated detail as part of the story's unfolding.

The implied status quo becomes a mirror reflecting itself back on itself while it ignores the narrative patterns and interests of most non-Western literatures, which often tell their story in a way different from much Western narrative (as Aliette de Bodard,[4] Rochita Loenen-Ruiz,[5] Joyce Chng,[6] and Sabrina Vourvoulias,[7] among others, have pointed out).

The implied status quo in denigrating descriptions of daily living and material culture denigrates the lived experience of so many people. It judges these details as unworthy of narrative in the same way colonialism, racism, and sexism dismiss other cultures and life-ways and life-experiences as inferior or exotic window-dressing. It does so by implying that a self-defined and often abstracted "universal" (of subject matter or of mostly invisible setting) trumps all else and can thereby be accomplished with none of this obsessive world-building, none of these extraneous details. This imagination is not contextless.

In the US/UK genre market, for example, it is exactly the marginalized landscapes that need description in order to be understood and revealed as just as expressive of the scope of human experience as that of the dominant culture whose lineaments are most often taken for granted.

Of course there is plenty of detailed world-building that emphasizes the status quo and expands on it, not always in a deliberate or thoughtful way.

Regardless, a well-described setting is good writing. There is nothing wrong with using (say) medieval Europe for your inspiration if you

3. http://aliettedebodard.com/bibliography/novels/on-a-red-station-drifting/

4. http://aliettedebodard.com/2013/04/08/on-political-and-value-neutral/

5. http://strangehorizons.com/2013/20130114/loenen-ruiz-c.shtml

6. http://crossedgenres.com/archives/018-2/growing-up-by-joyce-chng/

7. http://lareviewofbooks.org/review/dont-let-the-future-be-written-for-you-sabrina-vourvouliass-ink/

have a story to tell there. Judith Tarr's[8] deeply imagined medieval landscapes attest to that. The point of this essay is not to suggest what any person is required to write or how much or how little world-building they should deploy. A story needs to be the story that it is.

Meanwhile, as I don't have to tell most of you, there is an entire world literature of the fantastic, works of imagination set in the past, the present, and the future, most of which are embedded in the status quo of their particular culture and era. The examples are legion, such as the magnificent Sundiata cycle, the Shah-Nama, the Journey to the West, the numerous syncretic versions of the Ramayana that spread from India throughout Southeast Asia and the Indonesian archipelago, the Popol Vuh, and so many others, including all those I have never heard of and the many works being written today. However, speaking as I must from an American perspective, few of these works have penetrated into the Western consciousness to the degree that, say, Harry Potter has become a worldwide phenomenon.

So who chooses what amount of world-building is acceptable in fantasy literature? More importantly, from what place can such a demand be made?

The world can and will speak for itself, in a multiplicity of voices, not just in one.

Thanks to Daniel José Older, Liz Bourke, Rochita Loenen-Ruiz, and Joyce Chng for reading and commenting on early and late versions of this post. Special shout-out to this recent *Strange Horizons* roundtable arranged by Daniel José Older: Set Truth on Stun: Reimagining an Anti-Oppressive SF/F.[9] And a final link to N. K. Jemisin's excellent and important Guest of Honor speech at Continuum earlier this year: "SFF has always been the literature of the human imagination, not just the imagination of a single demographic."[10]

8. http://bookviewcafe.com/bookstore/bvc-author/judith-tarr/
9. http://www.strangehorizons.com/2013/20130923/1older-a.shtml
10. http://nkjemisin.com/2013/06/continuum-goh-speech/

ABOUT THE AUTHOR

Kate Elliott has been writing stories since she was nine years old, which has led her to believe that writing, like breathing, keeps her alive. Forthcoming novels are her debut YA fantasy, *Court of Fives*, described as "*Little Women* meets *The Count of Monte Cristo* in a fantasy setting inspired by Greco-Roman Egypt," and the first volume of a new epic fantasy sequence, Black Wolves. Her most recent completed series is the Spiritwalker Trilogy (*Cold Magic*, *Cold Fire*, *Cold Steel*), an Afro-Celtic post-Roman alternate-nineteenth-century Regency icepunk mashup with airships, Phoenician spies, revolution, and lawyer dinosaurs. Her previous series include the Crossroads Trilogy (starting with *Spirit Gate*), The Crown of Stars septology (starting with *King's Dragon*), and the science fiction Novels of the Jaran and the Highroad Trilogy.

Elliott likes to play sports more than she likes to watch them; right now, her sport of choice is outrigger canoe paddling. Her archaeologist spouse has a much more interesting job than she does, with the added benefit that they had to move to Hawaii for his work. Thus, the outrigger canoes. They also have a schnauzer.

For more information on Kate's novels, or to sign up for her new release email list, the author invites you to visit her website at KateElliott.com, to visit her Facebook page, or to follow her on Twitter at @KateElliottSFF.

About the Cover Art

The stunning cover painting by Julie Dillon illustrates a passage from *Cold Steel* (Spiritwalker 3):

> [A] sweep of color washed through the smoky sea.... Lights like fireflies twinkled against a black sky. The sea surged, lifting like cloth raised from beneath by a hand. A bright shape emerged, smoke spilling off it in currents.
>
> The dragon loomed over us. Its head was crested as with a filigree that reminded me of a troll's crest, if a troll's crest spanned half the sky. Silver eyes spun like wheels. It was not bird or lizard, nor was it a fish. Most of its body remained beneath the smoke. Ripples revealed a dreadful expanse of wings as wide as fields, shimmering pale gold like ripe wheat under a harsh sun. When its mouth gaped, I knew it could swallow us in one gulp.
>
> We had come to a place we ought not to be.